COMMUNE

COMMUNE

A Novel

Des Kennedy

HARBOUR PUBLISHING CO. LTD.
P.O. Box 219, Madeira Park, BC, VON 2H0
www.harbourpublishing.com

EDITED by Pam Robertson
COVER DESIGN by Anna Comfort O'Keeffe
TEXT DESIGN by Libris Simas Ferraz / Onça Publishing
PRINTED AND BOUND in Canada
PRINTED on 100% recycled paper

HARBOUR PUBLISHING acknowledges the support of the Canada Council for the Arts, the Government of Canada and the Province of British Columbia through the BC Arts Council.

LIBRARY AND ARCHIVES CANADA CATALOGUING IN PUBLICATION
Title: Commune : a novel / Des Kennedy.
Names: Kennedy, Des, 1945- author.
Identifiers: Canadiana (print) 20230473555 | Canadiana (ebook) 20230473563 | ISBN 9781990776519 (softcover) | ISBN 9781990776526 (EPUB)
Classification: LCC PS8571.E6274 C67 2023 | DDC C813/.54—dc23

For all true islanders.

Prologue

WHAT'S THAT BLASTED MAD BANGING? STUFF BEING BROKEN DOWN, torn apart. Wild wind, yes, wind slamming and slamming an unlatched door, imprisoned animals escaping into the frightening night. A moment's panic, but then, out of the gloom, a familiar scene assembling itself. Sturdy posts and beams. Old wood cookstove. Big kitchen table. Blessed assurances of home. But that wretched banging still. Oh, hell, someone knocking at the door. Dozed off again, I suppose. Why not? What's to stay awake for anyway. The evening news? Don't make me laugh. *Death creeping closer?* More likely. Could just ignore them, whoever's knocking. Persistent crapper though. I push myself up out of the big old armchair and toddle across to the door. Bleary-eyed and frumpish and hardly dressed for company.

Open the door and find a woman, a stranger, standing there. A muddled introduction and explanation of her purpose. Confused, I take her to be an agent of some government program targeting seniors, Better at Home or one of those, but I'm not sure. Truth to tell, I'm missing the finer points of what she's saying, only just back from the dreamworld and suddenly thrown into confusion by this unexpected visitor. Maybe forty years old, I'm guessing, large and obviously complicated, no shortage of attitude, a certain elusive ethnicity—tawny skin, sable hair, rose-red lips. She smells like I imagine frangipani does on sultry tropical evenings. Listening to her speak, I hear Odetta singing. Her brightly coloured tunic looks suitable for Arabian nights but it's about the most impractical outfit you could imagine for our rustic haunts. She's the first visitor I've had for days, and an instantly intriguing one, so naturally I invite her in. We sit together at the kitchen table. She lives down near the ferry terminal, she explains, in the old Cranston place.

"New to the island, though, are you?" I ask.

"We're all newcomers here," she answers cryptically.

She's looking around the disorganized kitchen as though sizing up the workload facing her. Cluttered counters, unwashed windows, flying trapeze spiderwebs. I tell her I really don't need anything done. And it's true. Apart from the cobwebs and dirty dishes piled in the sink. Really, I get by perfectly fine on my own. I can cook well enough to keep myself alive. Nothing like the meals we all used to have when a trug of homegrown vegetables would be transformed into a gourmet feast, but good enough. The government indifferently sends me cheques in the mail—Old Age Security, Guaranteed Income Supplement, GST Rebate—most of which I don't spend, so money's not an issue. I've no burning desire to go explore any roaring metropolis with homeless encampments squatting in the shadows of luxury condos, fear and frenzy on the streets. If necessary, I can putter down to the general store for supplies or to the clinic to see a doctor or dentist. A couple of muscular young bucks bring me enough seasoned firewood every autumn, and I've got a reliable handyperson—a non-binary character named Dragonfly—who'll clean the chimney and gutters or patch a hole in the roof, the kind of things I can't do myself anymore. So I've no pressing needs, really. No problems.

Except for wondering down what feral hole the confounded time all disappeared. And how fast. And to what purpose.

My surprise visitor—Rosalie, she tells me her name is, Rosalie Sloane—naturally wouldn't have a clue about any of this; how could she? Or whatever agency she's working for. No, it wouldn't be in the files, would it. How fiercely the winds of intensity used to blow through this little backwater. Wagnerian opera stuff. Course you'd never guess it looking around the old place now. This decrepit farmhouse. Enough listing sheds and outbuildings to house the Hells Angels. One hundred and sixty acres of toppling fences and encroaching forest with just me left to manage the whole shebang. Yes, it's true, some days the old place can feel overwhelming, not to mention awful damn lonesome with everybody gone. But I don't mind, not really. Truth to tell, the quiet's preferable to the worst of those tumultuous times. But not nearly as sweet as the best.

Letting go. Letting go. Like with the weeds mounting their assault out there. It would have driven Jess nuts, my darling Jess, seeing all those creepers rampant among her roses, strangling the herb bed.

She's been gone now for more years than I want to think about and her absence still leaves a great aching crater in my heart. She was the last of our group to go—there'd been just the two of us remaining for quite a while—and I've been mucking about here on my own ever since. Goes without saying it's not the same without her, without any of our gang, but especially her, no use pretending it is. As though the driving wheel just dropped out of everything. The externals all still happen the same—spring birdsong, say, or the first killing frost—but they don't signify, not the way they used to. Not the way they did, for example, when Jess and I and maybe some of the others would stand in the yard watching the full Hunter's Moon of autumn climb over the horizon. Primitive. Beautiful. Terrifying.

So you're left with the bedevilments of the aged—among nagging aches and pains, looking for patterns in the past, searching for whatever meaning can be gleaned from the fields of yesterday, ransacking the ruins of chronology for evidence of something more than an indifferent jostle of disconnected moments. All bets are off anyway, with Earth now exacting revenge for the damage we damn fool humans have done to her.

Seems pointless to me to waste much energy on the future, whether the remaining dregs of this life or the remote possibilities of an afterlife. I'm better in the present or, increasingly, in the past. The anthems of our glory days that still sound as good as ever—Pete Seeger, Joan Baez, Phil Ochs and all the rest, god bless 'em. I enjoy rereading favourite novels with an excitement as rich as the first time. Classic films to be entranced with all over again. Oh yes, I could tell you stories about the past alright. In fact there were a couple of university students came by not long ago to do an interview.

Bright young things, a boy and a girl, didn't look old enough to be out of high school, but armed to the teeth with smart phones and laptops and Christ only knows what other gadgets. Devices, I guess. Said they were researching the counterculture and the "back to the land" movement. Ancient history to them. "A paradigm lost," they called it. They weren't the first either; in recent years there's been a regular procession of earnest intellectuals from the halls of academe tramping around these parts, in pursuit of information about what the counterculture was up to fifty years ago. The big schemes we were scheming. You can change the world, rearrange the world. Hah!

I must have dozed off at some point, because when I stir myself and look around, there's nobody else in the room. What's her name—Rosalie—is gone. If she was ever here. Or anywhere. Had she visited me only in a dream? Increasingly these days I find myself wandering around in borderlands where dreams and not-dreams intermingle. She easily could have slipped across the dream frontier for a while, and then disappeared into the mists once again.

Within a day or two I'm convinced that the woman had indeed been only an extraordinarily vivid chimera. So when there comes a rapping on my front door a few days later, I'm startled all over again to find her once more standing there, an impudent grin on her face. Instead of the outlandish dashiki, she's wearing tight blue jeans and a black sweatshirt with bright vermillion lettering declaring "Pinch Yourself, I'm Real!" And is she ever. Dressed this way, she compels you to think of ancient goddess figurines—substantial breasts, bulging tummy, thick thighs like the sinuous limbs of arbutus trees.

We sit together in the kitchen again, this time in easy chairs facing the woodstove. I'd lit a fire earlier against the March chill, and we can see small flames dancing through the glass stove door. We exchange pleasantries for a few minutes, during which this Rosalie gives no indication that she's here to do housework or perform any other home support chores. Maybe I just imagined that was who she was.

4

ROSALIE SLOANE SPENDS SEVERAL DAYS ON-AND-OFF PONDERING THE possibilities of Mr. Shorter. He's the fifth, and decidedly most promising, old islander she's made contact with on her project. She's only been on the island a couple months, having left behind, at least for now, a disagreeable relationship she probably should have ended long before and a well-paying but spiritually anemic job. Public relations. The once-reputable firm seemed to her to be sliding toward image enhancement for highly placed predators. "Pubic relations" she'd taken to calling it. Plus she'd finally admitted to herself that she was locked in the tightening grip of addiction to life online. Social media, surfing the net, brainless browsing, any diversion the screen had to offer, no matter how vacuous. She'd become a slave to texts and tones, constantly awaiting something brilliantly significant that never did arrive but promised to on the *very next ping.*

Finally she wrenched herself free. After a particularly flatline meeting downtown one morning, she strode out of the glass tower and headed down Georgia Street toward Stanley Park. What took her in that direction, and why, she couldn't have said. But something had broken, something had snapped. Standing on the edge of Lost Lagoon, she fumbled in her pocket and pulled out her smart phone. She stared at it as you'd stare at a venomous spider on your hand. Resisting the urge to check her emails one more time, she hurled the goddamn thing as high and far as she could. It sailed in a graceful arc above the water, splashed down and instantly sank out of sight. She stood there triumphant among the Canada geese, almost giddy with relief.

Later she took to laughingly calling herself a cyber survivor. She would, she decided right there on the banks of the lagoon, take some time off to reclaim her authentic self, regain her bearings. Not so much a mid-life crisis, she told her closest friends, but a time of sanctuary, a rural retreat during which life's larger questions might be more productively addressed.

Through a convoluted sequence of circumstances, she landed on Conception Island—where she had found a smallish house at a reasonable rent. She sank into island life, the silence and serenity, the extreme lack of hassle, as gently as into a warm bath. Trouble was, after a sweet interlude of indolence she came to realize that reflective seclusion can fill only so many hours in a day. At least for her.

A creature of transactional habits, she instinctively needed to sink her teeth into something. She signed up for yoga classes, and tai chi, even qigong. They maybe gave her increased balance and enhanced mental awareness, but not the amped-up engagement the smart phone had deceitfully promised, which she still craved.

Then one morning a small inspiration blossomed. The island, she was well aware, had been one of many West Coast hubs of countercultural ferment back in the '60s and '70s. Remnants of it were still in evidence—tattered prayer flags hanging from trees, peace-and-love graffiti, pottery and poetry around every corner. With all the time in the world at her disposal, why not look into compiling a dossier of reminiscences by local veteran back-to-the-landers? What had become of them and of the ideals that fired their enthusiasms a half-century ago? She didn't concern herself at the outset as to what she'd do with the material, maybe feature pieces for a magazine, maybe a book, maybe just donating it to the island's museum. Gathering the stories might be gratifying enough in itself—no matter what, if anything, became of them.

She began by asking around at the general store and post office, going to a couple of senior's lunches as well as to Sunday service at the Anglican church, discreetly picking up information about potential sources, winnowing out those that were already dead or long gone. Eventually she had half a dozen names that offered possibility.

Starting out, it took only a few minutes of amiable conversation for her to realize that the first old gent she approached, though quite delightful, was suffering from an advanced dementia that enabled him to repeat verbatim a convoluted tale he'd already told her only minutes before. Charming in his mad innocence, he was entirely unreliable as an authentic historical source.

Undaunted, she next visited a tiny white-haired woman and her equally tiny and white-haired husband, the two of them huddled together in an immaculate double-wide mobile home. These two were extremely welcoming and seemed eager to assist her in any way they could, although nothing about them even remotely hinted at a connection to the Woodstock generation. Nevertheless, Rosalie settled in and began by asking a few preliminary questions, for each of which they tripped over one another in their eagerness to answer. Trouble was, every question she asked them, no matter the subject, provided them an opportunity to smoothly segue into a mini-monologue on the approaching Rapture, in which the Son of God would return to Earth in a Second Coming and triumphantly escort true believers directly to heaven. Anticipation of the Rapture seemed to underlie all of their reality. Rosalie found their singularity of focus really quite astonishing, but a little of it went a very long way and soon proved tiresome. She packed her gear and fled as soon as decency would allow, mystified by how fiery countercultural rebels—which she'd been assured these two had been—could end up as evangelical church mice.

Her third attempt, visiting an aging bachelor who lived in a crumbling log cabin overlooking the strait, proved even more dismaying. Although charming enough at the outset, the old geezer soon became absurdly flirtatious. Every question she asked seemed to elicit from him a salacious double entendre—some of them actually quite clever—followed by a brief bout of indecent snorting. Her skin crawled in his presence and she quickly bolted homeward to soak in her tub, to get the stench of him rinsed down the drain.

Visits to two other homes were less repulsive but not particularly productive either. She was close to packing in the whole project as misguided when she reached the final name on her list: Mr. Christian Shorter, reputed to be a notable member of the island's original and most prominent commune. On her first visit he was pretty fuzzy-headed and she concluded that she'd awakened him from a nap, but he disclosed enough of interest to have her return for another conversation. He mentioned a recent interview he'd had with a pair of college kids. Reminded him, he said, of his own college days pursuing a postgrad degree in English literature.

This unexpected literary twist gave Rosalie an entree she hadn't foreseen. Rather than a compendium of diverse stories from different sources, perhaps she could elicit from him a single version told with a bit of sophistication. Maybe the old fellow didn't need to be interviewed as much as nudged. Acting on the impulse of the moment, she introduced the notion that he might be interested in telling his story, the commune's story, his generation's sociological moment in the sun—tell it in his own words and at a leisurely pace rather than have it copied and pasted by academic enthusiasts who weren't here and didn't have a clue.

As expected, he straight away brushed the idea off. For one thing, he said, it sounds like a hellish amount of work. Rummaging around in all that old material, trying to make sense out of any of it. Plus how could he possibly remember even a small portion of what really occurred so long ago? The subtleties and nuances of ancient conversations. Sorting memories from imaginings. Revisiting old hurts and grievances. Ruffling the feathers of local villains, or their descendants. Not to mention the endless typing involved. "No, no," he dismissed her suggestion, "it's out of the question. Absolutely not."

She listened to his protestations without comment, other than a bit of discreet eye rolling. She'd already noted that a not entirely antique computer sat on a small table in one corner of his kitchen. Patiently she explained how he could talk to his desktop and have it do all the typing for him. Sort of. She offered to show him how.

But she doesn't insist, doesn't really press him in any way, so after a bit he imagines she's dropped this hare-brained scheme and they part on good terms, with her feeling she's adeptly gotten the thin edge of her wedge nicely driven in and him feeling the self-protective relief one does over having dodged a bullet.

A few days later she returns, carrying a packet of printer paper. Briskly she proposes that he begin at the beginning, set down whatever seems relevant, then print up the beginning pages for her to collect. As though she hadn't paid any attention to his previous refusal. Normally he has very little patience for people who don't listen, but this crazy lady is far from normal. She tells him she'll drop in the following Friday to see how he's getting along.

"Most critical," she emphasizes, "is that we closely examine those points in our story where a difference might have been made, wrong turns averted, future disasters possibly avoided. Would California be burning today if our species had chosen more wisely fifty years ago?" This strikes him as absurd overreach, the mouse that roared. He still doesn't know who this woman really is, who she's working for, why any of this is happening.

But somehow she's managed to hook him. The project seems unarguably under way already, such is the force of the woman. He fails to muster any effective objection. And, truth to tell, the whole idea, hare-brained as it is, does have a certain appeal. In fact, he's spent the few days since her first appearance, imaginary or not, mulling over the possibilities of unearthing the obscurities of his past in a systematic fashion. Foolishly, perhaps, he's positioning himself imaginatively alongside Proust's *In Search of Lost Time*. He catches himself beginning to feel something of a furtive excitement over the prospect of sharing his life story with this intriguing woman. No fool like an old fool.

Rosalie smiles winningly and finishes up by quoting Thoreau at him: "Say what you have to say, not what you ought. Any truth is better than make-believe."

Emphasis on *any*. Thus, against his better judgment, with a reckless excitement he hasn't felt for decades, he sets to work.

ONE

SO, TO BEGIN. JESS AND I ARRIVED BY CHANCE ON THE ISLAND AROUND noon on April Fool's Day, 1970. In memory at least, it was a brilliant morning of sunshine and rainbows and glittering water. We were driving a classic old vw microbus with the split windshield and double-gated side doors. Just like all the other originals—each of whom we'd salute with a peace sign when passing on a highway—we'd painted it in wildly psychedelic patterns, reminiscent of Further, the archetypal hippie bus of Ken Kesey and the Merry Pranksters. To distinguish ourselves from the crowd, rather than splashing on shrieking reds and blues and yellows, we'd used only shades of green—emerald, lime, jade, sea green and the rest. We called her Viribus in a nod to her viridescent splendour. Counter-culturing the counterculture, so we thought.

As you might imagine, we caused a bit of a stir when Jess nudged the bus down the cement ramp on the beach and onto the tiny island ferry that wasn't really a ferry at all, but a barge lashed by logging cables to a tugboat. I think it cost us $1.50 for the bus and ten cents for each of us, return. Once aboard, both of us jumped out to stand on the deck. "Wow!" Jess exclaimed, spreading her arms toward the water, mountains and sky. "How trippy is this!"

There were only three other cars on the ferry and two deckhands pretending to busy themselves with ropes and hawsers, but there wasn't an eye aboard focused on much other than us. On Jess mostly. She wore sandals, a pair of frayed blue jeans and a paisley shirt she'd pilfered from me knotted around her midriff, exposing a drumhead-tight abdomen and a suggestion of bosom that the weathered deckhands might have dropped their hawsers for.

Standing six feet tall, with her hair shorn close to her scalp and a face more wild than beautiful, she may, as she sometimes claimed, have been the great-great-granddaughter of Jesse James, not packing any heat at the moment but looking like she could.

As for myself, I was even taller, six foot seven inches in those days. My name's Christian Shorter, so just for the joke of it, everybody called me Shorter. Still do. I enhanced the vertical effect by wearing an old black top hat, a not uncommon affectation of the day. Beneath the hat, my silky brown hair, of which I was inordinately proud, hung down below my shoulders. I think I was sporting a tentative goatee by then and had what Jess described as disconcertingly blue eyes and an air of dismayed removal.

The two of us displayed ourselves like peacocks on the deck as we watched the mountains of Vancouver Island retreat behind us and the little island ahead draw nearer.

"Shorter, are you feeling some weird tingling of anticipation, or is it only me?" Jess said, laughing.

"Yeah, babe, I'm getting it too," I said. Something unaccountably arising deep inside me. Years afterwards I came to better appreciate how an entirely new place can do that to you, wisps of memory and imagination and dream somehow infusing a scene. A subtle type of intoxicant, for sure. As we stood on the deck together that glittering afternoon of arrival, we were getting something more than scenic astonishment; we were feeling that this unfamiliar place was somehow calling to us.

The plan had been to stay no longer than the afternoon. Jess needed to get back to her job at a sporting equipment co-op and I was still battering away at my master's thesis in English at the University of British Columbia. We figured we'd have lunch, do a quick spin around the island, catch this little boat back to Vancouver Island, then streak southward to be aboard the big ferry to Vancouver by evening.

We inched our way off the ferry and drove up a steep hill, at the top of which we found a small village of unpremeditated quaintness—a little general store and tiny wooden church straight off some soft-headed antiquarian's Christmas card, both painted

11

white, plus a sprawling old community hall and a scattering of vintage houses, also painted white.

Turned out the only place on the island to buy anything resembling a meal was the lunch counter at the general store. The little store was a classic: a handwritten sign saying "No caulk boots" scotch-taped to the front door, wooden plank flooring, a barrel of pickled herring, a huge wheel of cheddar cheese on the counter, gumboots on the highest shelves. All the place needed by way of authenticity was a pot-bellied stove with an old duffer sitting on a rocking chair in front of it puffing on a corncob pipe.

"Hello," Jess brightly greeted the middle-aged pair behind the counter, a miniaturized version of John Cleese alongside a plump lady with a magnificent beehive hairdo in bottled orange. The two of them just stared. By way of ritual ingratiation I doffed my topper and smiled down at them with my best you-may-be-little-but-you're-not-small smile.

"Can we get a bite to eat here?" Jess asked them as politely as she'd ever asked anyone anything in the two years I'd known her.

The storekeepers exchanged stone-faced glances. "We got sandwiches and coffee at the lunch counter," the woman said with a Midwestern twang and grudging tilt of her splendid head toward the back corner.

We perched on swivelling stools and ate white-bread devilled-egg sandwiches with coffee perked in an urn several hours, if not days, previously. Miscellaneous seedy-looking locals wandered in, principally seeking tobacco, and were greeted somewhat more warmly than we'd been. Most of them took a good gawp in our direction before shuffling out.

"Do you have a map of the island?" Jess asked the pair behind the counter.

"Nope."

"What about a tourist brochure or anything to indicate where we could or should go?" I said.

"No, we've nothing like that," the beehive said, as though it had been indecent of us to ask.

"You gotta love it," Jess said, laughing as we headed back to the van. "Tourist traps not included."

We took off down the road leading away from the ferry. Corny as it sounds, it really was like driving back in time. Narrow lanes edged with hedgerows and split-rail fencing. Old farmhouses and enormous wooden barns, gnarled apple trees in blossom. Stretches of big conifer forest and wooded cliffs dropping down to the glittering sea. You could easily have taken the scene for 1920, not 1970.

"Wow!" we both said together as we stopped the van at a vantage point overlooking the glinting sea. An enormous bald eagle perched on a snag just below us. "Can you believe it?" I said, laughing.

"Yeah," Jess agreed, "this is one mind-bending effing place. Don't you have a sense that, without even looking for it, we've somehow found home?"

We might have stayed right then and there if we'd had our camping gear and supplies, but instead we were back in Vancouver that night, back to the familiar comforts of our basement suite in Kitsilano, fine coffee at the Naam café, and the buzz of the Fourth Avenue hippie scene. After a week we wondered if we'd let our imaginations run a little too wild about the whole island thing. But at the same time we were getting bombarded non-stop with pastoral hippie anthems. Just a few days before, we'd picked up and compulsively played Joni Mitchell's *Ladies of the Canyon*, with its Woodstock imperative of getting back to the garden. We crammed into the Hollywood Theatre on West Broadway to watch the new film *Woodstock* with Crosby, Stills, Nash and Young singing Joni's song under the closing credits. Canned Heat were relentless in belting out "Going Up the Country". Bruce Cockburn's "Going to the Country" was everywhere that April too. Country-fried was definitely the flavour of the day, and both Jess and I kept having recurring images of the dreamy island we'd visited.

You'll remember that was also the spring when the immortal idiot Richard Nixon escalated the Vietnam War into Cambodia. Campuses everywhere were erupting in outrage. Then came the massacre of unarmed students by the Ohio National Guard at Kent

State. The student killings at Jackson State a few days later sealed the deal. When the news broke that day, Jess looked at me with tears streaming down her face. "Shorter," she asked, "what accommodation can be made with an authority that guns down its own unarmed children?" I had no answer beyond despair. "Fuck it!" she said, almost shouting. "Let's follow our hearts." We made up our minds right then and there that we'd somehow find a piece of land on that little island and get the hell out of the jaws of Moloch as fast as we could.

Two problems: one, tellingly, there was no real estate agent serving the island; and two, we didn't have any money. I was already up to my armpits in student loans and Jess's salary barely covered rent and food.

But we were determined. On a weekend trip back to the island, we chanced to meet one of the locals, a wiry woman of a certain age named Mercedes, who spoke with a thistly Scottish brogue and lived in a hopelessly quaint old house close by the general store. She invited us into what she called her parlour for a cup of tea with oatmeal biscuits. After a bit of polite conversation, she confided in us that she had just happened to learn that a certain old-timer was in fact interested in selling his farm if only he could find the right person to take it off his hands. Mercedes didn't wish to be directly involved in the business—"the very walls have ears around here," she confided conspiratorially—but gave us the name and location of the farmer (there were no street numbers in those days and he had no phone) and suggested we pay him a visit.

We found the place with no trouble, at the end of a narrow dirt road that threaded through a forest of big conifers for half a mile or so. At first glance, the farm looked decidedly unpromising. Almost derelict. A large wooden barn seemed to be listing to one side. The roof of the old farmhouse was blanketed in moss and its white shiplap walls were blistered with peeling paint. Various bits of rusting equipment lay scattered around the yard. Wire fences wobbled drunkenly off across weedy pastures. Mostly it looked like an insane amount of work.

We were expecting the owner to be some variety of crazed

hermit, but instead were greeted at the kitchen door by a beaming old chap named Willie Peave. Wearing striped coveralls and a threadbare hickory shirt, he was a grizzled little customer with thinning grey hair going off in all directions like Albert Einstein's. A half-dozen mongrel dogs of various sizes and colours snuffled away at him and at us until he banished them outdoors. Without any preliminaries as to who we were or why we had come banging on his door, he led us to his kitchen table and insisted that we have coffee with him. We were already sloshing with Mercedes's tea but felt we couldn't refuse. His method of serving coffee involved placing mugs of steaming water in front of us along with a jar of instant coffee, a mason jar of creamy but weird-tasting milk ("straight from the udder this morning") and a single spoon.

The kitchen itself was unreconstructed rustic with stout wooden posts and beams, mullioned windows, rough wooden counters and cupboards and an antique woodstove. We chatted briefly about this and that, but Willie soon cut to the chase. "You here about the farm then, are yeh?" He attempted a look of calculated shrewdness that didn't really fit on his cheerful face.

"That's right," Jess said with a smile that could have disarmed a foaming neo-Nazi.

"Could be I'd be willing to sell," Willie admitted, "to the right people." He eyed us cunningly. "And for the right price." He leaned back and folded his arms across his chest as though he'd just laid down a winning hand.

"And what might that price be?" I asked, saving Jess for the hard bargaining that was sure to ensue.

"Oh...," Willie said, dragging out the single syllable as though he was at that moment considering his price for the very first time, "I was thinkin' maybe—and we're talkin' cash here, right? Cash on the barrel?"

"Naturally," I said, as though I'd ever even seen enough cash to buy a farm.

"Had one of the locals approach me the other day," Willie spoke confidentially, taking a swallow of coffee while allowing this new wrinkle to sink in.

"And?" Jess prompted him.

"Had his eye on this place for quite a while. One of them kinda fellas, you know." We nodded knowingly.

"Offered me a certain figure."

"Yes," I said. Was Willie maybe the shrewdest negotiator this side of Henry Kissinger, and was mention of this other offer part of a crafty bargaining strategy?

"Way below market value," Willie snorted. Innocently, neither Jess nor I probed for the figure. "Took me for a fool, I guess," Willie added pointedly.

"Can we...," I began, but he cut me off with a wave of his hand.

"So you got the house here," he said, "maybe could use a new coat of paint and such but solid as Gibraltar, and the barn, full quarter section, fenced and cross fenced, forty-acre woodlot with prime timber, a real good well, plus a small lake holds water all year, two fine milkin' goats, dozen hens, reliable tractor, hay baler, tiller and stuff, two years' supply of firewood split and stacked, and them dogs."

"The dogs are included?" I asked, thinking perhaps I'd misheard.

"Yep. Place I plan to retire to won't take no pets. Not even a damn parakeet. Besides, them dogs all belong here. No dogs, no sale."

"I see." I looked at Jess, wondering if we really wanted to take on such a ramshackle place and a pack of mongrels as well.

"So, Willie, with all that in mind," Jess asked him gently, "what's your asking price?"

Willie paused for a moment, calculating. "Well, seein' as you're young folk just startin' out, and Lord only knows this place needs some young energy—I don't mean just the farm neither, I mean the whole damn community; way too many greyhairs here—that being the case, I'm prepared to give you a reduced price." He paused for a moment, then added, "Considerably reduced."

"How considerably?" Jess asked with a sweet smile.

"Very considerably," Willie replied with a wink. You could tell he liked Jess, liked playing along with her.

"We need a number, Willie," Jess prodded him.

He seemed reluctant to actually quote a price, almost as though he didn't really know what the place was worth. Or perhaps was embarrassed that he might ask too much or too little. It occurred to me then that we should have enquired what the assessed value was on his taxation notice, but just as I was about to do so, Willie asked: "How would you feel about eleven thousand dollars? Cash."

We just about fell off our chairs. Eleven grand for a whole farm, buildings, equipment and all? I don't know what sort of figure we were expecting, but for sure it was a damn sight higher than eleven thousand. (Nowadays around here you couldn't buy an outhouse for that, if they even let you have an outhouse anymore.) Jess and I were so confounded that for a moment we didn't say anything in response. Willie looked from one of us to the other for a minute or two, a worried frown gradually assembling itself on his face.

"Well," he said eventually, "look: if that's too rich for you kids, I might be arm-twisted into ten-five, but that's the bottom. Absolutely. Otherwise I'll be down to what that pompous ass Gilport offered."

"No, no," Jess said, recovering herself. "Say, would you mind if Shorter and I went outside for a minute or two to discuss things?"

"Not at all," Willie said with a magnanimous wave of his arm, "you talk all you want, take your time. I'll be right here."

We went outside and were instantly surrounded by the dog pack, sniffing and snuffling. All of us jostled our way across the yard toward the big barn.

"Can you believe it?" Jess asked. "All of this for eleven grand. I'm totally mind-blown." She had an almost rapturous look on her face at that moment, like Grace Slick in full flight.

For myself, I wasn't so sure. Suddenly I was thinking about my thesis, the comforts of the city. Colleagues. Career. I was pretty sure I didn't possess a single skill that would be useful in making a go of this tumbledown place. I was, I suppose, afraid. As one is at major crossroads, even if you're too dumb to know at the time that you're at one. Most critically, I loved Jess, loved her right down to the deepest twists of my DNA. Loved her in a way I'd never loved anyone or anything in my life before. Whatever she wanted, I wanted.

"Let's at least have a look around the place first," I said, temporizing, "just to be sure."

"Good idea."

We went back inside and asked Willie if he was up to showing us around the place.

"Sure thing," he said, getting up from his chair with sprightly enthusiasm. "I can see you kids aren't the type to buy a pig in a poke."

We wandered around with Willie for a good hour or more, the dogs trailing us at first, then gradually scattering for their own pursuits. Willie took us into the veggie patch, which he admitted had seen better days, what with the fence toppling and the rows of raspberry canes gone jungle. We looked at the henhouse and chicken run where about a dozen plump hens and a lordly rooster were scratching in the dirt. "Rhode Island Reds," Willie said, "darn good hens. Way more eggs than I can eat, of course, so I use the surplus for dog feed." A pair of goats mooched around in a meadow, ignoring our intrusion. "Alpine and Nubian," Willie told us, "cantankerous as hell, but boy-o-boy, they're great animals to have around. Calm your nerves kind of thing, you know? There's a couple of billies on the island, so these gals are easy enough to get bred."

"How come you don't keep your own?" I asked.

"What, a billy? Hah!" Willie laughed. "Go spend ten minutes near a billy with the hots and you'll know why. You talk about disgusting. Whew! Sours the milk to boot." Willie gave no hint that he thought he was talking to the damnedest fool of a greenhorn.

When we got to the woodlot at the back of the farm, Jess and I just about exfoliated, it was that beautiful. Dozens of old-growth Douglas firs towered over us, as big as anything in Stanley Park. Veteran red cedars too, as Willie pointed out (neither Jess nor I really knew one species from another back then), along with younger firs, western hemlocks and bigleaf maples, all of them widely spaced and splashed with slanting sunbeams. "Selection management, the foresters call it," Willie told us, "which is an educated way of saying you select individual trees to cut instead of knocking them all down at once. Takes a real genius to figure that out. Anyhows, forty acres is way more than enough to keep you in firewood and fence posts and everything without destroying the whole thing."

We stood in a small sunlit clearing staring up at the giant veterans. It was like something out of *The Lord of the Rings*.

"Eagle nest in that one," Willie said, pointing, "and we used to have a heron rookery back over in the far corner, but they've abandoned it for now. Ravens got too much for them, I guess. They'll probably be back in a few years' time."

He stared up into the canopy for a minute more, then he put on a solemn face and looked intently first at Jess, then me. "One thing I'd expect of anyone buying this place," he said, "is that they'd respect the trees. These big fellas were already old before anyone in Europe even knew about this continent. They deserve to stand for as long as they want and fall in their own good time. You understand what I'm saying?"

"Of course we do, Willie," Jess said, laying a hand on his arm. "These trees are incredible. Pardon my French, but you'd have to be a total asshole to damage any of them."

"Exactly right," he said, "they're a sacred trust, and whoever ends up getting the farm—whether it's you kids or somebody else—has to take a solemn oath to preserve this forest intact. That doesn't mean no cutting, it means no devastation."

Next he showed us a little lake—he reckoned it was just over five acres—bordered mostly by slender alder trees, but with one long meadow sweeping down to it. "Spring-fed," he told us. "Rises a tetch in the winter rains, but most of the year stays around the level she's at right now. There's a little creek on the far side drains down to the salt chuck. One thing you can't overestimate on any of these islands is the value of fresh water."

"Does it have a name?" Jess asked.

"Well," he said with a chuckle, "in fact it does. Old Pentlatch name, I believe, but no matter how many gol-darn times I had it said to me, I couldn't ever keep it straight. So rather than insult it with a mishmash, I call it Ponder." He stared across the pond to where a small creature was gliding through the glassy surface, creating a smooth V in its wake. "River otter, it looks like," he said. "The thing is, this was a sacred place for the local people. They'd have a summer camp on the beach down below. 'Til the smallpox just about wiped them out. There's a midden right down where this little outlet creek reaches tidewater, and they'd follow a trail along the creek up to this lake."

"Do you know why?" I asked.

"Not so's I could say. There was some sort of ceremonies involved and they were still happening in a small way when my dad was a boy. My dad and my grandpa got on with the original people well enough, which is not something I can say about everyone on this island." He stared pensively at the little lake for a while. "I remember my old man telling me there were human remains discovered up there when the land was first being broken for farming."

"And what happened to them?" I asked.

"Seem to remember him saying they were scooped up by some ant... anth... oh, what the hell is it?—anthropologists, that's it, who took them all off to New York or Chicago or one of them places."

We said nothing for a minute, and Willie continued gazing off across the meadow and pond. "You can see them here, sometimes," he murmured, almost to himself.

"See who?" I asked.

"The ones who lived here all those years, all those centuries. Down along the lakeshore. Ghosts, I guess, or—what do they call 'em?—wraiths. Kinda like mist people almost. If you're quiet enough, you'll maybe hear them singing and drumming."

Jess and I exchanged a glance, wondering about Willie.

We worked our way back to the house, Willie kinda hummuttering to himself, Jess with the silliest grin on her face and me pretty much in a stupor over how beguiling the farm was. I don't know if it was pure romantic delusion, but I could see myself living happily here with Jess forever, blissfully communing with Thomas Hardy and the Brontë girls. Nearing the house, Jess made a diversion under the guise of getting something from the van and beckoned me to follow.

"What do you think?" I asked her.

"No thinking required on this one, Shorter," she said. "If we don't grab this place right away, we'll be kicking ourselves ever after for pathological dumbness."

"But where can we possibly get the cash?" I asked, almost whispering, although we were a ways from the house and the mutts were making enough commotion to cover our conversation.

"Trust me," Jess said, with a wink.

Right then and there I stuffed my apprehensions into a hidden recess, looked Jess in the eye with more bravado than I was actually feeling and said, "Okay, let's do it."

We marched back inside and told Willie we wanted to buy the place for eleven thousand cash but it might take us a couple of weeks to come up with the money.

"No rush at all," Willie said. "I been here for almost eighty years; figure I can last a little while longer. And I want to tell you I'm real pleased that you've decided it's the right place for you. I have a feeling that you're going to do real, real well here." Then he stood solemnly in front of us, the way a rent-a-priest or rabbi might. "Now, you kids, I want us to shake hands on this, okay? Meaning she's a done deal. I'll talk to my lawyer and see about getting the paperwork all lined up, and you'll get the money. If you can't come up with the full price in cash within, let's say, a month, the deal will be off and I'll feel free to entertain other offers, as they say. That good with you?"

"Absolutely," Jess told him, and I nodded.

"Great," Willie said smiling. We both shook hands with him, as though in a ritual sanctified through the ages, then Jess and I shook hands, half solemn and half foolish. The die was cast, our future framed.

Willie slapped us convivially on the back as we were leaving. "I sure do hope we can close the deal. I'd feel real good about leaving the place to you kids, knowing you were going to make a go of it, unlike a certain vulture I could mention who'd log off all that prime timber, then flip the land to some slimy developer."

Funny to think of it now, all these years later, with me sitting here almost as old as Willie was back then. And in pretty much the same situation. All the crazy, painful, beautiful stuff that went on between that day and this. Unbelievable, really. I guess it's called life, but who the hell would have known at the time?

Jess was as good as her word. "I'm going to go see Daddy," she told me with remarkable calm on our way back to Vancouver. Remarkable because Jess, my beloved radical firebrand, was in real life the daughter of Richard Trimble, an executive vice-president with the oil company Mobil, which on our righteous ethics ladder put him only a few rungs above François Duvalier and Pol Pot. But however much each of them disapproved of the other's choices, Jess and her dad loved each other solidly. Jess was his only daughter, his only child, and she was absolutely devoted to him, albeit at a comfortable distance. With Jess's mother dead from brain cancer years before, there was just the two of them, leaving love the only realistic option. Within a week, Jess had flown home to New York City and secured from her father a $20,000 advance on her inheritance.

There was, however, one proviso. Richard Trimble's affectionate largesse extended to Jess, but no further. It definitely did not include me. I don't believe the oil man actively disliked me so much as considered me a nobody, a misguided dreamer nowhere near accomplished enough for his daughter. Although deep down I might have more or less agreed with him, I resented his attitude. Eventually I would come to better appreciate his generosity in underwriting our scheme, one that surely fell far short of his ambitions for his only child. But at the time I was privately convinced that for him it was all about money. An investment. In his eyes the farm wouldn't represent a dream, but an asset. His beloved daughter wasn't so much throwing her life away as acquiring a potentially valuable commodity at a rock-bottom price and would come to her senses in due course. The money was advanced with the express understanding that title to the farm would be in Jess's name alone.

We—I should say Jess—closed the deal with Willie the following week. We sat in his kitchen drinking tumblers of blackberry wine in celebration while he regaled us with tales of growing up on the farm, and the larger-than-life characters who'd homesteaded the island, when big timber was being felled by axe and saw and hauled to tidewater on narrow-gauge rails.

"Oh, you wouldn't believe some of the pot-lickers they had around here in those early days," he laughed.

"Like who?" I asked him.

"Well, there was one old crank lived not far from here, lived alone, of course, but he hardly ever came out. You wouldn't see him for months on end. People said he didn't wear any clothes in his house and he never shaved or cut his hair. 'The hairy hermit' folks called him."

"Sounds like a hippie ahead of his time," Jess laughed.

The more he drank, the more Willie got after Gil Gilport, the islander who'd tried to buy his farm. "Took me for a gullible sucker," Willie snorted. "Offered me eight thousand dollars. Eight thousand, can you believe it? I wouldn't have sold to him if he'd offered me three times that. Damn fool thinks he's entitled, just because his grandfather got here a couple weeks before mine."

Suddenly serious, Willie continued, "But I'll tell you one thing for you to remember: watch him! And watch your backs around him. He'll resent you getting this farm when he couldn't. And if Gilports are known for anything around here, it's for holding an almighty grudge."

ON ROSALIE'S NEXT VISIT, SHORTER SHYLY PRESENTS HER WITH WHAT he's written thus far. "It's a start, anyway," he says.

She settles in by the woodstove and reads the pages through while he putters around self-consciously in the kitchen. She's disconcertingly solemn and silent as she reads, with only an occasional sigh or giggle. Shorter's unclear why the assessment of this woman he barely knows is of any importance to him, but it is. He realizes that what's under consideration here is not just the felicity of his writing, but the wisdom of his life choices. His worth as a person.

"Mr. Shorter!" Rosalie exclaims once she's finished. "This is absolutely brilliant! I love Jess already, the strength of her, and of course old Willie is perfect. I do so hope he doesn't disappear from the story." Truthfully, she's delighted with the level of detail he's included, the characters introduced, all of it. "Vastly beyond my expectations," she tells him. "A solid start, wonderfully redolent with possibilities."

In reality, Rosalie hadn't known quite what to expect. Perhaps a dozen or so sketchy pages with a complex history boiled down to a few predictable observations. But Mr. Shorter is plainly capable of far more than that. The care he's taken to describe those long-ago days gives her hope that he might, just might, with the right encouragement, produce something truly memorable.

For his part, Shorter hadn't particularly wanted to show her what he'd written, or anyone else for that matter, at least not until he'd gotten more of the disparate pieces put together in his own mind. He's fully aware that at his age you recognize that memory's pockmarked with sinkholes, requiring that you move cautiously along any byway peopled with ghosts from fifty years ago. Plus, as he tells her now, he's uneasy about putting down verbatim conversations from that misty past, incidents where he can perhaps remember the essence of what was communicated but certainly not the precise words. Or even who half the characters were.

But Rosalie urges him not to trouble himself about these details. "Just be true to the truth of the moment," she tells him, her disconcertingly dark eyes staring into what Shorter can't help but feel is the shallow pool of his soul. "The history of your own emotions—that's your touchstone," she assures him. "The guardrail that will help prevent your being sidetracked early on and wandering off course disastrously. The surrounding clutter of who exactly said what exactly is far less significant than who you were and what you were feeling at that particular moment."

To hear her talk this way, you'd think she was a tenured lit professor at Yale rather than a freelance spirit out here in the boonies, but he feels he can't argue the point.

"I particularly like the character of old Willie," she tells him, "because he so reminds me of my own dear father."

This, he realizes, is the first tiny wisp of detail she's provided about her own circumstances, who she actually is. He's been reluctant to pry, but naturally has taken to speculating, as you would. She's such a commanding figure, he can't help but wonder what the hell she's doing on this little crapshoot island visiting old relics like him. By now he's completely abandoned the notion that she's any kind of home support person. There are such people on the island, women mostly, commonly referred to as angels, who do wonders in making life easier for aging old-timers. But this Rosalie is obviously a different piece of work entirely. And intriguingly enigmatic. Where does she come from? She may have mentioned Barcelona at one point, or maybe it was Barbados? Is she, or was she, married. Does she have kids. Has she suffered through hardships, losses, disastrous love affairs—he'd really like to know. Now, with the mention of her father, he thinks that perhaps she's going to begin disclosing something of her own story, who her people are, how she comes to be sitting improbably in his kitchen, concerning herself with his story. But no: the window momentarily ajar is firmly closed. For reasons best known to herself, Rosalie has no intention of muddling up her own story with his. She can hardly wait, she tells him, for what comes next.

TWO

BACK IN VANCOUVER, WORD THAT WE'D BOUGHT LAND AND WERE PRE-paring to move to one of the islands drew very mixed reviews. My thesis supervisor, for one, was supremely unimpressed. An incred-ibly brainy little guy, rumoured to be somehow distantly related to Malcolm Muggeridge, he shook his head in dismay. "No, no, no, no, *no*," he intoned, "this you cannot do. You have an unbounded future ahead of you. You can write, publish, teach, be and do any-thing you want. Travel the world, engage with the best minds of our time. You can and should live in the world of ideas, not be slopping around in mud and manure."

My problem was I kind of agreed with him. I had a nig-gling suspicion that what we were planning was more an act of cowardly disengagement than any meaningful blow against the empire. How would militarism and racism and grotesque inequality be confronted through our retreat to sylvan glades? (Not that these urgent concerns stirred the tranquil waters of the English department either.) I attempted to argue that as soon as we got the farm up and running I'd get right back into my thesis work, though I knew I was fooling myself. But not him. "Mr. Shorter," he addressed me formally, "if you choose to depart the university in order to go live on a remote farm, without means of livelihood, you'll leave me no option but to dissolve your supervisory committee and advise the graduate committee that I have done so."

If it had been just me, I probably would have buckled at that point and gone back to my master's program rather than "back to the land." But it wasn't just me; it was me and Jess, and her voice, her energy, was vastly more persuasive than anything my primly bow-tied supervisor had to offer. When I got back home that evening, I found her sitting at the kitchen table glancing through the *Whole Earth Catalog.*

"Listen," I said to her after a ritual kiss, "I'm feeling really twisted about this whole back-to-the-land thing. I mean, I'm conflicted about abandoning my thesis. About all of it."

She stood and gave me one of her grade-A comforting hugs, then looked me straight in the eye. "Shorter," she said, holding both my arms in her firm hands, "I feel for what you're going through. Truly. But you know as well as I do that academia has long since abandoned its high calling, the quest for knowledge, in favour of careerism, unseemly grubbing after tenure and craven departmental conniving. Not to mention the endless spewing of abstruse blather specifically designed to be unintelligible to any but a small cadre of specialists huddled at narcissistic conferences in expensive hotels." This was perhaps overstating things a bit, but Jess was not a woman given to half-measures.

"Yeah, I agree with all of that, as you know," I said. "I get that we both view the city in general and the university in particular as part of the capitalist colossus that's destroying the earth."

"And wreaking havoc upon millions of impoverished victims," she said. "It's more than an academic question, Shorter. I believe we owe it to ourselves, and to the well-being of the planet, to get as far from the crap and corruption of this sick scene as we can."

I could feel myself buckling before her forcefulness.

"Shorter, love you as I do, I know in my heart the farm will set us free."

This fierce determination of hers came as no surprise. We'd originally met in Chicago, both of us eager undergraduates at Northwestern. I'd come down from Toronto on a basketball scholarship, although the basketball program had fallen on lean times back then, which was why it was recruiting even lightweight Canadians like me. Jess was there because her uncle Benjamin Trimble, Richard's older brother, sat on the university's board of trustees and could theoretically keep an eye on his niece so far from her New York home. Good luck with that, as they say.

All the credit for bringing Jess and me together belongs to Mayor Richard Daley and his goon squads. Famously, the Democratic convention was happening in Chicago in August of '68 with thousands of protesters in the streets. Yippies, SDSers, Hare Krishnas, you name your crazy. Prudently conscious of my student visa and scholarship status, I had no intention of getting myself involved in any protests, but after Jerry Rubin and Phil Ochs and the rest of them nominated the pig named Pigasus for president, I had to go downtown to have a look.

I'm jostling through the multitudes piling into Grant Park and am front and centre when a young guy decides to tear down the American flag. The cops charge in and start beating on the guy with batons, then the crowd takes to pelting the cops with rocks and bottles and whatever they can get their hands on. People are screaming "Hell no, we won't go!" and soon there's tear gas drifting everywhere. Bodies surging in all directions. Total pandemonium. I'm fumbling my way out of the park, eyes burning from gas, when I see a beefy cop swinging a billy club and viciously battering a girl curled up on the grass. Something in me snapped; prudence hitched up her skirts and fled. Totally out of character, I charged the unsuspecting cop and hit him broadside with a bodycheck that knocked him flat on his ass. Jubilant, I then kicked him so hard in the groin his reproductive rights might have been permanently compromised.

The girl looked up at me fiercely. She had a nasty gash above her left eye and blood was streaming down her face. She looked at the writhing cop, then back at me, and laughed crazily. "That your idea of peace and love, dude?" she shouted wildly over the bedlam. I helped her up and together, arm-in-arm, we staggered out of the park. Although she was brutally bloodied, she insisted she didn't need medical attention, so I helped her clean off the worst of the blood and bought some disinfectant and bandages at a drugstore we passed. As I gingerly wiped her bruised face, I saw that although she wasn't particularly beautiful, her eyes gleamed with a kind of lightning, and I found her fiercely attractive. We stuck together for the rest of the afternoon, during which I had a hell of a time

28

trying to dissuade her from rejoining the demo. Instead we went to her place.

She had an apartment in the basement of an old house midway between downtown and the campus. There was none of that silly Hollywood awkwardness of those times about whether or not I should come in with her. "Yeah, we at least gotta watch what's happening on TV," she said to me, "like true revolutionaries." Her voice was pitched low, way beneath any shrill girlie giggle, and deftly brushed with sarcasm.

At least to my ears, she sounded supremely sexy. Her cluttered living space was tiny, dominated by a single large poster of Che Guevara thumbtacked to a wall. Flopped together on her old couch we watched live coverage of cops running amok in front of the Conrad Hilton Hotel while Senator Ribicoff gave Daley a dressing-down and Hubert Humphrey smiled desperately. By tiny increments our first tentative touchings evolved into serious fondling. It was the weirdest way to fall in love, but that's what happened that evening. Curled up together on the couch, watching in disbelief as cops viciously beat anyone they came across, we felt protective love simply and gently enfold us like the wings of a nesting bird.

When I awoke the next morning, I spent a long time studying the captivating woman lying beside me. A gash on her forehead had reopened overnight, smearing the bandage with fresh blood. Several bruises on her shoulders and arms had ripened to a nasty purple. Even at rest she was unmistakably a warrior. I felt like I never wanted to get out of that bed, never wanted to not have this fiercely lovable woman beside me.

We stuck together like burrs after that, fucking like crazy by night and by day, supposedly preparing for the school year, but really thinking and talking about everything else. The assassinations of Kennedy and King that past spring. Blacks rioting in the ghettos. Daley's goons. Body bags from Vietnam. Enough already! More than enough of Chicago, and Northwestern, and the whole fucking U.S. of A. for both of us.

"Let's get the hell out of here, Shorter," Jess said one torrid evening. "We can do better than this." Without a whole lot more discussion, we recklessly packed our bags and caught a Greyhound heading north and all the way west to Vancouver. We travelled as man and wife, having hastily gotten married by a semi-sober justice of the peace, primarily for the convenience of getting Jess landed in what felt like a more civilized country. We hardly knew each other, really. But we knew love when we saw it, or thought we did. Crazy, young, heart-pumping love. Now, two years into that hasty marriage, here we were, packing and moving once more to what promised to be a better place, and a purer way of living.

One morning while we were sorting through stuff that might or might not be useful on an island farm, Jess paused for a moment and said to me, "Shorter, how would you feel if we were to ask Elizabeth if she wants to come with us?"

"To help with the move, you mean?"

"No, no, to come live on the farm with us. Her and maybe some others as well."

To be honest, my gut reaction at the time was really negative. Of course, the buzz back in those days was all about communes and "intentional communities," notwithstanding the fiascos created by hordes of Summer of Love retreads withdrawing from Haight-Ashbury to the backwoods of Oregon for terminal romps of sex, drugs and acid rock. Jess's suggestion wasn't totally off the wall, but it wasn't something we'd ever discussed. All our times snuggling together in bed, chattering excitedly about how we'd do this, that and the other thing once we got to the farm—all of it had been about the two of us, me and Jess. Which suited me just fine.

My instincts have always been toward solitude, which is why I don't so much mind being here on my own at this point. I don't associate aloneness with loneliness. Back then I didn't really know this about myself—hell, I didn't know much of anything about myself—though I think I was aware of some subliminal discomfort with the notion of tribal life. For me, a commune was perhaps intellectually correct but not especially appealing.

30

Nor was Elizabeth Alcorn someone I wanted to spend a whole lot of time with. Jess's new best friend Elizabeth was also American, from Virginia aristocracy. A couple of years earlier she'd fled to Toronto with her then boyfriend, an sds firebrand, so he could avoid the draft. They'd split up within a year, but in the meantime she'd become a landed immigrant in Canada, same as Jess.

At the time I didn't bother trying to analyze what it was exactly about Elizabeth that turned me off. Sure, she was a bit of a prima donna, but not outrageously so. No question, her quick wit and clever quips enlivened things immensely in our crowd. But, although she was sophisticated and at least outwardly self-assured, she wasn't even remotely close to attractive. Heavy-set, pasty skin, wiry hair. I like to think that my resistance to including her in our grand scheme had nothing to do with her appearance; but honestly, had she been a beauty—a statuesque, long-legged, bosomy beauty—would I have had the same reluctance?

In reality, behind its shaggy self-congratulation, the counter-culture was pretty much a cesspit of male chauvinism, and I don't exempt myself from that description. Despite the best efforts of the second-wave feminists, guys still bragged about "balling a chick" as somehow being rad behaviour. Pretty girls, not clever ones, and certainly not strong-minded ones, were what dudes desired. Notwithstanding all of that, on a personal level there *was* something about Elizabeth that I found off-putting, but just how or why I couldn't have said. So I was torn about the question of having her come to the farm with us for reasons I couldn't precisely pinpoint.

Jess never pulled any "It's my farm, so I'll decide" kind of crap; nevertheless, elements of that troubling motif had already established themselves in the back alleys of my brain. If she wanted Elizabeth along, and others too, did I have any prerogatives in the matter? It *was* her farm, after all, though we always talked of it as ours. And intellectually I could appreciate she'd want some female company, women of her own age and outlook, rather than being confined to the redoubtable grannies of the island's Women's Institute. So, yes, for good or ill, we decided to invite Elizabeth along. And some others. We'd have ourselves a commune. We'd live together in the big farmhouse, pooling whatever money and resources we had and sharing equally in household and farm work. Piece of cake.

Remarkable in hindsight how glibly we skipped into this consequential decision. Same as our slam-bang impulse to get married. Or to abandon college in the States. Profound life choices determined as casually as though we were deciding which restaurant to choose for dinner. Stupid or honestly instinctive, who's to say.

"Who else should we invite?" I asked Jess, knowing sure as hell I didn't want Elizabeth alone.

"I'll ask Elizabeth if she's interested first," Jess said, "and if she is, the three of us can discuss who else might be a good fit." So already a certain amount of power was being devolved to Elizabeth. Just like that.

Elizabeth came for dinner the following evening, having earlier in the day yelped with joy over the phone when Jess invited her to join the putative commune. We ate burritos with homemade salsa, one of the few dishes I could reliably prepare. The Moody Blues album *On the Threshold of a Dream* was playing on the stereo.

"So, Shorter," Elizabeth jumped right in, "you cool with me coming along with you guys?" I had more than an inkling that her feelings toward me were as mixed as mine toward her. No denying the instinctual sense I had that I was being pulled into something I would later greatly regret.

"Absolutely," I lied mid-mouthful. Jess was watching me with an amused smile on her face, I'm sure at least partly aware of my misgivings, though I'd said nothing explicitly to her. It would take me a fair while yet before I recognized how adept Jess was at reading my inner thoughts. "I mean, intentional communities are what's happening, right?" I said blithely. "Like, that's the future."

"Right on," Elizabeth said with a ritual fist pump.

All three of us were probably conscious of a fundamental dishonesty beneath this insincere exchange, but did any of us have an inkling of its depth or its potentially painful consequences? Looking back now, the whole thing seems like a youthful pipe dream unfettered by common sense. Which is maybe what it needed to be.

After dinner, sprawled on our old overstuffed furniture in the living room, we smoked a joint and began to discuss who else should be invited to join us. Since we'd all be sharing a living space, we decided, righteously, that tobacco smokers would not be asked. A couple of names came up and were instantly vetoed by one or the other of us. Then Jess proposed a young couple we knew named Enzo and Lena, largely on the basis of Lena being a co-worker who regularly fantasized aloud about getting back to the land. Plus she had some Aboriginal blood in her veins and that counted hugely. By way of counterbalance, her partner Enzo was overweight, myopic, laughably hypocondriacal and maybe the most impractical person any of us had ever met. He was also incredibly funny in a self-deprecating kind of way. Everybody loved Enzo, though he was the absolute last person you'd want around in any kind of emergency. We all agreed they would be a good fit and should be invited.

I then proposed Angus McLeod, who I didn't really know all that well. Nobody did. He was a man of few words and a bit of a solitary oyster, never hooking up with anyone and apparently not wanting to. Although his manner was as quiet and steady as stones, his looks gave the impression of a colourful character, compact and muscular, with his hair shorn short, ridiculously bushy eyebrows and an extravagant red beard, meticulously clipped, in which hummingbirds might have nested. He worked as a mail carrier, delivering door-to-door in Kitsilano. Mostly he held considerable social cred from his evocative playing of Scottish smallpipes. Our crowd had enjoyed many a fine night lying around stoned while Angus beguiled us with mournful laments from the Islands of the West. Sometimes Jess would join him on her banjo. He wasn't one to talk about his past, but we did know that he'd grown up on the Outer Hebrides, meaning he was the only one of us who knew anything at all about island life or rural self-sufficiency.

Elizabeth balked at first. She didn't, or couldn't, disclose why she'd prefer Angus not be invited. But Jess and I both wanted him included, and so eventually he was.

Several other possibles were discussed, some of whom were rejected and some who subsequently said thanks but no thanks. So for the moment we stabilized at a wobbly half-dozen: two couples, two singles, median age late-twenties, except for Lena, who was barely twenty, and Angus, who was into his thirties but in fact looked timeless behind his Gimli beard. Other than Lena, who'd grown up in Prince George, and arguably Angus, we were all children of privilege—Elizabeth and Jess inordinately so. Enzo's financial status was a mystery; all we knew was that his family was based in Andorra, the well-heeled principality and tax haven sheltered somewhere in the Pyrenees, and that he was currently working the till at a BC Liquor Store.

Looking back, you could hardly credit what a bunch of damn fools we were, knowing virtually nothing about one another, even less about rural living, less still about the stresses and perils of communal life. No consideration given to how we would support ourselves out on the island, buoyed as we were by a near-mystical belief in self-sufficiency. No problemo, man. We were, we felt, good to go.

"GOOD MORNING, MR. SHORTER!" ROSALIE EXCLAIMS JOVIALLY ON HER next visit. "What a gorgeous morning we've got! Here, I've brought us a treat," she says, presenting him with a platter of homemade oatmeal cookies. Straight away she sets about preparing a pot of mint tea for the two of them. Maybe it's the bright sunshine, maybe the snowdrops blooming in her yard this morning, but she feels a bright enlivening, for sure.

For his part, despite her cheerfulness and her enthusiasm last week, Shorter's apprehensive about what she will make of chapter two.

"Ah, yes," she says, settling into a chair across the kitchen table from where he's sitting. "The engaging foolhardiness of the young! Your generation especially. Born into unprecedented privilege—if you were the right colour, of course. How wonderful to come of age in such intoxicating freedom. Empowered to shout into the face of authority, and to rage against repression."

At the time, Shorter didn't view the scene as quite so triumphal, but he holds his tongue.

"Oh, I do love your Jess already, Guevara poster and all!" Rosalie says. She's gazing out the kitchen window as though history itself was at that moment holding a noisy parade across the barnyard. Once again, Shorter doesn't know quite what to make of her. She's plainly not cut from straight cloth, though she's not really alternate either. A strange hybrid of some sort. "What opportunities you enjoyed!" she continues. "I envy you that, though not perhaps what your generation eventually managed to make of them."

Sensing a rebuke in the offing, Shorter sits calmly across from her and says nothing. After decades of hippie mocking and boomer bashing, he's pretty indifferent to this sort of thing.

Rosalie has decided beforehand that this morning she'll be deliberately provocative, a preliminary test of how far she can safely push Shorter. "Yes," she continues, "Muggeridge may well have been prescient with his denunciations of your pot and pills." Rosalie picking up on his passing reference to Malcolm Muggeridge strikes Shorter as odd. Surely she doesn't align herself with that crusty old curmudgeon. Not to mention notorious groper. Yes, he's feeling a tad defensive about her slagging his generation, naturally, but he resists the urge to slap back with the mud on Muggeridge.

Although Rosalie doesn't explicitly say so, Shorter wonders if she perhaps disapproves of the melee in Chicago. Which gets him thinking perhaps he should tone down the bit about his clobbering the cop who was beating on Jess. Not exactly Martin Luther King material. Maybe Jess and him tumbling into the sack before they hardly knew each other's names has struck a sour note. He really wants to tell Rosalie that both of those events were completely anomalous for him. In the half-century since, he wants to tell her, he's never done anything else close to either one of them. He doesn't know why it's important to him that he disclose any of this to a person he scarcely knows, but it is.

Switching tracks seamlessly, Rosalie says, "Oh yes, I quite appreciate the specific details you've given us about your fellow travellers, forming as they did a small component of the 'back to the land' migration. It really was a significant sociological event, wasn't it? Well before my time, of course." Truthfully she's feeling optimistic that his cast of unlikely characters is sufficiently diverse to maintain reader interest. "A touch more ethnic diversity wouldn't hurt, would it?" she says. "But in reality I guess it was what it was." She takes a sip of tea, musing. "Still, the choices you all made, or failed to make, and your reasons for doing so—these are precisely the nuts and bolts of the whole apparatus that need to be examined."

Though she doesn't mention it, she's feeling a growing confidence that Shorter's not only up to the task but plainly quite capable of exceeding her initial expectations.

Perhaps as a sidebar to the project, she's also experiencing a gratifying sense that she's coming to feel herself a smidge more deeply rooted on the island.

THREE

OUR HUGE RENTAL TRUCK, STUFFED WITH EVERYBODY'S PRIZED POSSES-sions, barely squeezed onto the little ferry, taking up most of the deck, which meant that several vehicles occupied by less-than-happy islanders were left behind. I was at the wheel with Angus riding shotgun, as we road warriors said. On the trip up from Vancouver I'd managed only narrowly to avoid maiming several innocent bystanders due to inexpert handling of the monster truck. Jess and Elizabeth had caught the previous ferry in Viribus, also stuffed with gear. Enzo and Lena had failed to arrive at the ferry terminal in their dilapidated Datsun pickup, but we figured they'd be along sooner or later.

"You'll have to take her real slow and easy getting off the other side," one of the deckhands advised, "or you'll be scraping bottom on the ramp." I thanked him and he asked me where we were headed.

"Peave Farm," I told him, then added with a fatuous note of pride, "we're the new owners."

"Oh, yeh," he said. "Heard there was new people had bought out old Willie. So, slow and easy, okay?"

"New people" is how we'd be known for at least several decades, us and the mini-horde of back-to-the-landers who'd be arriving in our wake over the next few years. "Oh, yes," our friend Mercedes told us with a wry smile when we dropped in to thank her for steering us to Willie in the first place, "you have to live here at least forty years before you're accepted as one of them."

What did we care. We had our farm, we had our tribe and we had our freedom. Willie greeted us in the barnyard wearing his Sunday best and carrying a small suitcase. He departed almost right away, after giving us some rudimentary instructions that mostly involved the dogs, each of which he hugged with a tearful farewell. "Good luck, you kids," he said to us before going.

After the sadness of watching old Willie take his leave, everyone in the group was over the top with how gorgeous the farm was. We ran around the meadows and woodlands like a bunch of crazies, with Willie's mad hounds dashing around too. But soon enough Angus reminded us we had to get the big truck unloaded so we could get it back to Vancouver the next morning.

As high as we were about the farm itself, we were forced straight away to get into the challenges of animal husbandry. The chickens were well set up with a snug little henhouse and a large fenced coop. "Don't let them wander, especially at night," Willie had warned us, "or the mink will tear them to pieces. Savage bastards, them mink."

The goats—Gracie the oldest, Sara her daughter—were supposed to live in the barn but steadfastly refused to go in it. We quickly learned that goats do precisely what goats want to do. They'd taken up temporary residence in an open machine shed off to the side, and we dutifully moved their milking stand over there. Sara had given birth that spring and, for reasons of his own, Willie had already weaned the kid and taken it elsewhere. Straight away the goats made it clear that they approved of Jess and Lena while maintaining a dignified contempt for the rest of us. The feeling being pretty much mutual, this arrangement suited the rest of us just fine. Most of the time we just turned them loose in an over-grown pasture where they could browse on encroaching salal, wild roses and trailing blackberry.

Right from that first day, Lena did most of the milking. "Oh yeah," Willie had advised, "milking females definitely prefer a regular person pulling on their teats. You'll probably find they'll refuse to let their milk down for anyone else, or decline to mount the milking stand, or kick the bucket over or just generally indicate you should fuck right off." Sure enough, the goats let us know straight off that they were happier with milkmaids than milkmen, so Jess served as backup when Lena couldn't do it.

Lena instantly loved the goats. Loved the ripe musky smell of them, their warm breath on a frigid evening, the satisfying plash of milk in the pail as she gently worked their teats.

"She loves those wretched creatures more than she loves me," Enzo joked.

"Only because they're so like you," Lena laughed back.

Truth to tell, the milk took some getting used to at first. Undeniably it smelled and tasted goaty. But eventually we'd come to appreciate the stuff—except for Enzo, who broke out in a rash at the sight of it. Pretty soon, all three women got into making yogourt as well as a wonderful soft cheese that became staples of our diet. Perversely, Enzo wouldn't touch the yogourt but could wolf down what he called the *fromage de chèvre* with the best of us.

Of all our creatures great and small, Willie's dogs were definitely the most problematic. There were five of them, three biggish ones and two miniatures. They were the rattiest-looking pack of mongrels you could imagine, unwashed, unbrushed and always underfoot. And always hungry. We were soon spending more on dog food than on grub for ourselves. They obviously really missed Willie and didn't much take to any of us, any more than we took to them. Willie had kept them indoors most of the time, but we routinely booted them out of the house, especially at night. If nothing else, we figured their presence in the yard would deter mink or other marauders from harassing the chickens. But, worryingly, they'd sometimes run off overnight, eventually reappearing covered in mud and burrs.

We'd scarcely been on the farm a few weeks when, early one morning, a battered pickup came screeching into the yard with a young guy at the wheel.

"You lookin' after Willie's dogs then, are yeh?" he calls from the cab to Lena, who's just on her way back from the henhouse carrying a basket of eggs.

"That's right," she tells him, coming up to his truck. "Willie couldn't have them at the retirement home."

"Yah, well, they were runnin' sheep in my pasture this morning."

"Oh, I'm so sorry...," Lena starts to say, but the guy cuts her off.

"I see 'em again and they're dead dogs, okay?"

"Of course, I..."

But before Lena can finish her sentence, he guns the truck and peels out of the yard, tires spraying gravel and dust.

So that evening we were forced to sit around the kitchen table and hold a What-Are-We-Going-To-Do-About-The-Dogs meeting. We discussed but abandoned the idea of contacting Willie for advice. We had already tried keeping them chained up, but they'd howled and bayed all day and night. Various ideas were floated and discarded.

Finally, after sitting quiet through the discussion, Elizabeth pipes up to tell us that she's a dog person, something she's never bothered to mention before.

"Absolutely," she declares, tilting her head sideways like the queen on a postage stamp. "My mother used to raise bichons frises" (she pronounces the name like *BEE-shawn FREE-says*, just so we'd know) "and I would help her with baths, exercise, training. Believe it or not," she scans the group of us as though looking for doubters, "I'm actually quite an accomplished dog handler."

"So how come you haven't paid any attention to these mutts?" I ask her, slapping the tabletop with an impatient hand. Even after so short a time I was already feeling a nascent dislike for the smug self-congratulation of the woman.

"Well, just take a glance at them," she says disdainfully.

"I'd rather not," I say. "But look: we're stuck with them, like it or not. They're getting to be a real pain in the ass and now we've got the local hillbillies threatening to shoot them and maybe us too."

"A bit of an overstatement, don't you think, Shorter?" Jess puts in. "We're not exactly in the North Georgia wilderness."

It's true I'd just recently finished reading James Dickey's *Deliverance* and was maybe a bit ramped on the theme of murderous backwoodsmen. But it wasn't a total overstatement. I'd learned from Mercedes that the slackjaw who'd accosted Lena was part of a goofball gang that specialized in getting liquored up and roaring around the island on Saturday nights, smashing down mailboxes and firing shotguns into the air. The Desperados, they called themselves.

"But we obviously do have a problem. Elizabeth," Jess said, putting a hand on her friend's arm, "what would you recommend?" Dear Jess, always the adept facilitator.

"Well," Elizabeth said, "I do think building a run for them would be a good start. We obviously can't have them running loose."

"Wouldn't want to see them all shot, for sure," Enzo said cryptically. He'd been given to thunderous sneezing over the last few days and made no secret of the fact he believed it was being triggered by sarcoptic mange on the dogs.

Everyone looked at Enzo, uncertain if he was being funny or not—except for Lena, who gave him a quick kick under the table.

"Not fair to keep dogs caged the whole time," Angus put in, "especially dogs that are used to running free. They'll need some working and it seems to me Elizabeth's the one knows how to do it. I'm willing to help with giving them baths and stuff."

"And picking up their crap?" Elizabeth asked. The dogs did have a dismaying habit of defecating as near to the house as they could get away with. Hundreds of acres in all directions, and every mutt has to shit right outside the front door where you're most apt to step in it.

"Maybe we should each take turns on that," Jess said, "rotating days." There was a group groan at the prospect.

"Looking on the upside," I said, "Willie told us they've all been neutered, so at least we're not going to have subsequent generations to deal with."

"Elizabeth?" Jess asked.

"Oh, alright, for fuck's sakes," Elizabeth said grudgingly, "I'll take the mutts on. But I'll need help with building a run."

"Lots of old posts and wire fencing out back of the barn," Angus said, "and there's a post hole digger in the toolshed; they probably got staples down at the general store, so how about we get at it

41

tomorrow." All were in agreement and we wrapped up the meeting feeling far more pleased with ourselves than when we'd started.

"That was great," Jess whispered to me as we snuggled into bed that evening, "almost like we know what we're doing here."

In bed we were compelled to talk (and everything else) quietly because the others were all sleeping in adjacent bedrooms on the top floor of the old house and soundproofing had not been a prime consideration in its construction.

This lack of household privacy proved an inadvertent blessing in that it encouraged Jess and me to seek other locations for our lovemaking; throughout the summer months we delighted in some truly spectacular couplings in the mossy glades of the woodlot and along the sun-dappled shores of the lake, where ravishment suffered none of the constraints of a squeaky cast-iron bedstead.

"Yeah," I agreed before wafting off to sleep. We left unsaid what was obvious in hindsight: that in selecting our entourage we'd given zero thought to who had what skills. Who knew carpentry or electrical or plumbing, who was good with plants or animals, who could fix a tractor if need be. Cue Neil Young: "Helpless."

Next morning I drove down to the general store and, miraculously, found enough staples for our fencing job. The post office counter was open for business and I enquired of Cleesey whether there was any mail for us.

"What's the name?" he asked. Not your name, *the* name. I gave him my name and he riffled through a pile of mail in general delivery. "Nope," he said, not looking at me.

"Would you mind checking for my wife's too?" I asked. "Nothing under Shorter," he said.

"Yes, her surname's Trimble," I said with a smile.

He rolled his eyes as though he'd been done a great indignity. "Trimble," he muttered and thumbed through the general delivery pile once again. Sure enough, he extracted a couple of letters and flipped them onto the counter without a word.

Having survived Mayor Daley, not to mention LBJ and Nixon, I saw this ill-mannered Yank as an opportunity to have some fun. "Would you mind checking for Elizabeth Alcorn too?" I asked.

He exhaled through his nostrils with a passable show of exasperation. "Elkhorn?" he asked, as though it were a variety of rat poison.

"Alcorn," I clarified. "A. L. C. O. R. N."

Again the ritual thumb-through. A single postcard this time, similarly tossed onto the counter. "Anyone else?" he asked, attempting but failing to achieve telling sarcasm.

"Actually, yes," I told him with perfect innocence, "there's also Angus McLeod."

"Uh huh." He seemed as determined not to be provoked as I was perversely to provoke. "Anyone else while we're at it?"

"Only two more," I told him. "Would you like all three at once, or is it easier for you if we keep going one at a time?"

"Funny fella, are ya?" he said glowering up at me.

"Not at all," I said. "Just trying to be helpful, you know."

Hard to believe, looking back all these years later, but for almost a year after that, while we waited patiently for the potentates at Canada Post to approve having mail delivered to a mailbox on our road, whenever we checked for mail at the general store we were greeted with the same dyspeptic "What's the name?"

Cleesey was one for the ages.

As I was leaving the store that morning, what do I see pulling up in front of me but a VW microbus just like ours, plastered with bumper stickers and peace signs. Out of it jump three bona fide hippies-in-training, two girls and a boy, emblazoned with enough feathers and beads among them to stock a roadside stand in Arizona.

"Hey, man," the young guy hails me, "what's happenin'?"

"Life," I tell him, "and death too."

"Far out!" he exclaims, preening for the two girls, all three of them giggling.

One of the girls shimmies right up in front of me, cocks her head and stares up at me. "Wow!" she says, "you're really tall," as though I might not have noticed on my own.

"I think big too," I tell her, my stock response to uninvited observations on my height. Nobody ever says to little people, "Wow, you're really small" or to plump people, "Wow, you're really wide." But tallness is fair game when it comes to unsolicited commentary, perhaps because height is confused with ascendency and thus presumed not to be hampered by self-consciousness.

"Hey, man," the guy says, "anyplace around here we can crash for a couple of days?"

I tell them there's a campground down at the beach.

"Yeah, we checked it out," the guy says, "but they, like, charge bread, you know? Aren't there, like, any communes or crash pads or anything around here?"

So of course I end up telling them they can camp at the farm for a couple of nights, figuring maybe they can make themselves useful with the dog run or whatever.

"Far out!" they tell me. One of the girls, the one who'd taken note of my height, decides she'll ride along with me while the other two follow in the peacemobile. She looks no older than sixteen, a tangle of dirty long blond hair and the pouting prettiness of girlhood. Just as I'm pondering whether I should ask her if her mother knows where she is, she tells me the other chick's her older sister and is, like, sort of engaged to the dude.

They're all from Prince Albert, which they hate, their parents are in the middle of a vicious divorce, and the girls are just, like, anywhere but there. I nod knowingly during this disclosure, wondering if maybe I've sounded not all that much different to my thesis supervisor.

The three foundlings stayed with us for several days, dropping not-so-subtle hints that they'd love to join the commune, while furtively smoking cigarettes behind the barn as though no one would notice. But working long hours hauling posts and stretching wire for the dog pound project soon did them in. "Gotta keep rollin', y'know what I mean, dude?" the guy said to me as the three of them eventually clambered into their van and then sped away forever. They were the first of a steady stream who would show up over the years, seekers and wanderers, some only needing a brief respite in their travels, others no doubt wondering if maybe our farm might offer them an answer to their uncertainties.

Besides the drifters, that same first summer saw perhaps a dozen or so other "new people" settle on the island, then more the following year and more again the next. They came ashore as individuals, couples or small groupings determined, like ourselves, to establish an alternative lifestyle that would eventually, inevitably, transform Western civilization. Some rented old farmhouses, others had bought land, while the truly transitory simply squatted in out-of-the-way groves and alcoves. They ranged in both appearance and attitude from earnest to insane. Beards and bushy Afros on guys, long flowing hair and flowery gypsy dresses on the "chicks." While the deal Willie had given us was the last of its kind locally, raw land was still comparatively cheap, in part because the provincial government had imposed a ten-acre minimum lot size on most of the islands. This so-called "freeze" had chased off the speculators and developers, so you could pick up ten acres for six or seven thousand bucks and let the fun begin.

Almost overnight the island was swept up in a whirlwind of the Whole Earth phenomenon, featuring montages of what enthusiasts chose to call the "rural astronauts" and "new pioneers" at work and play. "Gimme Shelter" was the theme song as the hippies threw themselves into creating log cabins, geodesic domes, yurts, teepees, rammed earth houses and all the rest of it. Work bees abounded as everyone pitched in to help raise high the roofbeams. And whenever people moved from a temporary shack into their new owner-built home, a night-long, rip-roaring house party was sure to ensue.

Within just a couple of years, the island was sprinkled with owner-built homes displaying as much variety, character and flamboyance as their tract home counterparts have little. Anything but little boxes on the hillside that all look just the same. Because there was no building code in place, there was also no limit to how zany, impractical and even hazardous a house might be. While some would have lowered property values in the slums of Manila, many were, and the surviving ones still are, sensible and delightful homes. Fuelled in part by this manic building/partying phase, we Whole Earth Catalogers were developing our own breed of a countercultural community right here on the island.

Though we loved our old farmhouse, built with considerable skill from prime local fir and cedar two generations back, Jess and I initially kind of envied the experience many of our new friends were having in creating places of their own from scratch. Not needing to build a house for ourselves, that first summer on the farm we spent a lot of time larking around, swimming in the lake (clothing optional, naturally) and smoking dope. In fact it was the sacred weed that got at least some of us motivated to start reclaiming Willie's vegetable garden from the blackberries, stinging nettles and bracken that had overrun it. While still in Vancouver, Jess and I had made a point of hoarding cannabis seeds, and so had Enzo. Though already well into June, we got some seeds planted with high hopes of enough good bud to get us through the winter.

But all was not exactly well in paradise; a certain portion of the old community was far from thrilled at the sudden influx of weirdo newcomers. It didn't take long for serious head-butting to begin. The first big clash happened over nude swimming. The scene of the crime, Sunset Beach, was a secluded little bay on the north-western shoreline. Well out of public view, it offered an ideal spot to disrobe for swimming and lolling about *au naturel*. If you could get to it, that is, because a steep bank behind the beach made it all but inaccessible by foot.

Just south of the beach, perched on that same high bank, sat the impressive designer home of John and Iris Thomas, a pair of the community's more eminent citizens. Rumoured to be descended from the Christadelphian preacher of the same name, our John Thomas had occupied several important positions in the federal government, including a stint managing the Indian Affairs portfolio until his retirement to the island in 1969. Back then most of us had never heard about the Sixties Scoop, when thousands of Indigenous kids were stolen from their parents and adopted out to white families or sent to residential schools. It was only much later we learned that our man John Thomas had been close to the throttle of that nefarious episode. All we knew at the time was that he came across as an obnoxious wannabe British toff. His wife Iris was old family on the island and a cousin to Willie's nemesis, Gilbert Gilport.

John and Iris had installed an elaborate set of wooden stairs and platforms down the bank so that they and their guests could gracefully descend from their clifftop patio to the beach below, where for a short time they enjoyed exclusive access. However, several resourceful newcomers soon discovered that, on paper at least, there was a public beach access right alongside the Thomas property. The access had been dedicated when subdivision created the Thomas lot, but with an expectation that the steepness of the bank would preclude any public use and incidentally provide John and Iris with a charming tax-free scenic buffer. What had not been factored in was the ingenuity of the buff interlopers in getting from top to bottom. Working with a frenzied focus that not all of them applied to other undertakings, they hacked and chiselled out a twisting pathway down the bluff face. A thick rope attached to trees alongside the path helped with the sliding down and stumbling back up. Soon a regular cavalcade of nudies was making use of the site and, needless to say, John and Iris were livid over the intrusion.

Most of us at Peave Farm weren't directly involved, as we had our own lovely lake in which to take a dip if an aquatic mood struck. But, of all people, Enzo enthusiastically took up disrobing at Sunset

Beach. "Oh, yes, it's the western slant of the sun at that particular spot I find especially ravishing," he told us all at lunch one rainy afternoon, "so reminiscent of the golden light in certain Italian Renaissance paintings." We all glanced around the table, trying not to smirk. For Enzo, naked, was not an altogether attractive sight and we were bemused that he'd expose himself so flagrantly.

"No, he's got a kooky exhibitionist streak," Lena told us one time when Enzo was off revealing himself at the beach. "He imagines people admire his love handles. Personally I enjoy them," she made a sweet gesture with both hands, "but as a visual feature?" Mostly we were all impressed that he could manage getting down and back up the steep trail.

So there you had a small multitude of new people, including roly-poly Enzo, lolling around on the beach and cavorting in the water all summer's day without a swimsuit among them while John and Iris fumed in their clifftop redoubt above.

Although nobody else on the island was directly affected, nude swimming at Sunset Beach, thanks largely to the machinations of John and Iris, soon erupted into a *cause célèbre* that engulfed the community.

In those days Iris served as president of the Community Club, the volunteer group that ran the community hall and orchestrated events for Dominion Day, Thanksgiving and Christmas, among other things. The presidency conferred a certain level of local prestige, which Iris now proceeded to wield against the nudists specifically and the new people generally.

We first got wind of trouble coming when Enzo burst into the kitchen one afternoon indignantly waving a small poster. "Look at this," he declared dramatically, "the philistines are assembling against us!" The poster denounced the gross indecency of the skinnydippers, lamenting how their activities were a slap in the face to traditional island values as well as a source of corruption for island youth. A public meeting was arranged for the coming Friday evening to discuss the issue and formulate an action plan.

"We'll have to get everyone out to that meeting," Enzo told us earnestly, "defend our rights." I think we found it curious how our laid-back and laugh-a-minute Enzo had been galvanized by this particular issue.

"We could all take our clothes off, like the Sons of Freedom," I said drolly. "That would clear the room."

Just then Jess and Elizabeth returned from their daily dog-training session, looking all brisk and outdoorish. Amazingly, in recent weeks they'd gotten the mongrel horde neatly washed and clipped and more or less brought to heel through daily training sessions. "What's up?" Jess asked. "You guys look like a parlour game that's fallen flat."

Enzo explained the situation again. "Whoa," Jess said with a mischievous laugh as she poured herself a coffee, "sounds to me like first shot across the bow in an imminent culture war."

Jess and I reluctantly accompanied Enzo to the public meeting, the first one we'd attended on the island. Angus, Elizabeth and Lena all stayed home, each with a reasonable pretext, expecting that there'd be more than enough defiant beachgoers to carry the day.

Situated near the general store, in what everyone ironically referred to as "downtown," the community hall was a venerable old building deep with character but bereft of charm. An oblong box fashioned completely from darkly stained wood, it had narrow doors, very few windows and a depressingly gloomy interior. The air inside, ripe with sweat and cigarettes, smelled like old jockstraps, as though it had been trapped in there for decades. A small stage with faded velvet curtains squatted at one end of the cavernous room.

The three of us entered the hall cautiously. It was immediately obvious that of the several dozen islanders seated in the gloom, most of whom I'd never seen before, there wasn't a single habitué of Sunset Beach other than Enzo. Recognizing a stacked deck when we saw one, the three of us sat unobtrusively in the back row, exchanging smirks and winks while the moral majority went at it hammer and tongs. Iris Thomas chaired the meeting and proved an impressive driving force, with Cleesey from the post office contributing sour asides throughout. Another vocal contributor was a thick-necked, barrel-chested character who turned out to be

Gilbert Gilport himself, the schemer Willie had warned us about. The man had a disturbingly red face, suggesting suppressed rage or perhaps an incipient stroke. It was universally agreed that a stop must be put to the nudity. "Nip it in the bud," Gil Gilport recommended, which got Enzo snickering: "Keep your nippers off my buds, bud."

Following John Thomas's strategically informed suggestions, it was agreed that an appeal would be sent to the regional district to draft a zoning bylaw forbidding nudity in all zones on the island. The Department of Highways would be petitioned to restrict parking along the public roadway above Sunset Beach. The Fish and Wildlife Branch as well as the Department of Recreation and Conservation would be asked to assess whether wildlife values were being compromised by the unauthorized footpath.

But what was really being talked about was "those people." Meaning us. While our minority presence in the room likely dampened down the tenor of invective, it was clear that "the new people," "the young people" and "the hippies" were ruining the island for most of these folks and corrupting the morals of local youth. The notion of local hooligans like the gun-toting Desperados even having morals made for an amusing sidebar. But the mood of the room was firm: long-term strategies would have to be developed to discourage hippies from congregating on the island and to replace the riff-raff with "good people."

Just as the meeting is winding down and I'm thinking we'd gotten off rather lightly, all things considered, Enzo suddenly rises from his chair, arm upraised, and calls out "Madam Chair!" Every head in the audience swivels in unison to stare at this rude intruder.

"Yes?" Iris asks with enough vinegar to pickle a jar of cucumbers. Jess and I exchange a quick look while Enzo widens his legs like a spaghetti western gunslinger.

"As one of the offending parties," Enzo begins, "I really appreciate hearing what all of you have had to say this evening." The turned heads exchange quizzical glances. "And I fully understand," Enzo continues, "that the current situation is totally unacceptable." The swivelled heads appear bewildered. Exchanging a glance, Jess and I have no idea what Enzo's up to. "Happily," he carries on, joining his hands together and smiling benignly across the crowd, "I have what I believe is the perfect solution to our present dilemma."

"And what might that be?" Iris asks sarcastically.

"You mean you're all going to bugger off?" someone—I think maybe Cleesey—calls out.

"Nothing so upsetting as that," Enzo replies suavely. "No, here's what I have in mind: a compromise of sorts, if you will. It's plain to see we have two issues here. The first is the issue of naturism." At this point Enzo abandons the relative safety of his position alongside us in the back and begins strolling up the centre aisle toward Iris, talking all the while as though he were Socrates in the Athens agora. "Naturists," he tells the crowd, "are not evil, nor even immoral persons. They, we, are simply people who repudiate contemporary standards of modesty, as do many cultures elsewhere." Having reached the front of the room, Enzo turns to face the crowd and opens his arms the way the pope does. "So in the matter of divergent social mores," he says, "there must be room for compromise. I see nothing inappropriate about taking off my clothes in the privacy of Sunset Beach, but wouldn't dream of doing so here in front of you."

A derisive cheer erupts, but Enzo's unfazed. "The second matter with which we are confronted," he explains to the increasingly restive crowd, "is the problem of the footpath. And here I believe we are on far more common ground, questioning as you have so rightly done this evening the trail's potential impact on wildlife, as well as on slope stability."

"It's a lot more stable than you are!" someone calls out, to which Enzo responds, "I couldn't agree more!"

You can see on the faces of certain audience members, women especially, that they're having a hard time sustaining any real animosity toward our affable and pudgy Enzo. Bespectacled and with a head of light curly hair, he's one of those cuddly kind of guys, generally adored by their mothers, who have learned how to get away with murder by way of innocent charm. But then he pushes it over the top. "Here's what I was thinking: that we should permanently abandon the new footpath and set about replanting it with native plants." No one knows where he's going with this, including Jess and myself. "And what we naturists would agree to do instead is make use of the excellent stairway Iris and John Thomas have constructed to get down to the beach with minimum disturbance to the bank."

A gargled gasp runs across the audience and Iris looks like she's been struck by lightning. "What?" she shrieks.

"Well, I for one would definitely prefer a dignified ascent up your fine stairway over scrabbling up that godawful goat path," Enzo says guilelessly, "and rest assured, we would be fully clothed in both descent and ascent."

"Young man!" a drill-sergeant voice rings out. It's Gil Gilport, on his feet, his Gene Kiniski brush cut bristling. "I don't know who you think you are, coming in here and prancing around like some goddamn pansy, excuse my French," this in deference to the ladies present, "but what you need to get through your thick head is that we don't want any of you faggots and freaks on this island, with or without your clothes on, so why don't you just shut your yap right now and get the hell out of here before I lose my temper."

"Yeah!" a bunch of the other men call out, the way lynch mobs do. Shit, Enzo, I'm thinking to myself, let's get going.

"Thank you for your forthrightness," Enzo calmly says to Gil. "I can see that there are some unresolved issues still at play here and certainly a need for further dialogue."

At this point Gilport, fists bunched, is beginning to shuffle menacingly toward Enzo. Finally realizing that discretion really is the better part of valour, our champion briefly bows to the crowd and briskly exits down the aisle and out the front door with me and Jess right behind him, a chorus of outraged voices buzzing like a kicked hornet's nest behind us.

"Well, at least we know where we stand," Jess joked lamely, as we sped home. "You were magnificent, Enzo," she added. Lying quietly on the bed in the back of Viribus, he grunted thanks but said nothing. I suppose we were all feeling some variety of sadness as we reflected on the bitterness and, yes, hatred we'd heard at the hall that evening. And perhaps a shiver of dread as well over the menace of Gil Gilport. Willie's warnings about the Gilport grudge suddenly seemed apt, triggering fresh visions of James Dickey's sadistic hillbillies. The bucolic anthems of Joni, Bruce and Canned Heat hadn't quite touched on this component of going up country.

Resistance efforts were soon launched. There happened in those days to be an old wooden fence that surrounded the highways works yard, and within days it carried a screaming graffiti message in bold red lettering: *I'm not a faggot I'm a freak!* Several days later somebody else added: *I'm not a freak I'm a faggot!* The graffiti fence, thus born, has been, magnificently, with us ever since. Soon buttons started appearing on-island carrying one or the other message. It quickly became fashionable to wear both buttons. Then bumper stickers started appearing. Gil Gilport was rumoured to be apoplectic with rage, most of it targeting Enzo. More strategist than combatant, Enzo repeatedly let it be known that he was not behind any of this campaign; he had only innocently shared with his fellow naturists what had happened at the meeting, including Gil's now-legendary outburst.

Skinny-dipping continued but the frolicking no longer basked in the same untroubled innocence that had marked its early days. A time of reckoning, everyone seemed to sense, was still to come.

ROSALIE IS OF TWO MINDS ABOUT THE DISCORD OF ENZO'S CONFRONTA-tion with the old-timers. Like the conflicted housewives attending the meeting, she's frankly ambivalent about Enzo and his love handles. "I have nothing against nude swimming *per se*," she assures Shorter on her next visit. "Indeed I rather enjoy a solitary swim *au naturel* myself on occasion."

Shorter imagines her: naked, magnificent, submerging herself smoothly into untroubled waters. Simultaneously he can hear the "but" coming, sure as thunder. Rosalie takes to filling the kettle and rattling around with cups and saucers for tea. Perhaps a touch of transitory moodiness, Shorter thinks, something he's not seen in her before. He casually picks up last Saturday's *Globe and Mail* and pretends to read analysis of the latest lunacy from the American president.

After fussing with the tea things, Rosalie settles herself at the table and looks at Shorter appraisingly. "Remember those wonderful photographs of flower children inserting the stems of flowers into the barrels of rifles held by grim-faced national guardsmen?" she says. "Make love not war—wasn't that the whole idea?" she asks him provocatively.

Shorter could easily argue that the flowers of hope were trampled under the jackboots of Daley's goons, how they withered and died with Malcolm and Martin and Bobby. But, he reminds himself, his purpose here is not to try to convince Rosalie, or anyone else, of the rightness or wrongness of what happened on the island all those years ago, but merely to provide a straightforward description of events as he remembers them.

By not attempting to defend or justify any of what happened, he imagines he's outmanoeuvred her. He wonders if perhaps she's afraid that her remarks have disheartened him to the point of abandoning the writing altogether. Rosalie's actually not thinking that way at all, but certainly she wants to avoid discouraging him. As she can do, she now deftly switches tracks.

"But who would have foreseen back then," she muses, "the fate that awaited Sunset Beach and adjacent shoreline. You look down there today," she shakes her head sadly, "and what you describe as a formerly lovely foreshore bathed in golden light, to my eyes, is just a godawful sprawl of retaining walls and beach cobble berms, protruding rebar spikes, acres of predator netting and multiple truck tracks."

"Yes," Shorter agrees, "that's completely true. The travails of straitlaced Iris and John Thomas battling Enzo's naturists seem a quaintly faint echo, don't they, compared with the havoc now being wreaked along that shoreline by the shellfish industry. Too weird, really, that a few naked kids enjoying themselves in the sunshine was more abhorrent than the mess that's been made in recent years."

"Nevertheless," Rosalie says, "I believe that overall the project is proceeding brilliantly. The bit about the three aimless hippie kids wandering into the commune has certainly touched a chord, and the whole sense of a new generation moving en masse to the island has enormous promise." She feels Shorter is beginning to hit his stride and now needs only an occasional touch of judicious gatekeeping from herself.

After clearing away the tea things and taking a cursory swipe at the kitchen countertops, she checks to be sure that he has sufficient printer paper to continue. "I can hardly wait," she tells him, "to read the next installment."

FOUR

DESPITE OUR BEST EFFORTS, YOU COULD SCARCELY BLAME LOCAL regulars for being alarmed at the sudden influx of so many outlandish-looking newcomers. And Peave Farm seemed to be a particular magnet. How the hell most of them found us is anybody's guess. It's as though there existed a psychic precursor to today's social media whereby information spread like grassfire over great distances unaided by any technology. Out of nowhere, suddenly there'd be a burnt-out fire-eater from Newfoundland wanting to stay for a while or a wandering trio of Guatemalan musicians willing to perform ancient Mayan music on bone flutes, rattles and drums in exchange for dinner and a place to sleep.

The times were particularly flush with wandering evangelists of all stripes—Rastafarians, Buddhists, Hare Krishnas, you name it—some of whom faithfully followed the pilgrimage trails to Peave Farm. I've forgotten more of them than I can remember now, but certainly not one. Not Christopher Volts. Without question an unforgettable visitant, he single-handedly just about wrecked our utopian idyll.

Into the yard on a bright autumn afternoon of that first year rumbled this big old Mercedes-Benz hearse, and out of it emerged a slender young guy clothed entirely in black with a large silver pendant suspended by a fine chain around his neck. With a perfectly tanned complexion and supernaturally platinum-blond hair, his manner radiated grace and beauty.

Angus and I were working over by the barn at the time, peeling young fir poles for some project or other, with far more grit than grace. We laid down our drawknives and walked over, curious to see what this visionary new arrival was about.

"Blessings!" he said with the slight bow and pressed palms of the classic namaste greeting.

"Same to you, too," Angus said in his gruff but affable way, and I nodded in agreement. Dressed in dirty coveralls and boots and sweaty from the log peeling, Angus and I stood in grubby counterpoint to this elegant stranger. At least the dog pack wasn't there to maul him, as Elizabeth had taken the mutts off for a session of what she called fieldwork.

"What can we do for you, brother?" I asked him.

"Allow me to introduce myself," he said with an amiable smile. "My name is Christopher Volts. Briefly put, I am a sojourner."

"A sojourner?" Angus asked skeptically while picking several small fir chips from his beard.

"Indeed," Christopher Volts said. "I journey between that which lies to the Far East and that to the West, between that which is most ancient and that most modern, between the social landscape and untrammelled nature."

"Any good at peeling logs?" I asked, just to test his mettle, and to his credit he laughed heartily.

"The logs I peel are primarily metaphysical," he admitted. "Nevertheless, I do maintain great appreciation for the practical arts. I'm thinking of the accomplishments of Chan as manifest by the monks who laboured as farmers and builders and much else in the great Zen monasteries of the Orient. So too I'm very much drawn to rural enclaves like your little island here, where people are coming together to work on the land and on themselves, building and growing in harmony with nature."

"That's us in spades," Angus said, "but if you'll excuse us, we'd better be getting back to our poles." Angus was built more for doing than for fancy philosophizing about doing, and I wasn't surprised that he'd quickly lost interest in our polished visitor.

Christopher smiled at Angus's brusque remark, and I thought to myself: This fellow's got some depth to him. Just then Jess emerged from the house and I waved her over. I introduced her to Christopher and left the two of them to chat. Jess, I knew, would quickly get a measure of the man. He joined us for dinner that evening, during which he chatted at length about chakras and tantric yoga, Shakti and Shiva, Zen teachings and Hindu scriptures.

"Harmless, I'd say," Jess confided to me in bed that night. "Maybe not quite the guru he imagines himself, but really well versed in myth and religion. A Zenist with Taoist tendencies, he calls himself."

"As opposed to a Taoist with Zenist tendencies?" I asked, for which I got a pointed knuckle in the ribs. "So you're thinking we should invite him to stay around?"

"Let's see what the others think," Jess said. "I got the impression at dinner that Elizabeth wasn't too taken with him."

"Well, who's Elizabeth ever taken with other than Elizabeth? Ouch!" A follow-up knuckle poked deeper.

Christopher did in fact stick around and became something of a fixture for a while. Although he took his meals with us, he insisted upon sleeping in the back of his hearse. "Perfectly private and comfortable," he told us, "and most salutary for contemplating the great adventure of death."

"Bit morbid, though, isn't it?" Angus asked. I don't believe Angus actively disliked our visitor the same way that, as became increasingly clear, Elizabeth did.

"Morbidity exists," Christopher replied smilingly, "as a byproduct of the fallacious separation of life from death, whereas the Tao teaches us that both are aspects of a single unity." Observations like these, despite the cloying earnestness, often provoked stimulating group conversations that were a welcome relief from protracted analysis of compost heaps or chainsaws.

After being with us for a short time, I think observing us as closely as we observed him, Christopher announced one evening that he would like to repay our hospitality by leading those of us who were interested through a ritual evening based loosely upon those of the Huichol peoples of western Mexico. This proposition didn't excite much general enthusiasm until he added, "I believe I have sufficient peyote for our purposes," which got everybody's attention.

Lena was particularly keen, since she'd recently been reading Carlos Castaneda's blockbuster first book about the teachings of

Don Juan Matus. I was a little surprised that Elizabeth wanted to participate, though it may have been more for the peyote than the preaching, which was certainly my own inclination. Although I'd previously ventured happily into psychedelic territory with LSD and psilocybin, I hadn't tried mescaline before, but knew the high was considered similar to the other two. Only Angus declined to join in, on the grounds that he'd long since had his fill of "religious mumbo-jumbo." Plus, he said, someone would have to look after the place: dogs, goats, chickens and all. Jess and I were the only ones who knew that about a year earlier Angus had suffered a near-psychotic episode with LSD and had sworn off all psychotropic substances other then Scotch whisky.

First off we constructed a makeshift teepee using the recently peeled poles and several old tarps. We made a fire ring of large stones in the teepee's centre, directly beneath an outlet at the peak for venting smoke. I was designated guardian of the fire, responsible for maintaining an even fire throughout, and Enzo would be our peyote drummer.

Adhering to the group's tacit understanding that food preparation was best left in women's hands, it was agreed that Jess and Elizabeth would produce a platter of brownies and butter tarts to offset the peyote's bitterness.

On the appointed evening, Christopher prepared the peyote tea according to formulas he said he'd been given by a Yaqui shaman not unlike Castaneda's Don Juan. We sat cross-legged in a circle around the fire, sipping our tea while Christopher spoke in a soft, dreamlike voice. He talked of Western culture's estrangement from nature as well as from ourselves. Of how both human nature and the natural world are mistakenly perceived as things to be conquered and rearranged through the technology of rational intelligence. Of the corrosive divisions separating body and mind, nature and humanity, object and subject, between that which is controlled and that which is controlling. Of the isolated ego floating moon-like through disconnected space.

As his talk rambled on, I could feel the peyote begin to take effect, a kind of dreamy lifting-off, like the smoke spiraling from our fire up into the dancing shadows. A mesmerizing drumbeat began and I glanced sideways to see Enzo, eyes closed, an ecstatic smile on his cherubic face, rhythmically striking his drum. Everyone in the circle seemed to be swaying like a kelp forest in dreamlike currents. Christopher continued speaking softly, though the words and phrases began interweaving and coiling back around upon themselves. The natural wisdom of Lao tzu and Chuang tzu. The seamless unity of nature. A still point in the turning world. The cosmic complexity of artfully interwoven lifelines forming an infinite tangle of self and not-self.

The fire that I continued feeding began to glow with brilliance and intensity. I saw colours dancing in the flames as I'd never seen before—strange azures and ultramarines, crimsons and carmines and blood-red rubies. The faces of angels and devils glowed in the coals. When I closed my eyes, galaxies of dots and lines oscillated in kaleidoscopic geometries. The beat of the drum became the beat of my heart and then the pulse of the breathing earth beneath me. At some point from far away there came a wailing skirl that sang of tragedy and loss, and I knew it came from Angus playing his pipes beneath the lamenting sky. Eventually opening my eyes and looking up, I saw the teepee had disappeared entirely and instead endless constellations wheeled across the black fabric of deep space. I began floating up into the star-splashed void.

"C'mon then, lad," a strange voice said. Startled, I looked around in dim light. Dawn. The rooster was crowing. I lay sprawled on a bed of straw near the barn. Angus, on one knee beside me, was offering a glass of apple juice. I took the glass and drank, the cold juice sluicing smoothly down my parched throat. "The rest of them are in their beds," Angus said, "but trust you to make a night of it."

"I thought I heard your pipes calling," I said from out of the fog, remembering.

"Sure you did," Angus replied, "plaintive airs, all of seven hours ago at least."

"Wow. That was one black-footed ferret of a trip."

"Yes, you got your money's worth, I'd say."

"No kidding. Christopher around?" I asked.

"In his hearse, as usual," Angus said, nodding across the barn-yard to where the hearse was parked, "but not as alone as usual."

"Wha'?"

"Lena's with him."

"Lena? With Christopher?" My brain couldn't take this in properly.

"Not sure that she'll want to be seen once she wakes up, so thought I'd get you moving first."

"Thanks, Angus," I said, still not putting the pieces together. I scrambled slowly to my feet and wobbled off with Angus toward the house.

None of us were in fit condition for dealing with heavy stuff that morning. Enzo stayed in the bedroom that he and Lena shared, refusing to talk with her or anyone else. Lena, unable to stop sob-bing, was being comforted by Elizabeth, whose scowl was truly formidable. Finding the mood intolerable indoors, Jess and I went for a walk through green and bird-blessed meadows toward the lake. We didn't talk much, beyond agreeing that last night had been brilliant and this morning was the shits. Lena, or anyone, having a one-night stand was not that big of an issue really, Summer of Love adepts that we considered ourselves. No, the gloom that was hang-ing over us had more to do with the suspicion that Christopher had duped her and taken advantage, and in doing so duped all of us too with his enlightened-man shtick. Lena was the youngest of us, shy and not entirely sure of herself, but such a sweet soul that we all loved her protectively. I couldn't stand the idea of her being violated by a fraudster.

Had Christopher joined us in taking peyote last night, or sim-ply provided it for the rest of us while remaining perfectly (perhaps cunningly) sober himself? We didn't know. I suspect both Jess and I were madly scrambling for any explanation that didn't involve admitting that our precious mind-altering peyote ritual had been nothing more than a devious contrivance by a charlatan. Neither of us had detected any predacious scent coming off him, but he wouldn't have been the first clever predator to gull a bunch of credulous kids. Of course it had been obvious that he and Lena had a thing happening, but at the time it seemed inconsequential. Lena was turned on by the Castaneda story and eager to hear from Christopher any further details about the Yaqui "Man of Knowledge." No big deal. But had Christopher exploited her naiveté?

By the time we got back to the house, things were at a rolling boil. Still no sign of Enzo, and Angus had fled to go do something, anything, with the tractor. But voices were being raised. A very sour-looking Elizabeth was sitting on the big old leather couch in the kitchen, Lena huddled against her and quietly whimpering. Christopher sat upright at the kitchen table nursing a mug of tea and apparently unperturbed by the tempest he'd unleashed.

"Ah, I'm so glad you're here," he said to Jess and me as we entered the room. "Seems we're at a bit of an impasse."

"The only impasse," Elizabeth growled at him, "is your refusal to acknowledge that you deliberately manipulated Lena into a vulnerable place and took advantage of her."

"Elizabeth, I did no such thing," Christopher replied serenely. "Whatever occurred between Lena and myself was completely consensual. Wasn't it, Lena?"

Lena wouldn't answer. Humiliatingly, I felt we were all trapped on the set of *Days of Our Lives*.

Jess sat down at the table straight across from Christopher and I joined her. "Christopher," Jess began in her normal no-nonsense manner, "tell me, did you consume any peyote last evening?"

Christopher hesitated for a moment, immediately creating the impression that the truth was less important than the best answer.

"Did you or not?" Jess pressed him.

"Actually, no I didn't," he admitted. "I chose to keep myself perfectly clear so that I might serve as your guide without encumbrance."

Elizabeth snorted derisively.

"Can you tell us what happened?" Jess asked.

"Certainly," Christopher replied, ignoring Elizabeth and focusing entirely on Jess. "As you perhaps remember, I had been speaking to you all about sacred and profane love..."

Again there was a scornful snort from Elizabeth that Christopher ignored. "About the conceptions of pure desire," Christopher continued with what appeared to be complete sincerity, "and courtly love. About the idealization of the beloved whereby she transcends mere womanhood and becomes a goddess, a reflection of the divine."

I couldn't remember any of this and said as much, but Christopher explained I had left the circle by that point, presumably to go to bed.

"Was I still there?" Jess asked.

"I don't believe so," Christopher said, pausing momentarily. "In fact I think you may have left before Shorter did. I can't be entirely sure."

"I certainly didn't leave," Elizabeth said aggressively. She had her arm around Lena, fierce mother bear with cub.

"Indeed you did not," Christopher agreed. "You did, however, fall into a deep slumber, marked by considerable loud snoring."

Elizabeth glowered at him. "And Enzo?" Jess asked.

Again Christopher paused as though trying to recall. "No, actually Enzo was the first to leave. He had done his drumming work brilliantly for several hours. It was brilliant, didn't you think?"

Jess and I confirmed that Enzo's drumming had been excellent.

"Yes," Christopher continued, "but as Angus's pipes had begun their wonderful lament off in the distance, Enzo seemed to feel that his work was complete and withdrew from the circle, taking his drum with him."

"So what you're saying is only Lena and yourself remained?" Jess asked.

"Well, and Elizabeth, of course," Christopher emphasized.

"Quite so. But fast asleep, as you've just said."

"Well, for all I knew, she may just have been having a brief nap after which she might rejoin the group any minute."

"There was no group, you smarmy hypocrite!" Elizabeth snarled. "There was only you and this poor girl—you completely sober and her high as a kite on peyote."

Lena's whimpering had subsided now, but she remained curled within Elizabeth's embrace, her face still hidden.

"I believe she was having an extremely beneficial mescaline experience," Christopher replied, undaunted by Elizabeth's fierceness.

"So your discussion of sacred and profane love was basically only for Lena?" Jess asked.

"Not at all. It was for the entire circle, a part of the Huichol ritual."

"Courtly love's got nothing to do with Huichol ritual and you damn well know it," Elizabeth hissed. "In fact, most of this crap you've been spewing since you got here you've lifted straight out of Alan Watts. Tell me I'm wrong!"

Christopher sighed deeply, the perfect embodiment of a spiritual mentor beset by intractable disciples. Now that Elizabeth had mentioned it, there did seem to be considerable similarity between Christopher's language and that of Watts, his *Nature, Man & Woman* particularly. Jess and I had been to an informal talk given by Watts shortly after our arrival in Vancouver. We'd found him wonderfully articulate and erudite, although Jess had detected an underlying sadness about the man. Of course we had no idea that an early death would claim him soon afterwards. Now the penny dropped: Watts and Volts.

"The simple truth of the matter is you were seducing Lena with your clever words, weren't you?" Elizabeth demanded.

"Certainly not," Christopher replied haughtily. "There is no truth to that assertion and I deny it categorically." The serenity he'd maintained to this point seemed to crack momentarily, releasing a flash of anger. For all his talk of carnal bliss, the accusation of seduction plainly unnerved him.

"Do you also deny that you talked to her, and her alone, about the Grand Ritual of Tantra, the ritualized ecstasy of sexual union?"

"Elizabeth, you're putting words in my mouth."

"You mean like how you were putting your ugly cock in her mouth."

"STOP IT!" Lena suddenly screamed, pounding the couch with her fist. "Stop it! Stop it! Stop it!" Throwing off Elizabeth's sheltering arm, she jumped up from the couch and dashed out of the house.

The following few weeks were supremely shitty, to the point that we wondered whether our vaunted commune would even survive. Christopher slunk away that first dreadful morning and was never seen or heard of again. Elizabeth was insistent that sexual assault charges be brought against him, but Lena, withdrawn entirely inside herself, would not even discuss it. After a couple days she and Enzo left as well, not saying where they were going, unsure of when, or even whether, they'd return.

The remaining four of us wandered around in a weird state of suspended detachment, doing the chores by rote and scarcely speaking at meals. Jess later maintained it was only the goats that kept her from falling off the cliff. She'd sit for hours communing with Gracie and Sara, then bring their wisdom back to the rest of us. Angus sublimated what I think was suppressed rage into a Herculean bout of heavy labour.

Elizabeth drilled the dogs for hours like an obsessive marine sergeant. I went so far as to unearth my tattered thesis to see what I could make of it, which wasn't much. We held on, but just barely.

Some weeks after the crisis, a pair of square-jawed honchos in suits showed up, identified themselves as part of a special investigative unit of the RCMP, and separately questioned Elizabeth, Angus, Jess and myself about Christopher. We hurriedly decided among ourselves, over Elizabeth's objections, that we would say nothing to them specifically about that horrid night. Though they compelled us to cooperate, the cops refused to provide any information about what they were investigating or why.

SHORTER HAD FULLY EXPECTED ROSALIE TO DISAPPROVE OF THIS WHOLE sordid segment. In fact, having written it, he'd debated whether or not to even show it to her, imagining her disgust at the sex, infidelity and faux-shamanistic sleaze. But she's surprisingly upbeat about the new pages.

"Christopher Volts is a charlatan of no particular interest," she curtly dismisses him. "But you know, I'm increasingly intrigued by Lena. This girl," she says to Shorter, "you keep very much in the background, a shadowy figure, almost an appendage to others supposedly more powerful than herself, whether that's Enzo or Elizabeth or Jess. I think the reader's eager to know more about her—why, for example, she's drawn to Castaneda, and subsequently to Christopher Volts. Why she ends up sleeping with him, which seems quite out of character, then refuses to discuss it with anyone, even her partner.

"You might think me mad," Rosalie says to Shorter, "but personally I see Lena as a doppelganger for Castaneda himself: reclusive and enigmatic, roaming somewhere between the realms of fiction and non-fiction. I do hope she hasn't left the farm, and your story, forever."

Which is precisely what everyone on the farm was feeling back then. As though Lena and Enzo had taken a part of the commune away with them and might never be seen again. That the commune itself might simply implode from of its own ridiculous naiveté.

FIVE

ON A LUMINOUS FRIDAY AFTERNOON JUST BEFORE THANKSGIVING I looked across the barnyard and felt a leap of joy at seeing Enzo and Lena slowly driving toward me in their old pickup. Jess came dashing out from the house whooping like a wild woman. The two of us hugged the two of them shamelessly. Enzo grinned like a circus clown; sweet Lena smiled beatifically, even while wiping away an occasional tear. By the time Elizabeth and Angus joined us, happiness was flooding the place in a way it hadn't for months.

Once we'd settled down a bit, I was happy to see that our two strays seemed more or less restored to how we'd known them. Enzo's sly wit was definitely dialled down and Lena seemed dreamily absent much of the time, but there was now a sense of loving kindness around the place that we hadn't fully realized was missing in their absence. It was obvious to everyone that their leave-taking had shaken us more than we might have expected and had revealed just how entangled all of our lives were surely becoming. A scarily mixed thing, that power of the collective and the apparent ease with which it might be shattered.

Enzo and Lena made it unarguably clear they didn't want to talk about the episode, not now, not ever. That was more than fine with me, and needless to say with Angus too, but I knew Jess would have preferred to work through what had happened and why, and I could sense that Elizabeth definitely wanted to talk about it, not with all of us, or with Enzo, but with Lena.

Anyway, relieved that we'd more or less survived a first major crisis together, we flung ourselves gratefully into fall chores, harvesting and preserving whatever fruits and vegetables we'd managed to coax out of the earth, gathering wizened apples from the gnarled apple trees half-smothered with brush, searching for chanterelle mushrooms in our woodlot and the forested lands beyond. We hauled in wagonloads of firewood that we (mostly Angus and I) had cut, split and stacked during the summer, even though Willie had endowed us with an almost full woodshed. (We had no way of knowing back then that amassing and hoarding firewood was a particular fixation of certain countryfolk, particularly loony bachelors for whom an abundance of seasoned firewood was a holdfast to reality.)

This rush of pre-winter preparation reinvigorated all of us. It just felt so goddamn *wholesome* grubbing around in the dirt for burly potatoes or pulling up beautifully tapered and bright-orange carrots. We canned wild blackberries that we'd picked by the bucketload and Enzo assumed responsibility for several large vats of blackberry wine.

Measly though the produce proved to be, compared with what we'd learn to generate in subsequent years, it provided a fabulous updraft of hopefulness. Despite the odds, we were growing our own, living off the land, and evolving, as we saw it, a fresh paradigm for a better way of being on this planet. Scott and Helen Nearing sprang readily to mind, Wendell Berry down at Lane's Landing, even Henry David Thoreau and his piddling Walden Pond.

In that buoyant spirit we finally addressed the issue of renaming the farm. For three generations it had informally been called Peave Farm but no longer really was. We liked the historical connection with Willie and his forebears but not the intimation of peevishness. We took intermittent turns dreaming up something more suitable, at times frightfully listing toward unhappy hippie-isms like Astral Acres or Frodo's Farm. Then one morning in the kitchen, Enzo suddenly clapped his hands and exclaimed, "I've got it! Figurative Farm!"

After a moment's reflection we all acknowledged that this was indeed a stroke of genius, introducing as it did a metaphorical as well as an allegorical dimension to the place by referencing the astonishingly large fig tree growing behind the toolshed. Willie had planted it himself at least fifty years ago and allowed it to expand in all directions so that it now sprawled like one of those giants invading Angkor temple ruins. "Desert King, she's called," he'd told us, "like Lawrence of Arabia." For a couple of dizzying weeks back in August we'd stuffed ourselves with luscious ripe green figs and also canned dozens of jars of figs, as well as packed the freezer with cartons of fig sauce, both sweet and savoury. Any unwary visitor during that fig extravaganza would end up, whether willingly or not, leaving the farm weighted down with bags of squishy figs. Consensus came in a flash; henceforward this would be Figurative Farm.

One bright, clear October morning Angus and I strode over to the toolshed intent upon clipping and cleaning the goats' hooves, something Angus had half-learned to do as a boy, and a good thing too because there wasn't a reputable farrier for miles around.

Maintaining their boycott of the barn, the goats were still provisionally housed in the open toolshed, alongside the hay baler and miscellaneous machinery.

But as soon as we got to the shed that morning, it was look out: it's gonzo time. Gracie had the wildest look in her normally profound oblong eyes; she was pacing about, flicking her tail maniacally and vocalizing like Tom Waits after a heavy session with the bottle. You have to realize that Gracie was a steadfastly and brilliantly peculiar creature (we could never remember if Willie had named her after Gracie Allen or Gracie Fields), but even for her this was anomalous behaviour.

"I'd say she's coming into estrus," Angus said. "What do you think?"

"Fucked if I know," I said. "Let's check with Jess."

Jess came over, communed eye-to-eye with Gracie for a few moments and told us, "Yep, I know that feeling: this gal's hot for a bit of loving, ain't ya, honey?"

After making arrangements, we bundled our yearning lover into the back of the pickup, with me and Angus sitting alongside her and Lena at the wheel. We sped across to an island homestead-in-the-making that we knew had a buck in rut. Rob, the young guy who owned the place (white as a termite but sporting a magnificent Afro straight out of *Hair*), greeted us warmly and led us over to what looked like a primitive stockade for penning rogue rhinos. "There's big Bill," Rob pointed to his prize stud snuffling inside.

Christ almighty, it was a stinking, slobbery, hairy disgrace of a creature. The thought of him mauling defenceless Gracie was sickening.

"It's cool, man," Rob told us as we pushed sweet Gracie through the gateway.

Curling his lips satanically and urinating all over himself, Bill the beast lunged toward Gracie with a terrifying single-mindedness, his glistening red penis swollen hugely, balls swinging, tongue lolling dementedly. He roughly mounted her without even a flicker of foreplay. Despite his enormity and the ferocity of his thrusting, Gracie withstood him, even accepted him, with remarkable dignity. Lena looked as though she was going to be sick.

"Why don't we leave them for a bit to have some nookie," Rob said. "Come on over, I'll show you the house."

Lena said, "I'd rather stay and make sure Gracie's okay."

"Suit yourself, babe," Rob told her with a faintly lascivious smile.

So Angus, Rob and I made our way through a clutter of old tires and wooden pallets and broken-down machinery to Rob's half-constructed log cabin sitting morosely in a sea of stumps. Piles of peeled logs lay off to one side. "Yah, most of what I know about building log cabins I got from Bradford Angier's *How to Build Your Home in the Woods*," Rob told us proudly. "Total classic."

Returning to the goat pen, we found them (him!) fiercely copulating. Once Bill had sated himself again, Rob entered the stockade and herded his slobbering champion to a far corner, like Mike Tyson in full blood, while Angus and I retrieved Gracie. She instantly sought Lena's embrace, though more, it seemed, in affection than in any repugnance over the mating. Mighty as he was at copulation, Bill fell hopelessly short in the affection department, either before, during or after, leaving the more tender elements to Lena.

We paid Rob his fee, wished him well with the building, then loaded Gracie back into the pickup and returned home. All of us were sobered by the display of naked passion we'd witnessed, Bill's brute animality and Gracie's queenly acceptance of what was required of her.

Two weeks later Sara came into heat and we were faced with having to relive the whole unseemly episode. I thought to spare Lena from having to endure seeing sweet Sara violated so roughly. "No," she said firmly, "I insist on being there for Sara's sake."

We set our minds to hoping that both the goats had been successfully impregnated (if formidable Bill wasn't up to the task, who possibly could be?) and to thinking what a delight it would be to have baby goats frisking in next springtime's sunshine.

Not long afterwards the rains began. Monstrous low pressure systems came bowling down from the Gulf of Alaska, one after another, pummelling the coast with wind and rain like soggy brawlers going at it in an alley. Although Jess and I had already weathered two Vancouver winters and Angus had cut his teeth on North Atlantic gales that he said were vastly more brutal, we were all staggered by the ferocity of the southeasters now lashing land and sea. Enormous trees were ripped from the earth and flung down across power lines and roadways. Electricity was repeatedly cut for weeks on end, forcing us to rely on Willie's ancient wood heater for cooking as well as warmth, on smoky kerosene lamps for light and on rainwater caught in buckets.

Sequestered day and night indoors, we were forced to depend on a battery-powered radio for contact with the outer world, on which we listened through the static to CBC Radio—*My Word*, *Gilmour's Albums*, *As It Happens*. The abiding gloom and inactivity, combined with chronic sleeplessness due to storms roaring half the night, began to take a toll. Irritability, petty misunderstandings and flashpoint flare-ups marked the dark days. Heathcliff could easily have come barging through the kitchen door, soaked and deranged. We might have gone completely nuts during that stormy isolation if it hadn't been for Angus's pipes and Jess's banjo. Instead, we could pass a joint around and sprawl in the semi-darkness while the two of them played elaborate tunes that meandered back and forth between the Western Isles and Appalachia. Tentatively, Elizabeth began singing along on certain tunes, surprising and delighting everyone with her clear, pure voice.

As the storms continued, the dogs, sheltering in a lean-to shed alongside the barn, took up a mournful baying day and night, their howls commingling with the shrieks of the battering wind. "I can't stand having the dogs going through that," Elizabeth finally said. "I think we should bring them back inside."

"I agree," Lena said. The rest of us were less enthusiastic, largely because when they were previously indoors the mutts had been such a pain in the ass, being constantly underfoot and begging for scraps at the table.

"They're far better disciplined now," Elizabeth insisted, "but, most importantly, I think their distress is about more than the storms. Something else is upsetting them."

"Like what?" I asked.

"Well," she said, "call me a flake if you want, but I believe they're having premonitions of disaster. Maybe they fear that the barn is about to collapse on top of them."

"You gotta be kidding," I said, instantly recognizing my over-reaction. Not a new sensation. Of all the small annoyances to be had in the crowded house during those dark days, Elizabeth's pronouncements grated on me the most. It wasn't so much what she had to say that I found irritating, but her manner of saying it. A subtle but unmistakable hint of condescension, an intimation that any point of view divergent from her own could be flippantly discounted. Easy to see now, from the vantage point years provide, that there was obviously a class issue going on, along with a gender issue. At the time I just thought she was an arrogant bitch.

But there was also an element of manipulation in how she fawned over Jess and coddled Lena while being dismissive of us guys. Nothing directly confrontational, nothing you could really call her out on, just a subtle and persistent belittling—aimed, it seemed to me, at establishing herself as Jess's confidante and Lena's protector.

"Not kidding in the least," she said, addressing the group rather than me. "After all, it's widely acknowledged that many animals can foretell an impending earthquake. We have no idea how, but they can. I believe those dogs sense that they're in imminent danger and are crying for help." I knew better than to say any more, and nobody else disagreed, so we brought the bedraggled mutts back into the house. They charged in gratefully, shaking their sodden coats and yelping, then soon flopped on the floor in a semicircle around the wood heater, their steaming coats stinking up the whole kitchen.

Two days later, as we were all going to bed early through the kerosene gloom, wind gusts smacking the house mercilessly, we heard a horrendous groaning shriek. I thought the roof was being torn away. The dogs began barking frantically downstairs, and just as I started back down, there came another wrenching scream, then three or four seconds of suspended tension followed by a muffled thump. Christ, I thought, the barn! The bloody barn's come down. Silent for a moment, the dogs picked up their soulful baying. Several of us struggled into our raingear, grabbed a couple of flashlights and plunged out into the lashing darkness.

Sure enough, the old barn had collapsed on its side, boards and beams askew, leaving, even in the dark, an enormous black emptiness where it had stood. "Crap," Angus said, "that's put a bloody dent in things." We all muttered a bit but mostly just stared.

I lay awake for hours that night listening to wind and rain battering the house. Every so often there was a pistol-sharp crack as a big tree limb snapped off and came hurtling to the ground. A couple of times I heard whole trees come down with a tremendous thump. The old house creaked and groaned and shuddered at especially violent gusts. Several times I was certain that the house was being bowled over the way the barn had been. And this was no fanciful paranoia, because earlier in the autumn, following the advice of an old-timer, we'd raked piles of fallen leaves to form an insulating berm all around the open crawl space under the house and in the process discovered that the building had no real foundation. The builders—Willie's noble forebears—had simply cut a number of big western red cedar stumps to equal height and used them as no-cost footings to hold up the house. Now, as the storm raged, I could feel the building tearing itself loose from those untrustworthy stumps.

Who the hell did we think we were kidding, anyway, other than ourselves. A pack of damn fools, that's what we were, ignorant kids playing at being the new pioneers. Back to the land my ass. On and on I fulminated, raging in my head as the storm raged all around. Convincing myself that the best thing to do was to pack up and get the fuck back to the city, starting first thing tomorrow morning.

The amazing element was Jess. After the barn had toppled, she'd climbed back into bed with me, put her earplugs in, kissed me tenderly and told me not to fret, then curled up beside me and slept like a child through the whole enraged night of tempest.

I awoke the next morning to an unexpected calm. The eye of the hurricane, I thought, this singular silence. But, no, I could glimpse blue sky through the bedroom window and sunlight splashing the tops of trees. The storm had passed. Somewhere nearby a pair of ravens began volleying caustic calls back and forth.

Careful not to awaken Jess, I dressed quickly and tiptoed down the stairs. As usual, I found Angus sitting at the kitchen table calmly finishing up a bowl of porridge. A fresh fire crackled in the heater. "Morning," he grunted and I nodded in reply. Angus liked a solitary breakfast, as did I, and without any formal arrangement being made we'd evolved a quite elaborate early risers' minuet to accommodate our separate solitudes.

Angus had already let the dogs out. Pulling on a jacket and boots I slipped out the door. Low on the horizon, the winter sun was mantling the farmyard in gold, with misty steam vapours rising. I walked over to the wreckage of the toppled barn. It had not smashed into bits so much as subsided gracefully onto the earth, its skeleton of hewn timbers partially intact but twisted askew. Quiet for once, the dogs gathered around me and stared at the remains of their terrifying premonitions. Off to one side, equally prescient, the goats Gracie and Sara stood looking solemnly at the ruin with their strange knowing eyes.

"Well, she's beautiful still," Angus said, coming up behind me.

"Truth," I said.

We all agreed that Willie ought to be told first-hand about the barn's collapse and that Jess and I should be the ones to tell him. Because of the storms none of us had been off-island to the nearby small town of Spangler or anywhere else for weeks, so we were desperate for food supplies and needed to do laundry in the worst kind of way. It was decided that Lena and Elizabeth would come with Jess and me to do town chores while Enzo and Angus were left to start getting the farm back up off its knees from the battering it had taken.

Waiting for the ferry to arrive, we mingled with a bunch of other "new people" similarly hauling bagloads of dirty laundry. We looked like a tribe of bedraggled survivors from a cyclone in Vanuatu or someplace. And once we got to Spangler, it resembled a tribal rite for sure as we all trooped into the Purple Hippopotamus Laundromat on (ironically) Fifth Avenue and loaded every machine in the place with our soiled and soggy clothes and bedding.

After dropping Elizabeth and Lena off at the supermarket, Jess and I drove up to the Sunset Rest retirement home that was situated on a ridge overlooking town. We found Willie in his own little suite ensconced in an overstuffed armchair, watching a rerun of *I Love Lucy*. He was wearing pyjamas and a thirty-percent-senior's-discount-on-Tuesdays Goodwill housecoat.

Although he greeted us warmly, he couldn't quite disguise his disappointment that our arrival meant he'd have to abandon his show. He'd never owned a television on the island, he told us, but seemed to be making up for all that he'd missed. Still chuckling over some laugh-track antic of Lucy's, he clicked what he called his "new-fangled remote control" and the screen went dead. "You see that?" he asked us straight off, holding up the remote. "What an amazing thing. It's got a crystal inside it that's fed by an electric current at a frequency you or I can't hear, but the dogs could. Then there's a microphone in the TV tuned to the same frequency. Bingo! It's like magic."

"Far out," I said, intrigued by the little device.

"How are you kids anyway?" Willie asked. "Here, sit down wherever you can." Jess plopped on the end of the bed and I sat in the only other available chair. "You survived these little rain showers we been havin', did you?" Willie asked archly.

"Barely," Jess said. "The road was blocked for days and the power's been off way more than on for the last three weeks."

"Well, that's the thing, isn't it?" Willie said. "Island living. Person's gotta be pretty self-reliant to get through a bad winter over there. Not every year, of course, but some years. And you kids have got yourselves a doozy this year, looks like. Doesn't bother me in this place a'tall, but I can see the whitecaps comin' up the strait from here and figure the island must be takin' a hell of a lickin'. Course we never had the electricity over there until I think it was '49 or so. And even then there was a lot of bitchin' and whinin' went on. Most folks wanted it, but some didn't. Said it would change the island for the worse. So back in the day, we never lost the power in winter storms because we didn't have it to lose." Willie chortled as though this was a truly fine cosmic joke.

"Sorry to say we've got some bad news, Willie," I said.

"Not the dogs?" he asked with a sudden look of consternation. "Don't tell me it's the dogs."

"The dogs are fine," Jess assured him, "just as happy as can be, snoozing around the heater." She and I had decided beforehand that we definitely wouldn't tell Willie about our banishing the dogs outdoors and them howling mournfully in the storms before we brought them back in.

"Yeah, they love their winter warmth, don't they? Y'know, at this place here they have what they call comfort dogs they bring in once a week, to try to cheer us up and keep from going demented."

"Nice," I said. You had the sense that, for all its ease and comfort, Sunset Rest wasn't really what Willie had hoped it might be.

"Better than nothing, anyway. But I sure miss them mutts of mine. So they're all doin' fine, are they?"

"So fine you wouldn't believe it," I told him.

"And of course they miss you too," Jess put in. "Our friend Elizabeth's been training them to do the most incredible things."

"Well, bit of training wouldn't do that pack of rascals any harm, that's for sure," Willie chuckled. "Think I'm gonna ask the staff people here if you can bring a couple of them over for a visit. It'd give me a real boost."

"Great," I said.

"Maybe you bring little Suzy and Bandy with you next time, eh?"

Before leaving the farm, Willie had rattled off a couple of dogs' names to us but we hadn't thought to write them down at the time and now we had no idea who Suzy or Bandy were. We just called all of them names like "Big Mutt" or "Grumpy Mutt" or whatever we felt like at the moment. In her training sessions, Elizabeth referred to them by an assigned number.

"Oh, I do hope they'll let us bring one or two in for you," Jess said.

"Mean the world to me," Willie said, smiling at her fondly. "So what's the bad news?" he asked.

"It's about the barn," I told him.

"The barn? Don't tell me she's fallen over at last."

"Flat on her side, sorry to say."

"Come down nice and easy, did she?" Willie seemed surprisingly unperturbed by the news. Clueless about how elders may accommodate loss, we'd thought perhaps he'd take it really badly.

"Like a ballerina," Jess said. "She just gracefully folded herself down onto the ground."

"Going on a hundred years old," Willie told us. "Reach me that photo album over there, would you?" he said, pointing to a small bookshelf in the corner. I pulled out the photo album. Beneath its plastic cover was a glossy picture of a man and woman in western gear, each perched on a horse. "Roy Rogers and Dale Evans," Willie said fondly as I passed him the album. "But look here." The first few pages contained ancient, faded photographs, black and white or sepia-toned, several among them of the barn being built. "Look at them fellers," Willie said, pointing to a photo of the barn in skeletal form with about ten or twelve men proudly posed for the camera astride the highest beams. "Before my time, of course," Willie said, "but there's my dad up there." His gnarled index finger pointed to one of the workers. "And somewhere in that group of women down on the ground was my mother. They were courtin' and sparkin' in those days." He gazed wistfully at the photos for a moment more, then closed the album. "All of them gone long ago, of course. And now the barn gone too. Funny, I wasn't there to see it go up and I wasn't there to see it come down neither."

"But you put in eighty good years with that barn, didn't you?" Jess said to him tenderly, and he looked at her with mist rimming his old eyes.

"Yes, I did, honey," he said. "I surely did."

Our ride back to the ferry was a jumble of conversation. Lena and Elizabeth were almost giddy over the reawakened joys of grocery shopping. The bargains they'd scored, the treats they'd splurged on for everyone. "You two sound like you just got home from a weekend in Vegas," Jess said. "Nothing like a few weeks of confinement to illumine the run-of-the-mill."

ROSALIE COMES CLOSE TO TEARS WHILE DISCUSSING THIS CHAPTER WITH Shorter. Just as she did when she first read the pages at home. Mostly they'd put her back in touch with painful memories of her mother. The dreadful last days of her life. Cut short, cut far too short by a malignant cancer. She doesn't return very often to the pain of those final days, but Shorter's description of Willie in decline for some reason carried her there all the same. It's not something she wants to discuss with Shorter. Not now anyway.

By way of distraction, she sets about brewing a pot of ginger tea for them to sip while munching on her prized chocolate chip oatmeal cookies. "I have to confess," she tells Shorter almost shyly, "that I'm finding much to admire in your writing. And I especially enjoy discussing it all with you each week. You have to know that you're doing brilliantly."

Shorter tries his best to appear modest, but is in fact thrilled by her praise. Now that he's into a regular writing rhythm, he's also experiencing real enjoyment in remembering so many nuances of those long-ago days. And as pleasurable as the writing itself is, he's beginning to find the sessions with Rosalie a highlight of his week.

Furtively he counts the days down to when she'll return. Speculates about what costume she'll be wearing—like the queen, she never seems to wear the same thing twice. Shorter has even upgraded his own appearance somewhat, shaving as well as combing his hair before she arrives and wearing not-too-tatty clothes.

On this particular day Rosalie's delighted, as Shorter imagined she would be, that Lena and Enzo have not been lost. "I already love them both," she says, "and wouldn't want to have them disappear from our story."

"No, no," Shorter reassures her, taking note of the *our*. "Those two characters are in for the long haul."

The goat-breeding scene did not offend Rosalie's sensibilities, as Shorter had feared it might. "Savagely elemental" she calls it as she sips her tea. "And I can certainly relate," she says, "to the power of winter storms because my own little house, as you probably know, is angled to the southeast, fully exposed to both the beauty of summer sunrise and the ferocity of winter gales. With the least bit of wind, even this time of year, I'm awake half the night waiting for the old place to be blown to bits any minute." Which leads back to Willie's dogs, then segues seamlessly into an extended discussion of Rosalie's cats.

She has two of them, idiosyncratically named Astrophe and Aclysim, and loves them both fervently. Having already heard more than enough about the habits and enduring traits of each, being no cat enthusiast himself, Shorter has yet to figure out a mechanism for short-circuiting this particular topic. "They are," Rosalie tells him, "a great comfort and solace to me." She offers no hint as to why comfort and solace are required. Has some dreadful misfortune blighted her life, Shorter wonders again—the loss of a child, perhaps, or the foundering of a great love affair? But he feels he has no right to enquire. It's somehow understood between them that her personal affairs are none of his busines. Perhaps, he considers, she's referencing the sorry state of the world, the suffering of millions, where whole continents of comfort and solace would scarcely suffice.

He notes once again that a weird dynamic is evolving whereby he continues disclosing increasingly intimate details of their long-ago communal existence while Rosalie reveals nothing whatsoever of her own story beyond the antics of her cats. But Rosalie is not a woman given to mindless chit-chat of any sort. She is entirely purposeful in what she says, or doesn't say, to Shorter—a state of affairs it will take him considerably more time to fully appreciate.

SIX

I'D NEVER BEFORE EXPERIENCED THE SEASONAL FADING OF LIGHT AS acutely as I did that first November and December. As though life itself was being sucked out of the landscape bit by bit each day. Grey skies brooded over us for weeks on end. Both cold and damp, the air itself felt malicious. We all took to sleeping in far longer through the tepid light of dawn, Jess and I snuggled together under our blankets, giggling about whether we should get up at all or just remain there in cozy bliss. Even Angus, who slept alone and was normally the first one up and faithful to a fault at lighting the woodstove every morning, began to languish.

After a few featureless daytime hours, by three in the afternoon the pale light of day was already draining away, forcing us indoors. Other than for tending the animals, we'd scarcely venture out at all during the dirtiest weather. I found myself morbidly pondering T.S. Eliot's lines from *Burnt Norton*: "I said to my soul, be still, and let the dark come upon you. Which shall be the darkness of God."

A bleak moodiness settled over the house. The collective energy level sank to dispirited depths. Pathetic conversations. We mostly lost interest in doing much of anything except eating. We smoked a lot of dope but the highs got lower and the cumulative effect was blearily narcotizing. We seemed to catch a strain of attention deficiency the way you'd catch a flu, making it difficult to concentrate on anything for more than five minutes and just about impossible to make necessary decisions. Our several dozen LPs, played over and over, became tediously repetitive. Arlo Guthrie's *Alice's Restaurant* mysteriously disappeared and was never seen, or heard, again. Some of us developed a toxic reaction to Barbara Frum, and as a consequence dinnertime communal listening to *As It Happens* on CBC Radio no longer happened.

Only Lena seemed in any way impervious to the bleak mood—she maintained it had to do with her gloomy childhood in Prince George, although Angus didn't benefit from having grown up at a similar latitude. Mind you, Angus was a mournful sort a lot of the time anyway. Nowadays we'd probably all be diagnosed as suffering from degrees of seasonal affective disorder, but back then nobody had ever heard the term and it would be another dozen years before the big brains at the National Institute of Mental Health officially recognized, named and described the condition. In the interim, we were just fucked up.

"We're all going to turn into bloody mushrooms if we keep going like this," Enzo complained one day as we ate a desultory lunch of rice and beans together. A dense Dracula mist was hanging over the farm, muffling everything except the occasional forlorn lament of the foghorn down at the ferry.

"What do you propose?" Jess asked him. Even the most innocuous comments now bristled with a whiff of irritability.

"I'm thinking we should get a TV," Enzo said boldly, a suggestion greeted with unanimous groans and jeers. Television epitomized everything detestable about the mainstream culture we'd abandoned. Escapism, mindlessness, manipulative consumerism, religion's updated replacement as the opiate of the masses. None of us had watched TV back in Vancouver, not openly at least, and to start doing it here in our Aquarian collective smelled like unseemly moral compromise.

"I know, I know," Enzo said, holding up his hands in mock surrender, "we imagine ourselves on a pathway to higher things and other deities, but realistically we're gonna go completely crazy sitting here in the gloom for months on end. What would be so wrong with a hockey game on Saturday night or watching Monty Python?" He stared at us challengingly through his thick bifocals. "We need some diversion, folks, a bit of fun now and then. We need to lighten up."

"I think we need to deepen down," Elizabeth countered with that whiff of the superiority she had limited skill in disguising.

"What's that supposed to mean?" Enzo snapped back.

"Just this," Elizabeth responded calmly. "I think we're letting ourselves go here, and to start numbing our brains with televised garbage would be to accept that we've let ourselves go completely."

"So what do *you* propose?" Jess asked her before a TV squabble could erupt.

"Just this," Elizabeth repeated herself. (Even back in these early days I'd twigged on this little gambit of Elizabeth's, to pick up any current *mot du jour* and work it into her pronouncements at every available opportunity. "Just this" was just that.) "I believe these winter months give us a perfect opportunity to move beyond washing dishes and chopping firewood and start working on improving our mental and emotional selves."

This suggestion was greeted with a subtler disdain than Enzo's had been, partly because we recognized the germ of truth in it. Plus we all were very aware that Elizabeth was a closet devotee of the "human potential" movement, that she'd read her Maslow and Satir ("more joy, more reality, more connectedness, more accomplishment and more opportunities for people to grow"). She'd even spent time at the Esalen Institute at Big Sur, where she'd taken workshops aimed at helping her, as the brochures put it, "rediscover the miracle of self-aware consciousness." To her credit, Elizabeth didn't try to proselytize this agenda at every available opportunity, and less to her credit, she was burdened with a personality not noticeably marked by either joy or connectedness. But, hey, let the perfect ones among us throw the first stone.

What Elizabeth now proposed was this (Just This, in other words): that we devote one evening a week to holding a group meeting at which we would enhance connectivity by "getting past" those things that are hampering us as individuals and as a collective.

Back in the spring, in our initial days on the farm, we had indeed held regularly scheduled house meetings every week, mostly about practical matters such as bringing some semblance of organization around who was doing what for the following week. (Meal preparation had been a major concern, handily dealt with by having the women do virtually all the cooking.) But somehow the meetings had gradually lapsed and we'd instead taken to discussing practical arrangements on an ad hoc basis during dinner or whenever.

You could feel resistance to Elizabeth's proposal stiffen in the room even as she was presenting it. Angus made no secret of the fact that he was a deeply private person, so the prospect of baring his soul, even for the greater collective good, wasn't going to sit well. Enzo and Lena's relationship had scarcely survived the Christopher Volts firestorm, and there was no way they wanted to drag out that particular bit of dirty laundry for public examination. So it was up to Jess and myself to either drive a final spike into Elizabeth's proposal or attempt to bring the recalcitrants around. To be honest about it, I was kind of in the Angus camp. Not so much objecting to touchy-feely adventures per se, as simply not wanting to engage in them myself. Instead of saying anything, I attempted to appear profoundly conflicted and, as usual, deferred to Jess for clarity.

One of the many things I loved about Jess was that she was so fucking intelligent without ever wearing a "Look at Me, I'm Smart" button. She just was. "Okay," she said after a few moments' thought, "we've obviously got some divergence of opinion here." Everybody laughed. "So I suggest a compromise: we get ourselves a television..."

"Surely not," Elizabeth interjected. Jess was more attached to Elizabeth than any of us were, and would be expected to support her friend.

"We keep it in the living room," Jess carried on, "and agree that for one night a week the TV will be on for those interested."

"Only if it's curling," Angus said, which got a laugh.

"For decency's sake," Jess continued, "when not in use, the TV will be covered with an appropriately exotic shawl."

"I've got just the thing," Lena put in.

"Also for one night a week," Jess added, "we'll have a consciousness-raising meeting, again for those interested. I suggest we try this arrangement for a month, then discuss whether we want to continue with both, or with one, or with neither. What do you say?"

A brief interlude of deep thinking.

"Let's do a round," Elizabeth said, a possible foretaste of what was to come. "I'll go first. I personally am appalled at the prospect of having a TV screeching away in the house, even if it's only for one night. But I think Jess's suggestion is a reasonable compromise and I'm willing to support it."

"I don't like either option," Angus said. "I agree we should be doing something more creative than moping around the way we've been, but why not a book club or a poker night or something, anything other than these two options."

Enzo—who'd started the trouble in the first place—said he'd accept the compromise as reasonable.

Lena said she wasn't seasonally screwed up like all the rest of us and didn't care one way or the other, but there were certain personal things she definitely would not discuss.

Jess and I both said we were willing to give it a try for one month and then reassess.

That left only Angus as adamantly opposed. "How do you feel about the rest of us proceeding and you can simply opt out?" Jess asked him.

"Well, opting out of the TV is a no-brainer," Angus said, "just like opting in. But with Elizabeth's stuff..."

"It's not *my* stuff," Elizabeth interrupted him testily.

"You know what I mean," Angus said, stroking his beard for comfort. "With that stuff it feels like it has to be all of us or none of us. I mean, what the hell kind of collective holds regular meetings with one member never at them? So I'll swallow my misgivings for the good of the group..."

He was saluted with scattered "right ons" and "far outs" (mercifully, "high fives" hadn't yet been popularized) and thus our decision was made.

Within days Enzo and Lena had returned from town, the back of their pickup jammed with bags of groceries and laundry surrounding an enormous console TV. "Got it at Goodwill for only ten bucks," Enzo announced proudly. A 1964 Zenith Valencia colour TV, embedded in a wooden cabinet. The thing was a brute, so heavy it took just about all of us to lift it out of the truck bed and carry it indoors like the Ark of the Covenant. We set it up in the living room. Enzo plugged it in and fiddled with the rabbit ears until a grainy picture appeared. After considerable adjusting, it was established that we could receive (barely) two channels out of Vancouver, one CBC, the other CTV, plus, on certain benign days, a PBS affiliate out of Bellingham, Washington.

Subject to the whims of the atmosphere, we were able to pick up episodes of American hit shows like *Gunsmoke, Bonanza, Mission Impossible* and *The Beverly Hillbillies*, but of course they were scattered all through the week not confined to our one dedicated evening. Despite her initial misgivings about the television in general, Elizabeth led a strong lobby for *Here Come the Seventies*, a Canadian documentary series with episodes such as "Art in the Seventies: Search for the Inner Self" and "Medicine: Living to be a Hundred." Broadcast on Thursday evenings, these quasi-highbrow offerings enlightened more than entertained.

Having opposed the TV on principle and boycotted fluff like *The Hart and Lorne Terrific Hour*, Angus somehow discovered and became devoted to *The Pig and Whistle*. Another Canadian effort, the show was set in a fake English pub and featured British and Celtic musical acts. Most agreeably from Angus's perspective, a Scottish performer named Stan Kane was a frequent guest.

Getting consensus on what shows to watch on what evening proved impossible.

Then Lena totally upset the apple cart by discovering *The Trouble With Tracy*, a truly execrable situation comedy shot in Toronto but set in New York City. With cheesy sets, a hambone laugh track, missed cues and flubbed lines, the show appeared every weekday afternoon. Best of all, it had a hippie character. What more could you want? We quickly jettisoned the one-evening-a-week rule and for a couple of demented weeks clustered around the old Zenith most afternoons, all of us sprawled on the floor howling with laughter.

In the middle of one of these shows, just as hippie brother-in-law Paul was once again asking lead character Doug for a loan, the Zenith suddenly went BANG! and the picture instantly collapsed inwards like the core of a neutron star. Momentarily stunned, we stared in disbelief at the blank screen. It was like the death of God. Turned out the TV was totally kaput. Its cathode ray gun simply hadn't been up to the challenges of *The Trouble With Tracy*. Accepting the inevitable, with due solemnity we carried the big console back outdoors, much as you'd carry a coffin, and deposited it in the chicken run for the benefit of broody hens. Having barely survived several weeks of exposure, none of us broached the topic of replacing our dead Zenith. Ever.

The consciousness-raising group wasn't exactly an unqualified success either. We met for two hours every Sunday evening after dinner. Elizabeth acted as facilitator, although the eventual goal was to have facilitation rotate through the group. We'd begin with a "Check-in" round in which each of us would summarize what was going on for us. Early on, some variation of "I'm feeling pretty good" tended to predominate, though at the very first meeting Enzo spoke at length and quite graphically about the state of his hemorrhoids, a topic he said he'd felt reluctant to raise at the dinner table. In the collective memory this episode was thereafter forever referred to as the round of piles.

Rounds, it quickly became evident, were the fundamental rubric of the group process, for next came a round called "Unfinished Business" in which anything left hanging from the previous meeting was straightened out. I have to admit that Elizabeth was working really hard at keeping all of us on track, gently preventing people from talking out of turn or wandering off into cross-chatter and crazy diversions. Usually there wasn't much of a charge around the unfinished stuff, any real drama being saved for the next round: "Held Feelings." The idea here was to straighten out anything hurtful or upsetting that had occurred at the previous meeting or throughout the week.

But here too the formula was stringent. You couldn't, for example, just blurt out to someone: "You really pissed me off with that dumb remark about my dishwashing." Rather, proper procedure required: "When you accused me of leaving crud on the pots I washed, I felt hurt and undervalued for my work." Specifics, not generalities. Similarly, "you always" accusations were verboten. And one absolutely could *not* say that somebody's criticism "made me feel undervalued" (or rejected or whatever.) No one can *make* you feel anything; you may well feel undervalued or rejected or whatever from something somebody said, but it's *your* choice, and your held feeling must acknowledge that reality.

The next round tilted away from bruised feelings and toward the surreal. It was called "Paranoid Fantasies." Here you could give voice to apprehensions or intuitions you were having about the group as a whole or individual members. Elizabeth gave as an example: "I have a paranoid fantasy that you all think I'm a total control freak." This was followed by an awkward silence. I, for one, and I suspect the others too, didn't know if Elizabeth really did have that paranoia, or had just plucked it out of the air to serve as an example. The formula called for the person(s) involved (in this example, all of us) to respond by either disavowing the fantasy or validating it, in part or in whole. In this instance, none of us did either, though I really had to bite my tongue from saying to Elizabeth, "Of course you're a hopeless control freak."

The final round was for "Appreciations." Some people—notably Jess and Lena—were really good at this, offering heartfelt acknowledgement of other people's contributions. For others, it was a struggle, not necessarily because we didn't feel appreciative, but because we lacked the vocabulary for expressing it. Especially for that tricky subset: the self-appreciation. I, for one—although on certain days a legend in my own mind—was far too modest to give any hint at self-exceptionalism.

For the first six weeks we devoted an hour of each session to having one of us tell our life story and that was invariably the most illuminating part of the whole ordeal. We learned things about one another that might otherwise have never been revealed.

Elizabeth's pampered debutante upbringing came as no surprise, but the revelation that her father was an accomplished alcoholic and womanizer certainly did. As suspected, Enzo grew up with parents who doted on him, but what we hadn't known was that his mother had birthed three stillborn children before him and that both his parents had died in a spectacular train derailment in the Alps when he was a teenager. Lena's story was grim in its own way too: she the youngest of seven kids, her mother a devout Roman Catholic and her father a consistently unemployed labourer inclined to give his wife a quick fist to the face when provoked by her piety. Angus suffered, or at least revealed, no trauma in his childhood other than sharing with three siblings a mostly grim round of chores on a stony hillside farm. I naturally knew more about Jess's story, dominated as it was by her mother's prolonged battle with a malignant brain tumour, the repeated frightfulness of radiation and chemotherapy before an early but merciful death. I felt almost embarrassed by the comparative blandness of my own upbringing in an unremarkable Toronto suburb. My mother a lifelong homemaker and my father a chartered accountant at the same firm his entire working life; an older sister whom I adored and who was then living on a remote sheep station in the Australian outback; and an immensely brainy younger brother who taught at the London School of Economics.

So there we sat in our circle, each with a distinctive story and all the storylines now unaccountably knotted together like roots in the fertile soil of Figurative Farm.

Throughout the ensuing group meetings we each were who we were. Elizabeth controlled. Jess was thoughtful, precise and careful of others' feelings. Lena remained mostly quiet and somewhat wary. Enzo waxed flippant and funny. Angus might well have been a neolithic standing stone at Callanish. And I was engaged but ever-so-discreetly distanced.

The second week, Elizabeth brought into the group a large eagle feather she'd found several days previous in the forest. "We'll use this like a talking stick," she proposed. "Whoever holds the feather has the floor and others should not speak until the feather is passed to them." I instantly had a paranoid fantasy (I'm not sure I'd ever had one before being in this group) that Elizabeth thought we were an undisciplined rabble given to interrupting and cross-talking and in need of even stricter discipline than was imposed by the rounds. Maybe she was right.

The feather worked passably for the first week, but in the second week, during "Unfinished Business," Lena voiced a quiet but firm objection to us using the eagle feather. "You know," she told us, "I remember my granny telling me that for Native peoples, the eagle feather is a religious artifact; it has spiritual and cultural significance way beyond what we realize. I don't think we should be using it the way we are. It's like using a crucifix for a gavel at meetings."

"Oh, Lena, I do think that's overstating things a bit," Elizabeth said, trying her best to hide her hurt. Having introduced the eagle feather with such fanfare, she was obviously reluctant to admit she'd made a mistake.

"I kind of agree with Lena," I said, less out of principled conviction than a desire to take Elizabeth down a peg.

"Me too," said Angus firmly.

"Okay, okay, I'm having a paranoid fantasy here," Elizabeth said, slapping the table. "I feel like I'm being attacked for no good reason."

"That's not a true paranoid fantasy," Enzo put in mischievously, "that's just a feeling with a judgment tacked on."

"And you'd know the difference, would you?" Elizabeth snapped.

"Actually, yes," Enzo replied calmly. I suspect he was trying to shield Lena from Elizabeth's wrath—unnecessarily though, because Elizabeth would never be hurtful toward Lena.

"I don't believe anyone's attacking you personally, Elizabeth," Jess said. "How about we do a round?"

"A round on whether Elizabeth is being personally attacked?" Enzo asked.

"A round on whether we should continue using the feather or not," Jess said in a tone designed to shut Enzo up.

"Should it be a paranoid fantasies round or a held feelings round?" I asked, just to be troublesome. Jess gave me a look that could have killed a rattlesnake.

"Okay, I'll start," Angus said, startling all of us because he normally contributed a bare minimum. "First off," he began, "other than Lena, the rest of us really don't know sweet bugger all about Native traditions around here. To be brutally honest, we're nothing more than a bunch of wannabes pretending to know things we actually don't have a clue about. I'd prefer to follow Lena's advice, at least until we get some more clarity on the thing."

You could tell Elizabeth was hurt by Angus's words. I certainly would have been. She simply looked down into her lap and said nothing.

Jess rescued us from the awkward silence. "Listen, how about we stop using the feather, at least for the time being, and switch to using a talking stick instead. That will serve the same purpose without the cultural/spiritual complications of the eagle feather."

"Great idea," Enzo said straight off.

"I agree," said Angus.

"Me too," I said.

"Lena?" Jess asked.

You could see Lena was really torn. She was trying to catch Elizabeth's eye, but Elizabeth was still looking down, out of reach.

"Elizabeth?" Jess prodded gently.

"Yes, alright," Elizabeth conceded. Plainly she was smarting from the discussion. Jess asked us if there was a need for a closing round of held feelings. Nope. Instead we had a really hazy round of appreciations, trying to smooth over some of the hurtful vibes.

Following the setbacks of the imploding TV and the contentious eagle feather, good fortune intervened in the guise of the Christmas party season during which humdrum realities were largely set aside. Jess and I had been accustomed to a fairly robust festive party scene back in Vancouver, but nothing close to the sybaritic extravaganza that engulfed the island. Almost every night for several weeks, we all roamed like Mongols from one house party to the next. No matter that some of the houses were half-finished or had hardly any furniture or maybe no electricity, we swarmed into them bearing bottles of dubious homemade plonk and baggies of homegrown along with our potluck offerings. Porches and hallways were cluttered with gumboots, many of which would later depart on feet different from those on which they'd arrived. Primitive stereo systems got cranked to the max for LPs by the Stones, the Who, Hendrix and the rest. Little kids swarmed around underfoot and danced wildly in the crowded kitchens.

Flirtations and culminations ran rampant on a field of psychedelic dreams, all leading to a climactic New Year's Eve dance at the community hall, packed with mostly the young new crowd along with a smattering of ribald old-timers and veteran party animals like roads foreman Byron Latasky. The long dark days were at least temporarily partied down.

"HELLO AGAIN, MR. SHORTER!" ROSALIE GREETS HIM ON HER NEXT VISIT. "Beautiful morning!"

Shorter grunts in agreement. He's had a restless night that's left him feeling fuzzy-headed and out of sorts. Rosalie repeats the tea-and-cookies ritual, as though it were now an established feature of her visits. Shorter has come to suspect that she sees him as socially isolated (which he happily is) and woefully in need of companionship (which he contentedly isn't).

"Well, truth to tell," she initiates this particular session, "I must confess openly that I do in fact own a television. I wouldn't at all," she says, "were it not for the trove of superior content now available on Netflix and YouTube and all the rest." She proceeds, by way of example, to outline in unnecessary detail the plot-line twists and turns of an ongoing series about the British monarchy. "Absolutely brilliant," she says, "though I have to admit I'm not the least bit proud of my perverse interest in the doings of the British royals.

And I must admit," she confesses, "to becoming similarly fascinated by the life stories of your commune's group members, particularly by the occurrence of tragedy in so many of them. But," she tells Shorter between nibbles on her second cookie, "I can hardly relate at all to the prim formalities of your consciousness-raising group. Such fastidiousness! Such scrupulosity! Whatever happened to 'born to be wild?'" She contrasts the communards unfavourably with the freewheeling honesty of what she calls "my people."

Intrigued as ever by her social circumstances, Shorter enquires in a number of discreet ways as to who these people are, but she discloses nothing. Is she making an ethnic reference, he wonders, or possibly hinting at a religious connection of some sort? For just a moment Shorter entertains the absurd possibility that "my people" is simply a euphemism for her cats.

Rosalie purposefully leaves him guessing by moving the conversation seamlessly back to the communal experience. "I would really like to follow up on the group meetings," she says. "Whether they continued, whether they evolved, whether they helped."

After she's gone, Shorter remains unsure if Rosalie is one of the brightest characters he's ever met or a total nutbar. He questions whether he still has sufficient mental resources to make that determination. Oh, I'd give anything to have Jess here with me, he thinks, so that we could dissect the enigma of Rosalie at leisure. We wouldn't be mean-spirited in our gossiping, Jess and I, but we might allow ourselves a bit of wicked fun at Rosalie's expense. But of course if Jess was here there'd be no need for Rosalie's visits. Rosalie's entire *raison d'etre* is the absence of Jess.

For her part, Rosalie would love nothing better than to have the other commune members all present there with Shorter and herself, nibbling cookies and remembering those long-ago days. Most especially Jess, who was plainly an extraordinary woman and so obviously the linchpin of both the commune and Shorter's existence.

SEVEN

DURING A MILD SPELL IN FEBRUARY, WE PRIORITIZED GETTING A PROPER goat shed built using timbers and boards pried from the wreckage of the old barn. This was our first real building project and, all things considered, it went remarkably well. Within a few weeks we'd produced a tight and handsome little shed for the goats from which they could wander freely into the pasture beyond. With great solemnity we moved the milking stand and the does into their snug new quarters.

By early spring both goats looked like horizontal barrels on stick legs. Gracie was due first. Watching her swell to bursting, everyone kept a close eye on her, alert for any sign that birthing might be imminent. But Gracie the maverick outfoxed us all by calmly returning from the meadow one sunny afternoon with two little billies cavorting behind her. No well-intentioned meddling from us required, thank you. Hard to connect those frisking little beauties with the slavering beast that had fathered them and that they in turn would become if allowed. Determined not to also miss Sara's birthing, Lena and Jess hardly let her out of sight the whole next week and were rewarded with an "O holy night" experience when she gave birth in the shed by the glow of a kerosene lamp. A single kid this time, but also a billy.

It seemed appropriate to let Willie know that the goats had given birth, so Angus and I stopped in to see him during a trip to Spangler to pick up hardware supplies.

"Mornin', fellas!" he greeted us warmly in his trademark dressing gown and slippers. "No Jess with ya then?"

"No sir, gents only this morning," I told him. He had his TV tuned to a workout class for women in revealing leotards but with

94

the volume off. He kept casting sideways glances at the women as they stretched and bent and made it burn.

"Sorry we didn't bring any of the pups along for you, Willie," Angus said. "Not yet sure if it's permitted here."

"Naw, I asked the head nurse about it," Willie snorted in disgust. "Strictly forbidden, except for those comfort dogs they bring in. I told her my Bandy and Suzy would give me more genuine comfort than those pathetic little schnauzers, but she said if we allowed it for one person, pretty soon everyone would be wanting to have their dogs brought in and the place would be overrun with pit bulls and Rottweilers attacking the staff. There's just no talking sense to some people."

"We've got some good news, Willie," I told him. "Both the goats have given birth. Gracie had twins and Sarah a single."

"Well, that's mighty fine news," Willie said, just as one of his exercisers bent herself into an impossible pretzel. "Any billies?"

"Three billies, I'm afraid," Angus told him.

"Too bad," Willie said. "They'll get to be a godawful handful in no time a'tall. Ferocious level of energy them little bastards have."

"What do you recommend?" Angus asked.

"You got four choices" he told us, holding up four gnarled fingers. "You can shoot 'em and butcher 'em yourself, which is what I did all those years. Meat's not bad a'tall, especially the tenderloin roasted over a wood fire, damn fine eating. Or you can castrate 'em and keep 'em around as pets if you've got more money than brains, which I don't reckon you folks have. You can take 'em up to the auction at Black Creek where guys will buy 'em for the Greek restaurants. Or you could keep one of them for stud purposes, which only masochists or morons would do."

We laughed with Willie at this, remembering the abomination of Bill in rut. "Bring Jess with ya next time," Willie said to me when we were taking our leave. "The sight of that gal does my poor old heart good."

"He's a horny old billy himself," Angus muttered as we emerged from Sunset Rest back into the light of day.

"But I appreciate he's given us lots to think about with the billies," I said. "Sooner or later, we're gonna have some hard choices to make."

"True enough," Angus agreed. "Lucky we don't have to make any decisions until fall."

"Yeah. But I suspect the choices will be even harder by then, when those little twerps aren't so little anymore."

What we didn't mention to Willie was that we were experiencing extreme problems with our waste disposal system. Willie or his forebears had installed behind the house a do-it-yourself version of a septic tank and drainage field into which the kitchen sink as well as the bathtub, sink and toilet all drained. This set-up may well have worked passably for a single occupant, especially one averse to excessive bathing, but was being overwhelmed by our multitude. As the water table rose over winter, so did the overflow as well as the stench from the field. "Better get the septic tank guys in, like, yesterday," one experienced islander advised.

Within a few days of our call, the Gone With the Wheel Septic Services tanker truck pulled into our yard. The two operators, bearded guys in gumboots and coveralls and large rubber gloves, laughed and joked as they went about their business pulling a long flexible pipe from the truck to our homemade concrete tank and sucking its malodorous contents into their truck tank. "Think maybe you folks could do with a new system," one of them said jovially before they drove off. No kidding.

All other business was suspended at our next group meeting so we could make some hard choices about sewage. As a stopgap measure, some of us had taken to using the old outhouse that squatted under a bigleaf maple tree a short distance behind the house. The Crapper, we called it. With no light in it, but multitudes of malevolent-looking spiders, the biffy did not provide an aesthetic experience at the best of times, and a sprint to it during heavy wind and rainstorms, requiring boots and raingear, was sufficiently off-putting that fewer and fewer of us exercised this option.

Enzo, who was decidedly not an outhouse habitué, did a bit of research on septic tank systems and reported back to us at the next meeting.

"Not good news, kiddos," he told us. "Replacing that dilapidated tank with one that actually works plus installing a whole new drainage field that would be up to code would probably cost us upward of fifteen grand." We all kind of gasped, as that was far more cash than we had at our disposal. What to do?

Angus spoke up. "I think we'd be way better off if we moved to a composting toilet regime."

"How's that any different from the Crapper?" I asked him.

"Doesn't take an Einstein," he explained. "You have your booth, just like the outhouse, perched on top of a sealed concrete chamber into which the droppings fall. You cover each visit with a sprinkle of sawdust or whatever. The chamber has a sloping floor, and by the time the shit works its way to the bottom, it's just like compost."

"What about urine?" Elizabeth asked.

"No, you've got to piss separately, into a bucket or something. But remember that urine makes for a great nitrogen fertilizer. The grand houses back home used it all the time in the old days; they'd have the servants empty their bedpans for them every morning, then the piss would age for a couple of weeks in barrels before the gardeners would apply it to the gardens."

"But where are we going to find the servants?" Enzo asked guilelessly.

"I guess that's where we come in," Jess said. "This obviously is a hands-on option, but, realistically, do we have any other?"

And so a decision was made: we'd construct a composting toilet with a breezeway connecting it to the house. We'd take turns digging out the composted crap as well as collecting, fermenting and distributing the enriching urine. With this regime in place, use of the old indoor toilet wasn't exactly forbidden, but strongly discouraged. At the outset, none of us had any idea what a colossal volume of urine and excrement six adults can produce. Or that the composting feces required regular aeration. Diligent maintenance of our environmentally correct system soon pushed us into the servant class and sparked numerous arguments about who was or was not carrying their load.

We decided against using any fecal matter in the veggie patch, just to be safe. But the abundance of free nitrogen from pouring diluted urine on the veggie patch was like winning a lottery. Already by late spring we could see that we'd be harvesting bumper crops of beans and peas and all the rest. The beds required almost perpetual attention, what with weeding and watering, staking and thinning, but the whole undertaking was so promising and productive we didn't begrudge the labour at all.

Plus our six residents were about to become seven. "Enzo and I have something to tell you," Lena announced at the dinner table one evening. They both had sort of goofy looks on their faces and I think we all guessed right away what they were going to announce. "Yes, we're going to have a baby!" Lena gushed while Enzo beamed like a polished *paterfamilias*. This was fabulous news, of course, partly as a definitive banishing of the ghost of Christopher Volts, but more importantly as a gesture of continuance for the collective. The announcement introduced a component of new seriousness to our endeavour, a purchase on the future that surely confirmed we were something more than just a bunch of aimless hippies on a lark.

A few weeks after that, I heard the dogs raising a ruckus outside and saw Jess and Elizabeth returning from a meeting of the food co-op. Starting this past winter, a bunch of us had set it up so that every three months a big truck came up from LifeStream Natural Foods in Vancouver loaded with pre-ordered grains, flour, dried fruit, beans, cheese and dozens of other organic food items. Distribution day at the community hall was normally a festive collective event, but I could see straight off that Jess and Elizabeth were really upset about something.

"You won't believe what's happened!" Jess said as I came out. There was something slightly crazed about her, not a typical Jess state at all.

"What is it?" I asked, concerned that something majorly dreadful was coming down.

"The hedgerow, you know, all along Lower Road..."

"What about it?" I asked, thrown off at seeing Jess so undone. Unspoken though it may have been, Jess was our touchstone; if she were to lose her grip, the rest of us would be well and truly fried.

"They've cut the whole thing down!"

"What?" I said, not really getting what she was telling us. "Who?"

"Latasky!"

"Huh."

Roads foreman Byron Latasky hadn't been resident on the island much longer than ourselves, having previously worked in a similar capacity in New Brunswick, a posting that had apparently given him a singular attachment to widening and straightening every road in his purview in order to deal with massive snowfalls. In several instances last fall he'd taken it upon himself to scrape away the grassy verges of island roadways with his grader for no discernible purpose. There'd been some grumbling at the time, but nothing had come of it, mostly because Latasky was a really popular guy. For starters, he was quite undersized for someone who piloted around such enormous equipment, much like the little men in cowboy boots so frequently seen driving colossal semi-trailers and Winnebagos. Latasky loved a drink or two after a hard week on the grader and could be riotously self-effacing when in his cups. He'd shown up at several of the Christmas house parties and had famously needed to be restrained from taking all his clothes off at the New Year's dance.

"Why would Latasky cut the whole hedgerow down?" I asked.

"Shorter, would you and Angus go down and have a look at it and come back here and tell me if we're overreacting, okay?"

"Sure thing," I said.

"Hey," Lena added, "take your camera. This needs to be recorded."

I ducked into the house, retrieved my old 35mm Kodak, then Angus and I jumped into Viribus and headed down to Lower Road. This was a favourite place, one of the many pleasing vistas that had so entranced Jess and myself on our exploratory visit the previous spring. Back then we'd parked the bus and walked along the narrow paved road edged with hedgerows on either side. We'd been completely charmed by the hedgerows swathed with tiny, pale green growth and the shining white blossoms of wild plum. We'd laughed at throngs of officious little birds, busy with springtime courting and nesting, as they hopped from twig to branch among the young plum, dogwood and cascara. In June the wild roses bloomed profusely pink and fragrant. Last summer Jess and I would occasionally go for an evening's bicycle ride or walk along this half-mile perfumery, our minds set dancing among sweet memories and dreams triggered by the scents.

By late summer, clusters of blackberries hung thick and richly purple. Every so often we'd see some industrious islander gathering buckets of berries destined for jam-making or the wine cellar. In autumn the hedgerow leaves splashed a fine line of colour against the dull, cut hayfields beyond. And after the first frosts, bright red rosehips glistened beside clusters of white snowberry, again attracting pickers for rosehip jelly or tea. Wrens and sparrows seemed to be always hopping around, and on occasion you'd come upon a dozy grouse at the road's edge gravel, or perhaps a cock pheasant strutting in baroque plumage.

But as Angus and I turned onto the road this particular morning, we instead encountered a godawful muddy mess. On one side of the road the hedgerow had been hacked down completely. What had been a place of small mysterious rustlings and wonderful seasonal changes now stretched before us as a swathe of churned mud and debris. The remains of trees, vines and bushes smouldered in forlorn heaps. Where before mice and shrews had scuttled about, intent on their miniature business amid the dead leaves, a backhoe now squatted incongruously, caked in mud, its operator smoking a cigarette nearby.

We hopped out of the bus and strode over to the backhoe guy, somebody we'd never seen before.

"What the hell's this mess all about?" I asked him, way more aggressively than I perhaps should have.

"Don't lay your shit on me, bud," the guy replied laconically. "I'm just doing what I'm told. You got a beef, go talk to the foreman."

"And where might we find him?" Angus asked.

"He's at the highways yard. But you better be quick because I'm starting on the other side here just as soon as I'm finished my break."

"Like hell you are," Angus said, less politely than before. He and the backhoe guy bristled at one another.

We decided that I'd go find Byron Latasky while Angus stayed there to do the dirty if needs be. Sure enough, I caught up with Latasky at the works yard.

"Byron," I said, "what the hell are you doing down on Lower Road?"

"Just cleaning things up a bit," he told me. "Them old wire fences need replacing and such."

"But you've made a total bloody mess down there," I said.

"Well, of course it's a bit of a mess right now," he admitted, "but once we clean all the garbage up, widen the surface a bit, put some proper ditching in and reseed the edges, it'll be better than ever."

"Why would you possibly want to widen that road?"

"Safety concerns," he told me.

"What safety concerns? At most there's ten cars a day use that road."

"Maybe for now, but not in the future. You'll want some room for cars to pass safely at speed in the future. Plus there's the snow removal issue."

"I don't recall you having snow problems this past winter."

"Course not; it hardly snowed this year. But you just wait, we'll get a real dump one of these winters."

I could see it was hopeless trying to reason with him. "Byron," I said, "I want to ask you to please not do anything more down there until we've had a chance to talk with your people in town."

Somehow the mention of his superiors in Spangler quickly sobered Byron. "Okay," he said agreeably, "we've got other stuff we can do this afternoon, but I'll have to be back at that job tomorrow or I'll lose the backhoe."

Angus and I sped back to the farm and reported to the others.

"We need to call the Highways office in town," Jess said, "which I'm happy to do if you like." We all murmured assent. Calling Highways headquarters, or anyone else, had only recently become a convenient thing to do. We'd waited month after month to have a telephone installed. For almost a year, any necessary phone calls had involved driving down to the ferry landing and using a scuzzy public phone that was often out of order because local yahoos had vandalized it. Finally the potentates at BC Telephone authorized our phone line and we joined the twentieth century. Well, let's say the early twentieth century, because we were on a party line that we shared with three other customers, all of whom had been carefully selected for both volume and loquacity. No matter what time of the day or night you picked up the receiver, somebody would be chattering away, pausing only long enough to tell you, "We're on the line, thank you."

Jess went to the phone, fully prepared to tell any of our party-goers that we had an emergency call to make, but amazingly found the line free. With a bit of no-nonsense insistence, she got through to the district superintendent who confirmed that, yes indeed, there had been no problems with this particular stretch of road, no accidents or incidents. No, he told her, the road is not slated to be widened. He agreed to have the work stopped until the situation could be reviewed.

Several days later, one of the office underlings called back to tell us the only rationale these officials could give for destroying the hedgerow was the ineptitude of the local roads foreman. "He stripped the place like a bald prairie," the spokesperson admitted. Destroying the roadside vegetation was, in this official's words, "a mistake," "unfortunate," and "unnecessary."

No kidding.

That evening we all piled into Viribus and drove together down to Lower Road in some kind of dim memorial gesture. One side of the road still retained its hedgerow, only because we'd intervened when we did, but its charm was more than halved by the mess facing it across the road. We stood around quietly, like pilgrims at a desecrated shrine, each of us wondering what it is about humans that allows them to wreak so much stupid and unnecessary havoc. Why are the wild roses of summer, the pastel white of plum blossom in the spring, so casually abolished? Can a thing of beauty ever hope to be a joy forever, when we see so much of what is beautiful, living and mysterious chopped down, chewed up and spat out by machines.

At that very moment, as we'd heard on the CBC Radio news that morning, the Bangladesh war for independence was erupting. Over the next nine months, the West Pakistan military along with Islamist militias would murder upward of half a million people, rape a similar number of Bangladeshi women and displace millions. Alongside that obscene bloodbath our little hedgerow disaster seemed embarrassingly paltry.

But looking back now, I do see this minor incident as a seminal moment in our communal endeavour. For us it was a startling eye-opener, a sudden revelation that we were living in a fool's paradise. Looking no further than our farm, we'd assumed all along that the beauty of the island, the peace and integrity of the place, would simply endure with no effort on our part. But standing in the wreckage that evening, it was clear to all of us, as Jess articulated succinctly, that this little island we'd already come to love, to think of as home, was going to need some serious defending. It was our first inkling that escape to a simpler lifestyle was really no escape at all.

ROSALIE, OF COURSE, WAS NOT LIVING ON THE ISLAND WHEN THESE events took place. And even if she were, she'd have been a toddler at most. She's never given Shorter any hint of her age, though he can't imagine she's more than forty, if that. Nobody's fool, she's picked up enough clues to realize that the old guy's increasingly inquisitive

103

about her private self, but has determined that an elusive and enigmatic presence—whether regarding her age or history or personal circumstances—will best serve her purposes. "More than anything," she tells Shorter, "I'm delighted at the news of Lena's pregnancy. Hope renewed, don't you agree—trust restored in the strength of women and beauty of birth. Nevertheless," she tells Shorter now, "had I been here at the time, I would certainly have stood in solidarity with your group over the butchered hedgerow."

She goes on to speak at considerable length about the incident, by gradual increments becoming more and more incensed. "Tracy Chapman comes to mind," she says. "The rape of the world. Disgusting, as well as disturbing. I'm so tired of the power wielded by men of diminished vision. Surely you are too, Mr. Shorter."

A type of regal indignation animates her bearing during this tirade. She rises from her chair and paces menacingly. Reaching a crescendo of sorts, she stands above Shorter and asks fiercely, "What gives such people, such *men*, the authority to destroy whatever they choose? No matter the consequences for everyone else, for the Earth herself?"

Cowed by her intensity, Shorter feels absurdly complicit in what has occurred, as though Byron Latasky and he were malicious co-conspirators. Assigned a portion of blame on the basis of gender alone, Shorter in turn begins to bristle at what he sees as her unfair insinuations.

"Hold on just a minute," he says to her. "Don't forget I was there to witness and lament this loss. I've paid my dues, I feel, in a very long struggle against the idiots busily working to destroy Mother Earth." He has to restrain himself from saying he's seen no evidence at all that Rosalie has done the same.

"Surely by now," he carries on, "you've twigged to the fact that the whole underpinning of the commune from the get-go was to remove ourselves from the patterns of exploitation manifest even in the miniature stupidities of pawns like Byron Latasky."

"Of course I have," Rosalie replies haughtily, no longer looming above him, but not sitting back down either. The two of them remain silently at indignant loggerheads, equally nervous that they are edging toward their first real *contretemps*.

Rosalie breaks the spell. "I'm sorry, Mr. Shorter," she says. "I think it best if I take my leave at this point." She abruptly packs her gear, bids him a brusque goodbye and departs. Stripped of any other recourse, unsure if perhaps he's seen the last of Rosalie, Shorter eventually seeks refuge in continuing with his story.

EIGHT

SPRING PLANTING SEASON CAME AT US LIKE A HURRICANE. ALTHOUGH we'd been immoderately impressed by our gardening achievements during the previous year, in reality most of what we'd grown, other than turnips and potatoes, had been eaten by Christmas. We knew we needed to seriously ramp up our grow-your-own game, and that's how Amrapali came onto the scene. Jess and Lena had met her through the food co-op and brought her over one afternoon to assess our veggie patch. A redoubtable character, tall and full-figured with abundant blond hair, she was dressed in a vibrantly tie-dyed muumuu that caused her to resemble a Bedouin tent. She strode authoritatively around our patch, stooped on several occasions to crumble a handful of soil and made a considerable production out of tasting the soil for sweetness.

"A little on the sour side," she announced, dusting off her ring-laden fingers. "Needs lime for sure. Probably could use a pinch of boron and, unless I miss my guess, is potassium deficient too." All this was news to us, but given her assured manner, as well as the fact that Amrapali had just about swept all the blue ribbon awards for produce at last year's fall fair, we figured she knew what she was talking about. (Only much later was it revealed that a diminutive Filipina named Theresa, nominally her "assistant," did most of the actual gardening at Amrapali's place.)

Amrapali advised us to dig over the entire vegetable patch and convert it to raised beds. "It's from the French biodynamic system," she told us, "and, really, it's the only sane approach. Gets the soil warmed up and properly dried out after winter." This came as particularly welcome news to Elizabeth who, as we all knew, had picked up a smattering of ideas about biodynamic agriculture from her Esalen Institute days.

Elizabeth had not previously distinguished herself as a "hands-on" gardener, preferring to leave the spading and hoeing and so forth to the rest of us, but now she entered into a robust discussion with Amrapali about the ideas of Rudolf Steiner, with a special emphasis on the mystical perspectives of a garden's ecology.

"I'm a great believer in astrological planting systems," Elizabeth said, and you could see everybody else's eyes rolling like bowling balls, since Elizabeth had never before been known to put seed to soil during any phase of the moon.

"Quite so," Amrapali agreed, plainly delighted to have come upon a fellow traveller in the field of biodynamic agronomy. "And it's *so* important," she added "to work in harmony with the cosmic forces in the soil."

After Amrapali had taken her leave, we unanimously agreed to convert the whole veggie patch to a biodynamic raised-bed system and set about starting a grand dig-over, each of us (except Elizabeth) taking turns in excavating the soil. Within a week, the entire *potager* had been transformed into an expanse of raised beds running north/south and separated by symmetrical pathways. Barrowloads of rich compost, derived largely from goat and chicken bedding (and definitely *not* from the new composting privy) were folded into the soil along with wood ash from the past winter's fires. In accordance with Amrapali's prescription, Elizabeth made a grand show of sprinkling tiny amendments of boron and potassium across the beds. Flats of seedlings that had been germinated indoors during the previous weeks were transplanted to pots (Willie had left us enough old plastic trays and pots to pollute a mid-sized ocean). Standing back and surveying our marvellous *potager* we collectively experienced a tremendous upsurge of confidence that this year's garden was going to be truly outstanding.

The vegetable garden project continued to proceed handsomely until all work ground to a halt, so to speak, because of the Oyster Festival. A long-standing tradition, this was the island's major social event of the year, attracting hundreds of visitors and generating crucial income for the community hall. Iris Thomas (she of the anti-nudist league), as president of the Community Club, was coordinator for the event, assisted by a small committee of volunteers. Attractions included a beer garden and several food stands, along with booths set up around the playing field by local potters, weavers and other craftspeople. The feature event of the daytime activities was an oyster shucking competition at which professional shuckers from around the region competed to see who could open and extract the most oysters in a set time. Primarily young men of peculiar bravado, the shuckers showed amazing dexterity at prying oyster shells open with a dedicated knife, then (without inflicting a single nick) extracting and flicking the hapless oysters into a bucket so fast you could hardly follow. The gathered crowds whooped and cheered as one local favourite or other shucked ahead in the competition. (Needless to say, this was not an event during the course of which no animals were injured, but sensibilities were of a rougher sort back then.)

After that, kids' games started, mostly involving the half-naked and face-painted urchins of us "new people." We whooped and clapped mightily as the kids did their wheelbarrow races, balloon tosses and three-legged races. Then a major highlight: a massive tug o' war in which "the hippies" faced off against a team of beefy good-old-boys. A chorus of good-natured jeering arose when it became obvious to the onlookers that our team would include women while our opponents' would not. But we longhairs were brimming with confidence; we had muscular youth on our side, our women members—including Jess—were a sturdy bunch and, most weighty of all, we sported Billy Butler as our anchor man. Wearing only old denim coveralls and smiling out from a huge bushy red beard, Billy was a truly massive chunk of humanity, three hundred pounds at least, with arms thicker than oak roots and shoulders like a Brahma bull. Having him at the tail end of our rope, we imagined ourselves unmovable.

The starting whistle blew and our team began tugging with impressive youthful gusto. Several times we had the red flag at the centre of the rope pulled tantalizingly close to our winning. The crowd was roaring at what looked to be victory in our grasp. Only trouble was, the good-old-boys knew what they were doing. While our gang just yanked away randomly at the thick rope, our opponents were experienced enough to have a driver, in this case a flinty old-timer none of us had ever seen before. Each time we pulled to within inches of victory he threw his arm up in the air and shouted, "Hang!" They instantly all dug their heels into the grass to resist our chaotic tugging. Then the old boy would yell "Pull!" and following rhythmic gestures of his upraised arm his whole team pulled in unison, jerking us forward.

Youthful exuberance strained mightily against coordinated experience. The crowd roared with excitement as one team, then the other, gained the upper hand. But as the see-saw struggle went on, it became increasingly apparent that footwear was our Achilles heel. While our rivals all wore boots with heels ideal for digging in, most of our gang had chosen to go barefoot or wear sandals. Bad idea. Soon enough our team began running out of gas from enthusiastic but erratic tugging. With each new disciplined pull from our opponents we floundered forward a bit, our bare feet or sandals slipping along the grass. Even barefoot Billy, upon whom our hopes had resided, was sliding forward helplessly. Finally their driver ordered one last synchronized pull and we were routed, tumbling onto the grass in defeat.

It was all back-slaps and handshakes after that, but nevertheless we felt as though Peace and Love had been given a robust spanking. After the rude humiliation, and a few snarky remarks from select spectators, we dusted ourselves off and strolled over to the food booths where people were chomping happily on ulcer-inflaming hot dogs. For a good number of participants, the remainder of the afternoon was devoted to steady alcohol consumption in the beer garden, resulting in certain merrymakers eventually passing out on the lawn. Gearing up for the evening dance, we had no inkling of the mightier tug o' war awaiting us.

Things soured later in the evening with an outbreak of profanity-laced beer bottle smashing. The scene was screwy enough that Jess and I decided to skip the dance and head home early, but as we came around a corner of the hall we encountered about fifty or more young guys massed on the road in a jostling mob. The Desperados were in the thick of it, of course, and the Faverall boys, along with a gang of off-island associates, the whole pack of them shouting and smashing beer bottles on the roadway. This appeared to be an accepted feature of the festival because clusters of older islanders, including some parents of the young rowdies, stood around watching and laughing.

There was normally no police presence on the island, but because of incidents of lawlessness at previous Oyster Festivals, an RCMP officer along with an auxiliary constable had been dispatched from town specifically to keep things under control.

Jess and I realize at the same moment that the two cops are actually surrounded in the middle of the mob. The drunks are taunting the cops, shoving them around and flicking cigarette butts at them.

"Jesus Christ," Jess says, "what's this—the flip side of Chicago?" And it was indeed truly bizarre, after our epic clashes with Daley's uniformed goons, to now see the local cops as victims and the vox populi as a howling mob. "I don't believe it," Jess says, looking at me strangely, "but I'm feeling like we gotta help those cops. Whaddya think, Shorter?"

"Too weird," I say, not conscious of any especially heroic impulses, but just then one of the goons hurls a whisky bottle, smashing a big front window in the hall. The mob howls in delirious triumph, as though it's just successfully stormed the Bastille.

Suddenly Iris Thomas comes tearing out of the hall, wild-eyed and furious, her carefully planned event disintegrating into mob violence. She tries to get the rowdies to disperse, but their blood's up and they scream vile obscenities at her. In the middle of it all, the young auxiliary constable is pushed to the ground and one of the Faverall boys gives him a vicious kick in the ribs while the mob roars with drunken glee.

"Well, fuck this," Jess says. "You stay out of it, Shorter, they'll only want to fight with you." Before I can say anything, she wades into the melee, pushing drunks out of her way. She gets to where the young cop's on the ground and gets right up in the face of Butch Faverall. "Back the fuck off!" she tells him fiercely and, amazingly, he does. The crowd's still wobbling and jostling close, but somehow she forces them back by the strength of her presence. She helps the young cop to his feet just as the other officer elbows his way through.

"I've called for backup," the second cop says, "they'll be here on the next ferry. Let's just try keep a lid on things 'til they get here." He's talking more to Jess than to his bruised sidekick. Hazily perceiving that the riot squad's on its way, the yahoos retreat, eventually huddling on the far side of the road and snuffling like a dim-witted lynch mob.

Bursting with a jangled mix of love, pride and anxiety, I tell Jess how great she was. "Ah, shit," she says, a kind of crazy wildness about her, "this whole thing's too fucking weird. After Kent State and Chicago and Selma, here we are, waiting for the pigs to restore order in paradise."

Pretty soon half a dozen more cops show up armed to the teeth so that the scales of justice are re-established with a vengeance. They arrest Butch and four or five others, including two of the Desperados who they find hiding in the hall attic with several bottles of liquor they pilfered from the bar. The dance is shut down and the crowd dispersed. The festival grounds look like the aftermath of a riot, which they just about are.

As Jess and I are leaving for home, we encounter John Thomas and Iris, he with his arm protectively around his wife's slumped shoulders. She's plainly been crying, her mascara moistly smeared, her event a ruinous disaster. John Thomas glowers at us. "Happy now?" he asks us fiercely, as though the mayhem was all our doing.

The irony of this whole episode was that the festival beer tent had sold so much booze that the Community Club was suddenly wallowing in cash. Several weeks later an extraordinary general meeting was called, ostensibly to approve plans for the disbursement of this sudden windfall, but everybody knew the meeting was really about who would control the hall as well as the loot and, by extension, who was running this island anyway.

The executive was reportedly gridlocked. In one faction you had Iris as president, still smarting from the festival debacle and having suffered a series of setbacks in her campaign against the naturists at Sunset Beach—despite repeated prodding from the clothing-not-optional crowd, neither the regional district nor the provincial conservation agencies had prioritized developing legislative impediments to the nudies. Her loyal vice-president and treasurer was Waldo Gilport, Gilbert's cousin, who'd made good money running a little logging show off the west coast and was now burning his way through it by wining and dining whatever available women he could ensnare. Mable Sutcliffe, the Midwestern sourpuss beneath the beehive in the general store, served as secretary.

In the executive's opposite corner we had Charles Jimson, a young artist and firebrand who'd arrived on the island around the same time we did. Also Julie Getz, a retired librarian who'd lived here for a half-dozen years and about whom almost nothing was known other than her active dislike for certain members of the island old guard, whom she considered, in her own words, "as backward as they are bullheaded." To put the executive's dysfunction unequivocally over the top, we had another relative newcomer, Brady Lazarus, a handsome young carpenter who, rumour had it, previously worked as a bouncer at an Edmonton strip club. He and his companion Ethel had purchased a lovely little waterfront cottage on the western shore where they resided briefly in rural bliss until Ethel took up with a considerably older—and considerably wealthier—gentleman neighbour and ran off with him to frolic in the sunshine of Hawaii.

All of our Figurative Farm group except for Angus squeezed into the microbus and rattled down to the community hall for the extraordinary general meeting. The place was packed with animated islanders, as though Muhammad Ali and Joe Frazier were planning to go at it in the main event. Iris was enthroned at the head table with secretary Mable on her left and treasurer Waldo on her right. Having called the meeting to order, Iris announced that the Oyster Festival had been an unequivocal success, generating several thousand dollars in after-expenses capital. A round of applause erupted. No mention was made of the near-riot or the cops or the smashed window (replaced in the interim). She proposed that these funds, supplemented by a matching LIP grant from the federal government, be used to install an outdoor swimming pool on the community hall grounds.

This suggestion was met with a cacophony of discord encompassing jubilation, disbelief, outrage, excitement and mockery. Some members asked why the hell we would need a swimming pool when we've already got the salt chuck and two fine lakes for swimming. Others wanted to know if there would be a high diving board. Where exactly would the water come from, since the current supply to the hall from a shallow well was barely adequate for flushing the toilets. Would chlorine be required. Where would the chlorinated water be dumped. What about ongoing pool maintenance. Who would fish out the leaf litter. On and on the questions went, with Iris's supporters enthusiastically praising this brilliant initiative and her opponents heaping contempt upon it.

When it was eventually revealed that the pool would occupy a spot on the hall grounds currently serving as left centre field, I added my two-bit concerns, speaking as first baseman for the men's fast-pitch softball team and coach-designate for the new women's team, arguing that outfielders risked death by water chasing long fly balls toward the pool.

A number of the "new people" argued passionately that the funds should be used to build an addition to the hall to properly house a much-needed preschool. Earlier attempts to have a preschool established in the hall had been rebuffed on the grounds that a preschool was nothing more than an easy way for lazy and inadequate (i.e., hippie) parents to duck out of their responsibilities. "I

113

raised nine kids on the farm without any help from any preschool," declared Abigail Gilport, matriarch of her clan, to rousing applause.

Then, amazingly, our Lena boldly declared in her own gentle way that she was having a baby within a few months and that she stood alongside all the young parents of the island in supporting adequate facilities for early childhood learning. More partisan cheers and applause.

Eventually Iris called closure on public input. The matter would be put to a vote. Only bona fide members of the Community Club were entitled to vote, which immediately disqualified a segment of the preschool faction. However the pro-preschoolers had done their homework in getting a number of supporters to take out club membership. But was it enough? Two independent vote counters were now appointed.

"All those in favour of using Community Club surplus funds along with an LIP grant to construct a swimming pool on the hall grounds, please raise your hands," Iris directed. Several dozen arms rose to be counted. The official counters made their tallies, wrote them on scraps of paper and handed them to the secretary. Being as the counters were not entirely beyond suspicion of bias, several unofficial counters made their own tallies. "All those in favour of using Community Club surplus funds along with an LIP grant to construct an addition to the hall to house a preschool, please raise your hands," Iris directed again. All of us from Figurative Farm raised our hands, along with lots of others, in what seemed a greater number than the swimming pool set. An excited buzz rumbled among the preschool supporters.

The counters again presented their numbers to secretary Mable, who calmly received the results. She passed both tallies to Iris. "The vote by show of hands," Iris announced to the expectant crowd, "is fifty-two in favour of a swimming pool and sixty-three in favour of a preschool." A loud cheer erupted from the victorious side. I gave Jess a hug and Lena too. Our whole gang was exultant.

"Now, Madam Secretary," Iris continued calmly once the tumult had abated, "would you please give the tally of the proxy votes."

Proxy votes?

Mable Sutcliffe made a great show of putting down her pen and retrieving from a file folder a piece of paper that she stared at solemnly for a moment before passing it to Iris. Iris stared at it too, pretending she'd never seen it before. She cleared her throat and announced to the crowd: "The proxy votes are as follows. The votes in favour of the swimming pool total nineteen. The votes in favour of the preschool total one." Astonishment quickly gave way to a sense of seething insurrection in the hall as it dawned on everyone that Iris had obviously contacted certain carefully selected non-resident landowners to bolster their side. Barely containing her triumphalism, Iris announced: "The combined results of the proxy votes and the shows of hand are: those in favour of the swimming pool, seventy-one; those in favour of the preschool, sixty-four. Therefore I hereby declare the motion to apply the designated funds to the construction of a swimming pool is carried."

Well, if that little trick didn't put the shit among the pigeons, nothing would. The meeting broke up in disarray when Waldo Gilport and young Brady Lazarus got into a shoving match that threatened to escalate into a bona fide fist fight. By the following morning, Brady, Charles and Julie had all resigned from the executive. An informal boycott of the hall erupted. "Iris resign!" signs started appearing on the community bulletin board and on the island's one and only stop sign. Bad blood would continue to spill for months.

In the meantime an enormous hole was excavated in deep left field (immediately dubbed the "Black Hole"). A tremendous wire mesh fence was erected, along the lines of Fenway Park's "Green Monster," to prevent incautious outfielders in pursuit of high fly balls from accidentally plunging into the pool-to-be. But the pool itself remained a chimera, shimmering like a desert mirage in the imaginations of its proponents.

One immediate problem was lack of water. Old Jim Sawchuck, one of the island's most respected dowsers, was brought in and spent long hours traversing the ball field trying to find a flow of water sufficient to make his forked alder stick bend. Not even a twitch. At Jim's suggestion they brought in Lance McCaffery next and he worked the grounds as hard as any water witch can work, but again found nothing. Three other dowsers each gave it a try, though two of them were generally considered cranks. As one old-timer muttered, "Them two couldn't find water in a toilet bowl." In accordance with custom, the dowsers declined to accept payment for their labours for fear of losing the gift, but, as is customary, each readily accepted a bottle of whisky as a token of the community's appreciation, providing us with the minor irony of funds raised by selling booze at the Oyster Festival now being spent to supply booze to the failed dowsers. In a truly desperate final move, the executive had an off-island well driller drag in a ramshackle old rig to punch random holes down a hundred feet or more (@ $12.00 per foot). Still no luck.

Even more fatally, the anticipated LIP grant from the federal government failed to materialize. Speculation ran rife that certain malcontents had somehow managed to sabotage the grant application. The directors who'd resigned in protest—Charles, Julie and Brady—were prime suspects, but firm evidence was never produced.

(Years later, at a memorial celebration of life for Julie Getz, her younger brother Alfred confided to me that it had indeed been Julie who'd spiked the grant application through a second cousin highly placed at the Ottawa trough. By Alfred's account, circumspect Julie had in her own words said she "didn't appreciate being dicked around.")

So the great community tug o' war resulted in neither swimming pool nor preschool, though a preschool would eventually be established and the misbegotten pool would soon return in even more provocative form to sharpen our divisions once again.

SHORTER ISN'T AT ALL SURE THAT ROSALIE WILL EVEN SHOW UP ON THE following Friday, the two of them having parted on less than amiable terms. And if she does return, will she be at least slightly contrite following their last encounter? After all, Shorter tells himself, I'm supposed to be the doddering oldster in need of supportive encouragement and she the sympathetic assistant.

Rosalie, of course, sees things somewhat differently. She's been feeling a bit of a fool for having berated the old guy so severely last week. She wonders where the force of her indignation really rose from. The few meagre cookies she brings this time are charred on the underside and her attitude, if not exactly combative, is far from tenderly solicitous.

Once they've settled at the kitchen table, she grudgingly appreciates Shorter's treatment of Jess's bravery at the near-riot. "But, sorry as I am to have to bring the subject up," she tells Shorter, "overall I find your treatment of women thoroughly ignoble." She notes the small jolt she's given Shorter, but carries on anyway. "Yes, given the circumstances, I can understand your dislike of Iris Thomas and Mable Sutcliffe, although a refined sensibility never permits disagreement to curdle into contempt." Before he can mount a credible defence, she tells him that his attitude toward Elizabeth has been shameful from the get-go. But never more so than in the scene with Amrapali in the garden. "Such scorn and disdain on your part! Such snide asides. What is it with you and accomplished women?" Rosalie wants to know.

His dander well up by this point, Shorter informs her in no uncertain terms that Jess was the love of his life, and a vastly more accomplished character than either of those two self-satisfied poseurs. "I never in the least begrudged Jess her considerable accomplishments," he says. "Never. I actually basked in the glow of all she did. But Elizabeth and Amrapali's synthetic mysticism deserved contempt at best."

Rashly, Shorter suggests, "Perhaps this sharing of my story with you is not such a good idea after all." Furthermore, going to the very brink of the precipice, he proposes, "Maybe you'd be happier finding someone other than myself to pursue 'The Work' with."

Aware that she's pushed him a tad too hard, Rosalie calmly brushes his comments off like dandruff. "No call for rudeness," she admonishes. "Any writer worth their salt can withstand a few gentle observations that are something other than base flattery."

Reluctantly he hands over his next chapter with mounting misgivings, while she accepts it with relief that his sensibilities are not, as she had feared, too tender for a bit of honest feedback.

NINE

ANGUS AND I WERE STRIDING ACROSS TO THE VEGGIE PATCH ONE BRIL-liant June morning when suddenly, out of nowhere, the birdsong silence was shattered by a roaring of chainsaws.

"What the hell?" I said, trying to detect where the racket was coming from. It was a ways off, but not all that far. Angus frowned darkly into the distance.

Within minutes a pickup truck came careening into the barnyard. At the wheel was Luis Moya, a young guy I'd run into a couple of times at various gatherings. Luis looked like your classic Hollywood Latino loverboy, bronzed and smooth and handsome as hell. Trini Lopez nailing it with "If I Had a Hammer." I'd gotten snatches of his story in between tokes at various crowded house parties. He'd grown up in the San Joaquin Valley in California and eventually became involved in the United Farm Workers struggles in the '60s. That activity, he'd told me, had motivated the local draft board to become extra inquisitive about him. At that point he'd split for Canada. "I love this country, man," he'd told me, "except for this pale gringo sun in winter!" According to Jess half the young women on the island had the hots for him, but he was currently liv-ing with his sister and her kids. An interesting guy for sure, friendly enough but majorly intense, and one of the very few non-Anglos in our entire crowd.

"Yo," he said as Angus and I came over to his truck. "Just seen a logging crew starting work over on West Road behind your place. That's them we can hear now." We knew from mushroom hunting last fall that there were hundreds of acres of woodlands back there, mostly big sturdy firs. "Thought you might want to check it out, before they start moving down toward your back line."

"Sure thing," I said. "You going back up that way?"

"Yah. You guys want to hop in and we'll go have a look?"

Angus and I climbed into his cab and we took off down our driveway, then curved around to the right on a one-lane dirt road through the woods. Kind of dumb on our part that we'd never bothered to find out who owned the woodlands all around our farm. They weren't spectacular in the way Willie's woodlot was, and from the huge remnant stumps you could see, hairy with salal and huckleberry shrubs, it was obvious the original forest had been felled many years ago.

Luis explained that all the land we were passing through was a tree farm that had been owned by an old lumber baron from Vancouver Island, one of those legendary characters who'd come out here in the early 1900s as a young man with nothing but ambition and had ended up a gazillionaire and owner of his own logging company. The old guy had died a few months back, Luis said, and was rumoured to have left all his forestry holdings to some charitable foundation we'd never heard of.

A little ways up West Road, Luis pulled his truck to the edge of the road behind a big mud-splattered pickup. Off to our left a small swathe of freshly cut stumps led to where two fallers were dropping and limbing big trees with incredible rapidity. We watched as each tall trunk crashed down precisely alongside its predecessor like chopsticks in a tray. Something I'd never seen before, this strange amalgam of symmetry and havoc. A thin veil of blue gasoline haze hung above the fallers and the fallen.

As we got out of the truck, we were instantly hit by a pungent smell. "It's the blood of the trees," Luis said sniffing the air, "the smell of death mingled with their tears in the mud." And with their cries too, it seemed to me, the painful creaking wail of each tree as it toppled and fell. The whole scene—the sight of overthrown giants, the roar of saws and shrieking of the trees, the unmistakable scent of death—evoked a sense of savage battle. Not as image or impression, not as metaphor, but reality. Luis recognized it too. "It's our species attacking another with brute force," he said, "it's fucking genocide."

"Can I help you fellas?" asked a short burly guy in a red hard hat and bright yellow safety vest who'd appeared out of the truck cab. "Not looking for a job, I don't imagine."

"Just looking to see what all the noise was about," Luis told him. "We're neighbours around here and nobody said anything to us about these woods being cut."

"Well, son, you're maybe new around these parts," the guy said with a phony grin, "but all this land here is tree farm..."

"Yeah, we know that," Luis said.

"Very good. Very good. So then you'll also know that tree farms are places where trees are grown to be harvested and that's what we're doing here, y'see: we're harvesting the crop." If the guy had been just a smidgeon brighter you might have called his tone patronizing.

"We understood these lands had been bequeathed to a charitable foundation," Luis said.

"And you understood just right," the guy said, still grinning. "The Waddington Foundation, to be precise."

"And they're responsible for this logging?" Luis asked with a note of incredulity.

"One hundred percent." The hard hat seemed to be enjoying himself, effortlessly running circles around us credulous newbies.

"Do you know how we can get in touch with them?"

"I do."

"Could you give us their contact info?"

"I could."

"Well?"

"I could but I won't. Give you fellas something to do, looking them up in the phone book and all. Seeing as you have nothing better to do with your time, y'know, like a job or anything."

Angus hadn't said a word through all this, but I could feel him bristling alongside me and wondered if he might explode at any moment. Though mostly taciturn, Angus did have a volcanic temper that seemed to gain in force from seldom being exercised. I was also really impressed by how smoothly Luis was handling the situation, not rising to this lumpy fellow's bait.

121

"Well, thanks for your help," Luis said. "I'm sure we'll meet again soon."

"I'll be longing for the day," the hard hat said, chuckling to himself over his wit as he waddled back to his crew cab.

"*¡Chinga tu madre, cabrón!*" Luis muttered as we climbed back into his truck.

Speeding back to the farm as though being chased by the hounds of hell, Luis said, "No time for fucking around here; we gotta stop those crackers before sundown."

"Amen," agreed Angus.

"Shit," I said. "You know, we should have seen it coming."

"What?" Angus asked.

"When they put that new ferry into service this spring, only an idiot wouldn't have figured out that the new boat was plenty big enough to carry logging trucks. Back in the old days, Willie told us, there'd been a log dump on the shore, where logs were assembled into rafts and towed away, but it was shut down long ago and the land sold off. The only reason there's so much maturing timber on the island is there's been no way to get logs off. Duh!"

We burst into the kitchen like a windstorm and quickly gathered everyone around the table. Assuming control, Luis summed up what was happening and said immediate action was urgently needed.

"What do you propose?" Jess asked him.

"Only one way to stop the trees falling," Luis said without hesitation. "That's go stand right under them."

We all glanced uncomfortably at one another around the table. Shit. This meant hassle, no question. Cops, arrests, lawyers, trials. All the crap we thought we'd left behind. Nobody spoke for a bit, everybody calculating profit and loss. Finally Angus slapped the palm of his hand on the table and said, "I don't think there's any alternative. We need to stop the falling right now, at least until we find out what the hell's going on."

"Agreed," Jess and I said simultaneously. Enzo sneezed loudly; he'd been bedevilled by hay fever in recent weeks.

Elizabeth reminded us, "Of course, we have to consider the animals. We can't all be locked up in jail with no one to milk the goats and all the rest of it. I suggest that Lena and myself should stay away from the front line and act as support persons to those willing to risk arrest and incarceration."

But Lena said, "I'd prefer to take a stand along with the rest of you." The rest of us didn't agree.

Jess said, "For sure we need backup people, mostly to mobilize others in the community and to start dealing with the owners of the land, this mysterious foundation."

After a muddle of debate, it was agreed that Luis, Jess, Angus and myself would return to the logging site and prevent further falling by direct action. Lena would get on the phone (party lines be damned!) and start calling everyone we could think of to get involved. Elizabeth would take on organizing an emergency community meeting for the following Saturday afternoon. Sniffling Enzo would notify nearby news outlets about what was happening as well as find out whatever he could about the foundation. I think everyone felt great that we were all in, that there was no one in our group wanting to avoid involvement. You could sense Margaret Mead in her dotage sending us her blessing.

Luis, Angus and I sped back to the logging show gobbling hastily made sandwiches as we went. The plan was that Lena and Jess would follow in Lena's pickup, stopping on the way to pick up Luis's sister, Tonya. Then Jess would remain with us at the logging site while Lena returned home in the pickup and Tonya drove Luis's truck back to her place. Clockwork green.

I was amazed at how many more trees had been dropped in the brief time we'd been away. "Okay, *muchachos*," Luis said as he parked the truck, "let's go kick some butt." I have to admit I was emboldened by Luis's bravado, just as I'd been by Jess's fearlessness at the Oyster Festival. I don't know what it is that gives certain people a battling spirit that most of us don't have. Angus, although he was new to any form of direct action, emanated a kind of stolid determination that seemed well suited to the occasion.

We jumped out of the pickup. Angus and Luis strode purposefully across the road and waded into the sea of slash. The joker we'd spoken with earlier was instantly out of his crew cab and I moved to intercept him on the roadway. "Hey, you dumb fucks!" he shouted at Luis and Angus, but they ignored him and kept going. "What the fuck are those two morons doing?" he barked at me.

"Their civic duty," I replied with a congenial smile. Once again I thanked the gods in charge of such things that I'd been endowed with considerable size. Stubby and squat, the hard hat was compelled to look up at me and both of us could sense his disadvantage.

"They can't go in there!" he spluttered, kind of vibrating in place like a jittery marionette. "It's dangerous. Are they fucking crazy?"

"Actually, no," I said, "they're both remarkably intelligent men. Which helps explain why they're doing what they're doing."

"And what the hell is that?"

"Well, stopping the logging, of course."

"Stopping it?" he bellowed. "You can't stop it! It's totally legal and what those assholes are doing is totally illegal."

"No," I replied as calmly as I could. "Actually I would argue that what they're doing is totally moral and what your pals with the saws are doing is arguably immoral." The smell of the trees' blood still hung thick in the air.

"Fuck this!" he said and retreated to his truck. I could see he had a radio telephone in there and was soon yelling into it.

By this point, Angus and Luis had clambered a good way through the clear-cut and would soon approach the area into which the tree tops were crashing. Suddenly the scream of chainsaws went dead. I could hear angry male shouts and see the two fallers waving Luis and Angus away. But they kept right on scrambling toward the fallers.

Pretty soon the four of them were in a concentrated knot with much shaking of fists and waving of arms. One of the fallers at least seemed especially agitated. At a certain point he picked up his huge saw, raised it above his head and violently flung it down on the ground. Indicative of anger issues, I thought to myself.

Then the hard hat emerged from his truck. "Okay, wise guy," he said to me, "the cops are on their way and you fellas are gonna be dealt with pronto. You'll all be spending the night in the drunk tank breathing shit and piss. If it was up to me," he continued, showing me a gnarly fist, "we'd look after you clowns ourselves, you know what I mean?"

"Nah," I said blithely, "you wouldn't want to try that. One of those guys in there has a black belt in tae kwan do. He could flatten all three of you without even working up a sweat."

The hard hat's eyes bulged with the strain of trying to figure out if I was bulling him or not. "Anyways," he said, "the cops will be here soon enough and that'll be the end of your dumb-ass protest."

"Possibly," I said, "or quite possibly not."

"What's that supposed to mean?"

"We'll see," I said, "won't we?"

After locking his crew cab with a prickly show of vexation, my antagonist took off across the clear-cut to join the heated discussion. Lena's pickup pulled in a few minutes later with Jess, Lena and Luis's sister, Tonya, squeezed in together. They joined me, all three of them wearing boots, blue jeans and flannel shirts as though they were here for a log rolling contest. Three mighty attractive women, I thought to myself, but knew better than to say so. I filled them in on the latest.

Tonya, every bit as handsome as her brother, shook her head, laughing about how Luis had a terrific nose for trouble. "I think he was getting a bit itchy because it's been so quiet around here since that community hall silliness. Nothing he loves better than a good tussle."

"Hmm. Interesting," Jess mused in that faraway leaping-ahead-of-the-moment manner she had. "So we expect the cops shortly. They'll probably try to talk the boys into just going home with a promise not to return. Less hassle for all concerned. Problem solved."

"Except, of course, Luis and Angus won't play along," I said.

"Then what?" Lena asked.

"I guess they'll have no choice but to arrest them for trespassing or mischief or whatever and take them to town just to try to discourage the rest of us." Jess, I could see, was developing a strategy.

"So are you and Shorter going to get arrested too?" Lena asked.

"Oh, I should think so," Jess said with a smile. "Don't you, Shorter?"

"Looks like," I said. This impetus toward arrest and incarceration seemed to have a momentum of its own, moving us like chess pieces wherever it chose.

"Only not right away," Jess added.

"When then?" Lena, normally so placid, was plainly excited by the dramatic possibilities here.

"Given the circumstances," Jess said, "I believe our best bet is to have the cops take the boys away to town. The fallers will get back to work, but once we're sure the cops are safely on the ferry, Shorter, you and I can get in and stop the saws again. It'll be at least another hour before the cops can get back, probably more because they'll have to get a second squad car to fit all four of us in along with two of them."

"Unless they take Luis and Angus to town first, then come all the way back," I said, "in which case it'll be late afternoon before they get here."

"Either way," Jess said with a grin, "we'll have seen our last tree die for the day. Which is where you come in, Lena. Top priority once you get home is to line up whoever you can to continue the action here tomorrow morning."

"I can give you a hand with that, Lena," Tonya said. "I pretty well know who'd be inclined around here—and also who to definitely not involve."

"Thanks," Lena said, the two of them smiling like sisters.

"We'll plan on doing the same thing tomorrow," Jess carried on, "with staggered arrests throughout the day if necessary. Meanwhile, we'll need some press to start putting our illustrious foundation's feet to the fire."

"I'll let Enzo know what's going on so he can call the newspaper and the radio station in town right away," Lena said.

"Great," Jess said, "so let's wait 'til the cops arrive and bring the boys out and we know what's what. Then you can get to work."

Damnit, I couldn't help but admire how quickly Jess sized up the scene and figured out a short-order strategy. Some part of her definitely feasted on these high-octane events—I'd seen it at the Chicago riots and even our Oyster Festival mini-brawl. For the first time, with almost no real evidence, I intuited how alike she and Luis were in this, that they shared an activist vibe in a way that she and I really didn't. It was not the time or place for jealousy, but you could glimpse it slithering along some distance away.

Another half-hour or more elapsed before two cops pulled up in a squad car. And, wouldn't you know it, one of them was the young constable that Jess had rescued from the drunken mob at the Oyster Festival. He spotted her straight away and a broad grin spread across his boyish face.

"We meet again," Jess greeted him with a honeyed smile. They shook hands awkwardly, the young cop already looking hopelessly conflicted. Demonstrably in charge, the older constable was all business and wanted to know exactly what was going on here. I outlined the situation for him.

"So this is private land?" the constable cut to the chase.

"It's land bequeathed to a charitable foundation," I told him.

"And the foundation has chosen to log it, or at least a portion of it?"

"We're not certain, but that seems to be correct."

"As is their right?"

"Their legal right, yes, I suppose."

"So why are you folks interfering?"

"We're not convinced that this clear-cutting lives up to the spirit of the bequest," I told him, "and we need to have the cutting stopped until the situation has been clarified."

"I see." He paused for a moment, looking across the clear-cut. The two fallers were now sitting, each on a large stump. Luis and Angus were standing in front of them, arms crossed like circus strongmen. The hard hat from the truck was struggling back toward the road, his stumpy legs making poor progress through the slash.

Eventually the cops drove in using a skid trail around the back, and brought out Luis and Angus arrested, handcuffed and grinning victoriously in the back seat. We clapped and cheered as though they were the winning team in a Stanley Cup parade. But even before the cops had sped away with them the chainsaws resumed roaring. After hugs all around, Tonya took off in Luis's truck and Lena headed for home in her pickup.

"Well, that was a fuckin' waste of everybody's time," the hard hat said to Jess and me. "And how come you two are still here? Show's over."

We just smiled at him for the moment and he retreated to his crew cab muttering his thick lexicon of curses. Painful as it was to watch the trees crashing down again, we waited until we were confident the cops had left on the ferry. Then Jess walked over to the crew cab and rapped on the window.

"What now?" the fellow growled through the half-open window. You could see that behind his bluster he was unnerved by Jess. She explained to him that we were now going to halt the logging again and that it would be impossible for the police to return in time for cutting to resume that afternoon. So he did have the option of voluntarily ceasing work straight away and saving all of us a lot of unnecessary clambering through the slash.

"Oh, for fuck's sakes!" he bellowed, a man pushed beyond his range of comprehension. He rolled the window up as though a carjacker was menacing him and got back on his radio phone.

Jess and I stepped into the field of screams and began working our way toward the fallers.

ALL TRACES OF THEIR PREVIOUS SPAT HAVE DISAPPEARED WHEN ROSALIE appears the following Friday. In fact, Shorter hasn't yet seen Rosalie quite as pleased as she is on this visit.

"Brilliant!" she tells him, once they've settled together on the couch. "I love it, love it, love it!" she declares. "I was always a great admirer of the War in the Woods, even though I was only a child at the time."

"Really?" Shorter asks her, thinking back to those roaring days in the '80s and '90s when fierce anti-logging campaigns had raged across the coast. All but forgotten now, of course, though he'd enjoyed recalling and describing their own particular small episode in the sprawling struggle.

"Of course," Rosalie says, aware that she's touched a soft spot in the old guy's store of memories. "I admired all you tree huggers tremendously, especially so many of you islanders who were well ahead of the curve." As hungry for validation as the next person, Shorter's gratified by this retroactive acknowledgement.

By way of celebration Rosalie has brought along a small New York–style cheesecake for them to enjoy with their tea. Not even a sliver of the friction with which they'd concluded their previous meeting remains in evidence. Shorter wonders to himself if Rosalie's restored approval derives largely from his description of Jess's mastery of the civil disobedience situation, as opposed to his earlier unflattering portrayal of Elizabeth and Amrapali.

But no. Within a few minutes it's obvious that Rosalie is pleased primarily by the introduction of Luis and Tonya into the narrative. "An intriguing pair," she declares them as she takes a dainty bite of cheesecake and closes her eyes in exaggerated rapture.

So this is an interesting turn. Without saying as much, Rosalie is letting it be known that Luis's brashness appeals to her. Shorter hadn't previously associated brashness with cat-cuddling Rosalie, although the flash of imperiousness he'd seen at their last session had alerted him to how little of her emotional subsurface he actually knew. Or perhaps her enthusiasm stems from the welcome relief these two Spanish-Americans finally introduce to his white-bread cast of characters.

Sensing his uncertainty, Rosalie plays him like a harp. She makes no direct reference to ethnicities, but laughingly approves of Luis's hot-tempered Spanish obscenities. Belatedly Shorter realizes that Rosalie's outfit today looks decidedly Guatemalan.

Aha! he thinks, perhaps at last we begin getting some slight inkling of the grand secrets in her background. Cleverly, he enquires if Rosalie is fluent in Spanish. She smiles at him coyly, seeing right

129

through his artifice. "*Sé un poco de español*" she tells him in sly mimicry of a Yankee tourist footloose in Guadalajara. They look at each other for a long moment, eyes laughing, but with, or at, neither can tell.

TEN

THE FOLLOWING MORNING WE HAD ABOUT TWO DOZEN ISLANDERS SHOW up at the logging site before dawn. Mostly new people, some of whom I knew and others not. A gratifyingly countercultural crowd with young women in gypsy skirts and guys with classic "Isaiah the prophet" beards and hair. Three or four little kids cavorted around. There was only one older gent whom I'd seen around a few times, named Ian McKenzie, and who, it turned out, had long ago been a campaigner for the Wobblies. He seemed not the least self-conscious about being the only oldster or about looking so straight in the bizzaro crowd. Luis and Angus were being held in jail overnight but were expected back later in the day. We all blew on our hands and stamped our feet in the cool of the morning like horses eager to run. Threads of gold began slowly stitching themselves across the eastern sky.

We formed a circle on the road and Jess took the lead in summarizing what had happened yesterday and how our plan for the day was to cause enough repeated interruptions in the logging to make it not worth their while to continue. She outlined the basic principles for successful non-violent civil disobedience—strict discipline, no aggression of any sort, treating opponents with respect and all the rest. I was hoping like hell that Tonya had succeeded in ensuring we didn't have any loose cannons in the crowd. Even back in those days we already knew that nothing can mess up an action quicker than having some dingbat throw a tantrum and get themselves, or maybe others, hurt and the whole operation compromised. Scanning the group, I didn't see any likely candidates for lunacy, but you never knew.

Nothing happened. Seven o'clock came and went. Then eight. By nine we'd all grown really tired of standing around. People began drifting back to their vehicles to listen to the radio or read. A couple of cars eventually pulled out. Jess and I and several others remained on the road with our bold plan of action lying deflated all around us. Eventually the last of us went home, agreeing that we'd return straight away at the first cough of a chainsaw. "Real smart on their part," Jess said as she and I drove home in Viribus.

We found Lena, Enzo and Tonya working full tilt in the living room. They already knew about the no-show at the logging site and Enzo at least was prepared to accept primary responsibility for having scared the loggers off. Working the phone, he'd already come up with an impressive pile of information about the Waddington Foundation.

"Named for Alfred Waddington," he told us, "who was, like, this major player in what they used to call the Colony of Vancouver Island."

"That's calling a colony a colony," Tonya said.

"On the plus side," Enzo continued, "Waddington championed free public education, but he screwed up royally by trying to develop a shortcut to the Cariboo gold fields by building a road up to the Interior from Bute Inlet. Forgot to check with the locals first and ended up igniting the Chilcotin War instead. Workers got killed; way more Natives got killed; chiefs got deceived and hanged. Not exactly a noble chapter in the colonial saga."

"No kidding," Lena said with a grim smile.

"And the foundation?" I asked, knowing Enzo's susceptibility to sidebars. "Ah, yes," he leapt at the opening, "I'm only just getting started, but it seems there's quite a story here as well. Big money. Lots of the right names. Headquartered in Victoria, on Gordon Street, next door to the Union Club where the 'who's who' meet."

Enzo beamed at us through his bifocals. Not for the first time, I suspected him of living out some childhood fantasy of becoming a private detective. He had, after all, lobbied hard during our brief television debacle to have us all watch *The Mod Squad*, which at the time we had put down to his obvious infatuation with actress Peggy Lipton.

Apparently our little ruckus yesterday had already made the news with bits on the local radio station and even brief mentions in the Victoria media.

Nevertheless, we decided we'd better spend the day working in the veggie patch as we still had multiple trays of tomatoes, cucumbers and squash to transplant. But before we could get out the door, the telephone rang.

"Maybe the boys," I said going to the phone, hoping it was Angus and Luis needing a ride home. Instead a stranger's voice said, "Good morning, my name is Bernard Frankl and I'm calling on behalf of the Waddington Foundation. Is this Mr. Shorter?"

"That's right," I said, instantly wishing it was Jess, not me, taking the call. "What can I do for you?"

"I understand we've had a spot of trouble with our lands on your island."

"That's right," I told him. "We were all freaked out yesterday to find those woods being logged without any advance notice from you folks or anything."

"Yes, a regrettable oversight on our part," he admitted smoothly. "We were thinking it might perhaps be helpful if we were to sit down together and discuss the best way forward."

My brain was spinning like a slot machine. Did we really want to be sitting down talking to these people? I flashed back to that piece by Tom Wolfe about "Mau-Mauing the Flak Catchers." Is that what this guy was, a polished shit-smoother dispatched to settle the natives down?

I temporized. "Can you leave me a number and I'll get back to you?"

"Certainly," he said, "and, Mr. Shorter, please rest assured that we've temporarily suspended the timber harvesting until after our meeting, so I would appreciate your getting back to me at your earliest convenience."

"I'll do that," I told him. We exchanged thanks and hung up.

"Bingo!" Enzo exclaimed when I told them.

"I'd say we've got ourselves a foundation with a real high sensitivity to bad press," Jess said. "You know, I'm actually starting to like our chances here."

We were reluctant to commit to the meeting before discussing our position with Luis and Angus. Especially Luis, tellingly, for there seemed to be an unspoken understanding that he was a linchpin to our strategy, much as Jess was.

In the interim we plunged into the transplanting project with such a frenzy even Elizabeth lent a hand (along with a good deal of unsolicited advice on transplanting techniques derived from Taoist principles).

After the two criminals' triumphant return, we all huddled briefly and decided we would meet with the Waddington people. I called Frankl back and we set up a meeting for the following afternoon at a hotel in Nanaimo, halfway between Victoria and us. A spirit of compromise and all that. Lengthy discussion ensued about who among us should attend. Luis was an obvious choice, as was Jess. But we had no idea how many of them would show up—we didn't want to be outnumbered by a posse of pistol-packing lawyers and accountants, nor did we want our entire planting crew spending a whole day travelling to Nanaimo and back when they could be working in the garden. Lena said she would be just as happy transplanting and Enzo recused himself on the grounds he was allergic to Nanaimo. There was consensus I should attend, based less on my strategic genius than my intimidating height. Risking outrage from our telephone party-liners, Lena took on phoning everyone on our contact list to let them know what was happening.

Next morning Luis, Jess and I motored down to Nanaimo in Viribus with Jess at the wheel, the three of us chattering excitedly, not knowing just what to expect. Emissaries of the unknown. With only a couple of minutes to spare, we pulled into the parking lot of the Excelsior Hotel, a venerable old place in the heart of downtown. We weren't exactly wearing our Sunday best, but enough of an upgrade to look passably respectable. Well, by island standards anyway. The desk clerk, a considerably more respectable-looking young woman, said she was expecting us and directed us to a conference room on the second floor. Up we went, a little further out of our element with every step.

When we entered the small conference room, there were only two people present: a youngish woman who was dressed, coiffed and polished to perfection, and a slightly older guy who rose from his chair, greeted us warmly, thanked us for making the time, and introduced himself as Bernard Frankl and his companion as Rosemary Delz. Wearing a business suit and tie, hair clipped with precision, black-framed glasses, immaculate fingernails, Frankl shook each of our hands, bid us sit and jovially launched into an introductory monologue about how his uncle used to have a cabin on the island and how the whole family loved to visit there in the summertime. "Such a unique place," he recalled fondly. Icebreaker expertly executed, he was, he told us, the community outreach coordinator for the Waddington Foundation (pronouncing the name with a tone close to reverence), while Rosemary served as deputy executive assistant to the chief executive officer. Jess and I exchanged a knowing glance of acknowledgement that we'd been assigned minor players rather than the phalanx of corporate lawyers and top executives we'd imagined.

Rosemary Delz next passed each of us a glossy full-colour brochure boldly titled *The Waddington Foundation: Excellence in Action*. A quotation prominently displayed on the inside cover read:

> The opportunity to preserve what is good on earth, to support what feeds the soul or stimulates the intellect, to encourage a talent or save an endangered species or keep alive the dreams and aspirations of others is not only a privilege but a sacred responsibility. For organizations such as the Waddington Foundation, that responsibility is the source of incalculable satisfaction.

The quote was attributed to someone named Richard M. Ivey, who apparently had his own foundation elsewhere. I was having a hard time seeing any connection between these high-flown principles and the carnage back at our clear-cut and was just about to say so when Luis cut to the chase.

"We understand that your foundation now owns all of the lands on our island that were formerly held by Icarus Timber; is that correct?"

"Quite so," Frankl replied. "The previous owner, Mr. James Glass, unfortunately passed away last year, bequeathing all of his land holdings, including on your island some thirteen hundred acres in total, to the foundation. These assets form an endowment in Mr. Glass's name that the foundation manages in such a way as to help address current and emerging community needs."

"And how are those community needs determined?" Jess asked.

"Oftentimes, donors stipulate where they wish dispersals to be directed, so only a small percentage of dispersals will be discretionary on our part," Frankl said.

"Did Mr. Glass make such stipulations?" Jess was locked in, I could see. Our flak-catcher was going to have to be nimble.

"Not specifically, no." Frankl admitted.

"But generally then?"

"Yes, he merely stipulated that dispersals should be made toward maintaining wholesome, vigorous and sustainable communities on Vancouver Island and the smaller islands."

"And how does clear-cutting timber on our island fit that picture?" Jess wanted to know.

"That's simply our way of realizing the assets," Frankl explained in a tone he was working hard to prevent sounding patronizing.

"What does *realizing* mean?" Jess pressed him.

"Well, converting them into cash, of course."

You could see Frankl's "Hail fellow, well met" veneer begin peeling away at the edges.

"Let me get this straight," Jess continued with sweet reasonableness. "Trees aren't real until you cut them down and sell them for cash. Is that correct?"

"Well, of course they're real as trees, as *things*," Frankl said with just a whiff of testiness, "but as assets capable of being converted into dispersals, plainly they have to be harvested and sold."

"I see," Jess said, pretending to try to understand. "And what dispersals did you have in mind from these realized assets?"

The briefest flash of annoyance from Frankl, perhaps unsure if he was being goaded. "It is our policy to encourage community self-direction. We believe very strongly that communities have the right and the responsibility to determine their own priorities."

"So for example," Luis interjected, "I see here in your vision statement," he waved the brochure, "it says you wish to foster communities that, and I quote, *enjoy a vibrant economy, pure water and unpolluted air, abundant parkland and green space providing protection for native flora and fauna, and secure sources of healthy food.* That's what you're aiming for, am I right?" Luis smiled disarmingly.

Sensing the ambush, Frankl hesitated for a beat before replying, "That's correct."

"So suppose," Jess said, picking up the thread, "just suppose that our self-directed community, exercising our right and responsibility to determine our own priorities, were to conclude that leaving those trees upright would be by far the most effective way of achieving your admirable goals that Luis has just quoted."

By this point Frankl's laboured pretense of good fellowship had pretty much vanished. Rosemary Delz was trying her best not to glower.

"Folks, what you don't seem to realize," Frankl explained patiently, "is that the Waddington Foundation is not in the business of running parks and playgrounds. We administer funds and we disperse those funds to various charitable organizations to enable undertakings that they themselves have determined are most worthwhile for their communities. Speaking frankly, it is not at all clear to me that you people represent the island community as a whole or that the majority of islanders would necessarily support your perspective. If, for example, the foundation were to offer a substantial dispersal of funds to enable construction of a medical clinic, say, or a library, or a swimming pool, I'm not at all convinced that there wouldn't be more local support for such an initiative than for your point of view."

Not the goddamn swimming pool again, I thought, but Jess didn't miss a beat. "And we're not at all convinced," she said amicably, "that a blockade of your logging show, including grannies and little kids being arrested, the whole shebang, with all the attendant negative publicity, wouldn't cause your foundation far more trouble than it's worth. So may I suggest, with respect, that you skip the hardball and let's try to get a reasonable accommodation on this thing."

I loved watching Jess going toe-to-toe with this lackey. Her fearlessness was one of the great privileges of growing up in privilege. Her old man could chew up pipsqueaks like Frankl by the dozen, and Jess, while she wasn't that kind of attack dog herself, knew perfectly well how the power game was played.

We left Bernard Frankl and Rosemary Delz with nothing really settled. They would have to "consult with their colleagues"—meaning they themselves didn't have any real negotiating power—while we would do the same with our community. Neither logging nor protests would occur until we'd spoken further.

Back home we set to work organizing an emergency community meeting.

Normally this kind of issue would be dealt with through the Ratepayers Association, but in those days hardly anybody attended their meetings and the few who did were mostly aligned with the good-old-boys ruling elite. So instead we rented the hall and set up our renegade meeting.

The fifty or so people who show up are pretty much unanimous in opposing the Waddington Foundation's plan to clear-cut the forest. Various ambitious schemes are advanced, mostly involving having the woodlands brought under community control with different areas designated for park purposes or wildlife sanctuaries or working forest. Dreams are floated for having out-of-work young islanders employed in managing the community forest, selection logging for firewood, operating a small-scale sawmill and secondary manufacturing. Handcrafted guitars and mandolins are imagined. There's a tremendous updraft of optimism that something really special might be in the works here.

Before anything's decided, who shows up for an unscheduled visit but Jess's old man. This was his first-ever visit to the farm, facilitated by his having oil patch business in Alberta. I think I was a lot more nervous about his arrival than Jess was. She didn't seem at all concerned about what he might think of our ramshackle set-up, while for me it seemed to offer incontrovertible evidence that I was the third-rater Richard Trimble had judged me from the outset.

He arrived in the late morning, driving a rented luxury car and decked out in new denims, a rust-coloured flannel shirt and cowboy boots. "Hey, Pops," Jess greeted him in the yard with a big hug, "I love your Alberta look! But where's the white Stetson?"

Richard beamed at her lovingly. Jess had kind of done herself up too, although she always looked good in almost anything, and so had the rest of us, as though Richard was here to inspect the troops. The surprising thing was, we actually all got along like the proverbial house on fire. Elizabeth and Lena had prepared a terrific lunch of warm multigrain bread fresh from the oven with soft goat cheese, scrambled eggs and salad greens from the veggie patch, followed by fresh strawberries and homemade ice cream. "My God!" Richard enthused, "I haven't eaten better than that in Michelin three-star restaurants." I think he was being sincere. He and Elizabeth seemed to strike a particularly amiable rapport, bantering as though they'd known each other for years. She even took him out at one point to view the mutts on parade. I wondered if the immediate cordiality between them flowed from the resonance old money has with itself no matter the circumstances.

After lunch Richard and Jess went off arm-in-arm for a walk around the farm, then later on Jess asked if I'd join her and her dad out in the orchard. We sat together on wooden deck chairs under a spreading old apple tree that Angus had just about got back into shape through remedial pruning. Richard appeared way more laid-back than I'd ever pictured him in Manhattan and seemed genuinely enthusiastic about the farm. To his credit, he never once referred to it as "our farm" or made any allusion to his having helped Jess purchase it. I figured the reason for this little confab would be Jess's eagerness to pick his brain about the Waddington

139

Foundation. She had, I knew, already written to him about our situation. It turned out Richard sat on the board of one of the big eastern foundations and thus had detailed information about their inner workings.

"Your Waddington group's a fairly minor player in the foundation game," he told us, "but still not insignificant. Capital funds somewhere around thirty million and attracting some bigger endowments lately. Earnings on endowments averaging better than fifteen percent over the last five years, and that ain't too shabby. When you hit a certain plateau, which they've done, a foundation can diversify investments the way smaller outfits can't, so there's a snowball effect."

"The rich getting richer?" Jess said.

"It's what the rich do, darling; we can't help ourselves."

I outlined to him the community forest initiative and asked what he thought our chances might be.

"Somewhere considerably below zero," Richard said with a smile. "What you dreamers are proposing is totally outside how foundations are set up to function. They're capital-intensive entities, all about moving money. Their primary obligation is to protect donor interests and they do that through shrewd investments whose benefits accrue to the individual donors."

"And all the glowing talk about philanthropy?" I asked him, not wanting to sound accusatory but suspecting that I had.

"Not just blather," Richard said, smiling. "They in fact accomplish a tremendous amount of good, not by doing it themselves, of course, but by handing out cash to organizations set up to accomplish worthy projects."

Just at that moment, as if on cue, Luis came striding across the orchard and asked if he might join us.

"Of course," Jess said gaily. "Your ears must have been burning with all our talk of foundations." She introduced Luis and Richard.

"Dad was just explaining to us," she filled Luis in as he pulled up a chair, "that the way foundations function couldn't possibly accommodate what we've been talking about for the Icarus lands."

"Yeah, I've pretty much come to the same conclusion," Luis said. "Talked to some old friends who've had dealings with a similar organization in San Francisco that is like a way bigger version of Waddington."

"Probably the Schwab Charitable Fund," Richard said. "Assets in the billions. Huge and highly regarded."

"Total eye-opener," Luis carried on, leaning forward in his chair. "Bottom line is these outfits are part and parcel of the whole capitalist scheme."

I saw an amused smile flicker across Richard's face.

"Say more," Jess said.

"Well, on the surface it all looks like benevolence and socially responsible altruism."

"Which much of it actually is," Richard put in.

"Of course," Luis conceded, "hospitals and music schools and all sorts of needy organizations get regular infusions of cash from Waddington."

"And would possibly cease to function without that support," Richard said, "or at least be severely curtailed in their operations."

"Absolutely," Luis agreed. Although neither man was being in any way aggressive, you could sense beneath the politeness two icebergs on a collision course.

"But what we don't get to see is all the dirt lying underneath what looks like philanthropic generosity."

"What dirt do you have in mind?" Richard asked.

"Well, there's the investment strategy to begin with," Luis waved his arm contemptuously. "Basically all these foundations have a gigantic wad of cash for playing the stock market and money markets. So in effect they're helping underwrite exploitive mining outfits in South America and Africa, for example. Armaments for fascist thugs. Tobacco, big coal, big oil. Whatever makes a buck, no matter what dumb-ass peasants get trampled in the process."

"Now that's a bit extreme," Richard said. "There's lots of socially responsible investing involved, at least in the reputable foundations."

"Oh, yeah," Luis said, "but what portion of the entire trust fund is dedicated to ethical investing? You'd need a microscope to find it. Those investments clearing fifteen percent or more have about as many ethical strings attached as Richard Nixon. It's just a case of international capital on the move to wherever lucrative dividends are possible."

"Go on," Richard prompted him.

"So what you've really got is bare knuckle capitalism cloaked in charity—wealthy investors putting big chunks of change into what's basically a tax haven, generating income from ethically questionable investments, reducing their own taxes but coming out of it smelling like roses because they're seen to be supporting such worthy causes. That pretty well fits my definition of hypocrisy."

"Mine too," Jess said. "Sorry, Daddy."

Richard sat quietly for a bit, managing to both smile and seem wistfully sad at the same time. Just what was playing in his mind there was no way of knowing. Loss of his daughter's respect, perhaps. Behindhand regret over some of his own choices. Frustration that we simply couldn't or wouldn't see common sense as he did. Maybe a portion of each. Impossible to tell. This withdrawing into himself didn't at all fit my version of who he was, the muscularly proactive player who could be outright intimidating when he chose to. I was caught completely off guard by this other, softly musing side of him. His tanned and handsome face looked older than it had an hour before.

"Well," he said finally, abruptly rising from his chair, "it's been great to see you all, and the farm here." He gestured with his arm to encompass our dream. "Thanks again for that fabulous lunch; I'm going to tell those sirloin-chompers in Calgary all about it. You know, it's terrific to see what you kids are up to, and I envy you in many ways, I really do. However, sad to say, I best be on my way."

"Oh, Dad, I thought you were staying for supper at least," Jess said.

"Love to, honey," he said, drawing close to Jess, "but I have to catch a late flight to Calgary." He enfolded her in his arms and the two of them hugged long and lovingly. Then he shook hands with

Luis, telling him "I have a lot of time for men of principle." For once Luis seemed stuck for words.

Richard shook my hand as well, saying, "Look after her, Shorter, will you? Not that she needs much looking after." He smiled ruefully, then Jess and he walked arm-in-arm back to his car. They hugged again, reluctantly pulled apart, and then he sped hurriedly away.

Jess just stood as she was, looking blankly toward where her dad had disappeared. She did, at that moment, actually seem like someone who needed looking after. I walked over to her and took her in my arms. We hugged for a good long while without saying anything.

ROSALIE IS IN EXTREME MELANCHOLY MODE ON HER NEXT VISIT. "THAT poor man," she mutters, scarcely greeting Shorter before sitting down at the kitchen table. She's brought no treats today, as though guilty pleasures would be a form of disrespect. It's obvious to Shorter what poor man she means: Richard. Poor rich man.

"To receive a loving daughter's affection," she says, "but not her respect—that's a very cruel ambivalence to be trapped in. For myself it would truly break my heart." As is so frequently the case with Rosalie's reflections, Shorter's left wondering what lies beneath her words. Is she herself a daughter to such a father? Does she have such a daughter of her own? He knows enough by now not to ask. Their business together, she has made it perfectly clear, concerns his life journey, not hers.

"No," she carries on. "As much as I was admiring you and your comrades for your brave stand in defence of the trees, I simply cannot accept that Jess's father—who had, after all, given you the money to buy the farm, underwritten your whole enterprise really—should feel himself judged in this way. As an unethical hypocrite. Doesn't the memory of it make you cringe, Shorter? I mean, imagine yourself being the parent of just such a child. Someone you adore, someone in whom all your hopes for the future are posited, who looks into the essence of your being and finds it corrupt. Tell me how many varieties of pain are as merciless as that one?"

Rosalie stares directly at Shorter, her large dark eyes glistening with moisture, and he really has nothing to say. He doesn't tell her, for instance, how on the evening of Richard's visit, he found Jess sobbing quietly in bed and once again took her in his arms and held her while she continued crying softly until sleep claimed them both for the night.

ELEVEN

NOT LONG AFTER RICHARD'S VISIT I HAPPENED TO BE CHATTING WITH our friend Mercedes one morning outside the general store. Among her several gifts, Mercedes had an uncanny ability to confide in someone as though that person, and that person alone, would be privy to whatever she was about to reveal. The atmosphere of intimate exclusivity she could conjure thus encouraged a broad spectrum of islanders to take her into their confidence, each one secure in believing that their secret would go no further. And, generally speaking, she was indeed the essence of discretion. But every so often a particularly choice morsel would come her way that she believed simply had to be judiciously shared in furtherance of the common good.

"I don't suppose I'm telling you anything you don't already know," she said to me *sotto voce*, the way she usually spoke in these circumstances, "but I did happen to hear the other day that the Waddington Foundation people have been in touch with certain members of the Community Club executive."

"Really?" I said noncommittally. This was news to me, explosive news, but you wouldn't want to appear to Mercedes as being excessively eager or grasping. Both parties, after all, share joint responsibility for maintaining an atmosphere of discreet disclosure.

"Apparently there's been an understanding achieved."

"An understanding." I rolled the term around like a worry bead.

"A quite firm understanding, I'm told."

"As to...?" I prompted gently.

She glanced about to ascertain no snoopers were within earshot. "As to a resumption of logging on the Icarus lands." She pursed her lips perfectly.

"Now how would a resumption of logging possibly involve the Community Club, I wonder?" It's preferable when dealing with Mercedes to cast generalized queries to the wind rather than engage in unseemly prying.

She paused to enhance the dramatic effect. "I'm told by certain persons very close to the situation that, should the Community Club choose to publicly support the logging show, the Waddington Foundation would be prepared to consider an application from the club for funds sufficient to cover the cost for securing a new water system as well as a swimming pool."

Holy shit, I thought to myself, that slimy little bastard Frankl has gone behind our backs! Clever though, you have to admit. Fiendishly clever to get the reactionary hordes mobilized against us. Without the appearance of community solidarity our protest would be crippled and quickly doomed. Why we hadn't seen something like that coming, I don't know.

"¡Chingada madre!" Luis exploded when I told our hastily gathered group what Mercedes had divulged. We all vented for a bit, none of us gringos quite as graphically as Luis, and then got down to strategy. The plan we eventually formulated involved forcing a special general meeting of the Community Club, as the bylaws allowed a percentage of the club membership to do, packing the meeting with supporters and rounding up whatever proxy votes we could. Our aim was to reject by majority vote the sleazy deal that Iris and her gang had cut with Frankl. If nothing else, this would be a definitive test of the extent to which power had actually shifted in the community. Would this be the old guard's last stand?

Once we had the required ten percent of the membership signed up to request an extraordinary general meeting, Jess hand-delivered the petition to Iris Thomas. "All terribly polite," Jess reported back to us. "Iris couldn't keep herself from preening like the cat that's just swallowed the canary. She obviously feels she's got the votes to beat us down."

"Did she mention a date for the meeting?" Enzo asked. Ever since he'd been menaced by Gil Gilport on the nude swimming issue, Enzo had developed an aversion to community meetings, and I wondered if he was already scheming for an alibi so as to avoid what would likely be another contentious clash.

"There have to be three consecutive weeks of public notice," Jess said, "so the meeting won't happen until this time next month at the earliest."

"Plenty of time to get the troops out," I said.

"Yeah, for them too," Enzo added.

Enzo was not quite himself in those days but his mood had less to do with the logging fracas than with the looming responsibilities of imminent parenthood, as well as with consecutive setbacks suffered by the naturists. Having conceded that their steep-bank pathway down to Sunset Beach was environmentally untenable, but at the same time being rudely prohibited from using Iris and John Thomas's stairway to the shore, Enzo and most of his naturist companions had reluctantly abandoned the delights of frolicking *au naturel* at Sunset Beach and instead begun skinny-dipping at our little Ponder. This wasn't a big deal at the outset as several of us, without necessarily marching beneath the banner of naturism, swam there unencumbered by swimsuits. But as the number of visiting naturists increased, problems began to arise. It soon became apparent that an outhouse was needed, but several attempts to have Enzo and his associates construct one came to nothing. Eventually I grudgingly dug a pit, then Jess and Angus put up a primitive privy. Necessary though it may have been, the privy sat indecently in what we vaguely thought of as the semi-sacred precincts of Ponder.

Summer ripened beautifully and the volume of swimmers swelled. Not all were naturists, or even islanders, but word was out that this was the grooviest place to swim and party on island. Cars began creeping in and out of the farm at all hours. Gates were left open. The animals were freaking out, especially the goats, who had limited tolerance for even familiar humans. Litter drifted like tumbleweeds across the meadows.

A line was finally crossed when a carload of yobs, having consumed several cases of beer throughout the afternoon, set about lighting a lakeside fire into which they could spend the evening tossing cigarette butts and beer cans, oblivious to the fire hazard posed by acres of dry grass all around them. Our whole group strode down together, doused the fire and invited the grumbling lads to be on their way and not return. Though not a man of violence, Angus had taken along the big double-bitted splitting axe by way of emphasis.

Without a whole lot of discussion being required, next morning we closed the farm gates and posted some hastily painted Absolutely No Trespassing! signs. The irony was not lost on any of us that circumstances beyond our control had cruelly transformed us into a countercultural reproduction of John and Iris beset by undesirable outsiders.

It was Lena who rescued our mojo by reminding us what Willie had said about Ponder being a site of ritual for the Old Ones and how he had sensed their spirits lingering there. "I have that same feeling," she told us, "and I think we're perfectly within our rights to keep the place from turning into some hippie Coney Island. These last few weeks have been like a desecration." Elizabeth instantly backed her up, saying her own work with the dogs had been badly derailed with the incessant stream of people and vehicles. There'd even been an instance of a carload of party animals showing up with a pair of enormous bull mastiffs that had terrorized our poor mutts. Thus we dusted off our dignity and got back to the larger task of mobilizing against the Waddington/Community Club axis.

I was in Spangler for a doctor's appointment the following week and, with time to spare, thought to scoot up to Sunset Rest and say hello to Willie.

"Hiya, bucko," he greeted me from his armchair, hitting the mute button on his remote. He recognized me well enough but I don't believe he remembered my name, or any of our names other than Jess.

"Hiya, Willie," I said, "how's tricks?"

"Don't ask," he said sourly. "If I see one more bowl of tapioca pudding I'm going to throw it at someone. Hey, saw you on the local news here the other day." He pointed to the TV. "Looked like a pretty good dust-up."

"Yeah, they started logging back behind our place, your place, I mean."

"The Icarus lands, that would be."

"Right. They're owned by a fancy foundation down in Victoria now."

"Y'don't say. Old Glass sold out, did he? I couldn't make out what that little wisp of a reporter was talking about."

"No, he passed on a little ways back and bequeathed his forest holdings to the foundation."

"Huh," Willie snorted, "little late with the benevolence."

"How so?"

"Oh, he was a flinty fucker, that Glass. Picked up all that acreage long ago, bits and pieces on all the islands. Logged as much of it as he could like nobody's business. Knocked every goddamn tree down—that was usin' axe and two-man saw in the early days—bucked 'em up and loaded the logs onto rail cars that ran down to the salt chuck. You wouldn't believe the diameter on some of them logs. They had a log watering spot on the island in those days where they could sort and bundle the logs into rafts. I was just a kid at the time but I remember it, that forest disappearing. Must be big second growth they're cutting now. Anyways, good on you kids for sticking your noses in. I hope you can stop 'em for good."

The memories were obviously painful for Willie and I was glad that I'd remembered to bring him a photo. "Look here," I said, "I brought you a picture of the hounds in all their glory." I handed him a photograph I'd taken recently of the five mutts all sitting in a perfectly straight line, each of them in the begging pose. At the right margin of the print you could see Elizabeth's disembodied hand pointing directorially at them, each dog with its eyes focused attentively on her.

Willie held the photo in a trembling hand and stared at it for a good few minutes. A single tear escaped from his left eye and glistened on his grizzled cheek until he wiped it away with the sleeve of his dressing gown.

"Them pups look real good," he said. "I knew from the first time I met you that you kids would look after them proper. Not everyone would, y'know. It was a weight off my mind at the time."

"Well, they missed you terribly at first," I told him again, "but our friend Elizabeth has been doing wonders with them."

"I can see that," he said. "They'd never sit in a row like that for me. Course I wouldn't want 'em to either. What's her secret?"

"Something called operant conditioning. I don't quite understand it, except that it makes use of a little clicking device."

"I'll be," Willie said, staring fondly at the photo.

"One problem we have, Willie, is that in all the commotion we've kind of lost track of what dog has what name."

"Funny you should mention it," he said with a chuckle, "because the only ones who have proper names are these two." He pointed to the two smallest dogs. "That one's Bandy and this here's Suzy. I never got around to finding a name for the rest of them rascals, so you can call 'em whatever you want."

I loved Willie at that moment, the anarchistic loopiness of the old guy. He placed the photo tenderly on his bedside table. We said goodbye and I came awful damn close to giving him a hug before leaving.

Our weekly meetings on Sunday evening on the farm continued sporadically, but rather than smoothing out nicely with time, complications seemed to be getting thornier by the week. Having been avoided like venereal disease, the question of money eventually reared its calculating head. As a group we'd gotten by for a year and a half without anything approximating a sound financial plan, largely coasting on what remained of Jess's $20,000 and occasional, if grudging, infusions of cash from Elizabeth (we suspected her of having a sizable trust fund prudently tucked away somewhere). And indeed it was Elizabeth who addressed the problem directly during a "held feelings" round. "I think we all need to be contributing equally to the ongoing costs of this place," she said, gratuitously adding: "You can't run a farm on peace and love."

Everyone agreed that equitable cost-sharing was absolutely the ideal toward which we should be striving. Various plans were advanced for generating income uncontaminated by rank capitalism. Angus talked primarily in terms of maximizing the farm's potential by cutting and selling hay as well as getting into selling firewood. Lena was enthusiastic about increasing the number of laying hens in order to sell eggs and maybe having a farm-stand for selling vegetables and fruits. Enzo presented a surprisingly solid business plan for ramping up our dope growing and marketing in bulk. I imagined I could add to the kitty by bucking hay and picking oysters for some of the island growers. Jess said she had a notion to try writing a column for the weekly newspaper in town, being as the woman who'd been writing the "island news" segment had recently retired to Arizona. By these modest measures, we estimated, our financial situation could at least be stabilized without compromising our commitment to subsistence living and non-cooperation with corporate consumer capitalism.

But things didn't go nearly so well the following week when Elizabeth dropped a real bombshell in the "held feelings" round. Increasingly, she confessed, she was beset by feelings of frustration over our inflexibility on the logging issue. The rest of us kind of looked from one to another, not quite believing what she was saying or why. Her misgivings began, she explained, with how shabbily we'd treated Richard on his recent visit. "Such a lovely man," she said. "Pardon me for bringing this up," she said to Jess, "but I feel I must. And I have to think that Richard believes the work of charitable foundations, including the one he supports, benefit a tremendous number of deserving and disadvantaged people."

"They're disadvantaged," I interrupted her, "because they're victimized by an exploitive system that the foundations are an integral part of."

"Oh, spare me the Noam Chomsky lecture!" Elizabeth snapped.

"What's happened to our talking stick?" Lena wondered.

"Good question," Jess said. I could sense her disquiet over where this discussion was going. She'd been unhappy for days after her dad's visit and had written him a long letter attempting to explain her position and how it had nothing to do with her affection for him or her gratitude for all he'd done for her. Thus far, she'd not heard back from him.

"My point is this," Elizabeth continued. "I think perhaps we were a bit hasty jumping into the logging situation the way we did. Knowing nothing about the Waddington group, what their plans were, how the community might benefit from a cooperative rather than confrontational approach toward them."

"Well, in fairness, Elizabeth," Jess said, "they didn't leave much space for a cooperative approach with the way they just started knocking down trees without a word said beforehand."

"I hear that, and it was certainly unfortunate," Elizabeth conceded. "But, look, they've stopped the logging to engage in dialogue with us and with others in the community."

"Others being the Community Club gang," Angus said in his no-nonsense way.

"That's correct," Elizabeth said, "and I think perhaps they've come up with some very positive initiatives."

"How positive?" I asked her.

"Well, Iris says…"

"*Iris* says?" Enzo blurted out. "*Iris* says?"

"That's right, Enzo," Elizabeth replied firmly. "Iris Thomas is a member of this community, every bit as much as you or I, and a harder-working contributor than some."

Enzo ignored this sly dig at his gentleman's approach to brute labour.

"She's entitled to have an opinion," Elizabeth continued, "and I think she makes good sense in this particular case."

"How exactly?" Jess asked her.

"Well, as we've discovered, the foundation has made a quite generous offer to the Community Club…"

"You don't mean the fucking swimming pool?" Angus said. Angus seldom swore and we were all a bit shocked at his outburst.

"Not just the pool," Elizabeth answered calmly. "They'll also finance an upgraded water system for the pool as well as the hall."

"*Phff*," Enzo mocked.

"Plus the foundation has made it plain they'd be open to further applications in subsequent years," Elizabeth said. "We might be looking at a community library or a museum, maybe developing a network of walking trails."

"Through the clear-cuts, you mean?" Angus scoffed.

The discussion jolted on to no reasonable conclusion and we finished the meeting with a round of forced and phony-sounding appreciations.

Afterwards Jess filled me in on what she knew. It appeared that Elizabeth and Iris Thomas had recently struck up quite a friendship around their mutual affection for dogs. By weird coincidence, Iris owned three bichons frises, the very breed that Elizabeth as a child had helped her mother raise and to which she retained a sentimental attachment. Based on that shared interest, Elizabeth had become something of a regular caller at the Thomas home. Also by this point, as the photo I'd given Willie indicated, Elizabeth was well on her way to transforming Willie's unruly pack of mongrels into a superbly disciplined troupe capable of performing clever tricks and even complex group manoeuvres. In very short order, the two women had bonded solidly enough that Iris's madcap schemes now made perfect sense to Elizabeth.

But not at all to the rest of us, and particularly not to Luis, who was by now a frequent visitor. "Bullshit!" he replied when first told of Elizabeth's apostasy by Jess and myself. "That's what these fuckers are so good at: dividing and conquering. They'll always find some crack to slither through, some weakness to exploit. I've seen it over and over again in campaigns, where well-intentioned people get suckered into believing that compromise and conciliation is how you advance your agenda. It's not. All it results in is principled opposition being fragmented while the corporatist agenda marches forward unhindered. I say we hold firm. That we continue blockading the logging until they're forced to sit down with us and discuss the future of that forest in a no-preconceptions way."

Jess and I agreed with Luis. As did Angus. And Lena too, although it was obvious that Elizabeth had tried to cajole Lena into siding with her. Enzo adopted a kind of fellow-traveller position in our camp, mostly because of Lena. Luis's sister, Tonya, was really firm about not selling out to the Waddington crowd, and so was Brady Lazarus, formerly of the Community Club executive and currently, if base scuttlebutt were to be believed, subtly courting Tonya. Another strand of scuttlebutt suggested that Elizabeth had succeeded in convincing her pal Amrapali to join her in what we now called the collaborationist camp. Needless to say, the scene around our place was particularly tense during the run-up to the public meeting. Elizabeth was frequently elsewhere at mealtimes.

The extraordinary general meeting actually fell flat on its face. Two other events had been inadvertently scheduled for the same time and people's loyalties, not to mention cowardice, were divided in multiple directions. It turned out the hall was barely half-full. Iris and her executive put a bold face on things, but it quickly became apparent that they didn't have the horses to pull their wagon. Iris's motion to proceed with concluding an arrangement with the Waddington Foundation was decisively defeated. The table officers accepted their drubbing with the meagre dignity nature had allocated them, but the same couldn't be said for Gil Gilport. With his trademark bunched fists and pre-cardiac red face he thundered at us venomously.

"You idiots!" he called out, pointing at Jess and Luis and myself especially. "You turn down thousands and thousands of free dollars that this community desperately needs just so you can protect a scrawny stand of second-growth! Are you out of your frickin' minds? None of you geniuses know bugger all about these forests. You don't have the brains to realize that you can harvest this crop today and it'll grow back just the same. Fifty years from now it'll look just like it does today. And then you can cut it again. It's like picking apples, for Christ's sake! And why you bearded know-it-alls can't get that through your thick heads I'll never know. Save the Trees! Gimme a goddamn break!"

We sat serenely, as victors are entitled to do, while Gil roared his frustration. But I thought again of Willie's admonition to beware the grudges of Gilports.

ROSALIE IS NO HAPPIER WITH SHORTER ON HER NEXT VISIT THAN SHE WAS on her last.

Together they nibble for a bit around the circumference of whatever lies between them, but eventually the truth comes out. Or some portion of the truth at least.

"I don't much care for the centrality of dogs in your narrative," she confesses with a bit of a sniff. Shorter's uncertain if she's just winding him up or what. Of all the possible elements to dwell upon—Community Club machinations, that slippery foundation, unruly crowds at Ponder, poor Willie floundering—and she wants to squabble about dogs! She's made no secret of her predilection for cats, but it hadn't occurred to Shorter that she'd have a matching animus against dogs.

"Their significance is overplayed in general," she tells Shorter. "All this 'man's best friend' hyperbole. Do you seriously not question the appeal of a manuscript in which these inescapable dogs pop up at every opportunity but which contains, thus far at least, not a single reference to cats? Surely there were at least a few neglected barn cats active on the farm?"

"Of course there were," he tells her, "and they were damn useful too at keeping the rats in check. But they had no real personality to speak of; they tended to sneak furtively around the margins of the barnyard, creating an impression of deviousness."

"Pah!" Rosalie exclaims. "They were obviously neglected and mistreated. It's a very shabby performance on all your part, very shabby indeed." She's correct on one level, Shorter realizes, that the communards were woefully negligent toward the barn cats. They were essentially feral, probably the consequence of Willie having let his dogs run loose for years. Wily survivors, the cats managed to produce litters on a regular basis, and it took the rural astronauts far longer than it should have to recognize their obligation to control the numbers. Eventually a freelance vet showed up at the farm, partway through a visionary journey from Nova Scotia to Tibet, and with his help all the cats were summarily trapped and neutered. Not at all sure that this was an initiative Rosalie would approve of, Shorter doesn't mention it to her.

Over the few short weeks of their collaboration Shorter has learned to avoid trying to rationalize or justify any of the group's experiences to Rosalie, having no desire for lengthy disputations. She in turn has walked a very fine line between offering relevant criticism of either the style or the substance of Shorter's remem-berings while not discouraging him from continuing. Shorter has in fact begun questioning whether he's truly able to record his own story in his own words without falling prey to tweaking the facts this way and that to satisfy what he increasingly sees as an idiosyncratic collaborator. Truth to tell, from his perspective, her possessiveness around what she now calls "the manuscript" is beginning to chafe.

But apart from preserving the peace, no real purpose will be served by him massaging the truth in order to keep her contented. Similarly, she resists the urge to voice any negative appraisal, however gentle, for fear that it might discourage him. Despite appearances, Shorter has what she has come to realize is surpris-ingly thin skin. Both however remember that she was the one who started him off in the first place by quoting Thoreau about any truth being better than fiction.

TWELVE

WE SWELTERED THROUGH AN OPPRESSIVELY WARM AUGUST, OUR DIMIN-
ished energies more and more focused on Lena as she ballooned
beautifully toward birthing. Every morning she still waddled gal-
lantly across the barnyard to tend to her beloved chickens and
goats while the rest of us observed her nervously. She looked as
though she might burst any moment like a dropped watermelon.

As I trust I've made clear by now, Lena was a truly lovely person.
I don't think she had a mean bone in her body, and she accom-
modated Enzo's neuroses with near-saintly lightheartedness.
Even before her pregnancy, her shy tenderness evoked protective
instincts in the rest of us. Now, as she wandered about with a radiant
and abstracted smile, you felt like you wanted to quietly follow after
her with silk-covered cushions on which to catch her should she fall.

It was in this atmosphere of gentle anticipation that Luis and
Tonya came scrambling excitedly into our kitchen early one morning. Lena was resting on the couch while Jess, Enzo and I lingered
over coffee, even though there was a ton of work waiting to be done
outdoors before the day's heat built up. Angus was out working on
the never-ending barn demolition and Elizabeth had disappeared
with the dogs. "Did you hear the news?" Luis asked, wide-eyed.

"Let me guess," I said. "Nixon's confessed to Watergate."

"Nah, we'll have to wait on that one," Tonya said.

"But almost as good," Luis enthused. "The NDP won the election
last night!"

Jess and Enzo and I kind of looked at each other. I don't know
that we even realized a provincial election had happened. Or
maybe we did but it certainly wasn't top of mind, as they say now. I
can't remember if I even voted.

"A socialist government!" Tonya exclaimed. "Finally!"

"Unbelievable!" her brother added.

This was a truly Canadian moment. To have these two ex-pat Americans totally wired over a provincial election the rest of us had barely noticed. Indifference was understandable in the circumstances because the province had been exploited for decades by a pack of good-old-boys, totally subservient to logging, mining and real estate interests, and nobody expected that regime to change anytime soon. Plus with the ultimately abysmal failure of activism south of the border—the war still raging, ghettos burning, misogyny amok—who the hell had any remaining energy for trying to change "the system" from within. But Tonya and Luis obviously did and a residual part of me was abashed.

Just as we were getting into a spirited discussion around whether the new NDP government had any hope of making meaningful change, a cry from Lena silenced us all. Jess was instantly at Lena's side.

"I think my water's broke," Lena said. "Either that or I've peed myself."

"Okay," Jess replied calmly, taking Lena's hand, "let's get you set up."

Straight away Enzo began making strange squeaking noises and looked like panic personified. "Shorter," Jess said, "can you give Abigail a call and maybe offer her a ride over?"

"Sure thing," I said, relieved to have some way of contributing while still getting out of the house. Not unlike Enzo, I was in some subliminal way terrified by the prospect of birthing, its risks and possibilities for mischance.

There was no practising doctor on the island in those days, and the birthing options were either a home birth or a trip to the hospital in town. The hospital was not necessarily a safer choice—there'd been several cases of babies born on the back seat of a car waiting in the ferry lineup, not to mention a few on the ferry itself. (Rumour had it that an onboard baby was entitled to free ferry passage for life!) Luckily for us, an experienced midwife from England, Abigail Smythe, had recently moved to the island and Abigail's extensive experience in postwar Britain had helped solidify Lena and Enzo's leaning toward a home birth. As Lena's due date approached, Abigail had become a regular visitor, riding over on her ancient black bicycle.

I called Abigail. She told me she was prepared to come at once and readily agreed to my picking her up. I sped across the island in Viribus—it was a transcendental morning with meadows and hedgerows luminous in slanting late August sunshine—and found Abigail waiting on the front porch of her old farmhouse. She strode briskly to the van carrying a small suitcase and looking every inch the purposeful public health nurse upon whom all could rely. On the drive back to the farm she quizzed me on Lena's condition.

Any way you looked at it, Abigail was a peculiar piece of work, straight as a pool cue in manner and appearance, yet completely at ease among us longhairs and in serenely defying the medical establishment. "Men!" she'd say derisively in her lilting Lancashire accent. "As if they know anything about the business."

By the time we got back to the farm, Lena was lying in bed and experiencing regular contractions but still able to laugh and chatter between them. Enzo was sitting beside her on the edge of the bed, holding her hand and perspiring profusely. His breath was coming in funny little pants that may have been intended to assist Lena with her breathing. Elizabeth stood nearby also looking worried while Jess was purposefully arranging bowls, pitchers and towels. Abigail snapped open her little suitcase and arranged her kit on the bedside table.

"Alright, everybody out for the moment, if you please!" Abigail's directive sent us all trooping out of the bedroom. We went down to the kitchen where Angus was brewing coffee. Apprehension and elation danced around us crazily. When we were allowed to return to the bedroom, Abigail told us Lena's dilation was "just as it should be." She'd drawn the curtains, transforming the little bedroom into a dim and cozy nest.

Jess moved to the far side of the bed and took to rubbing Lena's back and shoulders and hips. "Oh, that's lovely," Lena kept saying in between her intensifying contractions. On the other side of the bed, still holding Lena's hand, Enzo was quietly crying.

In a meeting earlier on, it had been determined that only Abigail, Jess and Enzo would attend the actual birthing, and Abigail now announced that it was time for Elizabeth, Angus and myself to withdraw. Partly you wanted to be there and partly you didn't. Later Enzo would describe the events to us in detail: seeing the tiny head crowning, agonizing over Lena's pain, the midwife's calm instructions to push harder in order for the head to emerge, then the little face revealed and Abigail's sure hands catching the child, then laying it on Lena's bare chest, the suckling and nuzzling sounds from the little creature mingling with Lena's sobs of bliss. "I went from hell to heaven in an instant," Enzo later told us. "Nothing in my life will ever match the terror and beauty of that moment."

The child was a tiny girl, born with the power to steal all our hearts. Of course in the wash of excitement we weren't even vaguely aware that our precious collective had undergone a tectonic shift. That we weren't the kids anymore, or the true future.

Enzo and Lena had previously compiled two lists of names, male and female, and now insisted that we all have a voice in the naming. A particular name would rise to the surface with a gush of enthusiasm, hold sway temporarily, then eventually subside and be replaced with another. Megan. Robin. Christie. Stacy. Erica. Erin. Holding the newborn tenderly, papa Enzo would ask: "Does this look like a Robin to you? Seriously?" After several exhausting sessions, we'd narrowed the possibilities down to two that seemed appealing to everyone: Angie and Josie. A final vote was called and Josie narrowly nudged out her rival. Josie it would be then, tiny Josie in whom more of our future was invested than we possibly could have known.

Meanwhile, the logging controversy had conveniently simmered way down, largely because the woods were crackling dry from summer drought and all chainsaw work was prohibited. But fall rainstorms were not far off and we for sure didn't want to be caught flat-footed a second time. Jess called the Waddington Foundation and asked for Bernard Frankl but got Rosemary Delz instead. Frankl was on holiday but would be returning to work next week. Jess asked Rosemary to set up another meeting.

"For what purpose?" Rosemary asked.

"To continue our discussion of the highest and best use of our island forestlands," Jess told her.

"I see." A pause. Jess was making ugly-mugly faces at me.

After consulting with somebody else in the office, Rosemary came back on the line and said that a meeting could certainly be arranged for the following week at the foundation's head office in Victoria. No halfway mutual accommodation here. A date and time were set.

Once again Luis, Jess and I piled into Viribus and trekked southwards down the eastern shore of Vancouver Island. Victoria was a full three hours away in those days and we had to heavy-foot it to get into the city and parked before our eleven a.m. meeting. We threaded our way through downtown Victoria, which was still in full-flush tourism mode. Swarms of portly Americans posed smilingly for photographs outside the Parliament Buildings and Empress Hotel while others were being trotted about in horse-drawn carriages. We parked in a big lot alongside the harbour and hurried up to Gordon Street where the Waddington Foundation headquarters occupied a tastefully old red-brick building partly covered with English ivy. Entering through a heavy wooden door with polished brass fixtures, we announced ourselves to a young receptionist in the foyer. The potted plants were real and the air had the distinctive, crisp scent of money.

The receptionist led us on clicking high heels to a small meeting room on the ground floor, invited us to sit and told us that Mr. Frankl and Ms. Delz would be with us momentarily. After about fifteen minutes the two of them arrived, Frankl looking tanned and happy, Rosemary Delz looking neither.

"Good morning," Frankl said matter-of-factly. No handshakes or breaking-the-ice pleasantries this time around. There was a component of mastery in Frankl's manner, though I couldn't have said how.

We seated ourselves around the smallish conference table. "Let me see now," Frankl muttered, opening a thick file and pretending to peruse it, intimating that he had so many files on the go he couldn't possibly be expected to recall the details of one as insignificant as ours. "Oh, yes," he said, "so I see you fine islanders have rejected our offer to provide substantial funds for the construction of recreational facilities. How very peculiar." He looked at us, as though for signs of derangement. Rosemary Delz seemed already convinced. "And," he added, again consulting the file, "in my absence, the board discussed this situation at some length and made the determination that we would continue to realize the assets of this portfolio, but regrettably without any funds being directed to island organizations."

"With all due respect," Jess told him, "that would not be a wise decision. The majority of islanders who turned down funding for the proposed swimming pool are the very same people who'll blockade your logging show and cause you a great deal of public embarrassment."

"Possibly so," Frankl conceded, "but the board seemed persuaded that support for your position in the matter is not quite as widespread on the island as you purport. That there are at least as many islanders, largely from the older, established families, who would like to see the logging proceed."

"Bullshit," Luis said firmly. We three had agreed beforehand that Jess would do the talking for us, but Luis's restraint had its limits.

"I regret we haven't been able to arrive at a mutually satisfactory resolution," Frankl said as he closed the file and stood up. "As I believe I mentioned previously, I have a great affection for the island from my time spent there as a boy and I would have liked to have seen us achieve a compromise that served everybody's purposes. But what will be will be. Safe journey home. Good day." He held the door for Rosemary Delz and both left the room.

From the look of rage on Luis's face, I was afraid for a minute that he might start smashing the place up. Hell, I felt like trashing it myself, bloody potted plants and all.

Maybe sniffing an excess of testosterone, Jess kind of herded Luis and me out of the conference room, across the foyer, past the indifferent receptionist and back out onto the street. To say that we were royally pissed off during the drive home would be putting it politely. We'd gotten up early to catch the first ferry, driven non-stop for three hours and now had another three-hour drive and ferry ride ahead of us. All for a meeting that lasted barely five minutes. For something that could easily have been said over the phone. Oh, we were roaring as we fled the city and climbed up over the Malahat. "Fuck them!" Luis growled fiercely, "Fuck them up, down and sideways!"

"OH, I FIND THIS CONTINUAL HEAD-BUTTING WITH THE WADDINGTON Foundation really rather distasteful," Rosalie says on her subsequent visit. She's wearing a black T-shirt with a large image of Harriet Tubman staring out at him. Shorter's instantly on his guard.

"I really don't care for demonizing," she says, "no matter how justified. I'm sorry to say I'm sensing a disappointing obstinacy on the protesters' part, an unwillingness to work toward a realistic compromise."

"I don't think that's exactly what was happening," Shorter tells her, "because…"

But she interrupts him peremptorily: "As fond as I've become of Luis, he's now unhappily revealed as more of a hothead than I'd imagined. Yes, I admire a man of principle," she continues, echoing Richard's words, "but I don't care in the least for stridency. Despite his obvious charisma, Luis is revealing himself to be an unappealingly strident character."

Part of Shorter wants to rebut this sharp assessment; another part of him doesn't. He says nothing for the moment.

"On the other hand," Rosalie continues with her first smile since arriving, "I really am thrilled to bits over the emergence of little

Josie. Such a beautiful birthing experience! And I love the image of Abigail Smythe pedalling around the island on her ancient bicycle, wearing practical outfits and sensible shoes while doing the good work of bringing babies safely into the world." She pauses for a moment, considering.

"Actually, I spent quite a few years championing the demedicalization of childbirth, and I've nothing but admiration for the skilled women everywhere who practise midwifery." Rosalie speaks with such force of feeling, Shorter's again tempted to question her further about her experiences. Was she coaxed into the world through the ministrations of a midwife? Has she perhaps given birth, herself aided by a midwife? Or, intriguingly, has she actually practised midwifery? Her obvious fervency around the topic readily lends itself to all three possibilities.

But, as inquisitive as he is, Shorter again holds back from questioning. He still nurtures a tentative expectation that, as their relationship deepens over time, Rosalie will gradually reveal much more of her own story. Then he stops. Why on earth does he continue imagining a deepening relationship with Rosalie? All they're doing is working on a little manuscript together, a project that will soon be completed, and it's hardly likely to result in any deepening relationship.

THIRTEEN

BY OCTOBER THE ENERGIES OF AUTUMN WERE UPON US. THERE WERE bumper crops of fruits and vegetables to deal with and we thrilled to be bringing in barrowloads of squash and potatoes and all the rest. The old root cellar was packed to the rafters with produce, including dozens of jars of canned tomatoes, peaches, green beans and pickles. The rejuvenated orchard overwhelmed us with heritage apples and pears. Then early rains coaxed up abundant chanterelle mushrooms in the woods. The whole business was, we felt, an indisputable triumph of self-sufficiency.

In the middle of this harvesting and preserving frenzy, goat activity pushed its way forward as well. The three billies definitely needed to be dealt with, and each of the does would soon be requiring another visit to lascivious Bill.

As involved as she'd been with last year's servicing, Lena, with babe at breast, excused herself beforehand from the expeditions this time. Care of little Josie occupied her days, and to some degree occupied all our days, even busy as we were with other chores. The baby's comfort and well-being was, without question, of paramount importance in the collective. All of us spent inordinate amounts of time gazing at the child, fondly holding her, as well as changing her nappies and putting her to sleep. Other islanders—whether Tonya or Mercedes or whoever—repeatedly found flimsy reasons to visit and get in on the cooing and burbling.

Meanwhile our billies had dramatically morphed from cute little tykes into a trio of energetic and destructive hellions, regularly cannonading around their enclosure with boundless energy. We knew they had to be dealt with, but how? We reviewed the options, reconsidering those Willie had outlined last spring: take them to the auction, castrate them and keep them around for no good purpose, remove two and keep one as a stud, haul them all to the slaughterhouse, or butcher them as Willie himself had done. Needless to say, a broad spectrum of opinions was expressed.

"Well," I said, "the smattering of milking goats on a half-dozen farms scarcely requires another stud on the island so long as randy Bill is standing ready." In fact, Bill's odiousness in rut went a long way toward dampening down whatever enthusiasm there may have been for keeping any of our males around.

"We could look at the castration option," Jess added, "but realistically, who'd want to take knife to scrotum? Enzo?"

Enzo crossed his legs in horror. "Much less have three hairy eunuchs wandering the farm for years to come," he said.

Dragging them to the auction, with all the trauma and eventual slaughter involved, seemed to everyone a cowardly dereliction of duty. Finally we arrived at the unsatisfactory decision to butcher them ourselves. We all looked to Angus as the only one of us with the cojones to take on the actual killing. He stroked his bushy beard and eyed us craftily. "I'll do the dirty alright," he said, "but on one condition: that we get some pigs on the place as well."

"Pigs?" Elizabeth said in a horrified tone. With the logging fracas having simmered down, Elizabeth had gradually reintegrated herself into the group.

"Farm's not a real farm without pigs," Angus said. "If we're going to be butchering goats we may as well have a pig to butcher too. Bacon, ham, sausages, all grown pure and clean right here."

Angus's clever ultimatum rudely kicked open a door that had been slightly ajar for some time. The eating of meat. Along with her friend Amrapali, Elizabeth had become a confirmed vegetarian, eschewing meat, fish, dairy products and eggs. She'd tried to persuade Lena to do the same but, while Lena's love for her chickens had made eating the culled young roosters increasingly difficult for her, she couldn't imagine not eating fresh eggs. It had become a bit of a ritual that every Sunday evening Lena would cook for everyone a huge frittata in the big cast-iron fry pan. Angus sat unabashedly at the carnivore end of the spectrum and had for some time

166

been advocating that we put down some venison in the fall, as the island was swarming with smallish but well-fed deer. Both he and I enjoyed fishing for the little rainbow trout that flourished in Ponder. Enzo, Jess and I kind of waffled around in the soft-core omnivore centre.

Now here was a fork in the road. If we used the old Boer War rifle Willie had left us to put down the billies, as we'd agreed to do, we'd now have pigs as part of the package and maybe venison as well, pushing our diet firmly into the carnivore camp.

Predictably, we entered a phase of impassioned discussion that lasted for days.

However, our deliberations were rudely cut short by a bomb-shell announcement from the Waddington Foundation: they'd be resuming logging the following Monday morning.

Luis brought us the news. "Those motherfuckers!" he exploded, "All their fine talk about consulting the community to determine the highest and best use. *¡Chingada madre!*" I don't know what was more disturbing, the news itself or the ferocity of Luis's reaction. He seethed with a disquieting rage.

So, reluctantly, we geared up for battle all over again. As we'd agreed at a hastily organized strategy session, several dozen of us gathered on the road early Monday morning to blockade the loggers. But this time they were ready for us. Unexpectedly, Bernard Frankl showed up backed by a phalanx of burly security guards. Frankl announced to us through a bullhorn that he had a court order forbidding any attempt to thwart or hinder legal activities on foundation property. Anybody breaking the order would be detained by the security people and handed over to the RCMP. Two police cruisers were already on the island. A charge of criminal contempt of court would be laid and conviction could result in substantial fines, a criminal record and possible time in prison.

"*¡Vete a la chingada!*" Luis shouted. Frankl seemed to know, or suspect, that this meant "Go fuck yourself!" but he just smiled at the insult. The prick knew he had us by the short hairies.

As the fallers prepared to get to work, we huddled on the road to figure out what the hell we were going to do. Plainly our previous strategy of shutting them down for the day wouldn't work anymore. Everyone was babbling until Jess took control, herding us into a circle on the road and introducing a talking stick, a forlorn-looking cedar branch rescued from the roadside ditch. Some of the people who'd been willing to chance arrest previously when the most they faced was a mischief charge were not willing to risk criminal contempt of court. Several spoke about their fear of losing their homes and land. But a handful of young types who had no money to speak of and no land to lose said they were ready to get arrested.

Ian McKenzie, true to his old Wobbly roots, stepped forward and said, "I don't have any money either, least not to speak of. Though I own a nice little parcel of land and a cabin I'd sure hate to lose, but goddammit I'd rather chance losing them than lose my self-respect by letting greedy elites ravage this place. I love this place. It's home."

"Right on!" shouted the enthusiasts.

Luis spoke up too, saying, "I'll be damned if I'm gonna stand by and watch these capitalist bloodsuckers destroy a place they have no moral right to."

I could tell that Jess was itching to go for it too, but I took her aside and said, "Look, you're sole legal owner of the farm and you'd be nuts to risk losing it." I could see her resisting right away. "Angus and I have nothing to lose," I said. "We can carry the banner for Figurative Farm. We obviously can't expect Lena and Enzo to expose themselves to imprisonment with their newborn, and Elizabeth's out of the question. So are you." It was messing Jess up to agree, but she finally did.

So Angus, Luis and I, along with old Ian and five young characters, three women and two guys, all stood with arms locked together to prevent the loggers from accessing the site. Frankl read his court order and the security guards escorted us off the road until the cops arrived a few minutes later. Then it was off to town in the squad cars again and overnight accommodation in the drunk tank. Though we realized our gesture was futile, our spirits stayed high. Old Ian regaled us with stories of strikes and marches throughout the Pacific Northwest back in the days when the working class was still charged with revolutionary zeal. He even taught us some old Woody Guthrie tunes that we bellowed at the top of our lungs to make that fetid little jailhouse rock.

But, as we'd known, we couldn't sustain the blockade. While the Fine Nine (as we branded ourselves) awaited our day in kangaroo court, the trees continued to fall. If it wasn't for the golden light of autumn and the beauty of little Josie in our midst we might have sunk entirely into gloom. But then Jess landed a position as freelance features contributor to a new newspaper in town named the *Valley Voice*. A pair of disgruntled old CCFers had recently started publishing it as a progressive alternative to the twice-weekly establishment paper. Secluding herself in our bedroom with a honking big black Remington Rand KMC typewriter we had picked up at the Goodwill thrift, she began clattering away at its keys. The following week, the paper ran her first piece as a full-page spread, front page of the second section, including several grisly photos of the logging carnage. A bold headline ran: "Can this be charity? Roughshod logging in the name of the poor lays waste to Conception Island."

When our whole gang was assembled for lunch, I stood and read her piece aloud. She pulled no punches, but neither did she rant. She just meticulously detailed the facts of the case in clear and uncompromising language. I read her concluding lines with a swelling sense of pride:

> It would be churlishness indeed to recline in one's pastoral surroundings and begrudge needed funding to many of the worthwhile projects assisted by the Waddington Foundation. Nevertheless, it's hard to avoid the conclusion that Conception Island is simply being exploited in the finest robber baron tradition. And it sets one wondering whether we really need this brand of aristocratic benevolence that makes a killing and calls it charity.

169

"Wow!" everyone whooped at the end of the reading. We cheered and congratulated Jess for telling it like it is. Perhaps a bit embarrassed, she mockingly struck the pose of a boxer, with raised fists clenched. I felt colossally proud of my brave, smart companion who dared to publicly speak such uncomfortable truths.

The following morning, the local radio station called to get an interview with Jess. CFOK was a typical small-town station jammed with schlock rock, hyperventilating commercials for cars and mattresses, and a newsroom whose abiding first principle was never to annoy the chamber of commerce. Jess calmly put down her coffee cup and, leaning against the kitchen counter, did the interview right on the spot. She absolutely aced it, notwithstanding several interruptions from impatient party-liners. Shortly after, the editor of her paper called to tell her that the major daily in Victoria wanted permission to reprint the piece, for which they'd pay her fifty bucks. "Fame and fortune both!" Jess exclaimed with smiling irony.

Two days later, a crew from an independent Victoria TV station showed up at the farm wanting an interview. The crew consisted of a cameraman, a sound guy and Bernadette O'Hare, a reporter with beauty-queen looks and, it turned out, a flashing-quick mind. Now we were starting to get some real traction in the public opinion battle. Bernadette wanted to shoot the piece up at the logging site, so Jess and I drove ahead, piloting their van up to the scene of the crime.

Once again we parked behind the big pickup truck and instantly the same stubby hard hat hopped out of the cab and glowered. Two shaggy security guys in uniform glanced across at us but remained sprawled in their lawn chairs on the road's verge. The fallers were hard at it, much further from the road, the clear-cut between us and them already vastly larger than it had been.

"What the hell you want now?" the yellow-vest growled at us just as the TV truck pulled in behind Viribus. "Oh shit," he said, "what are they doin' here?"

"We're just going to record a little piece for the evening news," Jess said sweetly. Typically, she hadn't bothered to change out of her work clothes or fix her hair or put on makeup. "What would be the point when you're standing beside Miss Universe?" she joked later.

And indeed, when Bernadette O'Hare strode forward with her perfect everything and million-dollar smile, poor Stubby just stood there with his mouth hanging open. The security guys sighed in their lawn chairs like deflating tires.

Stubby raised a half-hearted objection to their doing any filming on "his" site, but Jess pointed out to him that we were standing on a public roadway over which he had precisely zero jurisdiction. "Am I right, boys?" she called over to the security guys who just gawped self-consciously. Then she asked Stubby if he perhaps had a few words for the camera, but he only growled that he had a few words for her that wouldn't bear broadcasting and retreated to his truck.

The camera guy, Buzz his name was, set up a tripod, mounted his camera on it and attached a lens that looked like a grenade launcher. He then proceeded to zoom in on the distant loggers. "Sweet," he kept saying as each tree smashed down to earth. The sound guy, whose name we never did get, propped his huge boom mike aloft and adjusted knobs on a small pack held by a strap over his shoulder.

The shoot was set up with Bernadette and Jess in the foreground and the logging going on behind them. Bernadette's questions were perfectly on point and Jess was brilliant in conveying the essence of what she'd written in her piece. Smart, succinct and passionate without a whiff of fanaticism. They only needed one take, but did a second one for backup. "You're great," Bernadette said to Jess when they'd finished.

"Not too shabby yourself," Jess replied and the two of them laughed.

"Thanks for all your help," I said to Stubby in his cab with what I considered penetrating irony. He just stared at me, radio phone in hand, uncomprehending. Jess and Bernadette waved mock-flirtatiously at the security guys, then hugged each other. Jess and I said goodbye to the TV crew, then we got in our respective vehicles and sped away.

ROSALIE ARRIVES IN VERY FINE SPIRITS ON HER NEXT VISIT. "WHAT A PER-
fectly lovely morning!" she exclaims to Shorter. "Here, I've brought
us a few cookies to nibble on while we work." Good omens thus far,
Shorter thinks.

But no sooner have they sat down together than Rosalie looks
at him appraisingly. "I do have some difficult observations to make
about these recent pages," she says.

"Oh?" Shorter says. "Such as?"

"Well, to begin with," she says with a disarming smile, "I have
to confess to being a wee bit shocked at how cursorily baby Josie,
scarcely out of the womb, has been relegated to the sidelines by
this ongoing logging saga." Before Shorter can respond—and he
doesn't really have a credible response at hand—Rosalie continues:
"Sorry to say it, but in fact I'm feeling some serious misgivings about
your preoccupation with the whole logging brouhaha. Not the
issue itself—you know I'm a closet tree hugger—but its potential to
distort the larger questions in play. Your depiction of Stubby, for
example. Isn't it a touch too patronizing, too superficial a cliché
to be credible? The dumbbell hard hat outsmarted at every turn
by these clever revolutionaries. Jess's uncompromising exposé of
the Waddington Foundation rings similar alarm bells. Terribly well
done, no doubt, but chafing nonetheless. And I'm still not recon-
ciled to the residue of Richard's unhappy visit to the farm. Plus the
whole current fixation-of-the-moment on forests—logging blockades, the secret life of trees, forest bathing and all the rest—haven't
we had more than enough of all that for the time being? Don't we
risk having our deeper story sidelined by political posturing?"

Shorter's at a loss for words, but it doesn't matter because
Rosalie suddenly switches tracks and heads off in another direction: what she describes as the thorny issue of eating of meat.

"If you don't mind my asking," she says, "where do you stand on
the question now?"

"Well," he tells her, honestly enough, "I don't eat much in the way of meat anymore." Of course he doesn't each much of anything anymore, compared with those long-ago days when he'd shovel in heaped mounds of grub in order to keep the engine running through long hours of arduous work. "Of course I'm disgusted over veal and hot dogs and other certifiable abominations." She nods understandingly when he mentions that every so often he'll still toddle down to Ponder in order to catch a few small trout for dinner. Perhaps a bit defensively, he adds, "I still keep a little flock of chickens—they give me a steady supply of eggs along with repeated fond memories of Lena, our lovely mistress of the hens." Then for no good reason he blurts out a shameful little secret: "I have an appetite for bacon. Canadian back bacon to be precise. I simply can't let go of my Sunday brunch habit of frying up bacon and eggs, along with hash browns and whole-grain toast. It is," he tells Rosalie, "the culinary highlight of my week and in my opinion the essence of fine dining—and vastly preferable to the finicky niceties of *haute cuisine*."

"But I have to think that you're fully aware of the havoc being wreaked on the planet by meat eaters," Rosalie says in what she hopes is a non-judgmental tone.

"Oh yes," he tells her, "I respect and admire all vegans and I'm delighted to see their numbers multiply. Even the memory of Elizabeth and Amrapali, preening vegans both, touches me with a melancholy fondness."

He doesn't mention for the moment the disastrous consequences of the commune's pig-raising efforts, but he knows it's something he'll soon have to address in these pages. But will any of this curtail his appetite for a modest portion of bacon? So sorry, but no. He sits appropriately mortified beneath Rosalie's empathetic gaze. But, on this at least, like the tree standing by the water, he shall not be moved.

FOURTEEN

NATURALLY, EVERYBODY WANTED TO WATCH JESS'S TV INTERVIEW, BUT with our old Zenith now crumbling in the chicken run beneath a drumlin of droppings, we were forced to look elsewhere. It was common knowledge that Brady Lazarus had installed a huge colour television with remote control by way of partial compensation for the flight of his fickle wife. A short-lived loss, as it turned out, because by now the long-rumoured amour embracing Tonya and Brady had shed all traces of secrecy and the two of them could be regularly spotted in semi-private canoodling. So it made sense that we should assemble at Brady's place to view our televised triumph. Our whole gang packed into Viribus and motored over there. I was a tad surprised that Elizabeth came along with us, given her tacit support for Iris and the pro-logging faction.

Luis and Tonya were already at Brady's house along with Tonya's two kids, a little girl of three named Teresa and a five-year-old boy whom everyone called Pepe, though that wasn't his real name. Both kids had totally taken to Brady and everything seemed to be feeling cosily familial.

As the evening news hour approached, we all hunkered down on the floor in front of Brady's outsized television. An enormous antenna towering over his little house resulted in considerably clearer reception than we'd ever achieved with our old Zenith's rabbit ears. The news began with a late-breaking item about a massive drug bust in Nanaimo followed by a prurient account of a prominent member of the legislature having been caught trying to lure underage girls into his car. We segued smoothly into a commercial break largely featuring flashy automobiles splashing through clear mountain streams and gouging scenic grasslands. Then, suddenly,

174

there was a graphic visual of a big Douglas fir tree slowly toppling over and crashing to earth amid smashing branches and swirling debris. We all gasped at how amazingly that zoom lens had gotten right into the teeth of the logging action.

Quickly the scene switched to down at the ferry wharf, capturing the large wooden sign that proclaims "Welcome to Conception Island." The camera slowly pulled back to show flawless Bernadette O'Hare speaking straight to the camera about how logging operations by a charitable foundation have bitterly divided this once-bucolic small island.

"Uh-oh," Jess said straight off and I too felt a thematic wobble under way. After briefly outlining how the Waddington Foundation came to own the tree farm, Bernadette said the logging had "set islander against islander in a way perhaps unique to small island communities." Then who pops onto the screen in his full authentic-old-islander guise but Gil Gilport!

"What the fuck?" Luis barked, speaking for us all.

You could sense that Gil was more than a bit smitten by the lovely O'Hare because he was smiling and toadying to her in a completely uncharacteristic manner. No bunched fists and stretched neck tendons just now. More to the point, Bernadette was pandering to Gil in a way that immediately smacked of treachery.

"Can you tell our listeners, Gil," she asked, "why it is that you and so many of the old island families don't object to this timber harvesting, while certain newly arrived residents are horrified by it?"

I glanced across at Jess, who was staring at the screen with an expression I couldn't read. The smug little smile on Elizabeth's face was easier to decipher. Luis looked absolutely murderous. It was becoming hard to avoid the feeling that we'd been double-crossed by Bernadette, because while she'd been with us she'd managed to portray herself as implicitly sympathetic to our cause and we'd, perhaps naively, expected that her story would reflect the validity of our point of view. But her cozy colloquy with Gil projected the opposite—that she in fact sympathized with the authentic locals for whom logging was a way of life, rather than with us newbie upstarts. Gil sang the praises of the Waddington group, the

175

tremendous humanitarian work they do, with surprising restraint and near eloquence.

In a flash the visuals cut back to the logging site and Bernadette standing on the road beside Jess. Now Bernadette's winning charm seemed less authentic than it had, her questions more conniving than we'd noticed at the time. Was there an intimation of deviousness behind that glittering smile? Nevertheless, Jess was brilliant in her articulation of the issue. And looked brilliant too. Alongside Bernadette's maquillaged perfection, Jess conveyed, at least to my biased eyes, the authentic beauty of truth. Her calm passion for our cause, for the wisdom of touching the earth with care, resonated unmistakably.

Back at the wharf, Bernadette concluded the segment by informing viewers that the Waddington Foundation had declined a request for an interview and signed off with: "On the embattled shores of Conception Island, where opposing camps remain miles apart and a peaceful resolution seems a very long way away, this is Bernadette O'Hare for Island News."

We trooped out of Brady's place a considerably deflated version of the exuberant group who'd arrived. Jess was the one exception; she maintained that the coverage, while far from what we'd hoped, had in fact strengthened our hand because the one thing outfits like the Waddington gang couldn't tolerate was public controversy. "Nobody remembers the particular facts of these cases," Jess said, "but they will retain a general impression, and in this case the lingering image is the Waddington Foundation destroying a forest."

Back at the farm things didn't get any easier, because we were pressed with one outstanding item of business: putting down our three rambunctious billies. On the appointed day, Angus retrieved Willie's old rifle and a box of .22 Long rounds from a locked closet. "Yep, she's a Marlin 39-A," Willie had told us proudly when he'd handed the gun over. "I got it back in '39, first year they produced this model, though it's not a whole lot different from when they started making them in the 1890s. Sold a shitload of them over

176

the years. Black walnut stock, forged steel components, thing of beauty." He'd let his fingers run tenderly over the stock and barrel before handing the gun to me.

"Annie Oakley herself used one, the original model. One time she put something like two dozen rounds through a single bullet hole in an ace of spades playing card. Can you beat that?"

Angus and I had consulted with Willie again before attempting the detestable execution. None of us liked the prospect of ending these animals' lives prematurely. Lena was so distraught about it she announced that she'd be taking baby Josie away for a few days to visit her sister. Elizabeth fled as well, to spend time with Amrapali. "Well," Willie had told us, "like the old sayin' says: if you got livestock, you gotta expect deadstock. No two ways about it." He'd filled us in on how to proceed, which was pretty much the same as what Angus had learned about killing sheep back home.

"Yah, sheep and goats both," Willie had said, "they got thick bony plates down the front of the skull. You shoot them there and the damn bullet's like to bounce right off, might not be enough to even stun them much less kill them. Way better to shoot through the back of the head, pointing down toward the jaw. Easy enough too—just place a bowl of feed on the ground in front of them. The goat'll put its head down to eat. You just stand right behind, with the barrel a few inches from its head. Instant kill. No pain or suffering. But make bloody sure that bullet can't ricochet back at you!"

Stiff with foreboding, Angus and I went out to the paddock where the billies were cannonading around like mad creatures. We made sure their mothers were far away, grazing in the meadow, then lured the young ones close with buckets of grain and, while they single-mindedly gobbled it, slipped a noose around each of them. Hearts shadowed with treachery, we led two of them off, kicking and straining, and tied them behind the toolshed, well away from where their brother was about to die. Then we fastened the third one to a stout post near the compost piles, figuring the deep earth and mounds of compost could absorb a bullet without any ricochet. I poured a small pile of grain onto the ground in front of the billy, guiltily unable to look it in the eye. I was glad at that moment that we hadn't named any of them, but still couldn't avoid recognizing it as a unique and beautiful creature, spirited with precious life.

As the unsuspecting billy wolfed down the grains, Angus quietly drew close behind it, cocked the rifle, aimed and shot it in the back of the head. The animal fell dead instantly, just as Willie had said. The astonishing fact of life extinguished, just like that, the eyes staring blankly, blood mingled with grain gushing from the gaping mouth. We stood away for a bit to avoid any thrashing limbs, then Angus unsheathed a sharp knife and slit arteries and veins on both sides of its neck to bleed the carcass out.

We repeated the grim procedure with the remaining two, all three executed without mishap. I congratulated Angus for his expertise. I doubt that I would have felt up to doing the actual killing myself. Certainly not three times. Fierce adrenalin was pumping through my body and I could taste something weirdly metallic in my mouth that wouldn't leave for the remainder of the day. I asked Angus if he was okay and he nodded abstractedly but said nothing.

Everyone was pretty quiet at dinner that evening. Mercifully, Jess had cooked up a big stir-fry of garden vegetables over rice and tofu, so there were no animal parts to taste of accusation.

"Maybe the abattoir or the auction is a better bet after all," I said at one point, mostly to rescue Angus, who still had an abstracted look about him. But nobody offered an opinion.

Nothing was said about the killing when Lena returned with Josie several days later. We were thrilled to have them back, and the gloomy spirits that had lingered about the place gradually seemed to melt away. It was remarkable how that tiny Josie could enliven all of us. Her serenely innocent eyes and little bubbly mouth, the pre-philosophical pronouncements she could utter and the way her miniature fingers grasped at airy nothings—she held us all captive to unfamiliar tender feelings.

We each took a regular turn at child care and there wasn't one of us who didn't love our day spent with Josie. We'd snuggle and nuzzle and giggle with her throughout the day and then at dinner share all the brilliant things she'd done under our watch.

Naturally, all of this got Jess and me talking about whether or not we wanted a child ourselves. "God, Shorter," Jess said with a laugh, "I am so of two minds about it, I don't know which way to turn." We were lying together on a grassy bank over near Ponder, watching voluminous white cumulus clouds float like galleons across a brilliantly blue sky.

"I feel exactly the same," I said. "Sometimes, looking at Josie, I say to myself: Absolutely! This is what I want more than anything. But then, lying awake at night, I realize that as much as I love little Josie being here, I'm really not all that anxious to be a father myself."

We'd had and continued to have variations of this conversation intermittently for several years, to the point where it got be our standing preggers joke. Ultimately we decided to just let nature run its course, which is what we'd been doing up until then any-way—we'd carry on making love whenever we felt like it, neither attempting to prevent pregnancy nor scheming to try to ensure it. If the Fates were to send us a child, so be it, and if not, so be that too.

"BIRTH AND DEATH," ROSALIE SAYS WITH A MEANINGFUL SIGH, "BIRTH and death, those twin imponderables. I've experienced both of them up close and personal," she tells Shorter, and for a moment her gaze wanders off toward distances and possibilities he suspects she won't disclose. "Yes, I was deeply moved by the anguish of hav-ing to kill those young goats," she says. "And I really felt the tumult Jess and you endured on the question of having a child of your own."

"Oh, we didn't agonize all that much about the child thing," he says. "In fact we felt ourselves blessed to have Josie in the house. Without her, and her brother later on, things might have been different for us."

"Most fortunate, I agree," she says. "And such generosity for Lena and Enzo to share their parenting with all of you." She laughs when he tells her that in later years Jess and he used to bemoan not having grandchildren far more than they ever did about not having children. "Oh, yes, Lord save us from doting grandparents!" Rosalie then launches into a description of a former neighbour who for the life of him couldn't desist from crowing about his grandsons, already destined for stardom in the National Hockey League. "Forestalling the approach of death," she says with a sigh. "Futile in the end, of course, but comforting for those in need of comfort." Shorter finds this conclusion surprisingly harsh coming from Rosalie, who customarily tilts toward the side of compassion.

Equally surprising, she's not at all appalled by Shorter's description of their killing the young goats. "No, I agree wholeheartedly with your Farmer Jones: that if you're going to keep livestock you must take responsibility for both births and deaths. I far prefer the trauma-free death you visited upon your billies to dragging them to a distant abattoir where the stench of death would terrify them long before their dying. So, good on you bunch for doing what's proper in the circumstances.

"Of course," she adds with a wry smile, "whether or not you ought to have been keeping goats in the first place is another question entirely." This, as might have been expected, leads her directly to the matter of cats. She goes on at length about which of her pair is faring well, which poorly, and related complexities.

Shorter can't quite believe she sees no concurrence between the besotted grandad and her own feline fixation. He says nothing for the moment.

FIFTEEN

WHEN LUIS SHOWED UP AT THE HOUSE UNEXPECTEDLY ONE RAINY Sunday afternoon, my instant reaction was to imagine some disaster in the making. Luis and crisis, it was becoming evident, seemed to go pretty much hand-in-hand. But the Waddington situation was, for the moment, simmering in abeyance—the loggers had finished the initial cutblock, then mysteriously left the island. The Waddington people weren't saying anything. Islanders of all persuasions remained in a state of twitchy watchfulness.

Meanwhile, we Fine Nine arrestees had expended a lot of time and energy preparing to defend ourselves against the imminent criminal contempt of court charges. A pair of bright young lawyers up in Spangler had offered their services in our defence, pro bono. Jess was sharpening her pencils to cover the trial in depth for her newspaper. Luis in particular was looking forward to the trial as a perfect opportunity to publicly expose the furtive sleaze of the Waddington Foundation.

Then, with the trial date only weeks away, we were informed that the charges had been stayed. What? Yes, some anonymous official from the court explained, Waddington and the Crown had in consultation decided not to proceed with the charges.

"Why would they drop the charges?" Lena had asked. She was sitting at the kitchen table nursing Josie. Jess and I were washing dishes.

"I'll tell you why," Jess had said, holding up a soapy spatula. "More negative publicity, something to be avoided at all costs. They're not doing any logging just now, and we're not blockading. Why would they want to stir up any more public mudslinging?" So that was that. Poof! The trial of the century gone like a puff of wind.

We were all still in a state of guarded watchfulness on that rainy afternoon when Luis came calling.

"Yo, man," he greeted me at the back door, "you got a few minutes hanging?"

"Sure thing," I said, happy enough to get out of the house without having to go work in heavy rain. We drove down to the ferry wharf in Luis's battered pickup, making small talk as we splashed through muddy puddles. But Luis isn't a small-talk kind of guy and once we were parked he quickly cut to the core.

"Big changes coming down," he told me. "You know my sister and Brady have been having a thing…"

"Yep."

"Well, turns out they're getting mega serious."

"Really," I said, with no idea where this might be going. Domestic concerns weren't normally top of mind for Luis. Rain continued drumming heavily on the roof and blurring our windshield view of the sound.

"So Tonya's been carrying a heavy mortgage on that place of hers."

"I didn't know that."

"Yeah. I been givin' her whatever I can to help out, but she's still kinda stretched on her payments."

It was plenty obvious that neither Luis nor his sister was rolling in dough. They were scraping along like a lot of the rest of us, wearing poverty as a badge more of honour than disgrace. Another of the great freedoms of youth. And, for some, of privilege. Luis freelanced as a handyman and Tonya worked basically for nothing at a makeshift preschool that rotated around different homes. Maybe she got welfare, I don't know. Luis had told me bits and pieces of his own background but I knew less about Tonya—who the kids' father was or any of that.

"She's thinking of selling her place," Luis said, "and moving in with Brady."

"Ah." This instantly struck me as not a great idea, given current economic realities on the island. Land prices were constantly creeping upward. If you already had a place of your own, my instinct advised, best to hold on to it. Lose a place now and you may have lost your toehold forever. Plus, for all his finer points, Brady was not exactly Captain Stability. But what the hell did I know about being a poor single mom with two kids to raise? I considered Tonya a really smart woman not given to rash impulses, and possibly she detected some fine balance in Brady that I couldn't.

"Yah, I'm not crazy about the arrangement either," Luis said, recognizing my hesitation, "but it's her life."

"And the kids' lives too."

"For sure. But he seems really good with them. I know Tonya wouldn't go for it if he wasn't. Those kids come first with her. Always."

"Yeah, I get that about her," I said. "Has she thought about renting her house out rather than selling? You know, in case things don't work out."

"We talked about it," Luis said, "but she doesn't want the hassle of being a landlady, especially with that place. Between you and me it needs a shitload of work—a new roof for starters, needs to be jacked up and a proper foundation put under it, the wiring and plumbing are a fucking nightmare. I know because I been working at it whenever I can find the time and have seen up close how much more needs doing."

"Couldn't you maybe take it on yourself, work on the house in exchange for rent?"

"Yeah, that maybe works for the labour side," Luis said, "but not materials. The roof alone is thousands of bucks, which is thousands more than either she or I have."

"I hear you," I said.

The ferry had just pulled in and was now disgorging a cavalcade of vehicles.

Through the streaming windshield they formed what looked like a long and colourfully glistening metallic caterpillar.

"So she and the kids move in with Brady," Luis said, "and the property goes on the market. I can still crash there until it's sold, but that might not be all that long."

At last I was beginning to suspect where this was headed.

183

Luis looked me straight in the eye with the kind of intensity I'd seen from him before. He really was an extraordinarily handsome character, and vaguely disturbing as well. "What I'm asking, bro," he said, "is whether there'd be room for me at the farm. I know your house is full already," he hastened to say before I could, "but I was thinking maybe I could put up, like, a hogan or something, out of the way. I'd be no hassle to anyone and I could really help with all the stuff you guys are trying to get done over there."

"Well, it's true we're not exactly overrun with practical cats," I said. The truth of the matter was that without handy Angus, and to some degree Jess, maintenance-wise we'd be up the creek named Shit without a paddle, but I didn't say that. Luis was, I knew, super accomplished at both building and repairing things. One of those guys who can fix almost anything.

"I feel like we're pretty copacetic," Luis proffered his rationale. "I like you folks and I think most of you kinda dig me too."

This was true, but not necessarily persuasive. I knew almost for certain that Elizabeth would likely oppose having Luis move in and I wasn't sure that Angus wouldn't too.

"Listen," I said to Luis as the rain lessened its battering on the roof a bit, "we have a farm meeting this evening; I'll put it on the agenda and get a sense of what the group thinks."

"Thanks, man," Luis said, briefly putting a hand to my shoulder. "Would it help if I came and pled my case in person?"

I paused a beat for diplomacy's sake and pretended to consider the question.

"Probably work best if I present it to the group, then everyone can say exactly what they want without fear of offending."

"I hear you, man," Luis said with a smile, "but I'm pretty thick-skinned, you know what I mean? Or maybe I could give my pitch and then leave so everyone can discuss it."

"Hmm," I pondered this suggestion, again mostly for appearance's sake. All my instincts warned me to keep Luis's forcefulness well away while we discussed whether or not we wanted him to become a part of the commune. The mere possibility of it thrummed with nervous energy.

Jess and Lena were making the meal that evening, involving perhaps excessive dollops of squash, cabbage and rutabaga, which meant I didn't have a chance to discuss the situation privately with Jess before the meeting. Complicated issues were invariably clearer for me after a talk with Jess. And any way you sliced it, this was a complicated matter. I chose not to introduce the topic of Luis into the dinner conversation, figuring that the strict protocols of our meetings, though rudely disparaged at times, might serve us better in dealing with a decision as thorny as this one.

That particular evening it was Enzo's turn to facilitate the meeting. To put it gently, Enzo was not our ablest facilitator. While the meetings he led were often the most fun, they frequently lacked much semblance of structure, as logical linkage of component parts was not really Enzo's bag. He could wobble off topic, often hilariously, and lose all track of the thread, so that we would have to either let chaos rule or drag the discussion back to whatever topic was at hand. On this particular evening I would have far preferred that Jess, or even Elizabeth, was in charge.

After the dishes were cleared and Josie had been settled in her crib close by, we reconvened around the dining table. Before Enzo could get us launched into the initial round of check-ins, I told the group that we had a large and possibly contentious issue that might take most of the meeting to deal with. Of course that got everyone's attention, the same way Held Feelings frequently did.

"I think maybe we should postpone the normal order of business and deal with this extraordinary item first," I said. We did a quick round but without benefit of the talking stick because it had been misplaced somewhere. Again. Naturally everybody spoke in favour of getting after this mysterious new item.

"In a nutshell," I explained, "Luis has approached me with a request that we consider having him join the commune." A couple of subdued gasps, then silence for a moment. I gave them a thumbnail précis of the situation with Tonya and Brady and of Luis's proposal, then tossed our non-existent talking stick back to Enzo.

185

He stared around the group for a moment, the way you imagine time travellers staring at unforeseen worlds, then cleared his throat but said nothing.

Jess jumped in to rescue him, as she typically would. "How about we do a round on our initial response to Luis's proposal," she suggested, "knowing that we'll almost certainly need subsequent rounds to clarify our feelings." Everybody murmured assent.

"It goes without saying, of course," Elizabeth added, "that we would, as with all major decisions, absolutely need to achieve consensus."

"And," Enzo said, reclaiming his role as facilitator, "that we are, as always, bound by strict confidentiality."

As expected, opinions were all over the place in this opening round, some more considered than others. Most of us were scattered along the mushy middle, neither strongly in favour nor fiercely opposed. I was interested that Angus seemed reasonably accepting of Luis joining us. My cartoon of Angus was that the fewer people around the better he liked it. Perhaps his getting arrested and jailed with Luis had forged a bond of sorts. Or maybe on a practical level he simply valued adding a skilled worker to our labour pool. "Luis," he said pointedly, "knows which end of a hammer to pick up."

"You mean more than I do?" Enzo said and everyone laughed.

Eventually Jess and Elizabeth took up polar positions. It came as small surprise that Elizabeth was adamantly against having Luis join us. "He's a cool enough guy in many ways," she said, "and I admire how loyal he's been to his sister..."

You waited for the "but" and it came straight away. "It's his politics I have a problem with, or rather his extremism around political issues. I believe he's sincere enough in his convictions, but sincerity doesn't excuse fanaticism."

A palpable tension circled the table as we approached the great divide. Elizabeth's defection from our ranks over the logging had simmered down somewhat during the excitement of Josie's birth and the killing and butchering of the billies, but Jess's article and TV interview had certainly stirred the embers again.

"I'm sorry to say it," Elizabeth carried on, "but I find Luis too much of a zealot for my taste. All the Cesar Chavez posturing. Endless denunciations of the capitalist overclass. The anger and aggression." She looked around the group, focusing especially on Lena. "But we all know that nothing is ever solved that way. Anger begets anger and, before you know it, hostilities break out. It's what I believed we left behind by coming here in the first place. That we were looking for a new and better way. A path of peace and cooperation, exploring commonalities rather than divergences, not continuing this dominant male antler-clashing we've seen far too much of already. I believe we need to focus our energies on developing higher consciousness and I don't think Luis has much of anything to offer in that regard. In fact his tempestuousness could seriously hamper the rest of us getting on with important inner work."

We all sat silently for bit, considering what Elizabeth had said. I was fascinated by how scrupulous we were now being about what characteristics we needed to see in a potential new member, compared with the slapdash manner in which we'd first all come together. A couple of years in the trenches had taught us a few things.

Continuing the round, Lena wanted to listen and think some more before speaking and so did Enzo, which brought us to Jess at the opposite side of the table from Elizabeth. The two of them looked directly at each other before Jess began.

"I agree completely with Elizabeth about the hostility and anger," Jess began, surprisingly. "I too believe we're trying to create a different paradigm here, a way of being in community based upon mutual respect and caring. Not in trying to overpower or outwit anyone."

Was Jess deciding against Luis? I wondered. That would come as a surprise because I knew there was chemistry between them. I'd seen it first-hand during our Waddington expeditions, the way their minds clicked, the quick concordances of perspective, a similarly bent sense of humour. Never flirtatious, at least not that I observed, but an unmistakable attraction. I'd found myself keeping an eye, as they say, but never brought it up with Jess. For the moment anyway.

"But you know," Jess continued, "this whole Waddington thing has really got me rethinking a lot." All of us around the table were super dialled in, as though we sensed we were at the edge of something momentous. "We left the city," Jess continued, "believing we could distance ourselves from the worst of what was happening there, and to some degree we have, and I love all of you for being a part of what we're trying to do here." She glanced around the table with unconcealed affection. "But I also think the Waddington experience has shown us that, unfortunately, physical distance provides no lasting safety from the crappiest aspects of society."

I could feel Elizabeth bristle, but she said nothing for the moment. "And let's not kid ourselves," Jess went on, "this little island fracas is nothing compared with what's happening all over the globe. The devastation of forests and waterways, millions barely able to scratch out a living in abysmal slums. On and on—you don't need me to bang that same old drum again. What's changed for me is I've come to realize more and more strongly that active resistance is still required. Maybe required more than ever. That simply removing ourselves, opting out, is not sufficient. Not a tenable moral stance. That we must put at least some of our energies into beating back the malignant forces loose in the world."

Jess and I had talked much of this over between ourselves in recent months, fumbling our way toward some kind of morally acceptable position. The clarity and determination with which she was now speaking made me realize that she was glimpsing a way forward.

"Luis does not come problem-free," she continued. "None of us do, of course, but we've seen enough of Luis to know that he has an energy that makes everything, including his excesses, extra large. You'd be nuts to imagine his presence here would be smooth and easy all the time, but I do believe that his passion for social justice and environmental health is genuine. And that it would offer a net benefit for Figurative Farm. He would, if nothing else, help ensure that we weren't falling asleep at the wheel, becoming dedicated only to our precious selves. So, all things considered, even with the risks involved, I believe we should accept him."

Now we were up against it. We carried on through several more rounds, concluding with Elizabeth remaining adamantly opposed (despite repeatedly inserting her latest turn of phrase: "I hear that") and the rest of us more or less in favour. In other words no consensus. We talked about maybe having a trial period for three or four months after which we could reassess, but couldn't agree on that either. Eventually, with still no decision made, we took the low road of vacillation and booted the question forward to our next meeting.

I wasn't especially buzzed about having to report back to Luis that we were at an impasse, but a couple of days later our paths happened to cross outside the community hall. People were bustling around, getting set up for the school Christmas pageant, a seasonal highlight now only days away. I was relieved to bump into Luis because, with party season already in gear, I didn't want to be encountering him with maybe both of us under the influence, and nothing for me to say about his situation.

"Hey, man," he greeted me. But before I could say anything he asked, "You heard about the shitstorm coming down?"

"What's that?" I asked.

"You haven't heard?"

"About what?" I was already accustomed to how Luis liked to swagger a bit if he knew something you didn't. Usually people with this conceit I find completely off-putting, but not Luis for some reason.

"Our champions of the indigent at Waddington."

"Haven't heard a peep," I said. "What are they up to now?"

"On the local news this morning; they're selling all their land here."

"Selling it?"

"The whole shiteree. On the grounds that radical elements on Conception and several other places are making it impossible for them to conduct their affairs in an orderly fashion."

"Oh, for fuck's sake!" This really was a shocker and I instantly felt that we were a bunch of schmucks for not seeing it, or at least the possibility of it, coming. That insultingly abbreviated meeting in Victoria, the foundation's underhanded negotiations with Iris and her gang—what kind of stupid does it take not to see deviousness in plain sight.

"Rough translation: the negative publicity's gotten to them," Luis said. He didn't seem nearly as discomfited as I was feeling, as though the prospect of imminent battle with a fresh opponent was something he readily embraced.

"Hmm."

"So, guess what, it's out of the dumpster and into the dump for us."

"Yah," I agreed. "Could be the buyer proves worse than the seller. Any word about potential purchasers?"

"Not yet."

"Oh, hell," I said. "Looks like a rocky road ahead."

"Well merry fucking Christmas to you too!" Luis shouted across the empty roadway to no one in particular.

"WELL, YOU'VE CERTAINLY SET THE FOX AMONG THE CHICKENS AT THIS point, haven't you?" Rosalie asks Shorter almost before she's through the door. "Oh, yes," she says as she takes her customary seat beside him, "I admit it: initially I was quite enthusiastic over your introduction of Luis and Tonya into the narrative."

"Yes, I know that," he says. Shorter realizes that in recent weeks her attitude toward Luis, though not toward his sister, has steadily worsened. "Is it the expletives?" he asks her. Luis was uninhibited in his hurling what smug pundits now call F-bombs.

"I'm no prude," she tells Shorter, "but I do find vulgarisms are drained of their forcefulness if overused. Luis's profanities sound more and more like the tantrums of a troubled child." Luis's swearing never sounded obscene to Shorter, just a part of who he was, his passion and power.

"Well, language aside," he says, "what do you make of Jess's argument that having Luis join the commune would bolster it in remaining committed to activist principles? Or do you believe that having the commune align with Elizabeth would have meant settling comfortably into what's now derided as addiction to 'the cult of the self'?"

Rosalie doesn't answer straight away, but sits staring out the kitchen window. She's thinking of her own recent obsessions before leaving the city, her powerlessness, her magnificent hurling of her phone into Lost Lagoon and withdrawing to the blessed sanctuary of Conception. "I imagine," she says at last, "that back then you wouldn't have dared suggest that yoga, meditation, Pilates and all the rest might be merely the indulgences of privileged elites eager to hop on any self-absorbed bandwagon rather than get to work trying to prevent the pillaging of the planet."

"No, that's right," Shorter agrees. "Any more than you'd maintain today that Occupy Wall Street, Idle No More, Black Lives Matter, Me Too and all the rest are cheap activist escapism preventing any serious examination of our inner selves."

"And where do you stand now on all those kinds of issues? Do they still concern you?" Rosalie's remembering several of those old revisionist back-to-the-landers she approached before good fortune brought her Mr. Shorter.

"Well," he says, "like Jess, I always leaned more toward the activist camp."

"Nevertheless, you didn't wholeheartedly endorse having Luis join the commune. Like Jess did."

"No I didn't," he admits.

"For other reasons perhaps?"

"No, I don't think so," Shorter says, unconvincingly.

"It's all a bit dizzying, isn't it?" Rosalie smiles.

SIXTEEN

ONE THING WAS FOR SURE: THE SIMPLE LIFE WAS GETTING AWFUL DAMN complicated. We Figuratives were caught in gridlock over what to do about Luis while at the same time, like the rest of the island, growing more and more jittery about the impending Waddington sale. Our esteemed friends at Waddington headquarters were pointedly not returning calls. Rumours were constantly circulating that the tree farm was about to be purchased by one nefarious speculator or another. People entertained fantastical visions of suburban tract homes and shopping malls, luxury hotels with spas and golf courses, even a maximum security federal prison. Alarmists were already scouting the hinterlands for new locales they could move to once Conception was lost.

Out of this primeval stew arose the notion that we, the community, should buy the lands ourselves. Off the top this seemed absurd. The asking price was purportedly in excess of three million dollars and how the hell could we raise even a fragment of that amount. Typically fundraisers on the island were heavier on fun than funds. The volunteer fire department had instituted an annual auction for which islanders donated truckloads of old furniture, tools, building supplies, accessories and oddments that were auctioned off at bargain-basement prices, trucked home, stored in barns or sheds and frequently returned the following year to be auctioned again. Amid the hooting and hollering a few thousand bucks was raised to help equip the firefighters. Other worthy causes benefited in a modest way from the raffling of quilts and gift baskets, and sometimes the proceeds from a talent show or dance would go to help neighbours who'd lost a house to fire or incurred extraordinary medical expenses. But most of this worthy work involved hundreds, not millions, of dollars.

So the talk in certain quarters about raising several million bucks to buy out Waddington was discounted as pipedreaming by almost everyone. But then, out of nowhere, a previously low-profile character named Johnny Spriggs was suddenly leading the charge for community purchase of the tree farm. Johnny and his wife Grace—newcomers, mid-forties, obviously (some whispered) obscenely wealthy—had bought an expansive acreage down at the south end overlooking a picturesque lighthouse and impressive stretch of the Strait of Georgia. They'd hired every available back-hoe and Bobcat to clear and landscape the acreage and had erected, employing mostly local labour, a palatial home that was in turns discussed, envied and derided.

Johnny had never before shown any interest in community affairs but now he was everywhere, urging us all to get onboard with his vision. "Some folks got more money than brains," more than one old-timer grumbled about Johnny's ambitious plan. The rest of us just went about our business, scarcely wondering what, if anything, would ever come of Johnny's outlandish schemes.

"You know," Lena announced at lunch one day, "I was thinking it would be a good idea if I took Josie to town for a visit with Willie. The baby might help lift the old guy's spirits." Everyone agreed. It had been far far too long since any of us had seen Willie, but we shared a sense that he was likely withering in the confines of the retirement home. At the other end of the life cycle, the baby had single-handedly added an outsized new dimension to the collective household. For one thing, we were all hyper-alert concerning threats to the child's well-being. The faintest cough or distressed cry about a wet diaper or whatever would have everyone within earshot trying to determine what the problem might be. None of us had any expertise or insight into child rearing. Any number of times we had panicked scrambling over what turned out to be nothing at all. Relying primarily on her maternal instincts, Lena seemed to be the most sensible of us.

But mostly, Josie's smiles and burblings were delightful gifts to all of us. "Yes, I think we'd have to concur," Jess said at dinner one evening, "having the baby in the house seems to make all of us a little more mellow than we'd been. Gentler and kinder." We all agreed the child had come to us with a special gift for spirit-lifting, and so a visit to Willie made perfect sense.

As Enzo was nursing a strain of everlasting flu at the time and didn't fancy introducing it into Sunset Rest, Lena asked if I'd drive her and the baby into town. I was happy to do so, especially to have an overdue visit with Willie.

The morning of our trip was splendid. A piercingly blue sky set off the Coast Mountains gleaming with fresh snow, the waters of the sound shimmered with silvery grey light, and a promise of spring was palpable in the air. Having Lena and the baby sitting alongside was immensely sweet and I could feel my cares and worries peeling away across the water, such was the power of that child, her gurgled promises foretelling splendid possibilities. When Lena unbuttoned her shirt and held Josie to suckle at her breast, I felt a peculiar shiver of lust. For the briefest of sentimental moments I imagined myself the beaming father with lovely Lena my wife and our darling child in her arms.

Where did that all come from, I wondered, that hopeless mashup of lust-driven sentimentality? Bushed. I shook my head.

We found Willie in a poor way. I couldn't believe how much he'd greyed and faded in the few months since I saw him last. Slumped in his armchair, he was watching the Brier on TV. This was not a good sign because I distinctly remembered Willie telling me that he despised curling. Something about the sweeping didn't sit well with him. But he livened right up when he saw us, fumbled for his remote and clicked the TV off. "Stupid curling," he grumbled, then glanced from Lena to me and back again. "What have you done with Jess, though?" he asked with a worried look. "Surely you've not..."

"Relax, Willie," I said with a laugh, realizing he thought I'd switched partners. "As much as she wanted to, Jess couldn't come see you today, but Lena was anxious to visit and show you her baby."

"Hi, Willie," Lena said with the sweetest smile. "Look, here's baby Josie. She was born on the farm." She leaned forward and gently laid the swaddled babe onto Willie's lap. Josie was in a particularly transcendental mode at the moment and stared gravely up into the old guy's whiskered face. Willie stared back at her, transfixed.

"Hello, my sweetheart," he whispered dryly, and I saw small tears trickle one by one down his withered cheeks.

They stayed like that, he and Josie, gazing into each other's eyes, ancient and neonate, neither of them making any sound for a long while.

Eventually Willie looked up at us, working his lips but unable to speak. His eyes were wide open, the palest blue of glacial ice, and he gestured for Lena to take the baby back. I hated leaving him in that frail a space but he made it clear that he needed to be alone. Just as we were saying goodbye, a male nurse bustled in, excusing himself but saying it was time for Willie's toilet break.

Although Lena and I were troubled by seeing Willie's descent into darkness, we were convinced that taking the baby to connect with him, fraught as the visit had been, was beneficial. On the drive home, I had a sudden brainwave. "What if we were to sneak in one of the little dogs," I suggested to Lena. "Don't you think it would completely cheer old Willie up?"

"Oh, that's brilliant, Shorter!" Lena laughed. "I'm all for it." We so wanted to see Willie alive and laughing, back to the mischievous old guy we'd known at the outset.

Plus, to be honest, we were seriously under the influence of Ken Kesey's *One Flew Over the Cuckoo's Nest*. The film wasn't out yet, but a tattered copy of the book had been circulating around the farm for weeks and now sat high in our rebellious canon. The thought of busting Willie out of that grey-inducing institution had appealed to me, but realistically what the hell would you do with him once you got him out? Sneaking one of the dogs in offered a fillip of subversiveness without any entanglements.

Back home I consulted with Elizabeth as mistress of hounds. "Excellent plan!" she pronounced. "It needs to be one of the smaller dogs, of course, and I'd highly recommend Bandy for the mission because between her and Suzy, Bandy's the quieter and less excitable." So Bandy it would be.

I couldn't at that time pretend to any great affection toward Bandy. She had bulbous dark eyes protruding from a pug face and a turned-up snout that always created the impression of having been recently immersed in fecal matter. "She's a cross," Elizabeth told me, holding Bandy against her chest, "almost certainly shih tzu, a most noble breed, but mixed with whatever else I'm not sure, possibly an apple head chihuahua. One thing's certain: she's a supremely smart and very loyal little dog, aren't you, honey?" Bandy licked her lips and wriggled appreciatively. I chuckled to myself at how far removed we were from those chaotic early days when the mongrel horde ran amok and Elizabeth particularly sniffed at them with disdain. Nowadays the dogs lived comfortably in their cozy kennel with attached run and, thanks to Elizabeth and Lena, benefited from regular exercise and training sessions.

In preparation for the Bandy caper, I retrieved from the attic an old black leather satchel that, as a scholar, I'd carried around campus stuffed with heavy loads of books and manuscripts as evidence of academic achievement. Bandy fit inside it easily and, at Elizabeth's suggestion, I spent a bit of time each day getting the little dog accustomed to lying noiselessly in the satchel as I carried it around. Within a week or two she had it down pat, so Jess and I headed back to Spangler with the satchel and contraband Bandy.

The day was dripping grey, and during the drive in I smiled to myself, comparing it to the brilliant morning of the previous visit. Bandy in place of the baby, Jess instead of Lena. We gave Bandy a brief run on the beach, cleaned her paws and snuggled her inside the satchel with a biscuit.

After checking in at the front desk we made it to Willie's room without incident. We found him sitting on the edge of his bed, shoulders slumped, gazing vacantly through the window. The cluttered room had its usual cloying scent of disinfectant but the television was off. Glancing up, Willie smiled with pleasure at seeing Jess and she stepped over to give him a long hug.

"Little surprise for you here, Willie," I said placing the satchel on the bed beside him. "Go ahead, open it up." His wizened hands shook as he fumbled with the clasp and I reflected again on how dramatically, and in so short a time, he'd shrunk from the boisterous character we'd first met. He got the satchel open and peered inside. Bandy must have recognized his scent because she was making a tiny keening noise I'd never heard from her before.

As Willie reached in to lift her out, his wrinkled face was suffused with rapture. He clasped Bandy to his chest and kissed her unlovely little face with withered lips. Jess and I smiled together, catching a glimmer of the mischievous free spirit we'd first encountered at the farm. Following our plan, I loitered near Willie's door to run interference in case any authorities showed up while Jess and Bandy visited with Willie. We had a good half-hour or more before a nurse hove into view and Bandy was quickly secreted in her satchel.

"I knew you kids would do right by me," Willie said, near to tears as we were taking our leave. "You know I could lie down tonight a happy man and not wake up in the morning." We each hugged him warmly and said we'd be back in no time.

"OH GOODNESS, YES, I REALLY AM INTRIGUED," ROSALIE SAYS ON HER next visit. "At your choice to put the two visits with Willie alongside the Big Idea of purchasing the tree farm. I wonder if the juxtaposition is a clever analogue of you purchasing Willie's farm in the first place?" This hadn't occurred to Shorter, but much of what Rosalie comes up with hasn't occurred to him, so he puts it out of mind for the moment.

"On another matter," Rosalie says, "I have to confess that I'm very unsettled by your allusion to imagining Lena as your wife and Josie as your child. This, as I'm sure you don't need me to tell you, is the type of apparently trivial intimation that can have explosive consequences. I certainly hope that it's not a forerunner of tormented times ahead."

She notices how Shorter quickly shunts her off that track with an offhand reference to Bandy in the bag. "Oh, yes!" she tells him enthusiastically, "that little escapade was absolutely brilliant. Such a gift to give old Willie. I can just imagine myself in his position and some caring soul like yourself bringing me one of my cats. Yes! I'd be just as you describe Willie. Rapturous to the point of tears. I think our readers will be truly moved by both those vignettes involving Willie. A bit of a respite from the political thickets, at least."

Our readers? This is a group to which Shorter has given scarcely any thought at all. He's comfortably slipped into a mental groove of assuming that Rosalie is his one and only reader, that her response to what he writes is the only one that matters. He's spent almost zero time considering that hordes of strangers might someday be poring over his dim memories, picking out evident contradictions, lapses and lacunae. He feels a shiver of resentment that Rosalie is now moving the goalposts on him. That it's his story, to do with as he chooses, damnit.

But Rosalie's become increasingly convinced that his tale merits a far wider audience. That it would be a disservice to the history of the island to have it fade into oblivion. And although she doesn't say so just now, she recognizes that the history of the island, indeed the island itself, has gradually become more important to her than it was when she offhandedly began her little project. She registers the stiffening in Shorter and knows she'll have to finesse this aspect a bit.

"Oh, yes, you must be diligent in considering your wider readership," she tells him, smiling widely. "Not shaping your narrative to accommodate their imagined preferences, of course, any more than you do for mine, but nevertheless being conscious of them as the recipients of your accumulated wisdom."

Shorter suffers a further moment's panic at this, a horrid vision of prying eyes, judgments, criticisms. Eager postgraduates, like the one he himself once was, sharpening their knives on the old bones of his story.

SEVENTEEN

THE GRIDLOCK OVER WHETHER OR NOT LUIS SHOULD BE WELCOMED AS a full member of the commune was finally broken in dramatic fashion by Elizabeth of all people. Having failed to hold a group meeting for several weeks, we were gathered on a Sunday evening when Elizabeth fluffed herself slightly and announced, "I have to tell you that I've recently come into an unanticipated little windfall." Elizabeth generally favoured opacity when it came to her financial affairs, which was understandable as she was the only one of us who really had financial affairs. For my own part, I'd occasionally receive a letter with a skimpy cheque enclosed from my parents, by then retired in lower Florida and still nursing grievances over my academic bellyflop. I received the pittance with an ill grace similar to theirs in sending it.

"Yes, I've received a small inheritance from a dear old aunt whom I loved very much," Elizabeth told us. This was the first we'd ever heard of the dear old aunt. Whether or not she'd died Elizabeth didn't say and we didn't ask. "What I would like to do is just this," she continued. "Put that money toward building a small place of my own here on the farm."

This proposal sent a little shock wave rippling through the group, resonating like Tolkien's Fellowship of the Ring being broken. "I've felt for some time now," Elizabeth continued, "that I'd prefer more private space, more solitude, than what this house allows." There couldn't have been a person at the table who wouldn't say something similar. To be honest, the collective jam and jostling, for all its ideological merit, was a royal pain in the backside a lot of the time. Earlier in the spring, simply to get some psychic elbow room, Jess and I had taken off in Viribus for a couple of weeks to camp in

200

Death Valley. We'd adored both the desert landscapes and the glorious emancipation of not having other people breathing down our necks every waking minute. Sitting at a small campfire one evening under a spectacularly bright sky of stars, coyotes singing from the far hills, we'd both guiltily confessed diminished enthusiasm for returning to the confines of the collective.

Now here was Elizabeth actually proposing a radical break. "Additionally," she said, "I'm very conscious that it has been me alone blocking Luis from joining us on the farm. I'm still of the opinion that he would not be a constructive addition to the group, but if I were living separately, his presence would be far easier for me to accept."

Ah-hah. So we might be inclined to think of this gambit as a strategic trade-off. Or a bribe. Agree to Elizabeth having her own place and she'll lift her veto of Luis. But the implications were considerable. Once the bond was broken, would others want to do the same? Would a soon-to-be-screaming two-year-old be as welcome in our echoing house as sweetly burbling baby Josie? Would our vaunted collectivity be scattered like so many autumn leaves?

"Okay," Jess said, "this obviously puts us at a crossroads. I suggest that we each give the whole thing some thought before discussing it further."

Meanwhile the world came calling. The new provincial government, its socialist pennants flapping, had only been in office for a few months, but progressive legislative changes were occurring at a breakneck clip. For one thing, free dental coverage was extended to anyone living below the poverty line. That would be us. We discovered a hip young dentist in town who took us all on, so that pretty soon our long-neglected molars and bicuspids were cutting, grinding and shining perfectly. On a broader canvas, the government got started on establishing an agricultural land reserve to prevent loss of farmland, something that previously had been happening at an alarming rate. Now soil types were being assayed and maps drawn.

It was fairly obvious that Figurative Farm would likely be included in any credible farmland reserve and this pushed us into a flurry of discussions over what restrictions might be imposed. Would Elizabeth's proposed new house, for example, be permitted? Would we be required to generate a certain level of agricultural output? Despite lofty intentions, at this point our primary agricultural product was Enzo's burgeoning pot business, but that wasn't likely to qualify. So while we celebrated the prospect of speculators and developers being chased off precious farmland, we weren't so crazy about Big Brother's boots tramping around in our own back forty.

Next thing we knew, a poster appeared on the bulletin board at the general store announcing that a committee of the legislature would be coming to Conception to "gather public opinion on matters affecting the islands." Okay. We were seldom, if ever, visited by persons of high rank, certainly not ones interested in our opinions, so you'd think this visitation would have stirred considerable excitement, but in fact hardly anyone nibbled. Luis, of course, was all over it. "They want our opinion?" he snorted. "Let's give them an earful!" Jess agreed. So the three of us huddled several times to come up with what might be said to the visiting dignitaries.

When we showed up at the community hall on the appointed afternoon, almost all the vehicles parked out front were a few expensive-looking sedans without any dust or dirt on them. Inside we were surprised to find eight MLAs, all middle-aged white gents, arrayed along a front table from which they faced row upon row of mostly empty chairs. They were a peculiar-looking bunch, several of them bearded, all dressed in what appeared to be recently-purchased authentic country outfits suitable for urbanites touring the boonies. Their shining boots, blue jeans and flannel shirts resembled uninspired choices from the costume department of a campus production of *Oklahoma!* Despite the fact this was an all-party committee, with representation from across the political spectrum, the uniformly countryfied threads meant you couldn't differentiate the socialists from the capitalists.

More formally attired, locals Gil Gilport and John Thomas were sitting together up near the front, whispering animatedly. The chairperson, a portly fellow with a winning smile, rose and called us to order. After introductions and preliminary remarks as to their purpose for being here, he invited public input. Immediately John Thomas stood, cleared his throat and began reading from a prepared text. Nobody's fool, John Thomas was hampered in formal public utterance by a vocal delivery bereft of nuance. Every perfectly enunciated word slid from his mouth as smoothly indistinguishable from its predecessor as from its successor, creating a composite impression of uninterrupted meaninglessness. He might have been proposing the most outlandish and incendiary undertakings imaginable, but none of it would stick, nor a word resonate anywhere. In conclusion he thanked the committee for their attention and sat down.

And it must be said that the committee offered an admirable impression of dutiful listening, although not one of them was inspired to ask John Thomas a question of clarification. You couldn't clarify what John Thomas had presented because he himself had clarified and reclarified to the point of invisibility.

Missing only a couple of beats in the awkward silence that ensued, Gil Gilport got to his feet and launched into an unscripted tirade that had all of the punch and passion missing from John Thomas's effort. The prospect of a rumoured agricultural land reserve was not at all to Gil's liking. "I own a full section of prime farmland," Gil growled to the suddenly attentive MLAs, "and I run it exactly the way I please. I wanna grow turnips, I grow turnips. I wanna run cattle, I run cattle. You understand what I'm saying?"

Yes, the MLAs all nodded, they understood Gil. The brighter among them might also have begun to understand that they'd probably have fared better if they'd shown up in their business suits. You can't fake Gil's brand of rustic authenticity. Gil's monologue rumbled forward like a Sherman tank. "Nobody's going to put my farm in any damn socialist reserve. You understand what I'm saying?" Yes, the MLAs all nodded.

"Nobody's going to tell me I can't subdivide it into quarter-acre lots if that's what I have a mind to do, right?" Right.

As usual, it was impossible to know what was actually going on in Gil's brain.

Did he really have a fear of imminent collectivization? That his land might be taken from him or at least put under some Stalinist regimen in which he was no longer master in his own house? That his fields would be overrun with morbid-looking Tolstoy peasants staring at him with baleful menace?

The bizarre thing was that Gil, who to us personified selfish individualism and right-wing narrow-mindedness, was in this slippery committee context transformed into a champion of personal liberty, a bulwark against the vile encroachments of state meddling in private lives. I almost broke into applause as Gil's comments drew to a close with a badly mangled quote from Barry Goldwater about how those who seek absolute power end up creating hellish tyrannies.

The next speaker was Slips Gainsborough, a pinkish and balding little gent of considerable dignity who owned several hundred acres of prime waterfront on the southeast side of the island. Slips's grandfather had been a remittance man back in the day, but unlike so many other problematic sons of English gentry, he had declined to return to the mother country for the purpose of sacrificing himself in the slaughterhouse of the First World War, opting instead to remain on Conception so as to continue developing a rough approximation of an English country estate. In its heyday, the property, replete with lawn bowling greens and tennis courts, had served as a gathering place for the island's elite, but in later years, under Slips's rather more private proprietorship, the estate had subsided into a picturesque locale for steady sipping of gin and tonics.

Although the reclusive Slips wouldn't have had a clue who we were, we happened to know a good deal about him and his family because our friend Mercedes had, as a teenager, sometimes been hired to assist with food and beverages when there were festive gatherings at the estate. We had come to learn, in the most discreet manner imaginable, that Slips had long ago suffered through a tragical romance, the melancholy ending of which had left him irrevocably downcast.

The primary focus of Slips's presentation was eliminating the temporary freeze on small lot subdivisions imposed by the previous government. "If a man decides he wants to subdivide his property, then for God's sakes he ought to be allowed to do it properly," Slips told the MLAs. Jess and I exchanged a glance. Was Slips planning on carving up Brideshead West? John Thomas and Gil applauded softly as Slips resumed his seat.

Next up came Johnny Spriggs, who was still doggedly persisting in his campaign to buy out the Waddington group. Although unprepossessing in appearance—shortish, prematurely balding, eyeglasses, wearing jeans and an Arnold Palmer mauve sweatshirt— he nevertheless exuded a confident charisma that was probably nurtured in private schools and executive offices.

Speaking without notes, he outlined for the MLAs the situation as he saw it—a willing seller with an acute consciousness of its public profile, an activist community with the panache to pull off this one-of-a-kind deal, and sufficient sources of ready liquidity to enable it to happen. When one of the legislators questioned him about the available liquidity, he launched into a long and convoluted exposition involving debt equity ratio, arbitrage, incurred but not reported reserves, scheme options, statutory liquidity ratio, accrual accounting and a whole bunch more. (I don't rightly remember if those were the terms he actually used, or if these are all newfangled monetary gimmicks fabricated during the intervening years.) His presentation was so bewilderingly abstruse, my head was ringing like an old cash register and, looking around the room, I suspected nobody else, including the panel, had a clue what he was talking about either. It wasn't at all clear what, if anything, Johnny expected the legislators to do. He thanked them for their consideration of his ideas and resumed his seat.

Saving the best for last, Luis rose as our spokesperson. Dressed entirely in black except for a vermillion bandanna knotted around his neck, Luis faced the MLAs like the spirit of Zorro lacking only a

205

sword and mask. "Gentlemen," he began firmly, "unlike the previous three speakers, my primary concern is not subdividing land for personal profit. Nor should that be your concern. In fact, quite the opposite. What we most urgently need to do is put a permanent stop to the exploitation of the islands by fast-buck artists." You could just about hear John Thomas and Gil Gilport straightening their spines, but Luis charged ahead full bore.

"These islands are special places that need to be recognized as such and protected. Period. I applaud the government's stated intention of removing agricultural land from speculative development. That's a start. But I believe we should also be moving toward maximum public ownership of the islands so that sizable portions of them can be set aside as working farms and nature reserves. What we don't need here is a shoreline ringed with waterfront cottages owned by rich city folk who come for a frolic for a few weeks of the year. Intelligently planned development as part of a larger conservation strategy is the smart way to go, in fact it's the only way to go if we don't want every island to become a third-rate Coney Island."

I was hugely impressed at how articulate Luis was sounding. Yes, he was forceful as usual, no surprise there, but not at all brash or abrasive the way he could get. I'd had misgivings about him presenting our perspective today, thinking that Jess was a more reliably skilful and convincing speaker. But Luis had said he could do it and Jess had supported him. So here he was, knocking it out of the park.

It was readily apparent that Luis was far more of a socialist than any of the government reps. I'd already talked with him enough to know that he had a deeply entrenched hatred of the capitalist system, the whole arrangement of a few fat cats at the top of the pyramid and a sprawling mass of indigents at the bottom. "I'm for overthrowing the whole fucking shebang," he told me once, "though I don't see it happening until the middle class gets sucked completely dry and that's gonna be a while yet. But, sooner or later, sooner or later, the fucking beast is gonna rise, man."

I felt pretty much the same, or should I say I *thought* much the same. Luis *felt* it. You could see it roiling in him at times like an ocean current, a visceral anger and fierce determination. At the end of the meeting, Jess and I congratulated Luis and left the hall by one door while Slips, Gil and John Thomas exited by another.

Nobody really expected much to come of this little charade except perhaps that Luis's bravura performance would help solidify his chances of joining us at Figurative Farm. However, some time later, there arrived in the mail a large manila envelope from the provincial government. It sat unopened on a counter for several days, but one afternoon when everybody else was out and about and I was keeping an eye on Josie, I opened it up and extracted an impressive-looking *Report to the Legislature From the Select Standing Committee on Municipal Matters*. Expecting little or nothing of consequence, I was amazed to find the report actually read like a gussied-up version of what Luis had told our urban cowboys. At my insistence, we all got together that evening, including Luis, and, sprawled in the living room, everyone listened as I read from the document.

"Of all the problems, the committee identifies large subdivisions and overdevelopment as the priority concern," I read from the report.

"Right on!" shouted Enzo, inadvertently awakening Josie who was sleeping in his lap.

"The right start anyway," Angus grunted.

"Listen to this," I continued. "Our belief is that the Islands are too important to the people of Canada to be left open to exploitation by real estate developers and speculators."

"Whoa!" everybody whooped.

"Sounds to me like that's pretty much exactly what Luis told them," Jess said. Luis just smiled.

"Under its recommendations," I continued reading, "the committee urged establishment of an 'Islands Trust' to 'assume the primary responsibility for all Gulf Islands affairs within government jurisdiction, including land use; future growth patterns;

control of development; industrial, recreational and commercial activity; as well as parks and open space designations."

Again, whoops of delight. Yes! We were going to be protected by a land trust. Lena sprang to her feet and spun in a whirling dance.

"Time to rock 'n' roll!" Luis cried triumphantly, one arm raised in a true revolutionary pose. We gathered around and mobbed him with claps on the back and appreciative hugs.

ROSALIE IS NOT OVERLY IMPRESSED BY THIS POTENTIALLY PIVOTAL moment in the history of Conception Island. "I am," she tells Shorter, "increasingly concerned about the question of authenticity, since we're now dealing with official government business where errors of fact could have serious legal consequences." In that context, she looks at him intensely. "How securely can memory be relied upon to provide an accurate recall of undocumented events?"

"Oh, come on now," Shorter says, a bit vexed. "We hashed out this question at the very beginning of this project. Why would you possibly want to drag it out again at this late date?"

"Yes, of course," Rosalie concedes, sensing again a stiffening of attitude, "But back then we were discussing the details of personal interactions. Now we're talking about government ministers, which is an entirely different matter." She hastens to add, "It's excellent that you've included specific quotations from the legislative committee report. That certainly adds a ring of credibility to the account."

Shorter's a bit bemused, as he was the day he unearthed the dog-eared document in the attic, that he still had the damn thing lying around after all these years. "Well," he tells Rosalie, "the fact of the matter is I've got a couple of old filing cabinets upstairs that are stuffed to the gills with letters and speeches and petitions and Christ only knows what else going back to almost our earliest days at the farm. Not my doing, of course, no," he says, "it was mostly

Jess and Lena who undertook keeping important papers filed. Some of it's obvious stuff like land taxes, income tax, house insurance, that kind of business. But a lot of the files pertain to the crazy campaigns and issues we managed to get ourselves embroiled in over the years. Jess's newspaper clippings and other writings are a big part of the trove for sure. That's how come I'm able to provide some of these verbatim accounts."

"Yes," Rosalie agrees, "such documents are invaluable, but, much as you might not want to hear it, apart from the public policy angle, I'm increasingly concerned about how reliable your memories are of particular people and specific encounters. Nuances. Was Elizabeth quite the frump you make her out to be? Or Lena the sweet innocent? Was Luis really the lionheart you're showing us? Was Gil Gilport actually a threatening redneck, or just a simple farmer worried that the way of life he'd always known was now falling to pieces?"

Irritated, Shorter begins to explain once more that of course these are remembered impressions filtered through the hazy post-impressionism of passing decades, but Rosalie brings him up short. "Yes, yes, I realize we discussed this very thing at the outset," she says. "How legitimate can it be for us to present word-for-word conversations that occurred half a century before. Are we approximating? Are we paraphrasing? Or are we fictionalizing from mere wisps of memory and imagination?"

Vexed to say the least, Shorter reminds her that she had argued persuasively from day one that verbatim accuracy was neither possible nor necessary so long as we remained faithful to the underlying truth of the situation. "Surely you're not now moving the goalposts to an impossible position on the field," he challenges her.

"No, no, there is no value judgment attached here," she hastens to reassure him. "Only a desire for clarity in our own minds as to what it is we are presenting to the world. We could afford to be fairly nonchalant at the outset, before we considered the possibility of wider publication. But now, thanks to your wonderful work, we're looking at something vastly more ambitious, requiring that we examine our methods far more closely than we'd imagined necessary at the outset.

"Plus," she carries on, "we have to seriously re-examine the whole question of genre."

"Genre?" Shorter asks.

"Yes indeed," Rosalie says. "Is the material truly personal history, or is it muddled with fictional elements, some wonky hybrid of the two? I don't in the least want to sound critical," she hastens to add, "but you have to admit that some of your grand elaborations give the impression of being grounded in imagination at least as much as in fact." Shorter can again feel himself bristling. "Could we perhaps think of it," Rosalie wonders, "as semi-fictional nonfiction. Biofiction perhaps. Or maybe autofiction."

All of this annoying blather drags Shorter dismayingly back to those interminable academic discussions about history's meticulous tracking of events that supposedly actually happened, as contrasted with fiction's imaginative deviations from fact in order to plumb the deeper mysteries of human existence. Of course he can't remember who exactly said what exactly all these years after the fact. But the truth of the situation, the actualness of what occurred—this, he believes, he is rendering with perfect accuracy.

EIGHTEEN

AS SUMMER DAWDLED ALONG TOWARD FALL, ACROSS THE TAWNY MEAD-
ows bigleaf maple trees glowed golden in a wash of low-slung
sunshine. Bright days of ripening and harvesting, congregations of
small songbirds busy with seeds and berries in the gardens. Right
around this time, the island's fine-tuned rumour mill started
churning out stories about the new Agricultural Land Commission.
Talk at various gatherings told of government agents sniffing
around the region in order to flag likely farmland for inclusion in
the proposed reserve.

Then, one particularly luminous October morning, sure
enough, a pair of clipboard artists came banging at our front door.
Impeccably civil civil servants in the polished urban/white/male
mode, they toured the farm, took copious notes and discreetly
enquired about our agricultural activities. Equally discreet, we
outlined certain grand agronomic plans still in the conceptual
stage while tactfully steering them away from the shed inside
which Enzo's outstanding crop was hanging to cure.

This visitation jolted us into making several critical decisions.
The first concerned Elizabeth's proposed and much debated new
house. We still hadn't resolved all the issues it raised, particularly
around privatization within the commune, but now under dur-
ess we realized it was better to get the damn thing built, or at least
started, before it might become illegal. Deeper considerations
could be addressed at a later date. Elated, Elizabeth immediately
cast about for a reliable builder, but the best she could come up
with was Brady Lazarus, who was generally regarded as competent but limited in inspiration. Cabins not castles, that was our

Brady. He agreed to take the job on, subject to his hiring Luis as his right-hand man.

"Tonya's doing, no doubt," Elizabeth sniffed at this sticky ultimatum. But having no better option she finally acquiesced to having Brady design and build her new home. My own response was equivocal too. For sure I was pleased to have Elizabeth out of our house, the sooner the better (her latest attachment to "keepin' it real" was a clincher), but, truth to tell, I'd soured a bit about having Luis around full time. Yeah, no question he was a skilled worker, and on the political front an invaluable brawler, as he'd just shown in the legislative report. But. He had something on the go with Jess, I was sure of it.

Nothing you could put your finger on, nothing overt. I just sensed it the way you might sense a cougar or wolf somewhere silent in the woods behind you. Still I said nothing to Jess, and this wasn't like us, not to talk about a significant issue. I don't know what would have restrained me other than the fear of hearing what I didn't want to hear. Of course I raised no objection to Luis being hired on for the building project, how could I?

Part of Tonya's thinking, it soon became clear, was that she'd received an offer on her old house from people anxious to move to the island, meaning that she and the kids would be moving to Brady's place and her brother too would have to vacate straight away. What better angle for Luis to get a convenient toehold at Figurative Farm than by working here alongside Brady. Thus, by a kind of sticky osmosis, Luis got one foot inside the commune. The sale of Tonya's house concluded almost overnight and, with no place else to live, Luis asked if we'd allow him to park a trailer on the farm. Being on-site, he argued, would really accelerate getting Elizabeth's house closed up before winter. So, instead of his imagined hogan, he dragged in a decrepit old mobile home of sickly blue and set it up on blocks, mercifully out of sight behind the toolshed. Though Luis is long gone, the trailer's remains are still there, rusting and rotting in collapse.

Early on, perhaps conscious of his hazy position, Luis didn't frequently eat with the rest of us or participate in our fitful group meetings, but his energy vibrated around the farm, and even if he wasn't visible, you were aware of his presence. And his politics. One foggy morning I ran into him when he was freshly consumed with the mass murder of student protesters on the streets of Bangkok. A few days later it was Nixon's Saturday Night Massacre. Then the Yom Kippur War. From his perspective, this was an October of recurring tragedy. Of course these were unarguably horrid events, but Luis seemed to somehow co-opt them for his own purposes, extending a kind of weird proprietorship over them. Or so I thought. When I mentioned to Jess that I was finding the non-stop doomspeak a bit much, she looked surprised. "But he's spot on," she said. "We're living in troubled times."

Tell me about it.

Whenever extra bodies were needed on the construction— pouring concrete foundations, for example, or raising walls—Jess and Angus and I would pitch in. On these occasions it was pretty obvious to me that Luis, not Brady, was really masterminding the project. Since they weren't working from detailed architectural plans, the boys kept banging up against unforeseen complications. Luis proved by far the more perceptive at anticipating where problems might arise and suggesting how particular difficulties could be avoided. To his credit, Brady didn't seem to have a whole lot of ego around it and the two of them continued working together smoothly with only a couple hammer throw-downs at particularly vexatious points.

What was most intriguing in the process was observing the great conversion of Elizabeth. Being Elizabeth, she kept a sharp eye on how the construction was proceeding and didn't hesitate to say when she wanted certain things a certain way. Early on she conferred exclusively with Brady as her contractor and acknowledged Luis with a bare modicum of civility. But several times Brady couldn't figure out how to incorporate some new wrinkle she'd come up with—a glass room off the kitchen, an extended dormer in an upstairs bedroom—and would consult with Luis, who could quickly work out the logistics. Gradually, Elizabeth took to including Luis in these conversations and eventually she could be spotted sometimes conversing with Luis alone when Brady was elsewhere.

Naturally the rest of us had a good chuckle over the grand Elizabethan *volte-face* and weren't above sticking it to her whenever the opportunity arose. Freaky-deaky, as we'd say. Nevertheless, Elizabeth's little house steadily evolved toward a lovely, practical and enviably private small home.

A second consequence of the land commission types showing up was that it inspired Angus to push forward with his postponed pig-raising scheme. Although he was by far the most competent of us in terms of animal husbandry, he had no more experience than the rest of us in raising pigs. Nobody else kept pigs on the island in those days and we were too oblivious to wonder why. "I figure we should get a sow and a boar right from the get-go," Angus told us, "so we won't have any hassles with breeding." We tended to defer to Angus in practical matters, but when I mentioned this plan to Willie the next time Jess and I visited him he just about dropped contraband Bandy on her head.

"Oh, crap, no," Willie insisted, "you don't want a boar on the place. You think a billy's a handful, they ain't nothing compared with a boar. Way heavier than you are, tusks like meat cleavers, and unpredictable as hell. You'd need the Berlin Wall to keep him fenced. Boy-o-boy, you'd be better off with a rhinoceros in the living room. No, you don't want no bloody boar on the place!"

Rather than relying solely on Willie's assessment, we stopped at the public library and picked up a couple books on animal husbandry to bring home for Angus. They pretty much corroborated what Willie had told us, though in lengthier fashion. The manuals recommended that novice pig farmers start by buying "weaner" piglets a couple of months old and already weaned (duh!), then fatten them up for slaughter. At two hundred pounds or more each, the experts enthused, even a few pigs can net you a handsome profit. Alternatively, you can buy a pregnant sow that would give you as many as ten or more piglets, then you'd continue breeding her each year, same as with the goats. Unaware of the perils ahead, we left it with Angus to determine what would work best in our circumstances.

Meanwhile the Icarus lands had still not been sold, giving Johnny Spriggs and his committee elbow room to continue strategizing. We had something of a front-row seat because Elizabeth, along with Amrapali, sat on the committee and provided us with occasional updates. Community meetings were convened, at each of which Johnny repeated, essentially verbatim, his elaborate scheme for conjuring cash out of thin air.

Then he began pressing other island organizations, and even some individuals, to pledge contributions running up into six figures. This, he explained, simply demonstrated community support for the initiative and would never result in actual cash changing hands. Whether or not she sniffed fiasco on the wind, Elizabeth eventually withdrew from the committee on the grounds that her house-building project needed her undivided attention. Shortly after, Amrapali left the group as well, the speculation being that Johnny had pressed her for a pledge a touch too assertively.

Not surprisingly, the old guard wanted nothing to do with Johnny and his financial high-wire act. The Gilport boys, Gil and Waldo, were especially contemptuous, repeatedly referring to Johnny as Johnny Jump Up. Plus Gil was preoccupied with marshalling his resources against the socialists manoeuvring to confiscate his farm.

Then, suddenly, a lightning bolt: the Icarus lands had been sold! Cleesey down at the post office got word of it first and of course milked it for all it was worth, pretending he was far too busy sorting the mail to take time out to answer meddlesome questions about how much he knew and how he came to know it. Jess got on the phone right away to Bernard Frankl, who was infuriatingly tight-lipped about the business but finally did confirm that, yes, the Waddington Foundation had sold the entire tree farm to a logger from Sparwood named Spike Zlotnik. I immediately called an old pal named Harvey Young who lived up in the Interior. "Oh, shit, man," Harvey said to me after I explained what was going on, "that is one nasty motherfucker you got on your hands now. Zlotnik's a notorious cut-and-run artist, entirely unscrupulous and totally indifferent to community or environmental concerns." Harvey said Zlotnik specialized in buying large tracts of privately owned forestland, stripping off every last tree, then flipping the denuded acreage back onto the market and moving on. "Among his many crimes," Harvey told me, "he clear-cut a mountainside just up north of Harmer, eventually triggering a catastrophic land-slide into the Fording River. Good luck dealing with that asshole; I reckon he's a total hard-hat sociopath." It was hard not to conclude that the Waddington philanthropists had scoured the countryside to find the worst imaginable fiend to inflict upon us.

"Okay, gang," Jess said with a grim smile after I repeated what Harvey had told me, "looks like Fight Night in the Forest coming up."

ROSALIE IS FEELING PENSIVE ON HER NEXT VISIT. WEARING BLACK JEANS and a black hoodie, she exudes a funereal air. She seats herself wearily at the kitchen table, unable even to brew their customary tea, which Shorter sets about doing instead.

"You seem very troubled this morning," he says to her as he clatters with the cups. "Is there anything I can do for you?" She shakes her head no, as though she's beyond consolation and stares out the kitchen window to the barnyard.

A few sips of tea marginally revive her. "It's just that," she says eventually, "I fear we are on the cusp of tragedy."

"The logging, you mean?" he asks.

"That in part, certainly," she says. "But not just that. The forces coming into play within the collective itself. I so want your brave experiment to succeed, but unless I'm mistaken we're beginning to see the seeds of failure sprouting at every turn. Elizabeth mov-ing out, Luis nudging in. You and Jess in the desert, longing for

216

solitude. Was there nothing but naiveté at play here right from the get-go? I can't believe that's the case, but from what you've written lately, I fear we're on the brink of a piteous downfall." She sips her tea, pensive as a polymath.

"Plus the business with pigs," she continues. "Extremely disturbing."

"How so?" he asks.

"Well," she says after a moment's thought, "unlike your beloved chickens and goats, it seems to me pigs exist solely to be slaughtered. Fattened up and slaughtered, you said as much yourself."

"Sure," he says, "but you can say the same thing about beef cattle, lambs and the rest."

"Ah, yes," she says. "But don't you agree that pigs are somehow singular as highly intelligent creatures destined entirely for sacrifice?"

Before he can tell her that this is precisely the uproar that eventually engulfed the farm, she shifts focus again. "Tell me I'm wrong," she says, "but wasn't your great battle with the Waddington people eventually counterproductive in the worst kind of way?"

It's a question he and Jess debated for years afterwards. "Yes," he tells her. "Zlotnik and what he did to the community was monstrous. And Johnny Spriggs eventually proved himself a laughingstock. But how much of what happened back in those turbulent times sprang from our hubris or from the simple twists of fate, who's to say?"

"And this business with Luis and your wife," Rosalie says finally. "Who but a fool would fail to see heartache in the offing?"

NINETEEN

ONCE AGAIN WINTER CAME AT US LIKE A GRUDGE MATCH, BUT THIS TIME we imagined ourselves better positioned to withstand the onslaught. Our woodshed was reassuringly stocked with firewood; the pantry, root cellar and freezers were stuffed with food. All the animals had warm and dry places in which to hunker down. We'd even picked up an antique gas-powered generator for when (not if) the power lines went down.

Elizabeth soon decamped to her new house, although it was (as almost a prerequisite of new island homes) far from finished. She threw a housewarming party in November, just for our group, along with Brady and Tonya and their kids and Luis, plus of course Amrapali. We heaped Elizabeth with congratulations, then raised our glasses to salute the handiwork of Brady and Luis. Even we standby labourers got a token round of applause. Partway through the festivities, Elizabeth called us to order, then brought in the mutts, each of them wearing a large polka-dot bow tie around its neck. She had them perform a clever little choreographed dance routine to Lobo's numbing rendition of "Me and You and a Dog Named Boo." The sort of thing you'd see on *The Ed Sullivan Show*. As Jess said to me laughingly afterwards, just what every true-blue Trotskyite commune needs.

Somewhere beneath the cornball good cheer, envy was the true order of the evening—with big double-glazed windows, super insulation and a state-of-the-art woodstove, Elizabeth's cozy little abode made our dark and draughty old place seem all the more inadequate. As the days grew damper, colder and shorter, we bundled up in extra sweaters indoors and instinctively resurrected a familiar seasonal topic: whether we should seriously consider demolishing our rundown farmhouse and replacing it with something that better served our collective needs. A bigger communal kitchen and living area for sure, maybe serving as a central hub with private living spaces radiating out from it. Skylights and way more windows, like Elizabeth had. Eventually, as ritual required, someone threw cold water on the fantasy by reminding us that we didn't have any money for such an ambitious project.

Plus a powerful new voice was added to the mix. With Elizabeth's withdrawal, Luis had by small increments increased his participation in group affairs. Whenever talk turned to tearing down the old house, he was adamantly opposed. "This place is a classic," he'd insist, "it's beautifully built; the materials are priceless, all this old-growth fir and cedar. I mean, look at these posts and beams—you'd pay an arm and a leg for those at a lumberyard today." Whenever he was animated, which was a lot of the time, Luis spoke with compelling forcefulness. "And the workmanship is exceptional, far beyond anything Brady and I managed at Elizabeth's. No way, Jose, it would be like demolishing the Taj Mahal to build a burger stand." Of course it would, we agreed, allowing the chimera of a shiny new space with abundant light, warmth and privacy to recede into the gloom of November.

Lying in bed together on the night of Elizabeth's party, I asked Jess how she was truly feeling about her friend's departure from our household. Remember that our great communal enterprise had sprung into being with Jess wanting to include Elizabeth right from the outset. "Well, I'm really sad on one level," she said. "I thought back then that Elizabeth would be a soulmate, which obviously she never truly became. And I hoped that you would come to appreciate her, which of course you never did." I stirred uneasily in the bed, unable to deny that my attitude toward Elizabeth had been tainted with mean-spiritedness from the get-go.

"Why not, I wonder," Jess said. "Could it have been resentment from seeing her as a rival for my affection?"

"Hardly," I scoffed. "I knew all along you were smarter than that."

She snorted in response. "Well, I can't believe that you were dense enough to resent her as an uppity woman."

Well, I sort of did, but wasn't about to confess it. "No, I think it was more being turned off by her thinly veiled class pretensions."

"Or maybe you just had a gut-level distaste toward her?" Jess said.

"Maybe," I agreed, although my class analysis was slightly less shabby. I was ready to stop talking about Elizabeth. I rolled over and made a show of drifting toward sleep. I mused that on balance, I was happy to now have Elizabeth at arm's length from the commune, but there did linger a sour aftertaste of failure, both personal and political, as well as a nagging sense of foreboding that this could be the start of a larger unravelling.

We knew from bitter experience during the previous two winters that the seasonal dark days required a forceful response, for sanity's sake. A few islanders were in the habit of fleeing south to Mexico for the winter where they'd idle away time splashing in surf and tequila, but none of us had the instinct or the cash for it. Equitably divided, the profits from Enzo's cannabis crop would get us through the winter, but only just, and certainly wouldn't stretch far enough to include frivolous expeditions southward.

Instead we had little Josie. Right from the get-go, we'd all participated in her parenting so that she was completely comfortable with everyone. Even taciturn Angus could be turned into a sentimental melt with Josie cuddled in his arms. Now well into her second year, day by day she confirmed our collective conviction that she was a child of exceptional brilliance. Even while she was still babbling nonsense syllables, she seemed always on the verge of articulating shrewd insight. The first proper word she formed wasn't "mama" or "papa" or "doggy" but, amazingly, "Willie." Whenever any of us were visiting Willie, when possible we'd take Josie with us as well, both because Josie loved to see the old guy and because the tiny girl provided perfect cover for sneaking in little Bandy or Suzy. Truth to tell, Willie doted more on the dogs, but Josie loved him nevertheless. "Willie, Willie!" she'd cry excitedly on entering his dismal little room.

Soon she was calling each of us by name and using maybe a dozen other words, while plainly recognizing dozens more. Even at that stage, she loved listening to any one of us reading aloud to her, reading anything from Dr. Seuss (Enzo theatrically reading *The Cat in the Hat* or *The Sneetches* would put her in stitches) to Shakespeare. (I read her *A Midsummer Night's Dream* two or three times. She'd lie in her bed unaccountably enthralled by the antics of Puck, Nick Bottom and Tom Snout the tinker before drifting off to her own dreamland.) Enzo was already imagining a Rhodes scholarship.

From tentative initial steps before her first birthday, she was now walking confidently and, thanks to an early-developing taste for goat's milk yogourt with applesauce, seemed to be nearing the point of self-weaning. What didn't go nearly as smoothly was the whole teething ordeal. Starting from around six months, her gums became inflamed and she sometimes had a nasty rash around her mouth. She started suffering horrendous bouts of diarrhea, so that diaper washing and drying became a principal household chore. She didn't sleep well. Her bouts of irritability, while understandable, began getting on some people's nerves.

But the good far outweighed the bad, and looking back, I appreciate more than ever how generous Lena and Enzo were in sharing that baby's childhood with us all. Josie remained an abiding delight in the house, her tiny smiles and laughter a potent quick fix for seasonal gloominess. Then a wonderful thing: Lena and Enzo announced in the early days of December that Lena was pregnant again. Alleluia, we were high as kites!

While as unconstrained as ever, the Christmas party season was discordant with chatter about the expected arrival of Zlotnik's logging crew and what, if anything, we could do about it.

One morning as Jess and I are having a bowl of porridge together, Jess says to me out of the blue, "Shorter, I believe it's time we started a community paper."

"Cool-o-roonie," I say, just to be silly.

"No, I'm serious," Jess says, putting down her spoon like she's laying down the law. "We *have* been sort of spinning our wheels on this Icarus thing for the last couple of months, waiting to react to whatever comes next. So now it looks like the absolute worst *is* coming next and we're still kind of twiddling our thumbs."

"Spinning and twiddling, too—most impressive."

"*Shorter!*"

"You think a community paper would make any difference?"

"I do," she says, the way she does. "It would be a means of informing the community and galvanizing support against Zlotnik and whatever rough beast comes slouching after him."

She was right, of course. Moreover, the upstart progressive community newspaper in town, which had published her take-down of the Waddington Foundation, had folded ignominiously several weeks ago due to a gruesome lack of advertising revenue. As one of the dispirited old lefty co-owners put it: "If you can't sell advertising space during the run-up to Christmas, when the hell can you?" Jess had barely gotten under way contributing regular feature pieces (three cents per word) before the collapse. Unable to pay her the thirty dollars owed on her final piece—a searing exposé on the ludicrously inadequate sewage disposal system employed by one of the region's towns, involving a pipe disgorging raw sewage into a convenient hillside stream—the publishers had instead gifted her with an ancient Gestetner duplicating machine they'd had stored in the basement. Obviously this is what had given Jess her newspapering notion.

"We could call it the *Island Tatler*," she suggested, "you know, after the British society journal."

"I think that's still being published as a glossy lifestyles mag," I said, "and if so they'll sue the panties off you for copyright infringement."

"All the better!" Jess said with a laugh. "Think of the publicity!"

We rummaged around in a dark corner at the back of the pantry where we'd stored the Gestetner and lugged it out to the kitchen. The contraption was a real piece of work. You typed your copy onto special wax-coated stencils, the typewriter keys slicing precise perforations in the wax. Then you attached the stencil to a rotating drum and cranked the drum manually with a large handle. With rollers and drums revolving, ink bled through the perforations in the stencil, giving you page after page of identical copy.

You could envision revolutions being spawned in its spinning, hear the mutterings of Patrick Pearse and Mother Jones in the rumble of its drums.

We'd no sooner got the cumbersome beast set up on the kitchen table than Enzo wandered in.

"Ah, she's a beauty," he said, reverently touching the drums and rollers, the folding Bakelite handle and copy counting meter, the paper input board and output tray.

We told him our idea of starting a community paper and wondered how he'd feel about seeing his name prominently displayed on the masthead as head printer.

"With this baby?" he exclaimed, "Absolutely! How did that old poseur Archimedes put it? Give me a Gestetner large enough and a fulcrum on which to place it, and I shall move the world!"

And so the *Island Tatler* was up and running. Our ambition was to print once a month with a broad range of local content— news from the elementary school, sports events, credible (or not) rumours, poetry and recipes along with an adult dose of local politics. At the outset Jess and I took on much of the writing with the hope that contributions would begin to flow in from all corners. Tonya volunteered to organize the schoolkids' writings so that every issue soon had a sparkling page of student contributions, including poems and cartoons. Older poets of various pedigree heaped us with offerings. Julie Getz, relatively silent since the great Community Club debacle, took on contributing a book review every month, each one excellent but invariably critical of the book in question. Mordecai Richler, Margaret Atwood, Brian Moore—all suffered the iconoclastic lash of Julie's disapproval. (When I asked her once why she hadn't reviewed Alice Munro's *Lives of Girls and Women*, she looked at me with surprise and said, "Because I *love* that book!") Another Community Club emeritus, fiery Charles Jimson contributed a monthly column titled "Bring Back the Lash!"

in which he vented vehemently against evil and injustice locally, nationally and globally. I took on doing a column called "Tatler's Tales" in which I felt free to speculate on all manner of delicious morsels circulating through the community. (I'm sure my erstwhile thesis supervisor would have wept had he seen it, but I flattered myself that my insights were perfectly attuned to the celebrated style of the original "Tatler" journalist and editor, Richard Steele.)

Just how this exuberant printed potpourri was going to assist in withstanding the imminent onslaught of the loggers remained unclear, but the paper was mostly huge fun to produce. Lena became really adept at typing the stencils, and they demanded absolute perfection: any single letter incorrectly typed required meticulous resealing of the wax over the mistake and retyping across the seal—not something you wanted to do very often. Once the two dozen stencils were finished, Enzo assumed command and printed off the required eighty copies of each page. To have expected twenty-four different stencils to go through the Gestetner's rolling drums and squishing ink eighty times without mishap would be insane; mishaps we certainly had. On several separate occasions Enzo's frustrations boiled over. He'd throw off his printer's apron, denounce the Gestetner as an impossible piece of shit, declare his final and irrevocable resignation and storm out of the house. Hours might pass—on one occasion two days—before he could be lured back in to resume printing.

Collating the pages was far more fun than typing or printing. We'd lay out the two dozen stacks of pages, odd-numbered sides up, all around the big kitchen table, then each of us circled the table picking up one page after the next. Then we'd staple each complete copy three times down the spine until all eighty were done. Of course there were invariably more copies of some pages than others, and occasionally certain pages went in upside down or back-to-front, partly due to the frequency of toking that increased as the afternoon wore on. But by the end of the day we'd have our eighty copies, warts and all, and be feeling mighty pleased with ourselves.

Distribution was a tricky issue from the get-go. Because of the vagaries of the postal system, it was easier and less expensive to do a bulk mail-out to every postal box on the island rather than individually address fewer subscription copies. Down at the post office, Cleesey just about had a bird the first time Enzo and I marched in with two cartons full of copies for distribution.

"What's this then?" he asked, reminding me of Holden Caulfield's teacher holding out his essay like a turd. Of course as postmaster he couldn't refuse to distribute the *Island Tatler*, but the general store, specifically the redoubtable Mable Sutcliffe, could, and did, refuse to have it anywhere on the premises for sale to visitors.

Many of the straight islanders ignored the *Tatler*, undoubtedly hoping it would soon fold and leave them in peace, but several old pot-lickers couldn't resist the temptation to vent. What they lacked in coherence, they more than compensated for with depth of feeling, largely along the lines of "Why don't you people go..." with some truly colourful suggestions as to what we might go do.

I don't imagine Spike Zlotnik was trembling in his caulk boots over the emergence of the *Tatler*, but, if nothing else, the paper aided enormously in keeping that year's rainy and snowy midwinter blahs at bay.

FROM THE MINUTE SHE FIRST STEPS THROUGH THE DOORWAY ON HER next visit, it's obvious that Rosalie is a woman on a mission. "Tell me, Mr. Shorter," she says with unaccustomed formality while hanging up her coat, "what has become of this house that Elizabeth had built? Is it still standing?" Shorter tells her yes, it's still there, tucked away on the other side of the orchard well out of view.

"And is it occupied?" she wants to know.

"No," he says. "There's been nobody in it for years."

"But it's habitable still?"

"Certainly," he tells her, wondering where this line of inquiry is heading, for it's surely heading somewhere. He's already alert to the prospect of some long-lost nephew or cousin of Rosalie's needing a place to stay.

But no, turns out it's him she's got in her sights. "Wouldn't it be far more convenient for you to live in a smaller place?" she asks. "One that's well designed, easier to clean, keep warm and so forth?"

"Yes," he tells her, "it likely would be more convenient, but not sufficiently so."

"Why on earth not?" she asks in a tone suggesting that he's being unnecessarily difficult.

"Well, for one thing, it isn't home," he explains. "Never was and never will be. Plus there's too much of Elizabeth prowling around in it."

"What? Like Banquo's ghost," she says derisively.

He laughs this off, as one does, but the thought of sitting alone at night in Elizabeth's house with the ghosts of regret floating in every dark corner sends a shiver through him. "I prefer the ghosts in this old place," he tells her. "Simple as that."

"Yes, I suppose you do," she says offhandedly, then drops the matter with an unconvincing pretense of breeziness.

"I'm delighted of course by Lena's pregnancy," Rosalie says as she plops down alongside him. "And isn't that little literary Josie just the cutest thing imaginable?"

"Absolutely," Shorter agrees. He really did love having to recall and describe those priceless moments of Josie's childhood. Just as she loved reading about them. An affectionate connection runs between the two.

"Now about the *Island Tatler*," Rosalie asks. "Do you by chance still have any copies?"

"I do indeed," Shorter tells her. "In fact, it was only this week I unearthed a complete set of them up in the attic. Miraculously they hadn't been chewed to pieces by the mice."

"You've mice in the house, have you?" she asks.

"Hell, every house on the island's got mice," he says with a snort. "And roof rats as well in most of them. All tearing the insulation to bits."

"Yes, well I suppose I'd have them too if it weren't for Astrophe and Aclysim," she says.

"I guess," Shorter quickly agrees before any cat talk can get under way.

"So," Rosalie says, "the old copies of the *Tatler* must be proving extremely useful in providing tidbits for our purposes, are they not?"

"Absolutely," he says. "Stuff I've forgotten long ago. Stuff you'd think you'd never forget, but you do."

"Oh, yes, I know all about selective forgetting," Rosalie says.

TWENTY

ON ONE OF THOSE INFREQUENT BUT GLORIOUS MID-FEBRUARY INTER-
vals when winter's grip loosens, pale sunshine warms the earth
and hints of spring peep out like miniature green explorers, a
big half-ton truck rumbles into the yard and pulls up over near
the chicken run. Angus clambers out from the passenger side
and a stranger jumps down from the driver's side, a rangy character in cowboy hat and boots, torn jeans and fringed buckskin
jacket. Several of us watch with interest from the kitchen window.
"Shall it be male or female? say the cells," I muse aloud, cleverly
referencing Dylan Thomas, because you couldn't tell about this
driver. The back of the truck is boarded up with heavy planks,
and we can just make out through the gaps something very large
moving about.

As I believe I've made clear by now, Angus was by far the least
capricious of our group. Constancy marked his comings and
goings around the farm. When it was time to tip-prune the apple
trees, there was Angus, up on the orchard ladder artfully snipping
with his secateurs. He seldom went anywhere else or spent time
with anyone else. If a girlfriend had suddenly appeared, or a boyfriend for that matter, we'd have been both delighted and amazed.
So of course we were intrigued to see him appear in this unfamiliar
vehicle with its intriguingly androgynous driver.

"Omygod!" Jess exclaims excitedly. "I think Angus has found us
a pig!"

We hustle outdoors—Jess, Lena and I with Josie toddling
behind—and over to the truck.

"Greetings, friends," Angus hails us, "this is Jones."

"Hi," Jones says with a lopsided smile. Up close Jones is as indeterminate as at a distance. Tall and handsome in a weather-beaten way. Poor teeth. Dirty blond hair shorn short beneath the Stetson.

"And this," Angus announces grandly, while removing one of the planks of the truck's cage, "is Persephone!" An enormous golden-red pig looks out at us with alert and tiny eyes. Her ears stand erect, her snout's long and straight, bluntly ending with two magnificent nostrils. After surveying us all beneath her, she grunts wondrously. The odour I'd mistakenly attributed to Jones is plainly from the pig.

"She's a Tamworth," Jones tells us while caressing the pig's head tenderly. "A heritage breed. Super hardy. Does really well outdoors. Perfect for a set-up like yours."

"Oh, she's lovely!" Jess exclaims and reaches up to stroke the sow's head. You'd swear the pig was smiling at us.

Little Josie wants to touch this wonderful new creature too. "Is it safe for her?" Lena asks.

"Perfectly," Jones says. So Lena lifts Josie up and the girl stretches out a tiny hand to touch the pink protruding snout. Suddenly the pig's long wet tongue engulfs Josie's hand and the child squeals with delight.

"Sweet as sugar," Jones says, "but she's a four-hundred-pound handful still." And you're an enigma still, I think to myself about Jones. Even close up you can't tell whether this character is male or female; what's confounding is why it matters to me. But somehow it does.

Working together, each with a bucket of apples, Angus and Jones lure Persephone down planks angled from the truck bed and across to where, unremarked by the rest of us, Angus has already roughed up a temporary piggery giving onto one of the mead-ows. Persephone passes through the gate like a visiting dowager aunt, looks around her new digs with what appears to be approval, grunts a couple of times and flops on the ground, making herself perfectly at home. "She could bust out of the fencing if she really had a mind to," Angus says, "but I'm guessing she won't bother. She's free to wander in the meadow whenever she wants. Lots of food to grub for and lovely mud for wallowing."

"Plus she's got other things on her mind," Jones says, pointing to the rows of succulently swollen red teats lining the animal's plump belly. "She'll be having her babies before too much longer and then the fun really begins."

Persephone grunts, as though in agreement, and enthusiastically chomps down on her remaining apples. Drawn by the commotion, the goats Sara and Gracie saunter up from the adjoining meadow and stare across the fence line in apparent disbelief at Persephone. Though both are rounding nicely with babies of their own, the goats look like emaciated stick-critters compared to the enormous sow.

She really was a compelling specimen, soon showing herself to be super intelligent and endlessly inquisitive. Within days we'd all fallen in love with her. She'd excitedly greet any of us whenever we came down to the piggery (from the get-go we'd been unanimous in calling her abode a piggery rather than pigpen or especially pigsty), snorting and snuffling, frisking us for food, and rolling over to have her prodigious belly rubbed. Little Josie was entranced by her. "Purse-a-pee!" she'd call out, clapping her hands excitedly.

Queen of the underworld. Vegetation goddess. Cult figure of the Eleusinian Mysteries. That was Purse-a-pee, now reigning among us.

As chief architect of this great leap forward in our farmership, Angus permitted himself to preen just a bit. Turns out that Jones, whom he'd bumped into by chance at the feed store in town, ran a farm on Vancouver Island that specialized in raising Tamworths. By brilliant coincidence, Persephone was needing a suitable new home just as we were needing her. The timing couldn't have been better because the surveyor of taxes had only recently advised us that if we didn't generate at least $2,000 of agricultural product per year, our farm status for taxation purposes would be revoked and our property tax would skyrocket. Persephone the Pig would be our saviour.

I guess it was a season for saviours, because within days big news broke that the provincial legislature was creating an Islands Trust, putting most of the islands in the Strait of Georgia into a land trust with the aim of preserving and protecting them in perpetuity. The report of the Select Standing Committee, which we attributed mostly to Luis's fiery submission, had actually been taken seriously! Overnight we found ourselves suddenly, blessedly living within a land trust. Preserve and protect indeed. Take that, Spike Zlotnik! Duck and cover, all you exploitive assholes! By way of celebration, under a brilliant quarter moon, we lit a huge bonfire in the yard and invited everybody over for a corybantic dance party that carried on until dawn.

Still under the influence, we started putting together a special edition of the *Tatler* devoted entirely to the new Islands Trust. Which was right around the time the euphoria bubble burst. Jess got her hands on a copy of the freshly minted Islands Trust Act and read it through carefully. "Better put a hold on the champagne," she told us at lunch. "You know the section of the act that empowers the trust to acquire and hold lands?"

"Yeah," I said, "what about it?"

"Not enacted," she said. "It's in the act but not enacted."

"That's weird," Luis said. "Can they do that? Enact an act, but not a part of it?"

"Just the beginning," Jess went on. "Remember how the committee recommended that the trust should control everything under provincial jurisdiction, you know, be the decision maker on issues around forestry, land development and everything else?"

"Don't say it," I said.

"Yep. All the ministries—Forests, Highways, Lands and Parks, regional districts—still get to maintain their little empires. Nobody's toes getting stepped on here."

"Fuck!" Luis said. "What does the goddamn trust get to do?"

"Looks like consultations and referrals mostly. Each of the thirteen big islands will elect two local trustees and then—wait for

231

it!—the provincial government will appoint three general trustees and together they'll form a trust council to deal with general issues while a local committee will deal with stuff specific to each island."

"Not exactly *Viva la Revolución*," I said.

"Not quite," Jess agreed, tossing the emaciated Islands Trust Act onto the table.

"Just as well we got to party down before we'd read the act," I said.

Luis picked up the act and asked Jess if she was finished with it, which she said she most decidedly was. He fetched down a jar of peanut butter and spread a generous amount across the pages of the document.

"Lemme guess," Jess said, laughing. "Persephone?"

"Precisely!" Luis replied with a wicked grin. So we all marched down to the piggery, as though in ritual procession, and fed the dysmorphic act to snorting Persephone.

Our special *Tatler* edition veered considerably away from the triumphalist tone we'd started with. As Enzo summarized the situation while printing off the pages, the new Islands Trust, while falling considerably short of what we'd hoped for, was still better than hydrochloric acid in your coffee.

Which was about what we got shortly afterwards in the form of Spike Zlotnik. We never saw the man himself, so were free to continue picturing him as a low-life roughneck with snot running down his beard, but his crews descended upon us like a ravening horde, arriving in big pickup trucks, several of which bore a bumper sticker across the front hood warning "Think fast, hippie!" Chainsaws roaring all day, trees thumping down like a funeral march, gigantic loaded logging trucks shouldering their way along narrow roads and onto the ferry. The hateful days of the Waddington episode seemed by comparison almost genteel. And predictably there was no shortage of commentary about how some of us had brought this havoc upon ourselves by being so confrontational with the good souls from Waddington.

Much of the community was in a kind of dumbfounded shock. Emergency meetings were convened and different strategies debated. One group of gentle souls set up a kiosk at the ferry landing to publicly lament each truckload of dead trees that left the island. Jess spent her days pounding out condemnatory articles about what was happening and sending them to every newspaper and magazine she could think of. A few fitful blockades were thrown up, but the blockaders were roughly bundled off to jail with scarcely a beat missed in the logging. "No leverage in that," Luis said. "Zlotnik's got no reputation to protect, the way Waddington did." Plus, while Zlotnik may have been a scumbucket, he was a crafty one; he hired on a half-dozen local workers, including several from the Gilport clan, thereby cementing a faction of local support for the logging.

As the darkness deepened, one particularly gloomy afternoon Luis took me aside. "So what d'you think, Shorter?" he asked me in an undercover kind of voice.

"Screwed if I know," I said. "I hate what's going on and I don't know what the hell we can do to stop it."

"You thought any more about monkeywrenching?" he asked.

Yes, of course I'd thought about it. A paperback copy of *Ecotage!* by David Obst and Sam Love had been lying around the house for quite a while and I'd thumbed through it, but hadn't found a whole lot that seemed applicable to our remote situation. I said as much to Luis.

"I ain't talking about publicity stunts, man," Luis said, "I'm talking about seriously fucking up their equipment."

There was a fierceness in Luis's expression that somehow reminded me of the Chicago riots, the wild look on the guy who tore down the Stars and Stripes and the other dude who hoisted a Viet Cong flag. Something on the edge of crazy. The way I'd been myself, momentarily, when I flattened the cop who'd been beating on Jess. I wasn't all that surprised to hear this line coming from Luis, because I'd seen enough flashes of anger to realize that in certain ways he could be a pretty volatile character. I told him I thought destroying property contravened the nonviolent principles of Cesar Chavez, about which he'd previously been so vocal.

"Different strokes, man," Luis said.

"What exactly do you have in mind?" I asked. He drew himself really close, so his face was almost touching mine.

"Nighttime raids," he whispered, "just you and me. Those motherfuckers are leaving their equipment in the bush overnight. Chainsaws, Caterpillars, skidders. We slip in there and inflict some major league damage."

I thought about it for a moment. A cheap thrill, no question, but would it really get us anywhere? "Sorry, man," I said, "but I don't see that making much of a dent in the long haul, you know what I mean?"

"Maybe not," he shot back immediately, "but it makes a statement, right? Just like not doing anything makes a statement. One I'm personally not prepared to make, and I don't think you are either. The Weather Underground has it right: doing nothing in the face of violence is itself a form of violence. For sure civil disobedience is the right tool in some campaigns. But when it doesn't fit the bill, I say pick up a fucking sledgehammer!"

I flashed for a second on the old Yeats line: "the worst are full of passionate intensity." Personally I didn't consider civil disobedience as one tool in the tool box. From long talks with Jess, and listening to the speeches of Dr. King and reading Thoreau's *de rigueur* essay on the topic, I'd swung over to the point of view that civil disobedience was a way of life, not just a tactic. Now, pressed by Luis's intensity, I questioned for the first time just how committed to the United Farm Workers' campaign of non-violence he had actually been.

Damn, it was an uncomfortable few days as I wrestled with the notion of vandalizing the logging show. Luis had insisted we not mention it to anyone, not even Jess or others on the farm. Absolute secrecy. Which made me that much more uncomfortable. So I wrestled alone. Was clandestine smashing of equipment just another form of violence, doomed to failure? Or was it, as Luis urged, what you did, must do, when you had no other recourse? Visions of the French Resistance, Che Guevara, Black Panthers, all the revolutionary icons of our pseudo-revolutionary youth.

Luis pressed me for an answer. "Moonless nights right now, man," he said. "Primo conditions."

Still not convinced, but not unconvinced either, I finally caved. Jess happened to be away for a couple of days, which made things easier. But not easy; I was drenched in misgivings. But one night, dressed completely in black, and shouldering a small backpack of what I imagined were monkeywrenching tools, I slipped out of the house around two a.m. and made my way silently toward Luis's trailer. I couldn't see a single star through thick cloud cover. The night was so black you could touch it. I kept my faint flashlight beam aimed at the familiar ground immediately in front of my feet. Tree frogs erupted suddenly into intermittent croaking and just as suddenly fell silent. I felt as though I should be carrying a rifle, advancing stealthily with grizzled fellow partisans toward targeted enemy outposts.

Suddenly Luis loomed up right in front of me outside his trailer. Every light was out. All I could see were his eyes and realized he had blackened his face. "Here," he whispered urgently, pressing something into my hand, "I can see your shining gringo puss from fifty paces." I took the proffered rag and applied what turned out to be black boot polish to my face and hands. Absurdity seemed to press as close as the darkness.

We both mounted old bicycles and cycled slowly, silently out of the farm and along the tree-lined tunnel of West Road toward the nearest cutblock, not far from where we'd first confronted the Waddington loggers. With no farms or houses in the vicinity, not a single light was visible. Luis had scouted the place well and we soon came upon a landing in which sat several skidders and a big D8 bulldozer with a small Quonset hut off to one side. A stench of diesel oil and spilt sap.

"Hut first," Luis whispered as we dismounted. The hut door was secured with a large padlock. "Warded," he said with a contemptuous snort. He rummaged in his backpack and extracted a key ring holding a half-dozen large keys. He selected one and brandished it like a stiletto. "The lovely warded pick," he whispered to me, "a.k.a. the common skeleton key." He had me aim my flashlight while he inserted the key into the padlock and manipulated the key delicately for a few moments. I could hear clicking and rustling sounds coming from the nearby woods and felt a sickening jolt of fright when a barred owl suddenly shrieked close by. A few moments more, then the padlock sprang miraculously open. "Voila!" Luis whispered triumphantly. He was plainly enjoying all this in a way that I wasn't.

We opened the door and slipped inside the hut. Since it was windowless, we could shine our flashlights freely. Like silly undergraduates of film noir, we put on rubber gloves to avoid leaving fingerprints. Several large gasoline cans along with cartons of fuel oil and chainsaw oil sat stockpiled on the ground. Although tempted to, we realized we couldn't just dump them all, so we set about mixing the fluids freely, throwing in handfuls of sand from the floor. "I *don't* believe we have ignition," Luis said, chuckling. Then we attacked the chainsaws, several smaller ones alongside six Bunyanesque Stihl 090s identical to the one Willie had left us. Seriously sized saws. We feverishly dismantled all of them, breaking filters, pins, triggers and anything else vulnerable to the ball-peen hammers we'd brought along. We took the chains with us to dump in the woods.

Back outdoors we attacked the skidders, cutting whatever wires or lines our loppers and wire cutters could handle, smashing gauges, battery terminals and anything else we could, which wasn't much. Despite our best efforts, we failed to break the valve stems on the big tires. Luis tried but failed to drill into the tires with an antique brace and bit. The hulking machines were built to withstand far more punishment than puny humans could inflict by hand. Eventually we had to satisfy ourselves with pouring a generous dose of sand into each gas tank. The big D8 was even more impregnable and we scarcely inflicted much damage on it at all. We whispered about maybe lighting a fire under it but decided against the high-risk gamble of possibly igniting the whole forest in order to save the trees. "What we really need is a couple of propane bottle bombs," Luis said. Was it a joke, or was the guy actually wired to violent destruction?

Having done as much damage as we could, we brushed out our footprints using cedar boughs, remounted our getaway bikes and, flinging saw chains into the bush as we went, rode back through darkness. The entire ride home I was suffused with wild exhilaration over our audacity. We'd done it! Bloodied the fucking tyrant's nose. Truly delivered a blow against the empire.

IN THE COLD LIGHT OF SOBER SECOND THOUGHT, SHORTER IS MORE apprehensive about Rosalie's next visit than any previous one. The misgivings he's now feeling are strangely reminiscent of the doubts he'd started having shortly after the monkeywrenching episode itself. That it had been dishonourable behaviour in some way. The furtiveness of it a kind of dishonesty. As though we were really no better than the people we sought to hassle. And yet, at the same time, an undeniable thrill at having poked the monster's bloodshot eye with a sharpened stick.

When she does finally arrive Rosalie begins fussing about for several minutes, the whole time maintaining a disconcerting silence. Once again she's dressed entirely in black, as Luis and Shorter had been on their misbegotten raid, which strikes Shorter as her overdoing things just a touch. But, amused at how disconcerted Shorter plainly is, she calmly places their tea things on the table as though in preparation for the Paris Peace Conference.

They sit uncomfortably together without speaking. Shorter's convinced she's hugely disappointed, now imagining him a low-life vandal. As well as a coward. The very epithets he'd eventually directed at himself following the midnight mischief. Deceiving Jess was the worst of it and he wishes more than anything that he could have undone that particular strand of dishonesty.

Why on earth did he ever align himself with Luis's hare-brained schemes at the price of disloyalty to his life partner? Rosalie, he imagines, must surely be feeling the same way. Shorter's again forced to consider whether this whole memoir thing isn't a serious mistake. Maybe it's far preferable, certainly more prudent, to let all of this ancient detritus sink to the bottom of the pond and be forgotten. Then a dignified exit.

Just as he's about to say as much, Rosalie looks at him meaningfully and says, "You must realize, Mr. Shorter, that I consider the introduction of Persephone by far the most disturbing aspect of your tale thus far."

He can't quite believe she'd say such a thing beneath the looming shadows of far darker truths—his breaking the law, enraging Zlotnik, deceiving his wife and all the rest of it. "You don't seriously mean," he asks her, "that you think the arrival of a pig was more significant than our clandestine criminal activity?"

"Oh that," she snorts dismissively. "Boyish pranks! Superficial silliness. I'm actually surprised you even bothered to include it."

Boyish pranks? Is that all she thinks of their great derring-do?

"And feeding the Islands Trust Act to the pig—what were you numbskulls thinking?" she asks.

"Yes, of course you're right," Shorter concedes, "but that was mostly Luis overreacting and the rest of us just going along for a lark."

"No, no," Rosalie persists, "the appearance of Persephone resonates far more profoundly than that. Unless I'm greatly mistaken, this is a pivotal point in your entire communal undertaking." As things evolved, that turned out to be painfully accurate, but how on earth could Rosalie know?

"Dread Persephone!" she now declaims with perhaps excessive melodrama. "Goddess of Death carried to the underworld by the rapist Hades!" Then Rosalie gazes down from her rhetorical peak and pronounces: "You can't seriously imagine that a bit of schoolboy mischief dismantling chainsaws is of more consequence."

TWENTY-ONE

THE ISLAND AWOKE THE FOLLOWING MORNING TO A TRANQUILIZING silence. No roaring of saws and skidders in the distance, no wailing lamentations of trees in death throes. "Mighty quiet out there," Angus reflected as he and I ate breakfast. "Oh, by the way, you've got some funny black stuff in your eyebrows and sideburns, might need a little cleaning up." Good old Angus, grand master of understatement.

Word of the monkeywrenching spread like a grass fire in August. Rumours of who may have been responsible hopscotched across the community, with certifiable hotheads like Charles Jimson or old Wobbly Ian McKenzie topping lots of people's suspects lists. Luis wasn't beyond suspicion, for sure, but Figurative Farm didn't seem to be high on anybody's radar. CFOK radio up in town repeatedly led off their local news with breathless updates of what they were calling eco-terrorist attacks on Conception Island. The local RCMP detachment announced that investigations were already under way and that bringing the perpetrators to justice would receive top priority.

At the farm we spent most of the day fielding phone calls from hyperventilating news outlets in Vancouver and Victoria, the very places Jess had been sending her stories—which until then had been met with yawning indifference. Now everyone wanted the inside scoop on who the island eco-terrorists were and what demands were they making. I was half-expecting the feckless Bernadette O'Hare to show up at our front door with her film crew. Mostly I was wishing like hell that Jess was home to handle the calls, even though it might have involved breaking my pledge of secrecy with Luis. What a royal cock-up!

By default I ended up taking most of the media calls and of course dissembled shamelessly about who might be responsible for vandalizing the equipment. I suggested that this extremist response really should come as no surprise, emphasizing how dismayed many islanders were at the rate and scale of logging, the blatant disregard for waterways and wildlife. The wonder was that sabotage hadn't occurred earlier, I said, silky master of the disingenuous. Yes, the newshounds pressed me, but how much community support did I believe there was for this type of illegal activity? Did I think additional and possibly more flagrant actions were to follow? You knew they were all hoping so.

Zlotnik made the next move. By early afternoon two trucks carrying uniformed security guards and cages of fierce Rottweilers were spotted coming off the ferry.

The following morning dawned with the painfully familiar growl of chainsaws.

By the time Jess returned home that afternoon—and by God, I was relieved to see her—you'd almost think the whole episode hadn't really happened. Of course Jess was eager to hear about everything that had gone on and I talked at length mostly about dealing with the news outlets.

"Any idea of who actually did the dirty?" she asked me.

I mimed deep thinking for a moment, my inner self screaming, "Tell her! Tell her!" But my promise to Luis pinned me down. I squirmed between twin betrayals and, against every instinct and desire, against common sense and faithfulness, chose commitment to Luis over loyalty to Jess. For the first time in the four years we'd been together I broke the covenant that bound us, the one not mentioned in the marriage vows to love and cherish, the one that promises truth, undiluted truth, in all circumstances.

Luis approached me again a few days later. "Ready for a good counterpunch?" he asked me in his spy-coming-in-from-the-cold voice.

"What are you thinking?"

He had that same secretive, conniving aspect about him that I was beginning to recognize as a fixture of his personality.

"They'll have let their guard down now because nothing more has happened, right? Think we've been scared off by their dogs and fat-assed security. Perfect time to strike again."

I couldn't believe he was seriously proposing another clandestine raid. "What about the fucking Rottweilers?" I asked him.

"Piece of cake," he said. "Or should I say piece of meat. Like heavily laced with strychnine."

"You gotta be kidding," I said. But I could see he was being absolutely upfront. I tried to picture it: crawling stealthily through the woods, approaching where the killer dogs were prowling, throwing pieces of poisoned meat to them. The whole thing was so absurd I had to laugh.

"Count me out, man," I said to Luis. "For one thing I don't at all dig the idea of poisoning dogs; I'd prefer poisoning Zlotnik. Plus I'm not real big on suicide missions."

He argued forcefully that we could still do it, minimal risk, maximum exposure, but I held my ground, sensing that further duplicity toward Jess could be fatal in some way.

I'd let Luis down, I knew—almost betrayed him. Betrayal was becoming the subtext of this whole crappy episode, and all I wanted was out of it.

Not long afterwards, with fabulous irony, given the plunder and pillage going on in the woods, official notices arrived about local elections for the new Islands Trust. Two local trustees were to be elected to ensure the islands were being preserved and protected, but just who would be anointed was still very much up in the air. There was no shortage of speculation or rumour, just of hard fact. As I enjoyed doing whenever insider information was required, I arranged to drop in for tea with our dear friend Mercedes.

She greeted me at her front door with an expression of perfect innocence as though she didn't know full well just what I was up to. As usual when at home, she was wearing a flower-print apron over her dress.

"Oh, your May tree's divine!" I said to her, truthfully, but well aware of how she prided herself on its spectacular canopy of massed pink blossoms.

"Thank you, Shorter," she said drolly. "I have to admit it is quite fine this year." Which is what she said every year, except for once when a freakishly late snowstorm bent and broke a great many branches.

I followed her into her kitchen where she'd set out the tea things. She removed her apron before we sat together at the table. Although otherwise at ease, I always felt hopelessly oversized inside Mercedes's cozy home, as though any inadvertent movement might send a precious vase crashing to the floor. Typically, we began our conversation with her asking about little Josie. She was always interested in the child, and we Figuratives occasionally brought Josie to visit with her. I described Josie's electrifying vocabulary expansion in recent days.

"Oh, yes, at that age, so remarkable," Mercedes said, shaking her head and smiling inwardly, no doubt cast back to the days when her own children were toddlers. She enquired how Lena was progressing and I described as best I could the gentle grace of her pregnancy. Which led naturally enough to giving an update on our goats because Gracie was due to give birth any day now, and every summertime Mercedes made a point of bringing her young grand-daughters to the farm so they could frolic with the little kids. She was thrilled when I told her about Persephone and the likelihood of there also being a litter of piglets on the loose.

Then we inched discreetly toward the reason for my visit. I alluded to the Islands Trust elections in an offhand way. "Oh, yes," Mercedes nimbly picked up her cue, "quite a bit of jostling for position apparently."

"Really?" I said, as though this might not have occurred to me.

"Oh, yes. I have it on very good authority that at least one candidate has already filed."

I took a meditative sip of camomile tea. "Most interesting," I said, as though expecting nothing further.

"John Thomas, if you can believe it," Mercedes disclosed.

"Hm," I mused. "Well, not surprising really, is it, given his extensive experience at the senior government level." A patina of considered analysis can be fruitful in discussions with Mercedes.

"None whatsoever," Mercedes agreed, edging a platter of her homemade scones closer to me. "Married into an old island family, as he is."

"And implacable in his defence of common decency," I added drolly, thinking of Enzo and the skinny dippers. I took up a warm scone and spread on it some butter and Mercedes's irresistible homemade marmalade.

"A formidable candidate indeed," Mercedes said, leaving me an opening.

"Divine, as always," I said, indicating the scone, "but I would imagine that a shrewd operator like John Thomas would want to ensure that he had a compatible fellow trustee to work alongside."

"Ah, yes," she said, "and in that regard I have in fact only recently heard Waldo Gilport's name mentioned." This was a genuine surprise, given Gil Gilport's very public condemnations of the Islands Trust, the Agricultural Land Commission and the NDP government generally. His younger brother Waldo had the reputation of a troubled individual and not someone you'd automatically think of while discussing trustworthiness.

"The speculation being," Mercedes added, "that, as a pair, John Thomas could stickhandle through the legal technicalities while Waldo devoted himself more to public relations."

"Hm. Strange bedfellows, still," I said. "Now did I also hear that there'd been a flurry of excitement around the prospect of Mable Sutcliffe entering the race?"

"Can you imagine?" Mercedes said with a twinkle. "No, I happened to be in the general store the other day when Mable herself scotched that rumour with a tart comment that she had better things to waste her time on than this ridiculous trust."

Just as I thought we'd exhausted the topic, Mercedes threw in her showstopper. "No, for me the great surprise candidate has to be Slips Gainsborough."

"Slips Gainsborough?" I said in disbelief. We hadn't seen or heard from Slips since his unlikely presentation to the Select Standing Committee the previous summer. The scion of an old remittance man seemed the least likely candidate imaginable, but Mercedes explained that Slips had recently joined AA and taken to its restorative regimen with the same enthusiasm he'd previously devoted to his G&Ts. Treading the well-worn path of redeemed inebriates, he was now in search of a public good that he might do.

"No mention of Johnny Spriggs, though?" I asked Mercedes. We'd half-imagined Johnny might try reviving his faltering campaign by becoming a trustee.

"Not a peep," Mercedes told me.

I couldn't hope to match Mercedes's wealth of juicy information, but offered her the only tidbit I had: that our "Bring Back the Lash!" columnist Charles Jimson was poised on the brink of throwing his hat into the ring. He had, he'd told us fellow Tatlers a few days earlier, no expectation of winning, and would in fact be horrified if he did win, but looked forward to "skewering the establishment candidates" during the run-up. Needing something more to balance the ledgers, I finished up by describing to Mercedes the press tumult there'd been at our place after the monkeywrenching episode. As I took my leave, she gave me the most disconcertingly knowing smile.

Back home that evening our whole group had a lively discussion about who could make the best candidates to defeat the obvious front-runners, John Thomas and Waldo Gilport. We all agreed that neither Slips nor Charles Jimson had what it took to get elected or, even if elected, to function as a capable trustee. Jess would have been perfect, but being an American living in Canada for less than five years made her a non-starter.

The same would hold true for Luis if he'd had a notion to run, which he definitely didn't. We agreed Julie Getz could be listed as a maybe, and then Elizabeth suggested Amrapali would make a fantastic trustee but likely wouldn't be interested. As the conversation sputtered along, I could sense perimeters closing in around me.

Enzo lightened the mood momentarily by suggesting that we should run Persephone for trustee, the way the Yippies had nominated Pigasus for president in '68. Sitting on Enzo's lap, Josie shouted, "Purse-a-pee!" and clapped her hands. We all agreed with Josie that Persephone would win in a landslide, perform admirably as a trustee, but then likely abdicate in favour of returning to the muddy delights of her piggery. Then they all looked at me.

"What?" I said, laughing. "Next best choice after the pig?" I knew Jess had lots to say but wouldn't. Lena spoke instead. Her tummy was swelling noticeably now and everything about her glowed with a soft radiance. "Actually, Shorter," she said, "I think you'd make a brilliant trustee. You're incredibly smart and super articulate. You listen to people really well. You're seen as thoughtful and serious. Let's face it: you fit the job description perfectly. Doesn't he, Josie?" she asked and Josie again clapped her hands and shouted, "Purse-a-pee!"

Of course I was flattered by Lena's words, some of which I'd heard previously in our group appreciation rounds. I had little doubt that I could do the job, certainly more capably than Waldo Gilport, but would I want to work in close collaboration with John Thomas? Plus there was a broader unpleasantness involved, something about being in the public eye, being judged, challenged, disliked at times. And I really wasn't convinced that the Islands Trust in its throttled-down form would have sufficient power to be anything other than frustrating. Worst of all, I could perfectly foresee running a spirited campaign, scoring points in the all-candidates meeting, receiving pledges of support from all corners and then, within days of the election, suddenly being outed as an eco-terrorist, my candidacy sabotaged, leaving me humiliated like some Brylcreem politician caught in an illicit sex scandal.

Jess and I lay in bed talking late into the night about whether or not I should run. The pros and cons, the what-ifs, the gut feel of the thing. "Is there something you're not telling me?" she asked at one point, and there I was again on that fucking precipice, wanting nothing more than to come clean on the dumb monkeywrenching stunt but feeling that I couldn't. No question this had become a burden I no longer wanted to keep carrying. Just before floating away to sleep I resolved to speak with Luis about it tomorrow.

But tomorrow had other ideas. Early in the morning Lena came into the kitchen carrying a large basket of eggs she'd just gathered from the henhouse. Mostly under her watch our flock of chickens had expanded to several dozen hens and one lordly rooster. Egg sales now contributed a small but steady source of income. "I think Gracie's getting ready to have her babies," Lena said excitedly. Birthing days (or nights) were always special—sometimes chaotic, occasionally traumatic, but mostly exhilarating, with new life entering the world. Jess and Lena gathered what they needed and headed to the goat shed.

Late in the morning, the best of all outcomes—Gracie produced two perfectly formed and healthy female kids. No problematic billies to deal with, no wrenching breach births or stillborns. Not wanting to create a gawping spectacle, we took turns strolling over to the goat shed to admire our two new little beauties and congratulate Gracie. Josie and I went across together, hand-in-hand. She was mesmerized by the twins, who were already tottering around on spindly legs. "Baby gloats!" Josie cried with delighted laughter, "baby gloats!" I poured a small mound of special grains into Josie's cupped hands, which she then extended over the railing. Gracie stopped licking one of her babies and approached us. I was super alert because Gracie can be unaccountably cantankerous at times, responding aggressively to cues we're not even aware of. She sniffed Josie's hand, then delicately licked up the grains and stared at us knowingly with her peculiar oblong eyes.

"I VERY MUCH LIKE THE EMPHASIS YOU'VE PLACED ON SPRINGTIME BIRTH-ings in these latest pages," Rosalie tells Shorter. "The goats giving birth, Lena, the vernal basket of eggs. So appropriate for the season of regeneration. And equally appropriate that we don't have Persephone bringing forth her dread brood during the same interval." Shorter remains mystified how Rosalie keeps returning to this dire Goddess of the Underworld theme even though she has no prior knowledge of the unhappy events just ahead.

Aware of Shorter's puzzlement, she abruptly changes lanes into another familiar trope. "I've had what I think is a very fine idea," she tells Shorter, "Concerning Elizabeth's house." Now what? he wonders—it's already been established that he doesn't want to live in that empty house, for all its comforts. Nor does she.

"I strongly suggest that you not reject out of hand what I'm about to propose," she tells him, making Shorter all the more inclined to do so even though he hasn't yet heard what it is.

"You know that there's a severe shortage of affordable housing here on the island," she says, which he readily acknowledges, sensing now where this is likely going. "And you have to admit, Mr. Shorter, that you're no longer quite the strapping young fellow you were in your prime with respect to keeping this whole place running." No kidding. "So my thought is this," she says, "if you'll excuse my butting into something that's really none of my business. You make that house available to a young person, perhaps a young family, for little or no rent, in exchange for their providing you with a certain amount of labour toward upkeep and maintenance. It's a perfect convergence," she tells him, "one in which a good home is made available to someone who needs it while at the same time you no longer have to worry about fixing a leaky faucet or replacing a burnt-out light bulb."

He has to bite his tongue to keep from saying that those were the very chores he'd initially imagined she'd be doing on her weekly visits. Instead he promises her that he'll give the idea some thought. Which actually he has done already because Dragonfly, his very handy non-binary handyperson, had mentioned in passing the other day that they were looking for a new place because the owners of the house they'd been renting now wanted to move to the island themselves. Shorter senses that his beloved solitude is being put at risk, but perhaps, as Rosalie maintains, it's for the best.

Only after she's left does he consider that a line has been crossed, that Rosalie has, for the first time, involved herself in an aspect of his life beyond the writing.

Rosalie is equally aware that the pair of them are entering a new phase in their relationship and laughs softly to herself as she tools homeward in her old Volvo, humming "Where Have All the Flowers Gone?"

TWENTY-TWO

PERSEPHONE WAS BLESSED WITH AN IMMENSE AND CATHOLIC APPETITE, so we knew something serious was afoot when she stopped eating. She became restless and took to gathering straw as though building an unconvincing nest. "Farrowing behaviour, looks like," Angus said. "Think I'll give Jones a call." In the weeks prior to Persephone's due date several of us had managed to develop recurring panic attacks about all the things that can go sideways around pig farrowing. Piglets stuck in birth canals, disadvantaged piglets traumatized by the birth process, oxygen-deprived piglets, chilled piglets, splay-legged piglets, malnourished piglets unable to compete for milk, lactation failure, iron deficiency anemia, scour, scrotal hernias, congenital tremor, bacterial infection, mange and the dour Greasy Pig Disease—our pig-raising manuals ran rife with gothic horrors. So I was all for calling the experienced Jones for assistance in whatever ordeals awaited us.

Persephone entered her labours the following morning with a great show of snuffling, grunting and shifting about. She paid zero attention to Jess, Angus and me as we watched from a respectful distance. Jones arrived right on schedule with a satchel of implements and a couple of radiant heaters. "Gotta keep the little fellas warm for a coupla days," Jones told us. "Whoops, there she goes!"

Sure enough, with a magnificent grunt from Persephone, a tiny piglet popped out like a sausage onto the straw. Its umbilical cord broke away on its own and within a minute or two the piglet was up on its feet and stumbling around. "Looks good," Jones said, adjusting the radiant heaters to keep the newborn warm while not overheating prostrate Persephone. Bright beams of morning

249

sunshine were already warming the air around us, so at least our anxiety about fatally chilled piglets began to abate.

Persephone continued to rumble like an awakening volcano. Within a few minutes the piglet found its way to her teats and began suckling greedily, switching from teat to teat to gorge on the richest milk.

A second piglet emerged, then another and another and another. We were up to eleven by early afternoon. The mob of them suckled frenziedly, squealing and squabbling and tumbling over one another, through all of which Persephone lay like a prone punching bag with teats. At a certain point Jones suggested that we remove several of the larger ones so that the smaller and later-born ones got a sufficient share of the colostrum-rich first milk. Though a couple of the last-borns were noticeably smaller than the others, there seemed to be no real runt in the litter. "We have to be careful of the sow," Jones warned. "She'll be fiercely protective of her babies and may try to take a bite at us for removing them." We knew that Persephone didn't have a mean bone in her body, but just to be sure, we swung a gate between her and ourselves before picking up several of the larger piglets. They squirmed and kicked and squealed in distress and while Persephone took note, she didn't object.

Right around then, Lena and Josie showed up and of course Josie was ecstatic over the piglets. They really were cuteness chart-toppers, funny as well as ridiculous. Along with relief that none of our disaster anxieties had materialized, we all felt a great sense of accomplishment over the morning's work. Besides the sweet mysteries of birth, on the mercenary side, eleven healthy pigs fattened up for market could go a long way toward earning us enough cold cash for legitimate farm status. Naturally we didn't dwell unduly upon the eventual slaughter of these little beauties now cavorting around the pen.

We took turns maintaining an overnight vigil for the first few nights, because Jones had warned us that most piglet deaths occur during the first several days of life from either starvation or being accidentally crushed by the sow. But on our vigilant watch nobody starved and nobody got crushed to death.

Two days later Angus and I tackled the job of tail docking. No audience of enthusiastic supporters showed up for this brutal business. "Yah, you hafta cut their tails for sure," Jones had told us, "otherwise they'll get into tail biting and from there it's a short hop to cannibalism." Though they did have incredibly sharp teeth, "wolf teeth" Jones called them, easily capable of lacerating their brethren or their mum's udder, you could hardly imagine these cute little piglets morphing into savage cannibals tearing one another to pieces. We'd discussed, but decided against, clipping their teeth unless it became absolutely necessary.

Again, we boarded Persephone off with a gate and I took on catching each piglet—already the squealing little baggers were amazingly elusive—then holding it firmly while Angus slowly cut the tail with a special cutter Jones had loaned us. The knife had a heated blade that cauterized the remaining short stub of tail. Such blood-curdling screaming! Understandably, Persephone was hugely distressed by her babies' cries of pain. We worked as fast as we could and, after applying antiseptic to the wound, returned each traumatized piglet to their mum right away. We attached a leg tag to each of the five males so we could easily pick them out for the greater indignity that awaited them.

Jones returned some days later to initiate us into the solemn and more complicated rites of castration. Angus caught one of the marked males, cleaned its scrotum, then held the piglet upside down by its spread rear legs. Jones tightened the skin of the scrotum and then, wielding a surgical knife with a hooked blade, made a clean incision through the scrotum skin above the centre of each testicle. Then gently squeezed the testicle until it popped out through the incision. The finesse and delicacy of the operation, the dexterity with which Jones's slender fingers moved, made me think of a heart surgeon at work. The victim males screamed in agonized distress. Pulling the testicle sideways, Jones sliced its cord close to the incision, and when both testicles were lying pathetically in a small ceramic bowl, sprayed the wounds with antiseptic and returned the terrorized eunuch to the litter.

Only one of the five male piglets presented a problem: on this one we could find only a single testicle. "Cryptorchid," Jones muttered, "the testicle hasn't come down its canal. We'll have to earmark the pig and check it to see if the ball comes down the chute later on."

"Then remove it?" I asked.

"Yep," Jones said, "just like we did these. You up for that?"

I believed Angus might be but I wasn't the least bit sure about myself. Watching Jones slicing those scrotums and squeezing out the testicles, for all the finesse involved, had given me an extreme case of thigh-clenching. In fact the whole tail-docking and cas-trating scene, the blood and pain of it all, with multiple piglets squealing in terror and Persephone bellowing her displeasure, had left us all a bit shaken. Shooting the young billies last year had been harrowing enough, but at least had been quick and painless.

This business with the piglets, though there was no death involved (yet), had felt like more of a massacre. Angus and I, and even the others who hadn't been present, withdrew into a shell of silence for a while and scarcely looked one another in the eye.

Mercifully the following weeks were mostly spent in the vegetable patch with long hours of digging, planting and transplanting. Soul-lifting work. The compost bins were bulging with aged chicken, goat and pig manure that we lavished on the raised beds, dreaming, as springtime gardeners do, about sensational crops to come. Just being out there together, in various combinations, vigorous young bodies flexing and straining with honest exertion, bathed in sunshine, birdsong and springtime fragrances, set our spirits soaring.

Almost lost among the bedlam of piglets, Sara quietly birthed a single kid, unhappily another billy, but a problem that could be kicked down the road for now. The chickens were laying at pro-digious rates and the logging show had moved to elsewhere on the island so that we seldom heard it unless the wind shifted to a particular direction. In contrast to the grinding months we'd endured, communal life was starting to look pretty damn fine once again.

"Hey, Shorter!" Enzo called across the barnyard to me from the back door, "Phone call for you. Long distance!" Back then my instinct always was that a long-distance call meant bad news. No news, as my mom used to say, is good news. I set aside the chainsaw I'd been sharpening and sprinted across to the house. Enzo discreetly withdrew, leaving me private space in the kitchen. I picked up the receiver and said, "Hello?"

"That you, Christian?" My brother's voice, sounding a very long way away.

"Yeah. That you, Lawrence?"

"Yes."

"Hey, how are you, buddy? Where are you, in London?"

"Yes, I am. Listen, Christian, I have some terrible news."

"Oh, no, what's going on?" I was instantly shot through with anxiety.

"It's about Mom and Dad."

"What about them? Are they okay?" I knew already from his tone that they weren't.

"No, they're not. I'm sorry to have to tell you this, Christian, but they've both been killed in a plane crash."

"Oh, fuck no!" The news hit me like a blackout.

"Yes, it's a dreadful thing." Lawrence paused for a moment, possibly with his hand over the mouthpiece. "I was contacted just shortly ago by someone from the high commissioner's office or something at Canada House."

"How come they're involved?" Lawrence, for all his celebrated brilliance in the field of economics, was never an especially adept communicator. I wanted to shake him to find out what the hell was going on.

"Well, Mom and Dad were on their way over to visit Beth in Australia."

"Right, Mom told me they were going this year." I remembered her letter, rare in itself, containing an elaborate explanation of how the airline scheduling made it impossible for them to include a visit with me on this trip. At the time I'd been equal parts hurt and relieved.

"So they were flying Pan Am, en route from Hong Kong to Sydney with a stopover in Bali."

"Okay."

"So, you must have heard about the recent plane crash in Bali. It was all over the news."

"No, I guess I missed it."

A pause from Lawrence, as though he's wondering what manner of cave I live in. "Well, from what they can make out, the plane was supposed to land at Denpasar—that's the capital of Bali—but somehow strayed off course and ended up slamming into a mountainside on a remote part of the island."

"Jesus Christ," I said, forgetting Lawrence's strict religious scruples. "When did all of this happen?"

"The crash occurred on April 22."

"But that's weeks ago! How come we're only finding out about it now?" This whole thing seemed totally fucking bizarre to me. The pieces didn't fit together and I simply couldn't process the possibility of our parents suddenly being no longer alive. I wasn't feeling distress or grief so much as a muddled incomprehension.

"Long story," Lawrence said. "The plane was missing for a while. The crash site's about six hours from the capital, way up on a mountain covered with jungle. So it took several days for a US military team to get there. The locals had already found burned body parts scattered all over the place, but between the impact of the crash and the ensuing fire, most of the body parts were unidentifiable."

"Jesus," I said again, forgetting again.

"So the Americans started figuring out who was on the passenger list—I think there were twenty-six Americans in all, along with Japanese and French people as well as a few Canadians—and tracking down next of kin. It obviously took them a while to find me, and of course you and Beth are both out in the middle of nowhere."

"So you're quite certain Mom and Dad were on that plane? That they're dead."

"I'm sorry, Christian, but yes, they were booked on that flight and did in fact board it in Hong Kong. And they haven't been heard from since. I think we have to accept it as an absolute certainty."

"Oh, man, this is so unbelievably weird."

"I know. I simply couldn't focus on what those Canada House people were telling me. It was like they were talking Mandarin."

"Have you spoken with Beth?"

"Just a little while ago. She was completely distraught, as you'd expect. Couldn't stop crying. Said how much she had been looking forward to their visit, to showing off her kids, all of that."

"Yeah. Poor Beth. She was so close to them, to Mom anyway."

"Yes, she and Mom shared a special bond, no question. Maybe you could give Beth a call too. She's probably feeling awfully isolated stuck out there in that dreadful outback."

"I'll call her for sure," I said. Beth and I usually spoke briefly by phone every Christmas. Like Lawrence and myself, she lived in a space largely detached from the remnants of our little nuclear family. I thought of unidentifiable limbs and torsos scattered in the mountainside jungle.

Lawrence and I agreed that there was little we could do at the moment. Our uncle Francis, Mom's younger brother who was a barrister of some renown in Toronto, apparently would be handling the business end of things. There would, of course, be no funeral. Perhaps a memorial service of some sort later on. Perhaps.

After I'd hung up the phone, just as an intrusive party-liner had clattered on, I felt an enormous dislocation of spirit. An immediate rush of regrets, for one thing, that Lawrence and I hadn't spoken more at length and more from the heart about our shared loss. I hated that my parents had vanished from my life while that chilled distancing still existed between us. Talk about unfinished business. Over and over I envisioned their dreadful last moments of life as the errant plane hurtled toward the mountain. Were they even aware of it? Did they scream in terror? Clutch each other, sob a final "I love you" before the annihilating impact? So much left hanging, like the scattered body parts.

Instinctively, in a numbing stupor, I wandered outdoors and across the fields toward Ponder. I sat on the shoreline for what seemed like hours, turning over and over again in my mind a tumult of memories and regrets. Some good times for sure. The atypical excitement of Mom and Dad on their twenty-fifth wedding anniversary. Bumbling fishing trips Lawrence, Dad and I went on together. My parents' pride at each of our high school graduations. Occasions of family happiness I'd all but forgotten, discounted in the recent years of estrangement. More than anything I longed for a moment of redemption in which I could tell the two of them how much I appreciated all they'd done for us kids. A moment that would never now occur.

I sensed I should go talk to Jess, get some comfort there, give Beth a call, put this solitary nightmare in perspective. But still I sat on, gazing numbly at the smooth silken surface of water, distracted now and then by a belted kingfisher diving swiftly from a high branch cleanly into the water and emerging sometimes with a small fish in its pointed black bill.

Eventually I was startled out of my reverie by someone approaching. Enzo. He sat down on the grass close alongside me and put his arm across my shoulders. "So sorry, man," he said, but no more. Perhaps Lawrence had told him on the phone what happened, or he had somehow guessed. I remembered him telling the group how both his parents had been killed in a train crash when he was still in his teens. Glancing quickly, I saw tears at the edges of his eyes. Something inside of me opened, some blockage I'd been clinging to. The hopeless enormity of what had happened washed over me; then I was sobbing myself, crying probably for the first time in years, feeling the unholy fucking sadness of it all. We sat like that, Enzo and I, shoulder to shoulder into the mournful twilight.

ROSALIE IS IN A SOMBRE FRAME OF MIND ON HER NEXT VISIT. SHORTER'S account of his parents' death has touched her deeply, reawakening tragic memories of her own. "I feared the worst," she says, "with the introduction of Persephone, but I hadn't imagined anything quite so grotesque. Your poor parents. And you three siblings scattered as far across the globe as you could get from one another. It's all so terribly, terribly sad."

Shorter's not really in the mood for Rosalie's ruminations, however well intentioned, having sat alone in a cave of melancholy for several days replaying in his mind that gruesome episode. Back at the time, of course, he'd had the solace of Jess's affection and everyone else in the house being caring and solicitous. Particularly he remembered little Josie cuddling in his lap and whispering sweet messages of dreamy possibilities. So in a weird way the tragedy of that episode, which is not something he's much dwelt on over the years, now seems as disturbing in his solitude as it had when it happened long ago among friends.

Sensing this is the case and knowing that, following his time of postponed grieving, Shorter now requires a gentle leading out from the darkness, Rosalie breaks into his thoughts. "Families," she says with an affectionate smile. "What peculiar convolutions they're capable of sustaining. It's fascinating to me how isolated your family members were from one another, and yet you yourself chose to live in an intentional community, cheek by jowl with relative strangers, as though to create a new form of family."

"Yes," he tells her distractedly. Of course he's reflected on this paradox himself plenty of times over the years and he's still uncertain whether he was trying as an adult to create the family he'd felt he never truly had or, conversely, to develop a tribal form as an alternative to the claustrophobia of their nuclear family.

"Are your brother and sister still alive?" Rosalie asks him, unearthing another residual piece of his sadness.

"No," he tells her. "Lawrence, always the smartest one, and highly esteemed even early in his career, was stricken with early-onset Alzheimer's and forced to stop work in his fifties. He was dead before sixty."

"How sad," Rosalie says. As she has all week, she's quietly confronting painful memories of her own. Particularly the twins, her darling younger sisters, who died before their tenth birthday. The first tragedy of her young life, but certainly not the last. Like Shorter, she has kept that distressing memory in a deep recess seldom visited over the busy years.

"My sister Beth," Shorter adds, "dear sweet Beth, pretty much worked herself into the dust in that unforgiving outback and also died young." Although he's never adequately grieved for either his parents or his siblings, Shorter, like Rosalie, has for years carried a dark emptiness inside himself where their memories should be.

"There are seven nieces and nephews scattered in England and Australia," he tells Rosalie, "but I don't know them and they don't know me."

"And how do you feel about that?" she asks him, again setting aside her own concerns to comfort him in his.

"Oh, I guess it's okay with me," he says, "and with all the rest of them too. But it's a chasm nevertheless. One of those 'if only' things."

Each of them is appreciating the comforting presence of the other just now. For the very first time Rosalie gently takes his hand in hers.

TWENTY-THREE

THAT DISTANT TRAGEDY WAS JUST THE OPENING ACT OF THE TUMULTU-
ous summer of '74.

Still in a lingering fog of regret and grief, I needed to decide
about the Islands Trust election. I'd pretty much committed myself
to taking a run at it, less from any burning desire to do so than from
a sense of duty because nobody else in what we thought of as the
progressive crowd was interested. Except for mercurial Charles
Jimson. One of my numerous midnight misgivings was that he and
I would both be elected, meaning I'd spend the next two years trying to keep a leash on his "Lash." But with a large chunk of the
island now owned by an unscrupulous logger, it was blatantly
obvious that if land use decisions were left to craven yes-men like
John Thomas, the community was going to get royally shafted. So I
swallowed my misgivings, compartmentalized my tangled grief for
the moment, and entered the race.

We cranked out a special election edition of the *Island Tatler* in
which I outlined my platform—basically a call for rigorous control
of land speculation and development, strong measures to curtail
clear-cutting (though by the time Zlotnik's dark hordes were done
there'd hardly be a tree left to cut), and a mushy pledge to maintain
the rural character of the island. Charlie Jimson's column was vastly
more inflammatory, calling for, amongst other measures, expropriation of all summer cottages (there were only a few dozen at the
time) to provide homes for islanders who couldn't afford to buy
land. Not the worst idea in the world, but not exactly a vote-winner
either. I imagined any number of electors dumping me and wild
Charlie into the same basket. Although invited, the mainstream
candidates—Waldo Gilport along with John Thomas and Slips

Gainsborough had all filed—pointedly ignored the *Tatler*'s invitation to contribute information about their candidacies and platforms.

So there we were, five earnest white guys campaigning for two positions. The prospect of working in close quarters with any one of them for the next two years was about as inviting as testicular cancer. Everyone fully expected fur to fly at the one all-candidates meeting that was held, but it turned out to be less inflammatory than expected, partly because Charlie Jimson broke into a rasping cough every time he attempted to speak, so we never really got to hear his ideas for cottage expropriation. Even his most virulent detractors in the crowd had to feel sorry for the poor guy coughing his esophagus out. As usual, John Thomas sounded perfectly lucid without conveying anything of real substance. Waldo was his earthy self and whenever he faltered, which he did frequently, was buoyed up by supportive comments from big brother Gil in the audience. Slips Gainsborough provided a very smooth little dissertation that spotlighted his salvation through AA and basically called upon everyone to remain sober. I acquitted myself reasonably well, pushing the "rural character" button as often as I could.

Afterwards Jess and all the Figuratives heaped me with accolades which I easily recognized as the offerings traditionally made to sacrificial lambs. There'd be another couple months of campaigning before the fateful election.

Although we were sometimes too embroiled in trivial pursuits to properly appreciate it, the essential beauty of life on the farm, as Willie had alluded to any number of times, lay in the intimacy with which we were embraced by natural processes. Thus it was that haying season mercifully rescued me from the gloom of my parents' deaths as well as the tedium of local politics. Angus announced at supper one brilliant June evening that the hay was ripe for cutting and the weather forecast promised perfect conditions for the next week. Great commotion ensued as the ancient Massey-Ferguson tractor was primed for its biggest challenge of the year. We dragged out of the equipment shed the old-style sickle bar mower, the simple wheel rake and the miraculously complicated old hay baler. We'd used all this stuff the previous summer in a laughable trial-and-error introduction to getting in the hay. Novices no longer, now we were stoked for serious haying. Lena was exempted from the work because of her condition, but Enzo set aside his hay fever for the duration and pitched in valiantly. Luis added some welcome musculature as well as mechanical know-how.

The farm's two huge hay meadows sloped gently toward the southwest, their tall grasses dancing and shimmering like the sun-dappled fields of *Elvira Madigan*. True children of Tolstoy, we each took turns driving the clattering tractor across a meadow, the sickle bar mower cutting a wide swath with each pass. After initial drying, we'd do another pass using the wheel rake to flip and fluff the hay for complete drying. Then a final round with the hay baler whose multiple moving parts swept up the windrows, compressed them into rectangular bales, knotted them with black cord and discharged them back onto the field. A noisy, cantankerous, primitive kind of magic.

Then the real hot and heavy work began, as we'd have to gather the bales to keep them from getting damp overnight from ground moisture or dew. You'd throw each bale onto a flatbed wagon pulled by the tractor, with a couple people riding on the wagon to stack the bales. A bale could easily weigh sixty or seventy pounds, and "bucking bales" for hours on end, slimy with sweat and itching all over from hay dust, was a circle of hell all its own.

But exhilarating nevertheless. Notwithstanding the hazards of a sudden summer squall or vexatious equipment breakdown, the whole process formed a grand summer ritual, rich with camaraderie and invariably connecting you with long-gone agricultural ancestors. You felt like wholesome rustic worthies straight from the pages of Thomas Hardy, people of the land at last.

Meanwhile, Lena was drawing close to her due date. Just as with Josie, her belly swelled beautifully and her complexion glowed. She waddled around the farm with Josie in tow, tending her chickens, milking the goats and dutifully visiting Persephone and the squealing litter, much of the time with a beatific smile. Although still a nervous wreck, Enzo wasn't quite as whacked as he'd been with his first paternity. For myself, I'd come to a deepening appreciation of Enzo's worthiness, however eccentric, since his understated solicitude around my parents' deaths.

In the middle of July, impeccably on schedule, Lena began to go into labour and, seasoned veterans now, we kicked into gear the same routine as last time with me first driving over to pick up our redoubtable midwife Abigail Smythe. As before, Lena's labour was relatively brief and without complication. Josie sat alongside, holding her mum's hand, wide-eyed at the unfolding drama. Enzo sat close on the opposite side of the bed, whispering words of encouragement and trying mightily to help with deep breathing. In due course a beautiful and healthy little boy slipped gently into the world. We all laughed and cried and got gooey by turns, knowing that hope was once again alive and thriving in that tiny pink body. Lena decided straight off that she wanted to call the little guy Hollis because that had been her granny's name. Awesome cool, all of it.

Elizabeth was another story. Her new house, as I've mentioned, was situated across the orchard and was more or less entirely screened from the main house. She, or anyone else, could come and go without being noticed by any of us. We'd frequently see her at a distance passing between her place and the dog run. By this point the dogs were almost entirely her preserve and had ceased to be much of a presence around the farm.

Elizabeth seldom attended group dinners or meetings anymore unless there was a special occasion of some sort. So we were all intrigued to one day receive a rather formal invitation from her to attend what she called a "gala evening" at her place.

On a glowing late summer afternoon the whole bunch of us, including Luis and Tonya and her kids, strolled through the orchard to Elizabeth's. Josie ran excitedly among us and tiny Hollis slept in Enzo's arms.

We were greeted outdoors by Elizabeth and Amrapali, both of dressed theatrically in colourful gowns. Elizabeth directed us to a semicircle of lawn chairs set up below her back deck, then stood on the low deck before us. "Welcome, everyone," she said in a giddy tone. "I'm so glad you could all make it because this is, I believe, a very special evening. You are about to witness the world premiere performance of the Figurative Farm Dancing Dog Ensemble!" We all clapped and cheered as though she'd just introduced the Bolshoi Ballet.

The show started with all five dogs prancing onto the stage, each with a large pink bow tie around its neck, then executing a perfect circle around Elizabeth and ending up in a straight row facing us all. We clapped appreciatively and the dogs all lowered their heads as though bowing in acknowledgement. Elizabeth was beaming. The troupe exited in a line behind a screen to the left, and then little Bandy, Willie's favourite, seemed to tiptoe back onstage. Amrapali followed her out carrying a gaily decorated walking stick. Flourishing the stick, she tapped the deck once and Bandy immediately fell to the deck as though shot. Josie cried out in distress. Two taps and the little dog sprang up, somersaulting in the air and landing perfectly on all fours. Again we clapped and cheered exuberantly. Then we had dogs riding on each other's backs, dogs leaping over small fences, dogs wriggling through wide pipes and, as a grand finale, the whole troupe standing on their hind legs and waltzing to Patsy Cline's recording of "The Tennessee Waltz." Pure magic. Total hokey. We all loved it, of course, those mangy mutts from three years ago now performing like disciplined stars onstage. Elizabeth and Amrapali, holding hands, took a bow at centre stage, thanking us all.

The whole event was so irredeemably schmaltzy we laughed our heads off on the way home, questioning whether Che Guevara or Malcolm X would have approved.

The show also reminded me and Jess that, with so much on the go, it had been far too long since we'd last visited Willie. A few days later we drove into town and, after doing laundry and grocery shopping, went up to Sunset Rest with, as usual, little Bandy secreted in the satchel.

But Willie wasn't there. We enquired at reception and were told that Willie had been transferred to the nearby hospital where he was believed to be in the intensive care unit. "What's wrong with him?" Jess asked, but reception curtly declined to divulge that information. Hell. We sped across to the hospital, a sprawling old unit with enough religious statuary to outfit a mid-range cathedral. The reception area was strewn with old folks in wheelchairs, crashed athletes on crutches and distressed-looking families. After a lengthy wait in line, we asked the harried receptionist where we could find Willie.

"Are you family members?" the harried one asked. Before we could answer, her phone rang and she held up a silencing finger to us while taking the call. The lineup behind us continued to lengthen as we outwaited what developed into a very long phone conversation, then a second shorter one. I could feel poor little Bandy becoming restless in her satchel. "Family members?" the receptionist repeated at last.

"Not exactly," I said, "but..."

"I'm sorry," she cut me off, "the patient is in intensive care. Absolutely no visitors other than immediate family."

"But he doesn't have any immediate family," Jess explained. "We're it for him."

"I'm very sorry," the receptionist repeated just as her phone rang again and Bandy began to whine and scratch at the satchel. We fled outdoors and let Bandy have a bit of a romp on a patch of desiccated lawn beside the parking lot. We were totally stressed about Willie but also stymied as to how we could get to see him or at least find out what the hell was going on with him. I wondered if we should head home and try getting info over the phone.

"I'm not leaving until we know what's happening," Jess said. "Why don't you stay here with Bandy and I'll just go straight up to the ICU and plead our case." Off she went with that determined look I knew would be more than a match for any Big Nurse who got in her way.

For about a half-hour Bandy and I sat on a wooden bench near the front entrance watching the halt and the lame, the crippled and casted make their way in and out of the hospital. At one point a wizened old lady in a wheelchair rolled up alongside us and asked me if she could pet Bandy. She had tears in her milky blue eyes and when I asked her if there was anything I could do for her, she said, "I had a wee dog like this little feller long, long ago. I loved that little dog, you know?"

I said yes, I did.

She gently patted Bandy's head, thanked me, then manoeuvred her wheelchair away, crying softly.

Jess emerged shortly after and joined me on the bench. "Pretty grim in there, Shorter," she said.

"You get to see Willie?"

"Only through a window in the ward door. He was lying in bed like a mummy hooked up to all kinds of equipment—monitors and drips and even a machine that's doing his breathing for him. He's in a coma, they told me. Not expected to come out of it. They don't think he'll live more than a couple more days."

"Christ," I said. Bandy, still sitting on the bench, started whining again. It was, I realized, a sort of dirge she was singing, a kind of prescient keening. We drove home almost in silence, each of us coming to terms with the imminence of Willie's death.

A few days later, the sympathetic nurse that Jess had spoken with at ICU called to let us know that Willie had died without trauma or distress. She didn't have any information on funeral home arrangements but did say she'd heard that relatives of Willie had arrived to look after things.

For Jess and myself it was like Willie had without warning disappeared into a black hole, just as my parents had. The devious ways of death once again revealed.

Several weeks later we received a call from somebody at a legal firm in town asking for either Jess or myself. I took the call. The caller enquired if it was convenient that Jess and I attend an important meeting on the following Monday concerning the estate of Mr. William Peave. The caller was not at liberty to provide any additional information at the moment but urged that we attend. I said we would.

As usual whenever we went to Spangler in those days, which was as infrequently as possible, we had a list of chores at the laundromat, the credit union, hardware store and supermarket, so even if this legal meeting was a waste of time we'd still get lots of other necessary tasks done. And, as Jess had speculated, it was not unthinkable that Willie had left something in his will to do with his dogs.

At the appointed time, we wheeled Viribus into a parking space outside the offices of Chapman, McDonough & Spalding, Barristers and Solicitors, strategically located directly across from the courthouse. Inside we were directed to a budget-sized conference room where three people were seated at a long table. One of them, a man not much older than ourselves, wearing a dusty-looking suit and an unfortunate moustache, immediately stood and strode over to us.

"Ah," he said, extending his right hand, "Mr. and Mrs. Shorter, is it? How do you do? I'm Lance Chapman. Thank you ever so much for making the time. Do come in and sit down." He pulled back two chairs on the opposite side of the table from the other two people, a greying middle-aged man and woman, who appeared as taciturn as Chapman was ebullient.

"Permit me to introduce Mr. and Mrs. Shepley," Chapman said. "Mrs. Shepley being the niece of the deceased."

"Hello," the Shepleys said in flat-bottomed unison.

Jess and I sat down opposite the Shepleys while Chapman seated himself at the head of the table.

"Yes, well, to get right down to business," Chapman said. "First let me extend to each of you my own personal and our firm's collective condolences on the loss of William." Jess and I acknowledged the formality with an appreciative nod; the Shepleys stared impassively at the tabletop.

"Our purpose here today is to read the will of the deceased and to wrap up any remaining details concerning the estate," Chapman said.

"Was there a funeral already?" Jess asked.

"No," said Mrs. Shepley.

"And will there be one?" Jess asked.

"No."

"I should tell you," Chapman said, "that the body was cremated the day after Mr. Peave died."

"I see," Jess said. "And what about the ashes?"

"Disposition of the remains," Chapman said, "is among the matters we shall be discussing momentarily." He extracted a document from a file folder on the table, cleared his throat and began reading the last will and testament of William J. Peave with the usual blather about revoking all former wills, codicils and testamentary dispositions, payment of debts, duties, taxes, funeral and testamentary expenses. I was gazing out the window to the parking lot where a flock of industrious pigeons pecked at food scraps, and thinking how little of Willie's spirit there was in all of this legalese, when suddenly I was catapulted back into the present. "I wish to have my ashes scattered," Chapman read, "around my old farm on Conception Island. Furthermore, I direct that the sum of $12,000 be paid to Mr. and Mrs. Shorter, now resident on my former farm, to assist in maintaining the farm and in caring for my dogs for the remainder of their natural lives."

Holy crap. Jess and I looked at one another in disbelief. Crazy Willie was giving us back every penny we (Jess) had paid him for the farm! We couldn't believe it. Neither could the Shepleys. Especially when it became obvious that Willie's estate extended almost nowhere at all beyond the twelve grand. That the Shepleys, glowering now with thinly veiled contempt, were about to inherit basically nothing except some old family photos and a few keepsakes. In other words, just about what they deserved for their sustained indifference toward Willie while he was alive.

After the Shepleys had left with a rudely token goodbye, Chapman presented us with a cheque for $12,000 and said the funeral home just around the corner had been instructed to release Willie's ashes to us. We signed a couple of documents, thanked Chapman for his good services and burst out onto the sidewalk laughing like maniacs. Good old Willie! Fuckin' eh—good old Willie!

Back home, after the windfall excitement had abated, we decided we'd honour his passing in a way Willie would have appreciated. All of us Figuratives gathered on a Friday evening and walked across the farm, Jess carrying Willie's ashes in a bentwood cedar box Lena had gotten from a friend on the reserve. We entered the woodlot, which is just about like entering a cathedral anyway, and each of us scattered a bit of his ashes beneath several of the gigantic firs that Willie had loved especially well. I imagined the ashes slowly being worked into the earth, mingling among the mycorrhizal fungi, being gradually absorbed into the roots of the great trees, then eventually sucked up through the cambium layer, lifted skyward into the dizzying canopy with the farm and the whole island spread far below.

My heart rejoiced for Willie and gave thanks for the circumstances of our own story intersecting so brilliantly with his. Then we wandered in semi-procession to the grassy hillside near Ponder and sat in a circle around a blazing fire. Of course the newly endowed dogs were included and Elizabeth had them do a joyfully mournful little circling routine while we all sang "Happy Trails" just like Roy Rogers and Dale Evans. Long into the night we told stories about Willie and knocked back glasses of blackberry wine just as we'd first done with him. Then we lay back under a sky of dazzling stars while Angus's melancholy piping escorted Willie out into the universe.

"BIRTH AND DEATH, BIRTH AND DEATH," ROSALIE INTONES MEANINGFULLY on her next visit.

She is of course delighted with the introduction of little Hollis to our expanding cast of merry prankster characters. And touchingly emotional about Willie's death and him leaving them an unanticipated inheritance.

"I love the idea of Willie's remains being gradually assimilated by the big trees he loved so well," she says. "Yes, I myself have had certain dealings with both birth and death," she tells Shorter, and this is a turning point because up until now she has been resolute in her determination not to allow her own story to intrude upon his. But as they move toward the greater mysteries of birth and death, she's feeling an increasing convergence of life stories.

"Oh, I'm extremely pleased," she tells Shorter, when he mentions that his handyperson Dragonfly has indeed moved into Elizabeth's house.

"You can find them doing handy things all over the property. I can't tell you how great it feels that I don't have to worry about every pestilential chore that needs doing."

"A most wise decision," Rosalie nods knowingly, not bothering to claim at least partial credit for this happy outcome. "And incidentally," she says instead, "it lifts a considerable burden of anxiety from my own shoulders."

"What anxiety would that be?" he asks her, suspecting he knows already.

"Well, that there be someone close at hand to keep an eye on you," she says.

"So's I don't get into any mischief, you mean?" Shorter jokes.

She gives him what passes for her major league stare-down before smiling archly. "Mr. Shorter," she begins, but he interrupts her with a raised hand.

"How about," he says, "you drop the 'Mr.' and just call me Shorter the way everyone else does."

She appraises him for a moment. "Very well," she says finally, "and I'd be most pleased if you in turn would call me Rosalie, in place of the no-name strategy you've so stolidly maintained thus far."

Absurdly, Shorter feels his old heart do a little flippy-floppy thing, as though she and he have just declared undying love for one another. Shorter fears he might be on the cusp of saying something irretrievably stupid. But Rosalie rescues the moment by planting a sweetly chaste kiss on the top of his head.

"Birth and death," she repeats herself. "Birth and death."

TWENTY-FOUR

PERSEPHONE'S BROOD WAS RUNNING AMOK. GORGING ON WILD GLEAN-
ings, surplus garden produce and supplemental grain feedings, the
adorable little piglets of spring had morphed into stocky bruisers,
bundling around their field like meaty grinders playing Australian
rules football. The Dirty Almost-Dozen we took to calling them,
excepting Persephone, who moved amongst the rooting rabble like
a dowager empress.

"What do we call a collection of pigs when they've grown too
big to be a litter anymore?" Lena wondered one afternoon when
she and I were scattering baskets of windfall apples over the fence
into a maelstrom of porkers. Good question. We looked it up later
and found the options included a herd or drove or farrier of pigs,
or a sounder of swine or passel of hogs. We took a vote at dinner
that evening and settled on a farrier of pigs as the most elegant,
although the vote was non-binding and if somebody wanted to call
them a sounder of swine or passel of hogs they were free to do so.

Rooting around exuberantly all summer, our farrier had
transformed their grassy pasture into a five-acre mudbowl and in
their ebullience were now threatening to smash down the old fencing and begin excavating the rest of the farm as well. Endearingly
funny, the roiling mass of them was also a disaster in the making.
Rather than addressing the problem like adults, some of us took to
casually tossing off traditional pigisms whenever the opportunity
arose. "Oh, you're squealing like a stuck pig," I might half-jokingly
tease Jess in one of her moods, to which she'd sharply counter:
"In a pig's eye!" Enzo actively pursued opportunities to tell anyone who'd listen that he wasn't about to "cast my pearls before
swine," any more than he'd be fooled into buying "a pig in a poke."

Pigheaded, sweating like a pig, eating like a hog, pigging out, when pigs fly, greased pigs, silk purses from sow's ears, hamming it up, too many pigs for the tits—on and on the moronic comments ran, mostly to do with pigs being greedy, unclean, fat and stubborn, none of which actually applied to our handsome Tamworths.

Finally Lena put a stop to our silliness on the grounds that we were setting a really poor example for Josie, whose love for pigs embraced Porky Pig as well as the Three Little Pigs. We were reminded how fondly in our misbegotten TV days we'd embraced Arnold the Pig in *Green Acres*. In a more literary idiom, someone like myself would occasionally make reference to Golding's character Piggy in *Lord of the Flies* and the forbidding pig leadership in Orwell's *Animal Farm*.

All of this chatter, whether silly or serious, was transparently by way of denial, because our sounder of swine was in reality pushing us to make some tough, perhaps impossible, choices. Were we going to keep some of the females and breed them, thereby committing ourselves to getting seriously into the hog raising business? Or, alternatively, just keep Persephone and raise a single litter per year sufficient for our own needs as well as providing a modest farm income top-up? Or not have pigs at all? No matter which way we went, the implications were considerable. A decision by collective consensus was definitely in order.

Everyone, including Elizabeth and Luis, showed up for the great debate. Luckily, it was Jess's turn to facilitate the meeting, so at least chaos would be kept at bay. Barely. We started with a preliminary round as to where people stood. Uncharacteristically, Angus jumped in straight away by saying he favoured keeping the three best sows, along with Persephone, for breeding next year. The five males and one smaller female he said should go to the livestock auction next week and the remaining two sows we'd take to the abattoir and have butchered and processed for our own use. "Lots of bacon, ham and sausage," he said, "plus enough ground pork, roasts and chops to easily last us a year."

The expressions on faces around the table ranged from blank to horrified, but Angus was unfazed. Speaking briefly but firmly he

advocated expanding the operation, constructing a skookum piggery with concrete floors, lighting and proper drainage as well as
a sturdy hog wire enclosure. The raising of pigs would become the
financial backbone of the farm. "I don't believe we could find a better use for Willie's money than that," he concluded, "and I'm fairly
sure Willie would feel the same way." Willie's imagined endorse-
ment, combined with Angus's prowess in the piggery, added
considerable heft to that point of view.

I could tell by the clench of her jaw that Elizabeth was itching to
jump in with a counter-argument but restraining herself because
of her now equivocal status within the group. Jess thanked Angus
for getting us clearly focused and suggested we continue the round
with prioritizing what to do with this year's passel of eleven. Next in
line, as a confirmed bacon-head, I agreed with Angus about having
one or two pigs slaughtered for our own use as well as with taking
at least some of the remainder to auction. As to keeping additional
sows for breeding, I said I'd like to hear other opinions before
deciding. For sure the money-making aspect appealed, I allowed,
but part of me couldn't imagine having four times as many juven-
ile pigs roaring around all summer. Plus I suspected the chances of
getting consensus on that scheme were slim to zero.

Lena was next to speak. Holding baby Hollis in her arms and
smiling tenderly at him, she cleared her throat nervously and
transferred her smile to everyone around the table. "God," she
said, "I am so all over the place on this. You all know how much
I love having animals on the farm; the place just wouldn't be the
same without the chickens or goats or the dogs," she said, smiling
across at Elizabeth. "And I love Persephone, I really do...But I'm
sorry to say I'm having a real problem with sending those brilliant
young pigs away to be butchered. It feels heartless and cruel to
me in a way that culling the young roosters, say, never does." She
gazed around the table with a look of sweet bewilderment. "I don't
know why I'm feeling so strongly about it, but I am. Remember
the reasons we decided not to send our young billies to auction
or the abattoir. Moral reasons, not financial or practical ones. So
would those moral reasons not be the same for these pigs? I mean,

the way they'd be killed is horrible, the stun gun and squealing and everything. I'm almost certain I couldn't eat any of that meat. Persephone's babies. No, really, I couldn't..."

Lena's voice trailed away and you could see she was struggling not to cry. Angus was staring hard at the table. It was Elizabeth's turn to speak. She began by acknowledging that her position within the group was now ambiguous at best, but she'd say what she had to say anyway. And that she was speaking for herself, not attempting to convince anyone that her way was superior to theirs. She had, she told us, recently made the choice to become a vegan, meaning she now abstained completely from consuming any animal derivatives in her diet—no eggs, dairy products, honey, nothing. I'd never heard the term before, but my immediate thought was that a life without cheese was a life not worth living. However, she continued, "the issue goes beyond just dietary concerns; it has to do with the morality of exploiting animals for any purpose." Of course, I was itching to ask whether her little dog-and-pony shows weren't shameless exploitation of the mutts, but didn't. Partly because you knew, annoyingly, that way down at ground level, what she was saying was essentially correct. Slaughtering those endearing Tamworths so that we and others could scarf down chops and sausages? Come on.

Next in line to speak, Luis took a deep breath, exhaled dramatically and then shocked us all by more or less endorsing Elizabeth's point of view. Not that he'd become a vegan himself, yet. But, he told us, he'd just finished reading Frances Moore Lappe's recent bestseller *Diet for a Small Planet* which had totally turned his head around. "You gotta follow the arrows, man," he concluded cryptically.

This was a total head-slammer, to have Elizabeth and Luis now lining up as soulmates after she'd moved out of the commune because he was moving in. Dylan's great line occurred to me: "Something is happening but you don't know what it is, do you, Mr. Jones?"

Never short for words on the topic of food, Enzo had barely begun to explain his latest thinking when he was beset by a sneezing

273

fit that wouldn't quit. Depositing drowsy Josie in his chair, he took off as though pursued by demons. Jess finished the round first by acknowledging Angus's outstanding work with the pigs and then by saying she definitely didn't want to see us getting into an expansion of pig-raising on the farm. She wasn't sure she'd even support having Persephone bred again. 'We've got some really tough choices to make," she said. "Like do we want to go vegetarian? We know that the chicken eggs, along with milk, yogourt and cheese from the goats, are a huge part of our diet. Should we be talking about replacing those protein sources? And, if so, who among us wants to commit to the extra work of developing plant-based alternatives?"

If nothing else was clear by then, this much was: the majority opposed keeping any of the young sows for subsequent breeding. The grand plan Angus had advocated might as well have been hit by a stun gun. He contributed nothing to the subsequent discussion and you could tell that behind his stoic silence there lay hurt and disappointment. I tried to talk with him about it as the two of us ate breakfast the following morning, but he'd say only that he needed time to think. He disappeared for most of the day and later that evening sat outdoors playing what sounded like mournful laments on his pipes.

Two days later, a bombshell: Angus called us together to announce that he'd be leaving the commune the following day. Angus? Leaving? It was inconceivable. We all sat in stunned disbelief. He explained that he'd been in discussion with Jones and an arrangement had been concluded that he would move to Jones's farm on Vancouver Island. Both of them, he said, shared a passion for raising pigs and Jones badly needed an extra pair of hands on the place. "I love the time I've spent with all of you here," Angus said, his voice husky with emotion, "and I'll never forget having shared the last few years with you. But now our paths must diverge, as paths so often do. So I leave you with no ill will, none at all, only thanks and love." He smiled then and quickly ducked out of the room before more could be said.

We were reeling for days. Figurative Farm without Angus seemed almost a contradiction in terms. In his own quiet and unassuming way, he'd been bedrock from the day we all got here. Our only true rustic, instinctively at home with plants and animals, happiest working outdoors in all weather. A farmer. And, to me at least, the kind of friend too seldom found among men: absolutely forthright, generous, principled. No games. I was remembering how matter-of-factly he'd strode into that Waddington logging show and gotten hauled off to jail, calmly returning the next morning as though the whole episode was no different than an afternoon spent turning the compost heaps. Humility was the term that kept coming to me. Modesty. Old-fashioned virtues. A sadness crept over my spirit like swamp mist at the thought of not having him around.

The following week a large truck arrived from the livestock auction and our eleven handsome Tamworths were herded into the cage in back and driven away, leaving Persephone and the rest of us bereft.

"DAMNABLY CHALLENGING," ROSALIE SAYS WITH A SIGH, "WHEN PRINCI-ples run up against the dictates of the heart. I so feel for all you communards at that painful juncture." She and Shorter are sitting cozily together, as is their custom, in matching old armchairs by the woodstove. Although the days are beginning to mellow toward springtime warmth, Shorter still lights a fire in the stove most mornings, particularly on Rosalie Fridays. Despite the occasional tempest, these have become, he freely admits to himself, the absolute highlight of his week. By Wednesday he's already anticipating her arrival, and the weekend after she's come and gone is invariably sweetened by her having been with him.

Rosalie feels much the same, finding within herself a peculiar tenderness toward the old guy, something she doesn't often experience otherwise. Especially not with men. Now she looks at him with what he takes to be fondness and says, "You loved your friend Angus, didn't you, loved in that peculiar way many men seem to have—the 'love ya, bro' thing tossed off too quickly for embarrassment to get a toehold."

"Yes, I suppose I did," he tells her.

"But we knew from the outset, didn't we," she says, "that the Persephone episode was going to prove difficult."

"In hindsight, yes, of course," he agrees. "But back in the day we were completely blindsided by it. Knowing everything about everything and nothing about anything."

"Yes, yes," she says. "But let's not forget that the wisdom of the group did eventually prove correct, did it not?"

"I suppose so," says Shorter. "But still."

Sensing him slipping toward melancholia, Rosalie quickly changes tack. "And how fine is it that you were discussing veganism all those years ago, decades before it became fashionable."

"Well," he responds with a laugh, "we were discussing it more fervently than actually practising it. I mean, who in their right mind would voluntarily stop with the goat's milk cheese or an egg still warm from the body of the hen?"

"Nevertheless," Rosalie says, "nevertheless. But let's move on to other considerations, shall we? Because there's something I wish to propose that I'd like you to give some very serious thought."

"Okay," he tells her, wondering what sudden turn in the road she's going to take this time.

"I believe," she says, "that our manuscript, although far from finished, has arrived at the point where we need to start seriously thinking about the ins and outs of publication." She pauses long enough for Shorter to recognize that she realizes this is not a topic he particularly wants to entertain.

"What do you have in mind?" he asks her, already feeling a kind of trepidation stalking. From his perspective the unfolding story rests very comfortably in the mostly genial give-and-take of their weekly sessions together. How it would fare out there in the snake pits of commerce and criticism he hardly dares imagine. Instantly he feels a paternal protectiveness toward the manuscript. And, he admits to himself but not to her, he doesn't even want to think about the project being completed and his engagement with

276

Rosalie drawing to a close. In his imagination this woman and the writing have become in some weird way indivisible.

Rosalie has similar misgivings, but in her case counterbalanced by a firm conviction that Shorter's story deserves to be told to a wider audience. Deserves and needs, because she believes that it contains salutary elements for a society radically altered from what existed half a century before.

"If you'll permit me, here's what I have in mind," Rosalie says. "I happen to have a second cousin living in New York City who's very well placed in one of the city's leading literary agencies. I have every confidence that she'd be pleased to review the manuscript and, having done so, to represent it."

Holy crap, Shorter thinks. This is magnitudes more intimidating than anything he'd imagined. He'd thought maybe a decent small press in Victoria, or at best Vancouver. But New York? Surely not. He's so bowled over by the whole idea that he can't scrape up anything coherent to say.

"No need for an answer today," Rosalie reassures him, smiling. "Just thought I'd put the idea out there—plant the seed, so to speak, let you mull it over for a bit."

"Yes, yes, I will," he tells her. And he will. But cripes.

TWENTY-FIVE

A GREY MALAISE GRIPPED THE FARM FOLLOWING ANGUS'S DEPARTURE. We were missing him in the worst kind of way and missing those crazy pigs too. We spoke of neither and I didn't dare even think of our noble Tamworths stunned and gassed and slit open while hanging from satanic racks. Stripped of her offspring, Persephone wallowed like a listless remnant of herself. Even the goats, Sara and Gracie, had a questioning air about their faraway staring, as though barbarous rites were being enacted just beyond the visible horizon. Of all of us, only Josie seemed to sail above the sinkhole by spending long hours perched on her tricycle outside the piggery fence conversing with Persephone.

Zlotnik's logging show was now pushing into the most inaccessible crannies of the Icarus lands and the number of loaded logging trucks bullying their way out of the clear-cuts was finally diminishing. Our inability to have in any way curbed Zlotnik's assault on our homeland hung over us like dismal wildfire smoke. Generally dismayed and still off balance from losing Angus, by this point I was totally regretting that I'd put my name forward for the Islands Trust. The position of trustee had been stripped of all appeal and I'd lost any heart I may have had to do real campaigning. I half-heartedly tried going door-to-door for a bit but was dogged by a constant anxiety that I might break into tears any moment for no apparent reason. All I wanted was to be left alone.

Conscious of my disquiet, Jess suggested one clear morning that she and I go for a walk together. With so much communal commotion during the recent dismal stretch, we hadn't really spent as much time together as we should have.

"So, how are you bearing up?" she asked as we meandered across the meadow alongside Ponder. Stretched before us, the whole farm looked beautifully, deceptively placid. The enigma of problems in paradise. Instinctively our footsteps carried us toward the edge of the woodlot.

"Well, where to start," I said. "This trust election is kind of rasping my spirit; the thought of actually getting elected and shouldering all the responsibility involved gives me the shudders. And, like everyone else, I can't wait for that fucking logging to be over." In the middle of the general commotion, Jess had spent the better part of the year writing a string of killer articles about West Coast forestry issues for a number of regional and national magazines. She'd interviewed dozens of experts in the industry and academia as well as organizers and firebrands in Native communities and in the burgeoning environmental movement. Already she knew a dizzying amount about ancient temperate rainforests, raw log exports, loss of biodiversity, stumpage rates and Native land claims. My kvetching about the workload of a local trustee seemed pathetic by comparison, but I wasn't above pathos at the moment.

"And Angus?" she asked me.

"Yeah, I'm truly not at peace with his leaving," I said. "Part of me keeps thinking, hoping, that he'll just show up again one day and confess he made a terrible mistake and would we consider readmitting him. Just a stupid fantasy, I know."

"I have it too," Jess said. "I really miss him."

"And I'm worried about where we're headed, as a group I mean," I said. "With Angus gone and Elizabeth off in her annex, I wonder if we even have any core vision left of what it is we imagine we're doing. It seemed so clear and purposeful at the outset, that compelling perspective of how to make a better world, or at least create a form of living that made the world no worse. Now I wonder if we're not just a pack of privileged kids playing at being Thoreau."

Even voicing this little catalogue of woes, I could see how puny they were as we walked into the realm of the ancient ones. Giant firs and cedars engulfed us, shafts of sunlight angling down through gaps between their enormous trunks, swarms of illuminated insects flittering in the beams of light. I loved the ancient timelessness of those woods, their ability to shrink us fool humans down to proper size.

"What about Luis?" Jess asked.

"What about him?"

"Well, how will it be, do you think, with Angus gone and Luis becoming more central to the group? We know how forceful a character he can be."

It was at that moment I was smacked by the realization that, in all the recent commotion, I'd still not come clean with Jess about the monkeywrenching episode.

"Funny you should ask," I said, "because there's something I've been meaning to tell you."

"You and Alice Munro together?" Like Julie Getz, our idiosyncratic book reviewer, we'd both loved Munro's recent stories.

"Not exactly," I said, probing for an angle that would work.

"Who then?" I had an unfamiliar sense Jess was toying with me, playing cat to my mouse. "Not Luis, surely?"

Damnit, she'd found out. But how could that possibly be. I decided to play it straight. "You remember back last spring..."

"Around the time Zlotnik's logging equipment was vandalized, you mean?" Jess looked at me disarmingly.

"Well, yeah," I said, no additional evidence required, "but how did you..."

"Know that it was you and Luis?"

"But..."

"Luis told me, that's how. Simple." Her tone was light and her manner breezy, but I knew dark currents were moving under us. Magisterial trees loomed above us in judgment.

"He *told* you?" Now the pieces weren't fitting together at all.

"That's right. A little while ago. Said he was concerned that word of it might somehow get around and wreck your chances in the election."

"Fuck off. That stinking little two-faced prick." It was a thought not meant to be voiced, but I'd instantly felt blindsided by Luis's betrayal. Even if he hadn't consulted with me first, the least the scumbucket could have done was admit it to me afterwards.

"Shorter, don't you think it would have been preferable if I'd heard this from you, not him?"

Just at that moment a big pileated woodpecker swooped in shrieking hysterically, alighted on a nearby snag and started jack-hammering on the reverberating wood.

"Of course it would," I said, "and I had every intention..."

"But surely you remember when I came home right after the incident and asked you directly did we know who was responsible and you..."

"I know, I know—I told you we didn't, which was a lie. That was wrong, and stupid. And I'm sorry."

"So every intention hadn't quite kicked in at that point, am I right?"

"Yeah. Listen: of course I wanted to tell you. The only reason I didn't say anything was because Luis had sworn me to secrecy. Absolutely no one was to know. That way there'd be zero chance of it becoming public knowledge. Of course it went against my gut instinct, not to tell you, but stupidly I agreed to it. I went along with it and I can't tell you how sorry I am that I did."

"You know, Shorter, our marriage was a bit of a lark from the get-go..."

"Sure. But since then I've come to see it as the linchpin of my life. Seriously. I adore being with you—you know it's true—and I'd never do anything to jeopardize that. You gotta believe me."

"Well, what could jeopardize it faster than frosted flakes is one or the other of us not being absolutely upfront and above board. Are we clear on that?"

"Yes, I am. Absolutely."

"Meaning, for example, that if I ask you if you know who did something, you don't have to tell me. You can simply say that you know but think it's best that I don't, at least for the moment. What you cannot say to me is that you don't know when you damn well do. Because that's an outright lie and a lie's demeaning to both of us. Understood?"

"Perfectly." Oh, this was humiliating. How could I have been so fucking stupid? To put at risk the one thing, the only thing really, that underpinned everything. I felt more a schmuck at that moment than I ever had before.

"Excellent. So let's say no more about it, okay? If I'm not mistaken we're already late for lunch."

We walked out of the woods and back through the meadows in weighted silence. I paused near Ponder and told Jess to go ahead without me.

"Are you okay?" she asked, putting a hand lightly on my arm.

"Yeah, yeah," I lied, "I just need to be alone for a bit, okay?"

"I'd like it to be clean between us, Shorter."

"Me too. I just need to sort myself out."

"Okay," she said, giving me a perfunctory hug. "See you later." A chaos of feelings was roiling around inside me as I watched her walk away. I was so fucking angry at Luis I might have clobbered him if he'd shown his face right then. For him to have specifically insisted that I not tell Jess what we'd done, then turn around and tell her himself without even first checking with me. Why would anyone pull such an asshole stunt? The more I turned it over in my mind the darker the story became. Something picked at a scab, something about Luis demonstrating to Jess that he trusted her more than I did, and was willing to confide in her in a way I wasn't. That he and she were soulmates of a sort. The whole thing just stank of duplicity. I'd need to have it out with Luis, and have a further clearing with Jess sooner or later too. But definitely not yet, not while I was still whirling like a dervish.

For the first time in our few years together, I imagined living without Jess; the prospect settled like cold winter fog around me.

I walked back toward the woods alone and re-entered the vaulted basilica of trees. I wandered deep into the grove to a massive Douglas fir among the sprawling roots of which Jess and I had made ecstatic love in our first days on the farm. I reached out and touched the veteran's scabrous bark, charred and pitted from eight hundred years of survival, repeatedly stretched and cracked from the huge bole's incessant expansion. I could feel life forces surging upward as the giant pulled secret streams of liquid up into its canopy.

There was a sense of Willie's spirit moving nearby, something I'd experienced before when wandering alone in these hushed woods. I remembered him talking in tones of love about these spectacular trees. Their immense complexity, about which we know next to nothing. "They're not individual trees, you know," Willie would say. "Nossir, every one of these trees you see are all connected to each other." His gnarled old fingers spread out, dancing in all directions. "Their roots all interconnect and share resources and there's enormous tangles of fungus under there as well connecting all the roots, so that the trees feed the funguses and the funguses feed the trees and they're all in communication with one another. The whole thing is one big organism with a billion parts all working together, plants and animals and everything else all doing their bit to keep the whole shebang firing on all cylinders. It's more beautiful and whole than anything we ignorant humans have created up 'til now."

It's a marvel how Willie had come to comprehend the superstructure of a forest mostly by simply being in it. In his own earthy way he was decades ahead of many eminent foresters and forest ecologists.

As invariably happened, just being among the towering giants, presences that had survived fierce windstorms and wildfires for centuries, shrank my personal melodrama down to its true pathos. What Luis told Jess. What I didn't tell Jess. What Jess told me.

Oh, come on! No, the trees didn't whisper anything to me; they didn't have to. It would have been beneath their dignity.

In something of that sustained blue mood, I approached election day. Still tiptoeing around the unspoken truth, Jess and I drove down early to the community hall to cast our ballots. Already, we were told, the turnout had been brisk. I got the requisite "good luck" greetings from several regulars. Electors were free to vote for one trustee or two; I marked my own name and then examined all the others, wavering between not choosing a second name or taking the least bad of a bad lot. Rashly perhaps, I marked a second X for flame-throwing Jimson, Charles. Thanks to Mercedes, I was fully aware by then that the Gilport/Thomas faction had in recent weeks been actively spreading rumours that Charlie and I were in cahoots, together conspiring to expropriate vacant properties and give them to our friends, along with other socialistic plots. So, what the hell, Charlie got my vote, out of spite if nothing else.

The polls would close at eight, with results likely by nine. We'd already decided against throwing an election night party, though Elizabeth did let it slip that John and Iris Thomas were hosting a party at which she and Amrapali would "drop in just for a minute, for appearance's sake." Julie Getz and Enzo were serving as my scrutineers and would bring back the final vote count that evening. It was a thoroughly weird experience sitting around for hours waiting for a decision about what the next two years of your life might look like. Even weirder knowing that the entire community had just gotten through registering its considered opinion of you.

When Enzo arrived back at the house just after nine, his downcast expression told it all. "Sorry, man," he said to me, placing a commiserating hand on my shoulder, "you missed it by a whisker." It had been touch-and-go throughout the ballot count, he told us, with myself, John Thomas and Waldo Gilport running neck-and-neck-and-neck almost to the last ballot. Like thoroughbreds coming down the back stretch, Enzo said. A closing surge put John Thomas over the top at 112 votes, leaving Waldo at 103 and myself at 101. Slips Gainsborough had garnered only 47 votes and my erstwhile fellow trustee, Charlie Jimson, a disappointing 11.

"Well, that's that," I said to everyone, camouflaging as best I could my considerably mixed feelings of disappointment and elation. I accepted my rightful share of hugs and claps on the back as well as a sweetly tender kiss from Jess. Enzo proposed we demand a recount but I nixed the idea. Luis was all for tracking down three of our compadres who could have voted but failed to do so. And do what to them? I asked. Tar and feathers? Mostly I was just relieved that it was over and gave private thanks to whatever gods were

284

listening that I didn't have to spend the next two years headbanging with John Thomas.

But in the pitiless light of morning you couldn't get around the fact that this had been one depressing effing season of losses.

"WONDERFUL NEWS, SHORTER!" ROSALIE EXCLAIMS ON HER NEXT VISIT, seemingly oblivious to the pathos of marital turbulence and election defeat in Shorter's recent pages. "I've spoken with my cousin Hattie in New York and guess what? Yes! She's hugely enthusiastic about our story. There's an immense appetite for '60s and '70s nostalgia, she tells me, 'back to the land' stories especially. The tie-in with current concerns, climate change, saving the trees, all of it. Great marketing possibilities, she believes. She wouldn't be at all surprised if we don't find ourselves in the middle of a publishers' bidding war!" Rosalie's actually laying it on a bit thick, aware that Shorter's not exactly fired up about the prospect of big league publication. Plus she imagines he's likely depressed from having unearthed the gloomy business of this last chapter.

She's right about Shorter being far from convinced by the promises of a publishing bonanza. "But your cousin hasn't seen a word of it yet," he cautions Rosalie. "She has no idea what it's really about or, more importantly, how competently it's written."

"Well, I did give her a bit of a précis," Rosalie says. "And I assured her that stylistically the work is top-notch. No, this is no time for false modesty, Shorter; you've done such a bang-up job I'm convinced we've got a real tiger by the tail here."

The skimpy bit that Shorter knows about the publishing industry suggests to him that caution be the order of the day. He knows enough to know that wildly inflated expectations are common currency in that peculiar sphere where fame and fortune are imagined lurking around every bookstore corner. Until they're not. Increasingly uneasy about the whole publishing gambit, he says no more to Rosalie for the moment.

"Speaking of which," Rosalie says, "this most recent chapter is a bit of a downer, don't you agree? Angus leaves the commune abruptly, you and Jess have a falling-out—and don't say I didn't warn you about the Luis factor!—and then you proceed to lose the election. There's a note of defeatism creeping in, don't you find, and I'm not sure this is quite the tone we want to be setting."

"Well, the story is what it is," he tells her. "We're not going to start massaging the facts to manufacture a more upbeat version."

"No, no, of course not," Rosalie agrees. "It's not a question of concocting falsehoods so much as carefully selecting certain components over others in order to enhance the desired overall tone. And Hattie was particularly forceful on this point: our readers don't want pessimism or negativity—there's far too much of that already with all these climate doomsday scenarios, pandemic terrors and dystopian speculations. 'Dystopia is so yesterday,' she told me. 'What our readers want today is bullish, buoyant, hopeful.' Yes!"

Rosalie knows as clearly as Shorter that Hattie's expectations are bunk, but she also has real concerns that Shorter's story may be beginning a nosedive toward the tragic.

TWENTY-SIX

AS EXPECTED, FIGURATIVE FARM OFFICIALLY BECAME A PART OF THE provincial Agricultural Land Reserve and, as though by way of validation, the proceeds from selling off our pigs handily topped up the farm income necessary to ensure our farm taxation status. We were, we felt, legit at last, even though the loss of Angus combined with abandoning wholesale pig production certainly muddied our future prospects.

By this point Zlotnik's vile minions had all but disappeared from the island. The community hall finally had a fully functioning preschool, under Tonya's capable leadership, to which Josie went whenever she could pull herself away from her in-depth colloquies with Persephone. Whether or not we would breed Persephone in the fall remained an item of discussion.

To no one's great surprise, Elizabeth approached us ("as a courtesy," in her words) to propose that Amrapali be allowed to move in with her. Turns out the San Diego sugar daddy Amrapali had depended on for so long had recently become besotted with a Las Vegas showgirl, upon whom all his attentions and surplus capital would henceforward be showered. Embarrassingly caught without means, Amrapali had thrown herself on Elizabeth's (and our) mercy.

Meanwhile our freshly minted Local Trust Committee, composed of John Thomas, Waldo and three distinguished government appointees, set in motion developing a community plan and land use bylaws for the island. An Advisory Planning Committee was to be elected to carry this work forward and, having been outmanoeuvred in the trust election, we resolved to have the APC controlled by conservation-minded folks. Quietly but determinedly we squeezed every available supporter to get up, get out and vote.

Perhaps misjudging the significance of this nebulous advisory body, the pro-development crowd failed to do the same. Jess got herself elected and so did Julie Getz and, surprisingly, even flame-throwing Charlie Jimson. Mable Sutcliffe from the general store and a newcomer whom nobody knew anything about rounded out the committee.

With Jess appointed as chair, the committee roared into its assigned work. Subcommittees were formed, recruiting other community members. Questionnaires were circulated, community information sessions held, guest speakers with particular expertise consulted. Issues of the *Tatler* positively rattled with opinion pieces concerning what the island could or should or would look like under various imagined scenarios. Although ex officio members of the APC, trustees John Thomas and Waldo Gilport bobbed along behind like rubber ducklings in a fast-moving current. Within little more than a year, and after a spate of tempestuous public meetings, the island was finally endowed with a community plan and a set of land use bylaws aimed at protecting the environment and limiting growth to what the carrying capacity might absorb.

Not everyone was happy; perhaps nobody was entirely happy, as the process was necessarily one of compromise and mandated constraint. Certain free enterprisers, perhaps hoping to retire in luxury from the proceeds of subdividing speculative properties into small lots, were livid at having their inalienable rights curtailed. Ambitious enviros chafed to realize how few tools were really available for adequately preserving and protecting the watersheds and forestland. Although the two local trustees danced faithfully to the tune being called by Gil Gilport and his cronies, the three general trustees appointed by the government leaned more to the progressive end of the spectrum and frequently outvoted the two locals. Not exactly democracy at its finest but damned useful nevertheless. By the time the plan and bylaws were finally signed into law, planning fatigue syndrome had laid almost all of us low.

Meanwhile, back at the farm, for the first six months after Hollis was born, public health nurse Abigail Smythe continued faithfully cycling over every second Saturday to check on how the little guy was doing. Week after week, she could find no real cause for alarm, and yet she remained concerned. For one thing, Hollis was not growing at what was considered a normal rate. "There's no hard and fast rule," Nurse Abigail told us, "but a typical baby would double its weight in the first five months, just as Josie did. Hollis hasn't come even close to that. But, then again, some babies don't, do they, honey?" she asked, gazing down fondly at Hollis in his crib. "Some will even lose weight at certain points, so his size and weight are not themselves a major concern just yet."

"What is then?" Enzo asked her. Enzo's obsessive attention to his own health issues, real or imagined, had ramped up to extreme when it came to the health of his children.

"I confess I don't know quite what it is," Abigail admitted. "Over the years I've encountered babies of every conceivable sort, but never one quite like Hollis. And yet when I ask myself what precisely is it about the little fellow that's concerning, I'm unable to say. He's alert enough, certainly. He seems contented. No apparent distress or discomfort, and yet..." She gazed down at the subject under discussion and Hollis gazed back placidly.

"Yes, it's what I go through lots," Lena said. "He hardly ever complains, he sleeps contentedly, he suckles lovingly. And yet, half the time it feels like he's not really—oh, I don't know how to say it— as though he's not really *there*. As though he's floated off someplace that's at least as interesting as here. There's a kind of separateness, I almost want to say remoteness, that he has that I never saw with Josie."

"Absolutely right," Enzo added. "So much of the time he just looks weirdly solemn, like he's watching a production of great significance that none of the rest of us can see. When he really comes alive, when he seems to be most fully present, is when Josie's with him. Then he lights up in a way he seldom does otherwise."

All three of them gazed down perplexedly at Hollis and he continued gazing enigmatically back at them.

"I'll go get Josie, if you like," I offered. Jess and I had remained discreetly in the background during Abigail's assessment. With no need to ponder where Josie might be on a Saturday morning, I ambled down to the piggery. Sure enough, Josie sat straddling her tricycle beside the fence, on the other side of which Persephone lay sprawled in a wallow of mud, grunting in apparent agreement to whatever it was Josie was proposing.

I stood quietly in the background, listening to Josie's chatter. An active verbalizer almost from birth, she was now at the age where she could answer simple questions and easily converse in senten-ces of a half-dozen words. But whenever she was chatting with Persephone—which was as often as she could—her speech was all nonsense words strung together in an undulating singsong with-out any apparent sentence structure at all. Almost an incantation. She'd occasionally tilt her head sideways, shrug her shoulders or extend her hands questioningly while verbalizing an imaginative chant of *ongs, blurfur, pels, kistel, bant*. She was, she had told me ear-lier, concerned that Persephone was lonely with all her babies gone.

"Hey, Josie," I called to her, "sorry to interrupt, but we need you up at the house for a minute. Nurse A is with Hollis."

"Okay, sure," she said. "I'll be back later," she told Persephone and the personable sow grunted accommodatingly.

"Want a sky ride up?" I asked Josie. She eagerly dismounted from her tricycle and ran toward me with extended arms. I swooped down and hoisted her above my head as she squealed with delight and bicycled her little legs through the air. She perched high on my shoulders and clasped my forehead as I marched with magisterial solemnity up the hill, she riding like a maharaja.

When we entered the room, right on cue Hollis became ani-mated. "Hello, Nurse A," Josie said politely, then looked down at Hollis in his crib. The little guy's eyes beamed with excitement. Josie made a funny sweet burbly sound and Hollis laughed and flailed his tiny arms. All us adults watched without a clue as the two kids chattered and laughed together.

As the weeks went by Hollis remained mystifyingly abstracted. You could look into his dark and solemn eyes for a long time without him blinking or becoming the least bit agitated. Absurd as it seemed, it was difficult not to suspect a keen knowingness in his quiet depths.

We discussed among ourselves and with Nurse Abigail whether specialists ought to be consulted, rigorous examinations undertaken, tests administered, but we were pretty much of one mind that whatever the little guy was going through was a psychic rather than physical phenomenon. Yes, he was unduly small, solemn and silent, but not alarmingly so. He seemed not in any way ill, at least the way we generally understand illness. Amrapali became particularly fascinated with the case and we started seeing more of her and Elizabeth than we had for months. Amrapali had been reading some groundbreaking material on what were then being called indigo children, kids who from a very early age were surrounded by an indigo aura that was thought to signify a new and more elevated level of consciousness. They possessed, she said, a deeply innate spirituality. This was all the very latest new thinking, she stressed, and we certainly shouldn't rush into premature judgment, but it was entirely possible that our somber little Hollis was in fact an indigo child.

From there it was a very short hop for Enzo to begin speculating whether or not his son could possibly be a changeling. Nurse Abigail had inadvertently put this notion into his head when she'd one time reminisced, uncharacteristically, about the years she'd spent as a district nurse in rural Wales. "All sorts of peculiar beliefs in the old folks," she'd told us, "not the least of them having to do with fairies and changeling children." How an elfin child, substituted for a baby stolen by the wee folk, could eventually grow into an ugly and vicious youngster requiring some form of exorcism. "I remember one old maid," she said, "who insisted that immersing a changeling baby in a bath of digitalis water was the best method of all. Mind you," she added with a laugh, "that old one turned a pretty penny retailing ancient Celtic notions to the tourists, so let's say she was not the most reliable of sources."

Nevertheless, this was sufficient information to get Enzo launched into a full-scale investigation of fairy folk, child-swapping and the mystical kingdom of Elfhame. Lena did not join him in his quest, but remained both perfectly calm and cautiously fascinated with her baby's unusual behaviour. Josie carried on as her baby brother's lighthearted but steadfast confidante. For his part, little Hollis continued his benign surveillance of a world in which he did not seem entirely at home.

One Sunday afternoon Lena was visited by a Comox woman she'd recently befriended. Pauline was a robust character from the reserve in town, her conversation punctuated with deep, rich laughter. She had, she told us, known old Willie and visited the farm some years ago as a place of interest to her people. She said she was currently pursuing a degree in social psychology at the community college in Spangler. She and Lena planned to take a stroll around Ponder and into the big trees. But almost straight away Pauline gravitated to Hollis, who was sitting on Enzo's knee staring fixedly at this intriguing stranger.

Pauline stood for several moments looking directly at the child and he at her. "May I?" she asked Enzo, indicating she'd like to hold the baby.

"Of course," Enzo said, lifting Hollis toward her. She took him in both hands and held him in front of herself. She had the biggest grin on her face and Hollis grinned back at her happily, cycling his little feet excitedly. Those of us watching could see that the woman and child had identical dark brown eyes. You had the feeling the two of them were looking into each other's soul.

Pauline spoke to the child in her own language and he garbled back to her in his. Then the two of them laughed while she hugged him and kissed his tiny head.

"Thank you," she said to Enzo, carefully handing the baby back to him. "A most remarkable child, a special presence in the world, I think." Then she and Lena went walking arm-in-arm to Ponder, leaving the rest of us wondering if perhaps we'd just witnessed a moment of divine grace.

"OH, YES!" ROSALIE EXCLAIMS ENTHUSIASTICALLY. "THIS IS PRECISELY what we're after, that sense of tenderness and sweet hope."

"I agree," Shorter tells her, "and more readily experienced back in those simpler times than nowadays, I'm afraid." The past week's news has seemed particularly gruesome, rife with climate disasters, the plight of refugees and machinations of tyrants. Conditions in which instances of illumination, however fleeting, appear all the more precious.

Meanwhile the ever-handy Dragonfly's been literally under-foot all week doing repair work in the crawl space beneath the kitchen. Filthy work. When required, back in the day, Shorter used to squeeze under there himself, but now the thought of being wedged between bare earth and those big timber joists seems uncomfortably close to the grave. Feeling some guilt over fobbing off such a nasty task, he considered the least he could do was to offer his handyperson dinner following a dirty day's work. Soon enough Dragonfly and Shorter fell into eating supper together while watching the evening news on TV. Surprisingly, Shorter quite enjoys spending time with them, though he's wryly aware of his now playing an aging Willie to their young Shorter. Oftentimes some item on the news will set Dragonfly chuckling with derision while Shorter's oblivious to what was meant.

"But, dear me," Rosalie now says. "I did receive disturbing news this week."

"How so?" Shorter asks her.

"A message from the Billingtons," she says. "You know, the owners of my home."

"I've heard the name," he says, "but I don't believe I've ever met them."

"Extremely decent people," Rosalie says.

"But?" he asks.

"Well, the uncomfortable truth of the matter is they've decided to retire to the island. The city's become too dangerous, they say. Fascist thugs roaming the streets and trigger-happy cops chasing them. Theft and mischief everywhere. So they've taken early retirement and will be moving up this spring."

"Them and everybody else," Shorter grumbles. Any number of times recently he's caught himself nattering in his head about new arrivals clambering onto the island, just as certain entrenched old-timers did when he and the hippie hordes invaded a half-century earlier.

"That is a drag," he says. "So you'll be needing a new place."

"Yes, myself along with Astrophe and Aclysim," she says. "But you know how tight housing is on the island just now."

"I've heard that," he says. He realizes that all their grand work in the past on community plans and bylaws served passably well in helping conserve what remained of island ecosystems, but by restricting residential density they unavoidably limited housing options, leaving people in Rosalie's circumstance small hope of locating an affordable home.

Straight away Shorter sees where Rosalie's predicament is apt to lead, but between his deepening dare-we-say affection for Rosalie and his enjoyment of Dragonfly's company during what customarily had been his solitary suppers, he doesn't feel quite the dread he may once have at the prospect of Rosalie and her cats moving in. All his decisions now are viewed through the closing lens of mortality. Maybe companionship is preferable to solitude in these declining days.

Tenderness and sweet hope, yes. He says nothing more for the moment, nor does she.

TWENTY-SEVEN

THE SPRING OF '75, LIKE MOST EVERY SPRING WE EXPERIENCED ON THE farm, was just plain silly with updraft. The dawn chorus of songbirds greeted each morning like an especially brilliant overture. Fresh pink buds unfurling on the salmonberry canes seemed worthy of an alleluia chorus. What came first, the magenta blossoms on red flowering currant bushes or returning rufous hummingbirds searching them out to sip their sweet nectar? Fellow travellers back from the south, violet green swallows, chittering excitedly, swooped and glided across the meadows and fluttered around their nest boxes, delirious with plans for propagation. Emerging from our torpor, we fuzzy humans got busy tapping bigleaf maple trees for their sweetly vitalizing sap and clipping emergent stinging nettles for plates of restorative steamed greens. Newborn goats, baby chicks and eventually tiny spotted fawns joined the springtime parade, mockingly asking what all that worthless, morbid winter despondency was about, anyways?

We threw ourselves frenziedly into the springtime rounds: tip-pruning fruit trees (Oh Angus, wherefore art thou?), forking compost that seethed with wormy red wrigglers into the vegetable beds, then optimistically seeding flats of onions, peppers, tomatoes and all the rest. Throughout these elemental rituals, returning us to earth, creatures of soil and sunshine once again, you wouldn't for a moment question the eminent good sense of living this way, the brilliant correctness of what it was we were doing.

Not, that is, until the other world, the world of profit and loss and fiduciary duties comes trampling into the bucolic bliss. I was just emerging from the general store one particularly lovely morning when I spotted our friend Mercedes examining the big New

Dawn rose bush sprawling over her front fence. "The very person I was wanting to see," she said knowingly as I approached.

"This sounds either very good or not so good at all," I said. She cast a quick glance around in all directions and beckoned me closer. Not so good at all, I suspected.

"So much happening all of a sudden, it seems," she said in her enigmatic way.

"Well, that's springtime for you, isn't it?" I countered, striking what I imagined was an ironic Byronic pose and launching into Dylan Thomas: "Now as I was young and easy under the apple boughs..."

"Indeed," Mercedes said with a grin, "our season of sprouting purple prosody."

"And much else, I dare say."

"Yes, yes. For example some most interesting murmurs concerning certain lands and landowners," she said. "Have you heard?"

"Not a peep; mind you, we've had our heads so deep in the soil in recent weeks we probably wouldn't have heard a hurricane." Her allusion to the Icarus lands was enough to take the sheen off what had been up until then a perfectly pleasing morning.

"A grand scheme is under way, apparently," she confided in classic *sotto voce* fashion. "The snippets I've heard indicate that our enterprising Mr. Zlotnik has concluded a partnership with some sort of land development consortium."

"Oh, hell," I said, breaking my own rule to never use profanity when speaking with Mercedes, the same way you wouldn't with your mother.

"I've heard no specific details of what kind of development they might have in mind," she said, "but I suppose we might allow our imaginations some latitude."

Finishing our conversation with the requisite report on how our kids were doing and her grandkids, I thanked Mercedes for her heads-up and drove back to the farm in a funk. Will these fucking parasites never just leave us alone?

Luis joined us for lunch—Jess had prepared a pot of superb nettle soup, served with Enzo's homemade bread—and naturally the news from Mercedes was the talk of the table. "No surprise here, man," Luis said. "We've known all along that those scumbags would be back for a second helping." True enough; we'd known and chosen to disregard. Perhaps I was seeing what wasn't really there, but I had the sense at that moment that Luis was enlivened by the prospect of a brawl in the offing.

Jess said, "My money's on a replay of what happened on Obispo." A smaller island in the gulf, Obispo had recently been torn to pieces in a bitter dispute within the community over a land development proposal that would have seen several hundred inland acres dedicated as a community park in exchange for the developer being given a rezoning to accommodate a waterfront condominium development. What started as civilized discussion on the pros and cons of the proposal soon degenerated into a fierce debate, then outright hostility, that eventually severed lifelong friendships, split certain families apart and provoked a number of established residents to abandon the island forever. The kind of unholy civil war we might now be facing ourselves.

We got on with our springtime chores, but even on the brightest days a cloud of apprehension now hung like toxic smog over the green fields of home.

In early July the tension ratcheted up with the announcement of an important public information meeting being sponsored by an entity called Iverton Futures Inc. Despite having asked all the right questions of all the right people, Jess had been unable to discover what this outfit was up to. Now she was thoroughly pissed that her Advisory Planning Committee had been given no hint about the meeting's purpose or agenda. If local trustees Thomas and Gilport knew what was going on, they weren't saying. Yet somehow we all intuited this wasn't going to be some innocuous income tax information seminar.

It was always a matter of interest why certain public meetings attracted standing-room-only crowds while others were lucky to garner a handful of attendees. As Iverton Futures Inc. perhaps knew, one sure way to fetch out a good crowd was to shroud the doings in mystery. By the time Jess, Luis and I got to the community hall, it was already three-quarters full, with stragglers still arriving.

297

At a glance, the crowd represented a broad cross-section of the island, most people chatting amiably with neighbours. On the tiny stage up front stood a flip chart and an oversized map of the island flanking a table at which two immaculate young professionals, male and female, along with an older guy, sat exuding an air of relaxed confidence.

Eventually the older gent rapped on the table with an authentic gavel, bringing us raggedly to order. He introduced himself as Ralph Fazio, a senior vice-president of Iverton Futures, headquartered in Seattle. Fazio spoke with a kind of avuncular good cheer that seemed to presuppose we were all in the same boat and rowing eagerly in the same direction. He introduced his companions, Mr. Peter Cipilone, maybe thirty-five years old and polished like a pearl, and Ms. Aleisha Kateesh, also an attractive-looking specimen with dusky complexion and icy composure. These two represented a Vancouver consulting outfit called Visions Unlimited that would be responsible for steering Iverton's development proposal through what Fazio called "a rat's nest of regulatory impediments." No mention was made of Zlotnik Logging. The purpose of tonight's meeting, Fazio explained, was to ensure that the community—"you good folks," as he called us—was "fully informed and engaged right from the get-go" because Iverton Futures and our futures from now on would be inextricably and beneficially linked.

Through all of this bosh we good folks sat and waited noncommittaly. Fazio then thanked us for our attendance this evening and handed conduct of the proceedings over to Cipilone and Kateesh. The two of them conferred for a moment, then Cipilone took the hand mike, rose and walked to centre stage front. "Good evening, friends," he said with a toothsome smile. You could have taken him for a young Robert Redford. "With your forbearance, I should like to first briefly outline in the broadest of brush strokes the development concept that Iverton Futures envisions for the properties you know as the Icarus lands. After which, my colleague Ms. Kateesh will describe the various administrative steps required to see this quite extraordinary dream become a reality. So to begin: here, as I'm sure you don't need me to tell you, we have Conception Island writ large." Like a magician, he produced a small wand that suddenly shot out into a full-size pointer that he then aimed at the big map. "The Icarus lands, as you see," indicating with the pointer, "are shaded in pink. A total of approximately thirteen hundred acres with just marginally less than three miles of waterfront, all with a lovely southwest exposure."

"Lovely stumps, too!" someone shouted from the audience, a first indication of nascent rebellion within our ranks. Ignoring the jibe, Cipilone moved to the flip chart and turned the first sheet over, revealing an architectural sketch of a large and futuristic-looking building perched on the high bank waterfront with several matching but smaller structures scattered further along the bluff. The buildings featured big timbers, substantial stonework and large sheets of glass. Tidy deciduous trees were pictured among them. "This, my friends," Cipilone proclaimed dramatically, "is our vision of the Icarus Health and Beauty Resort!" The crowd made a noise something between a collective gasp and mutinous rumble. "We envision an upmarket facility capable of accommodating some two hundred guests with a top-of-the-line spa and exercise centre, along with a five-star restaurant, golf course and tennis court. In other words, ladies and gentlemen, a world-class facility of which every Conception Islander might be justifiably proud!"

We sat there like bumpkins for a bit, all of us, I think, bowled over by the sheer audacity of what was being proposed. On little old Conception Island? Where could sufficient clients possibly be found to even begin to fill such an upscale facility?

Thinking the absurdity was like something out of Monty Python, I turned to get a reaction from Jess sitting to my right, but she was leaning toward Luis on her right, the two of them whispering intensely.

"I know that you must have a multitude of questions about this bold initiative," Cipilone continued with a self-deprecating smile, while he shrank his magic pointer back to its initial size, "but may I suggest that my colleague Ms. Kateesh first outline to you the technical pathway by which this extraordinary vision might become a reality. Aleisha?"

Aleisha Kateesh stood, took the microphone from Cipilone and flashed us a dazzling pro forma smile. "Thank you so much," she said with a dusky voice in which the slightest hint of an elusive accent lingered. Like her companion, she was superbly composed in her manner and address, so that you could imagine the two of them earlier in life dutifully attending community college courses in public speaking and group dynamics until they'd perfected their craft.

"I can fully understand that some of you might have serious misgivings about what we are proposing," she said. No kidding. "To begin with, as you know, the lands in question," and here she tapped the coloured portion of the island map with an extravagantly elongated red index fingernail, "are currently zoned for forestry use only, meaning there is an extreme limitation on residential or other permitted uses." Murmurs of assent riffled across the crowd. Many of us had been particularly pleased with ourselves that in the community planning process we'd succeeded in limiting residential density in the forestry zone to one building per 160 acres of forestland.

"So, of course," she carried on smoothly, "we would need to apply to the Islands Trust for a rezoning of the property. However, the commercial use that Peter has described to you constitutes only one component of the development proposal. In addition, we will be applying for a rezoning of the remainder of the coastal strip"—her brilliant forefinger skated along the area—"to allow for the development of a certain number of townhouse units." Here she deftly flipped over another page of the flip chart to reveal a second conceptual plan, this one depicting townhouse clusters scattered along the high bank, facing the sea, with tasteful green spaces, complete with shade trees, walkways and benches between each cluster.

Now there did arise an audible rumbling and grumbling throughout the crowd. But Aleisha Kateesh floated above it, graceful as a gull above roiling waters. "How, you might well wonder," she continued, "would we expect you good islanders to countenance such a radical change happening within your peaceful community?" She paused to look us all over searchingly. "But here's the true brilliance of what Iverton Futures is proposing for your consideration. In exchange for the requisite rezonings to commercial and residential use, Iverton Futures is prepared to donate to the community approximately one thousand acres of land to be held in perpetuity as a community park."

Scattered hoots of derision, including Luis shouting, "A thousand acres of stumps and slash, you mean!"

But Aleisha Kateesh merely smiled benevolently while dealing her second card. "In addition," she said, "Iverton Futures will donate to the community the sum of four hundred and fifty thousand dollars to be dispersed in whatever way the community decides." This component of the proposal fetched far fewer jeers, as rapid calculations indicated this sum—if, say, divided equally among island residents—could amount to more than a thousand dollars per head. Figurative Farm, for example, could theoretically pick up close to ten grand, nothing to sneeze at back in those days when a dollar was still worth a dollar.

Thus was the fox set loose among the chickens. Iverton Futures and Visions Unlimited, having made their polished pitch, withdrew for the moment, leaving us to our own devices.

Well, needless to say, all hell broke loose. Battle lines were established with impressive speed, basically along the template of the nude swimming/community hall/Waddington Foundation precedents, pitting conservationist back-to-the-landers and miscellaneous agitators against the pro-development cabal of certain large landowners supported by unsuccessfully retired newbies desperate for more (any) civilized amenities, along with a rump of characters ineluctably drawn to the prospect of free cash.

Over the next several months a number of community information meetings took place, each of them facilitated smoothly by the Kateesh and Cipilone duo. These gatherings tended to be as long on boosterism as they were short on specifics—particularly when it came to what anticipated revenue Iverton Futures would be pocketing from the project. After a few stormy initial sessions, attendance began to dwindle noticeably from meeting to meeting.

Once again Mercedes supplied an intriguing snippet of information during a visit to the farm with her grandkids. While all of the kids were happily frolicking with the young goats, Mercedes asked Jess and me if we happened to know where the two Visions Unlimited reps stayed while on island. We had no idea. "Somewhat surprisingly to my mind," Mercedes said, "the two of them are put up quite handsomely in the guest house of Grace and Johnny Spriggs." Now this *was* a juicy morsel. Very little had been seen or heard of Johnny and his ambitious committee of late. The plan to purchase the Icarus lands with magically conjured funding had apparently come to nothing and we had assumed that Johnny was no longer in the game. Now this.

Masterfully orchestrated by Kateesh and Cipilone, for months the island simmered with scheming, intrigues and stratagems, everyone waiting for the moment when the other shoe would drop.

WELL, THE DIE IS CAST. FOR GOOD OR ILL, ROSALIE AND HER CATS ARE now a part of Shorter's household. After a period of gnawing indecision he had finally set aside his misgivings and extended the invitation. The thought of her possibly departing the island, leaving him, had proven far less palatable than his surrendering his cherished solitude.

For her part, Rosalie had grown misty-eyed and uncustomarily unable to speak when he extended the invitation. Far beyond the simple practicality of securing a place to live, she was recognizing her deepening attachment to island life and to old Shorter in particular. Although her plan had initially been to enjoy a brief restorative retreat on the island before returning to city life, she'd come to realize that there was now no place else she would rather be than right here. Upon reaching agreement, the two of them shook hands, then stumbled into an awkward semi-hug.

Dragonfly helped her get her possessions transported in their pickup truck, but there wasn't all that much to move, as the

Cranston place she'd been renting had come fully furnished. No shortage of clothing, however, as Dragonfly hauled in case after case of mostly clothes.

"Here I am then, Shorter," Rosalie said, standing like a mail-order bride among her personal effects and disturbed-looking cats. He escorted her up to the second-floor bedroom that had been Lena and Enzo's. The gabled windows offered lovely views of the orchard and meadows. "Oh, it's delightful!" Rosalie exclaimed. "Shorter, I can't begin to tell you how relieved and grateful I am to you."

"Not a problem," he said, almost stepping on one of the cats underfoot while wiping a treacherous tear from his cheek. She settled in nicely and even took to doing some of the domestic chores he'd mistakenly believed was her reason for appearing here in the first place. Far better in hindsight, he knew, to have had a muse than a housekeeper.

With her now at his elbow, they began bearing down ever more relentlessly on getting the manuscript finished. Cousin Hattie has indicated she now has three, and possibly a fourth, New York publishing houses wanting to see the full manuscript. And the sooner the better. Suddenly there's a tremendous rush to get the thing wrapped up and ready for various scheduling deadlines about which neither Shorter nor Rosalie have much comprehension. The sense is of a runaway freight train. Rosalie's the calmer of the two, repeating with gradually diminishing conviction that they must put their faith in Hattie's expertise in these matters. Shorter is suffering a squirmy feeling of things getting dangerously out of control, of forces far stronger than himself elbowing him out of his own story.

Plus this whole episode of the Futures Unlimited development proposal is really a slippery eel to try get a hold of. So many players. So many points of view. So much the same old same old. As with the logging conflicts that preceded it, Shorter's wary of dumbing complex issues down to disposable stereotypes. Old copies of the *Island Tatler* now prove invaluable, with page after page of articles, letters, poems and cartoons devoted to the Great Debate.

Only problem now is it soon becomes impossible for him to write at the kitchen table, as he's been doing up to this point, with Rosalie bustling around humming like a defective sewing machine and Dragonfly wandering in for coffee every few hours, both of them wanting to know how it's going, while the two cats, Astrophe and Aclysim (affectionately referred to by Rosalie as Trophe and Cly) spend their waking hours glowering at him from beneath the sofa.

He eventually retreats with all the computer claptrap to a small room off the kitchen with only one tiny window and an ineffectual baseboard heater. But blessed solitude and silence.

TWENTY-EIGHT

"OKAY, WE'RE READY TO BOOGIE," JESS ANNOUNCED AFTER RETURNING from an evening Advisory Planning Committee meeting. "They've submitted an initial application for a bylaw amendment to proceed with the rezoning. To be followed by what they call a three-month feedback loop so we can evaluate the proposal before a final plan is submitted to the trust in the fall."

"Feedback loop," Luis snorted. "How about we send them a bag of pigshit to put in the loop."

I caught just a fleeting glance of Lena's grimace. She was curled up on the couch with Enzo, the kids already put to bed. I knew that Luis's anger was starting to wear on Lena—starting to wear on most of us, truth to tell.

"We'll have to go over the application with a fine-tooth comb," Jess said, "but I can't imagine the APC recommending acceptance."

"Still, it's the trustees who'll decide," I said, "and I have to think that John and Waldo will be all for it. The You Can't Stop Progress drumbeat."

"Yeah," Jess agreed. "Our best, maybe only, hope will be the three general trustees outvoting our local yokels. Which will only happen if there's a tidal wave of community opposition."

What we got instead was a tidal wave of signage and flyers proclaiming the glories of the Iverton proposal. The formidable alliance in favour included Abigail Gilport, matriarch of the Gilport clan, along with her son Gil; the enigmatic Johnny Spriggs, though noticeably not his wife Grace; Iris Thomas, at a very skinny arm's length from husband and local trustee John Thomas; Slips Gainsborough; reliable Mable Sutcliffe down at the general store and a number of other notables.

305

The intensity of feeling was sufficient to cause people who'd never previously revealed much beyond contempt for the *Island Tatler* to now see the paper as an indispensable tool for disseminating their point of view. Our letters to the editor pages seethed with passionate disquisitions, admonitions and castigations. You had to be really quick on your toes coming out of the general store or community hall to avoid getting cornered by some zealot or other wanting to pronounce definitively on the issue. (In hindsight, you have to give eternal thanks that the perversities of Facebook and Twitter still lay decades in the distance.)

In due course the APC submitted a report to the Local Trust Committee recommending that the application be turned down due to its radical noncompliance with the community plan and bylaws. "Utter rubbish," snapped Mable Sutcliffe down at the general store. "I'll tell you one thing," she told anyone who'd listen, "I've already resigned from that thick-headed APC and I won't be returning no matter how much they plead." Within days she'd established an informal war room at the general store. The standing joke was that Mable and Cleesey were dreaming big dreams of how all the new money pouring onto the island would expand their quaint little store into a sprawling emporium.

When the Local Trust Committee held a public meeting in August, with the rezoning application on the agenda, the hall was packed in a way it hadn't been since the great swimming pool debacle. After various submissions, including a predictably slick presentation by Kateesh and Cipilone of Visions Unlimited and a meticulously mealy-mouthed report from the Islands Trust planning department, the pivotal moment arrived when the trustees had to vote on whether to accept the application. Suspense ran around the room like a mad dog. Trustee Waldo Gilport immediately raised his hand to indicate support and so did John Thomas. No surprise there. But then two of the general trustees—off-island people of supposed eminence—voted to deny the application. "Woah!" Jess gasped aloud.

An incredible tension gripped the crowd as the deciding vote fell to the chair, an urbane gentleman with a magnificent head of sleek silver hair who'd previously enjoyed a distinguished career on the BC Supreme Court. His name was Philip Travers. Playing the moment for all it was worth, he removed his rimless spectacles, pursed his lips, gazed meaningfully across the crowd and announced: "I'm afraid I'm compelled in good conscience not to accept the application." Wild whoops of triumph clashed with gasps of indignation. Jess leapt to her feet, absolutely jubilant, and we hugged in disbelieving celebration.

After the meeting, as people were streaming out of the hall, everyone jabbering excitedly, I happened to bump into the trust chairman emerging from the men's toilet. I introduced myself. "I really appreciate your vote," I said to him, "and your deft handling of what could have become an ugly spectacle." He acknowledged the compliment with a courtly smile. The shrewd look he gave me suggested that he'd developed sharp judgment of character from his long career on the bench.

"May I mention something to you in strictest confidence?" he asked.

"Of course," I said.

"I don't imagine we've heard the last of this development proposal. I suggest that you folks would do well to investigate just who you're dealing with in Iverton Futures."

"Uh-huh," I said. "We know more than enough about Zlotnik, and we've checked out Visions Unlimited in Vancouver, but we really know hardly anything about Iverton other than they're based in Seattle."

"Very polished operators," Travers said, "with a particular penchant for acquiring desirable properties, orchestrating their upzoning, then flipping them back onto the market for a quick windfall profit."

"You mean the whole health and beauty spa scenario might be a sham?"

"I wouldn't call it pie in the sky, exactly," Travers said with a smile. "It's not as though it might never happen. But we have to recognize that rezoning for commercial and high-density residential uses obviously has a considerable value. If I was a resident of your lovely island, I'd want to ascertain how that speculative value measures against the value of a thousand acres of clear-cut."

Feeling a bit of a rube that we hadn't already done that investigation, I thanked Travers for the tipoff and assured him we'd keep his name in confidence.

Next thing we knew there was a petition circulating through the community denouncing the Islands Trust as undemocratic and demanding that the rezoning application be allowed to proceed. Every imaginable old forewarning was dusted off and dragged out to feed the fires of indignation: that we risked losing the opportunity to have our very own Stanley Park right here on the island; that the declining school population and the volunteer fire department's problems in attracting new recruits were signs of community stagnation; that the voices of hundreds had been undemocratically silenced. One loyalist student of jurisprudence pointedly referred to British Lord Chief Justice Hewart's landmark speech from 1923 declaring that "Justice must not only be done but should manifestly and undoubtedly be seen to be done."

As had happened on Obispo Island, the furor pushed its way right into the kitchens and living rooms of feuding families, so it shouldn't have come as any surprise that Figurative Farm would eventually feel the sting of its slap too. We were dismayed to see that Elizabeth and Amrapali were both signatories on the petition. In addition, the two of them submitted a lengthy opinion piece to the *Tatler* outlining their extreme disappointment in the APC, especially its chairman, as well as the Islands Trust. Jess could have taken the criticism personally, as I did on her behalf, but she shrugged it off with a breezy "Everyone's entitled to their opinion, so long as they're not abusive in expressing it."

Following up on Travers's suggestion that we look into other projects that Iverton Futures had been involved in, Jess and I discovered that, while the company operated mostly in the States, they had indeed also recently done several projects up here in concert with Visions Unlimited. In at least two of these, the rezone-then-flip scam that Travers described had in fact taken place.

Armed with this information, Jess paid a visit to Elizabeth and Amrapali, hoping to convince them of the flaws in the application as well as Iverton's questionable business ethics. But the two women remained unconvinced. Elizabeth's loyalty plainly lay with her dog buddy Iris Thomas. "Obdurate as rocks," Jess said afterwards, shaking her head.

Luis, however, took a different approach. After seeing their signatures on the petition and reading their opinion piece in the *Tatler* (the gist of it—that a spirit of compromise was required for the greater good of all—being effectively sabotaged by their underhanded attack on Jess's integrity), Luis launched a rampage. Unbeknownst to us, he stormed over to Elizabeth's house to confront her and Amrapali. The rest of us were sitting in the kitchen eating lunch when we started hearing raised voices in the distance. Jess and I headed across the orchard toward where the commotion was happening, plainly at Elizabeth's. We found Luis standing on the lawn below her deck pointing an accusatory finger at Elizabeth and shouting in the mix of English and Spanish he resorted to when really aroused. "*¡Vete a la chingada!*" he shouted, "*¡Ya me tienes harto!*"

Nearby in their compound, the mutts were raising a cacophony of growls, whines and whimpers. Though Amrapali had a terrified expression on her face, Elizabeth stood defiantly unintimidated. "You're a hotheaded buffoon, Luis," she hissed. "You're like a third-rate parody of political activism."

"You don't belong in this collective!" Luis shouted back. "Why don't you go live in some fucking suburb where you'll fit right in with all the other fucking sellouts!"

"Piss off! Elizabeth shouted.

"Fuck you!" Luis shouted back while the dogs howled.

"Come along, Luis," Jess said, gently taking him by the arm and leading him back toward the house. And there it was again: Luis and Jess. Him seething, her soothing. A pair.

Something in me snapped. "What the fuck!" I suddenly shouted, startling them both. "Why don't you two just fucking get on with it!"

"Shorter, please: not now," Jess said calmly.

"When then?" I shouted. "How long am I supposed to put up with you two screwing around? Huh?" I was roiling with a blaze of jealousy and envy and suspicion and resentment.

"Hey, man," Luis said, sounding saner than I was.

"Don't 'hey man' me!" I raged at him. "You fucking little skunk, playing every angle, milking every situation for your own purposes."

"Like what?" he said. A smug challenge.

"Shorter, you're out of line here," Jess said firmly.

"Out of whose line?" I challenged her. "The line between you two hypocrites? Huh?" Oh, Christ, I was over the top, but I couldn't stop myself. A demon had me by the throat.

"You fucking played me for a sucker!" I raged at Luis, pointing an accusing finger, "and don't pretend any different."

"Shorter," Jess said, coming between us like a referee, "I think you should go for a walk, calm down, and we'll talk about this later, okay?"

I paused, trying to find myself. I looked into Jess's clear blue eyes. The eyes I'd loved from the outset. Suddenly, the devil went out of me. My rage died down like a brush fire that has passed. Yes, let this be over. Let this never have happened. Breathing hard, I watched as Jess returned to the house and Luis strode off toward his trailer.

I never really did talk the whole thing through with Luis. We circled one another tentatively for a week or more, like reluctant combatants, and gradually by small increments restored our normal way of being around one another, as though nothing unusual had happened at all.

Jess, of course, was more complicated. After a short spell of prickly mutual exclusion, we agreed that a clearing was in order.

"Do you love him?" I asked her right off the top.

"Not the way I love you, no."

"How then?"

"As a comrade."

"A comrade?"

"Yeah, a brother in the battle."

"Have you slept with him?" I asked. Not really wanting to know.

"No, I haven't, Shorter."

"But you've wanted to?"

"Of course. Same way you've wanted to sleep with Lena."

"What?"

"Let's not play games, Shorter."

I paused. "Okay. Yes, you're right."

And that's how we started, launching out into the words between us. Mistrust, for one, something I'd never thought I'd feel with Jess—we'd seemed so open and honest with each other from the start. Jealousy another. Fear, for a third. Over the ensuing days we spent many long hours examining the elements of love. Damned hard work, all of it. Gritty, greasy, hard work. Painful and humiliating at times. But we pushed our way through it, bruises and scratches and all, unearthing fragments of anger and grief and sorrow, all the shards regularly scattered by imperfect human feelings.

And we were far from finished when the commune was rocked by a couple of unforeseen seismic shifts.

Several weeks after the screaming match at Elizabeth's house, Elizabeth came over to visit Jess and Lena. I happened to be upstairs and could overhear their conversation.

"Amrapali and I have decided to leave the farm and return to the States," Elizabeth said.

"Oh, no!" Jess and Lena replied in unison.

"Afraid so," Elizabeth said, sounding close to tears at that point.

The toppling of Richard Nixon along with the landslide victories of progressive Democrats in the '74 general election had, they said, convinced them that darkness had passed from over the land of the free.

Shortly after, Elizabeth announced, rather than requested, that the dogs would be accompanying them to the US. Most of us agreed that seemed a pretty logical decision. The dogs were undeniably attached to Elizabeth and we all recognized what wonders she'd worked with them, so it would have been really unfair for her not to keep them. But Jess balked at the idea.

"No, I'm sorry," she said firmly. "Willie sold the farm to us on the express condition that the dogs would remain here as their true home. We can't renege on the promise we made him." This was unarguable, but you could tell from her manner that Elizabeth considered it a slap in the face. But Jess was right: we had given Willie a solemn undertaking to keep the dogs on the farm.

"Well, it's a miserable and vindictive approach you're taking," Elizabeth said testily. "Meanwhile, I insist that my house remain locked and unoccupied in my absence. I'd like to be certain that it was available for me to use as a 'getaway' if and when I was so inclined."

"So now we're supposed to maintain a summer cottage available for this freeloader whenever the fancy strikes her," I groused to Jess afterwards. I was thoroughly disgusted at Elizabeth's behaviour throughout this whole episode, but Jess calmed me down.

"It's perfectly natural," she told me, "that Elizabeth has adopted this high-handed manner. Because she's hurting. She's losing her home and her beloved mutts too. We shouldn't be holding anything against her."

I knew she was right, but still it would take me a while to surrender the simmering grudge I held against Elizabeth.

The morning Elizabeth and Amrapali were on the point of leaving, all of us except Luis gathered in the yard to see them off. Everyone was a bit awkward about what to say, whether or not to hug, but little Josie, fully understanding that their departure was final, ran over and gave them each a long loving hug, tears streaming down her face and theirs.

"Goodbye!" we all called, waving to their departing car. "Good luck!"

"Good riddance," Luis muttered, having come out to see the last of them.

We were a melancholy bunch after Elizabeth and Amrapali left us. Not that they'd played any substantive part in the collective for some time, so the break wasn't as sharp as when Angus left, but still, it felt as though another piece of the whole enterprise had fallen away. "Yes, I feel the same," Jess admitted to me. "Although I would probably be feeling more disheartened if Elizabeth hadn't publicly rebuked me over the Iverton mess."

"Unforgivable," I said.

"Most everything's forgivable," Jess replied. "I'm just really saddened that the relationship with Elizabeth crumbled so badly. For myself, of course, but for the whole group as well."

Lena was perhaps the most disheartened because Elizabeth truly loved Josie and Hollis, and they her. "I'll never forget how super kind she was to me those first couple of years," Lena said, "before I really found myself."

We didn't talk as a group all that much about this latest fracturing, not even Jess and I. For my own part, I can't say I was particularly saddened to see the two women depart. Yes, it represented a further diminishment of the collective, but on a personal level I was happy to see them go. I remembered keenly that evening back in Kitsilano five years earlier, when Jess, Elizabeth and I met to begin planning the imagined commune. On the edge of a dream. How at the time I'd felt some deep-moving discomfort over our including Elizabeth, a vague premonition, perhaps, that we were building our aspirations on an extremely shaky foundation. Subsequent events had now proven that instinct to be painfully accurate.

ALTHOUGH ROSALIE IS NOW A CONSTANT PRESENCE IN THE HOUSE, LEAVing her and Shorter free to confer at any point, they've agreed to adhere to their original schedule of him passing his pages to her each Friday for her feedback. However, where previously she'd provide her comments to him the following Friday, she now reviews the new work on Saturday or Sunday and gives him her feedback before he gets going on the next week's writing.

While still rigorous in her analysis, Rosalie's undergone a gradual transformation toward focusing more on production output than refinement of content. So long as Shorter hasn't included anything too outlandish or abrasive in the narrative, she's happy just to keep things moving briskly along.

"Well, certainly the loss of Elizabeth and Amrapali is a bit of a setback," she tells Shorter, "largely because it diminishes the communal living angle that is, after all, what Hattie continues to call our 'big hook.'"

But Shorter's concerns run far deeper. Unhappily, he's reached the stage of believing that most of what he's written is complete rubbish. Heartfelt and genuine as all get-out, perhaps, but in reality unmitigated drivel. He'd made the mistake of recently reading Tom Wolfe's *The Electric Kool-Aid Acid Test*, followed by T.C. Boyle's *Drop City*, both of them bubbling with clever countercultural exuberance vastly beyond his own experience or writerly talent. Finding himself exposed on very shaky ground, he abandoned his earlier plans to also revisit the demigods Kesey and Kerouac. He's reluctant to mention any of this to Rosalie for fear she'll see him for the shallow old fart he's currently imagining himself.

Rosalie considers him for a moment, as though she were intuiting his self-doubt. "You know, Shorter," she says, touching him affectionately on his shoulder, "I can't tell you how proud I am of the commune for helping stand up against the Great Pretenders at Iverton Futures. Lord knows what would have become of this blessed little island if those swindlers and crooks had been given carte blanche." Shorter's touched by her kindness. "We've enough gentrification going on as it is," she continues, "without having a toxic dose of it stuffed down our throats by bloodsuckers from Seattle."

But then she's abruptly back to business: "I don't want to distract you in the least from your writing," she says supportively, "but I'm afraid the time is fast approaching when we need to begin formulating a strategic marketing plan."

This notion strikes Shorter as both strange and repugnant. "I thought that's what the publishers do," he says.

"I imagined much the same," she says, "but Hattie raised the issue by email yesterday. According to her, everything's changed in recent years. To hear Hattie tell it, a handful of blockbuster authors still get the regal treatment—limousines, talk shows, high-profile lectures—but everyone else pretty much has to scrabble around on their own, generating whatever publicity and sales they can."

"How the hell are we supposed to generate publicity sitting out here in the boonies?" Shorter asks her.

"Social media," Rosalie tells him. "Hattie maintains that it has become the golden key."

"You mean TikTok and WhatsApp and all that horseshit?" Shorter says with contempt. "Clueless influencers?" He really is revealing more of a cantankerous streak than Rosalie has seen previously.

"Well, perhaps not those teeny apps," she says. "But LinkedIn. And Goodreads, of course. Wikipedia presence. Plus having your own website. Absolutely essential, according to Hattie, if we're to sell anything more than a few token copies."

"I don't know how to do any of that crap," Shorter objects, a tide of revulsion rising. "And I wouldn't particularly want to even if I did know how. Surveillance capitalism. Consumer capitalism, all of that shit is completely repulsive, and the less I have to do with any of it the happier I am."

"Ah, yes, but I suspect this is where Hattie will be of immeasurable help to us," Rosalie attempts to reassure him. But she's far from convincing. Or convinced. In fact, over recent weeks the suspicion has been steadily growing in Rosalie that the whole Hattie/New York/bestseller fantasy is just that: a fantasy.

She hasn't shared her misgivings with Shorter for fear he'll slacken and lose heart. Closing the project down prematurely would be the worst of all outcomes. Because she appreciates how beneficial it is for Shorter to be writing these memories. Putting his life in context as a way of reawakening for himself the blessings of the past as well as of the present moment. She's taken enormous satisfaction from watching his gradual enlivenment over the weeks, his apparent re-engagement with the wider world. And, to be honest, also feeling some portion of it within herself. So naturally she wants to avoid doing anything that will throttle his progress.

"Just you wait and see," she says unconvincingly. "But first things first; let's get the story wrapped up and take it from there."

TWENTY-NINE

ONE BRIGHT MONDAY MORNING, JUST AS WE WERE GETTING STARTED with the day, all hell suddenly broke loose at the farm. A helicopter came scudding in low over the treetops, thundering like Thor, circled once above the barnyard, then banked down, its rotors kicking up cyclones of dust, and settled right in front of the house. "What the fuck!" Enzo shouted, jumping up from the kitchen couch where he'd been cuddling Hollis. Josie came running barefoot down the stairs and Jess emerged from her study with a look of bewilderment.

"Christ almighty!" Enzo blurted, "it's a dope raid!"

Two uniformed cops emerged from the chopper just as Enzo, Jess and I came outdoors. Each of the cops brandished a large pair of loppers. They'd shut the chopper down and behind the sudden silence we could hear the chickens squawking hysterically. Off in the distance Persephone was grunting her indignation. "Just what do you think you're doing?" Jess said to the officers in her finest authoritarian voice, hands defiantly on hips.

"Good morning, folks," the older of the two cops said. "What we're doing is enforcing the provisions of the Narcotics Control Act. We have reason to believe that there are substantial plantings of marijuana on this property and we're here to seize and remove them."

Although she'd been asked to stay in the house, Josie came wandering over at this point, went right past the cops and began clambering onto the chopper. "Hey, hey, hey!" shouted the second cop, waving his loppers. "You can't go in there!" Josie looked at him and laughed, then hopped down from the chopper lithe as a little mountain goat. Just at that point Lena emerged from the henhouse

317

carrying her basket of eggs like Mother Earth's youngest daughter and came across the yard to us.

"What's going on?" she asked. "The hens are totally freaked out by all the racket."

"These officers think we've been growing marijuana," Jess said with a tone of finely fabricated incredulity.

"Marijuana?" Lena said with a straight face. "But that's ridiculous."

"Sorry, folks," the lead cop said, "but our infrared cameras definitely detected a significant number of plants in your garden over there. And, like it or not, we're taking them out."

"Do you have a warrant?" Enzo asked. He was still cradling Hollis. The baby stared at the officers with a perfectly inscrutable expression.

"No warrant required," the cop said. "If we have reasonable grounds to suspect that there's a breach of the Narcotics Control Act, we're authorized to take action."

"Why don't we go have a look then," Enzo offered. By now it should have been obvious to the cops that if we'd had any plants, they were no longer in the garden. The whole mob of us traipsed over to the veggie patch. I have to say the big garden looked truly impressive, laden as it was with late-season produce. Expansive butternut squash plants sprawled across the south end, dotted with handsome yellow squash. Rows of bullish parsnips and carrots awaited being mulched with straw before winter. Two big plastic greenhouses were bulging with ripening tomatoes, eggplants, melons and sweet peppers.

"Boy-o-boy," the older cop said, "you kids sure know how to grow your vegetables, don't you?"

"Well, they're not illegal yet," Enzo said drolly, "so we're growing them while we can."

"Here we go!" the junior cop announced triumphantly, pointing over to the far side of the garden. "Just like we thought." Loppers in hand, he marched purposefully over to a big patch of Jerusalem artichokes whose stems towered well above his head. "But, but...," the cop spluttered.

"Jerusalem artichokes," I announced, sounding more pompous than necessary. *"Helianthus tuberosus.* A splendid root crop. I'm surprised you don't know it." The cops looked part bewildered and part pissed off. It was common coinage among the grow-your-own crowd that Jerusalem artichokes could be planted to mask aerial surveillance of dope plants, but these two geniuses seemed not to have heard of it. I glanced across at Enzo who was sporting a subtle smirk. As usual, back in the spring he'd meticulously transplanted his cannabis seedlings among the emerging Jerusalem artichokes and had by chance only harvested the cannabis a few days previously. The trick now was to ensure that the flummoxed constables didn't go poking around in the sheds where the pulled plants were hanging to dry.

I resisted the temptation to pontificate to the cops about a significant downside to the consumption of Jerusalem artichokes, namely their potency in producing flatulence. Truth to tell, we'd pretty much stopped eating them ourselves with so many tasty and less gaseous alternatives available. But Persephone loved the tubers and would happily gobble whatever bucketloads of them we brought her. Whether or not they increased her mighty flatulence was impossible to determine.

We walked with the constables back to their chopper, trying to chat them up as we went. Josie was cavorting around us, singing one of her private songs. Enzo made a point of carrying Hollis close beside the older cop to reinforce the wholesome family motif. The cops had turned sort of sulky, knowing they'd made a spectacle of themselves, and we were mostly just hoping they'd get back in their chopper and piss off. But as we rounded the remains of the barn I glimpsed the tail end of a pickup truck peeling out of the yard and saw at the same instant that the chopper had been completely disfigured with black graffiti. Swarms of swastikas, "fuck you" fingers and stylized clenched fists.

"What the hell!" shouted the older cop in a rage. "Who the fuck did this?" He turned on us furiously. "Who was that driving out of here?" We told him we had no idea.

He clambered into the chopper and got on the phone, alerting someone to be on the lookout for a truck speeding away from our farm. Though I couldn't be sure, I was reasonably certain that it was Luis. "We'll get that son of a bitch, whoever it was," the cop said to us fiercely. "Luckily we've got lots of backup on the island today, and that idiot's gonna wish he'd never gotten out of bed this morning. I mean, look at this fucking mess! We only got the machine last month, brand spanking new, now just fucking look at it!"

At exactly that moment, a pair of large black ravens flying in formation just above us cawed down mockingly.

The chopper indeed looked really pathetic. You could hardly see its shiny blue and white surface under Luis's manic spraying. He must have worked with lightning speed to get the whole thing covered during the brief time we were over in the garden. Although it was a brilliant counterpunch against this vile invasion of our space, I kind of wished Luis hadn't bothered, so that the cops would be gone by now. Instead we were locked into a serious incident, and who knows where it might end. If they decided out of spite to search all the buildings and found Enzo's crop, there'd be some serious retribution coming down.

While we all waited for who knows what, I slipped into the house and got my camera. But when I started taking shots of the chopper, the older cop barked, "Hey! No photos, okay? You hear me?"

With sweet conciliation no longer much of an option, Jess slipped into Boadicea mode. "Excuse me, officer," she said firmly. "May I remind you that you've invaded our home space, terrifying our livestock and children for no good reason whatsoever." Terrifying the kids was a nice touch but a bit of an overstatement, as Josie was plainly enjoying the excitement and Hollis was not the least bit perturbed, but Jess carried on. "You had no reasonable cause to come thundering into our yard and make accusations based upon social stereotyping rather than factual information. The last time I looked, this was still a free country in which citizens are entitled to go about their lives free from police harassment and intimidation. And don't for one minute delude yourself into thinking that you have the power to forbid us from taking photographs on our own property. Now, I'm sorry that your equipment has been vandalized, but that's none of our doing, which you know full well, as we were all with you the whole time. I'd like you now to please get this machine out of our yard," she waved at the sadly defaced chopper, "and let us get back to the law-abiding tasks we were doing before you came blundering in here."

I loved Jess all over again at that moment. Her fearlessness, her strength of purpose. Her ability to keep a straight face.

The cops made some silly noises about having to get a forensic team in to go over the crime scene, but you could tell their hearts weren't in it. After a lot of chatter on the phone, they told us we'd be hearing from them in due course, then they strapped themselves into the laughable chopper, ascended through a windstorm of dust, banked to the west and disappeared over the treetops.

We all whooped and laughed and danced around the farmyard like crazy, as though an armistice had just been signed.

But almost right away we got to worrying about Luis and wondering if he'd been caught. It was impossible to get through to anyone on the phone as every party line on the island was jammed with excited chatter about the dope raid, warnings being passed to the unwary to get their plants out of sight. I volunteered to drive to the village to see if anyone knew what was happening, but I no sooner got over to Viribus than I saw Luis calmly driving across to his trailer. He had the biggest grin on his face as I came over to meet him.

"Hot damn!" he said. "Just my luck to miss all the fun."

"What do you mean?"

"Me and Brady are working on a place over on the west side, right, when suddenly a truck pulls in I don't recognize. It's some guy I never saw before and Charlie Jimson. They tell me they'd come over here to warn you guys about the dope raid, but when they get here, they find the chopper sitting all by itself in the yard and nobody around. So happens this new guy—Dirk or Kurt or something like that his name was—is deep into graffiti and has a bunch of spray paint right there in the truck with them. Well, *hello*, they're out of the truck and plaster the chopper with throw-ups in record time, back into the truck and gone before anyone even knows they were here. Woohoo, what I wouldn't have given to be here too."

"God, Luis, we thought for sure it was you. I spotted the back end of a truck speeding away and was certain it was yours."

"I wish, man. Those cops must have been royally pissed."

"It was an incident, no question."

I felt closer to Luis at that moment than I had in a good long while. For sure he was out on the edge far more than I ever was, and I remembered Jess arguing for his inclusion in the commune on that very basis, that he'd help us keep true to whatever counter-cultural roots we imagined we had. He showed a fearlessness similar to what Jess had and maybe that was part of what I resented in him, that commonality they shared and I didn't. Anyway, for that moment at least, united in our high at having routed the cops, we felt sort of like comrades again.

In the end, the Great Islands Pot Bust of '75 was a colossal bust itself. On Conception, a grand total of about two dozen mingy plants were seized and only one charge of cultivation laid, this against a newbie who didn't know enough to deny any connection to the plants flourishing in his yard, cultivation being just about impossible to prove in court unless you're observed actually tending the crop. The other islands that were raided produced similarly meagre returns. The day after our raid, a pair of RCMP flak-catchers visited every island home that had registered a complaint about the unwarranted intrusion. Publicly the RCMP proclaimed the operation a smashing success in preventing illicit substances from falling into the hands of innocent schoolchildren, but the abiding image in our minds was of the vandalized chopper fleeing in ignominy.

Nevertheless, as the great quotations repeatedly insinuate, victories are shifty creatures. Not long after the drug bust excitement had died down, we had another surprise visit from the Mounties. "Good morning," said the senior of the two uniformed officers standing at our front door. A grim-looking pair.

"What is it this time?" I asked them.

"Is Mr. Luis Moya here?" the cop asked.

"Afraid not," I said. Josie and I were the only ones home at the moment.

"Can you tell us where we might find him?"

"He may be at his trailer," I told them, indicating where it was. They headed in that direction just as Viribus pulled up alongside the cruiser. Josie bolted over to tell everyone about the cops. Within minutes the officers returned with Luis walking between them, handcuffed.

"What's this all about?" Jess asked them.

"We have a warrant for the arrest of this gentleman," the senior cop said.

"A warrant for what?" I asked him. I was waiting for Luis to explode but he was strangely silent.

"We're acting on behalf of US authorities," the cop said. "There's an outstanding warrant in California for Mr. Moya."

"A warrant for what?" Enzo asked. "He's been living here for years."

"For draft evasion," said the cop, as though this were a type of disease. Luis snorted contemptuously. This seemed totally weird, three-plus years after the fact and with the Vietnam debacle finally, mercifully over.

The cops had no explanations. "We're simply carrying out our end of a reciprocal agreement with the Americans," they said. Sure. You could smell that this was payback time.

We barely had a chance to say goodbye to Luis. Jess gave him a loving hug and I could see tears in her eyes. And maybe in his too. We each shook his cuffed hand and I was feeling a terrible roar of conflicting emotions as I did so. Luis as spark plug, as co-conspirator, as unspoken rival. I remembered the exhilaration of cycling home with him in the dark after our clandestine monkey-wrenching. The thrill of a recklessness I wouldn't have known without him. Then his betrayal of confidence. His attachment to Jess. I could see sadness in his eyes as I hugged him awkwardly

323

and said farewell. But also the hint of defiance on his face; they might take him down but he'd go down fighting. Then he was led away and pushed into the back of the squad car. We stood there in stunned disbelief as the cruiser disappeared down the lane.

"Let's go for a walk, Shorter," Jess said to me. Still dismayed and a little dazed, she and I wandered on, not saying anything, into the tawny western meadows glowing dreamily in the sunshine. Autumnal golds and ochrous reds. The colours of dying down. Hopkins's Goldengrove unleaving.

"Oh, I'm so sad, Shorter," Jess said in a wistful tone I didn't normally hear from her. "Poor Luis behind bars. I can't stand the thought of it."

"I know," I said, realizing for certain she was hurting far more than I was from Luis's departure. I had no interest in saying anything that would deepen her distress. "I'm so sorry I mistrusted you and Luis," I said after a long silence. "Stupid jealousy. Jealousy and fear."

"Yes," she gave me a sad smile. She took my hand and leaned in against me as we strolled along. "This loving thing is a crazy piece of work, isn't it?"

"Yeah, it is. But you know what, Jess? I wouldn't trade it for anything. Fame. Wealth. Anything. I love you, babe. I love you like crazy, way beyond anything I ever imagined."

She squeezed my hand gently. "I know. And I feel exactly the same. I'm absolutely crazy about you, Shorter, I truly am."

We paused and looked into each other's eyes. We were both kind of crying. We kissed. A deep, soft, surrendering kiss. Then we hugged and hugged like long-separated lovers.

Eventually we wandered back to the house, again hand-in-hand, curiously both burdened by what had become of Luis and unburdened at what had become of us. I never loved Jess more entirely than on that sweet and melancholy stroll home.

SHORTER HAD FULLY EXPECTED ROSALIE TO HAVE ALL KINDS OF STRONG responses to this chapter. For one thing, she hasn't bothered of late to conceal her increasingly sour feelings about Luis. But for the moment she ignores his arrest and instead goes back to the drug bust.

"How silly it now seems in retrospect," she says. "All that hysteria about illicit marijuana growing. Especially when you see today's corporate boardroom crowd squabbling over legalized marijuana profits." Shorter just smiles. "I think in hindsight I prefer the old renegade approach," she carries on. "These Rolex executives have taken all the fun out of it."

But Rosalie also realizes how distracted she's becoming from the storyline. She seems to Shorter increasingly bedevilled, almost obsessed, with this business of a book marketing strategy. At the same time, her enthusiasm for Hattie's suggestions has cooled considerably.

"I don't know at all about these once-venerable publishing houses," she says to Shorter out of the blue.

"Well, you know what my attitude has been right from the get-go," he tells her.

On top of it all, and perhaps most pressingly, she's been having difficulties with her cats. "They still haven't really adapted to the move here," she informs Shorter. "This big old house. Whatever spirits linger here. Cats are finely attuned to these things," she says. "Extremely sensitive. It's all rather intimidating for my darlings." She makes no comment on Shorter's obvious disinterest in the cats.

"But, you know," she says, switching tracks again, "I'm actually feeling increasingly optimistic about our marketing possibilities. About Dragonfly, I mean." She and Shorter had been sitting around one dull afternoon earlier in the week mulling over how they might apply Hattie's advice about harnessing the power of the internet to whip up enthusiasm for the forthcoming book.

"Well, we have to remember that we haven't got either a finished manuscript or a publisher yet," he'd pointed out.

"No matter," Rosalie told him. "We can start a subtle drumbeat of rising expectations about the book long before it's actually available. It's how things are done nowadays."

Shorter remained unconvinced, but at this point Dragonfly had wandered in, as they do, listened for a bit, and then casually mentioned, "You know, I actually have some experience in online marketing."

This struck Shorter as highly improbable, Dragonfly being who they are, but Rosalie pounced straight away, questioning them at length about their bona fides. They'd never mentioned it previously, given as they were to enigmatic musings on more metaphysical concerns, but it turns out by their own account that Dragonfly had enjoyed a brief but spectacularly successful stint at one of Toronto's biggest advertising outfits.

"Absolutely," they said. "Prestige clientele, power lunches, the whole top-of-tower scene."

"How did you possibly go from all that to this?" Shorter asked them.

"Up and quit," they said, snapping their fingers. "Just like that. Chucked it all—lakefront condo, racquet club membership, the whole shebang."

"Why?" Shorter asked them. Dragonfly had never even hinted at any of this previously.

"Well, to start a new life as a mendicant pilgrim," they said, "which got me eventually washing up on Conception's gentle shore. But still, yes, I know a thing or two about making digital moves in the marketplace."

Rather rashly in Shorter's opinion, and without any consultation, Rosalie then put it directly to Dragonfly: Would they be willing to act as our virtual publicist? Of course they would, subject to their reading and approving the manuscript. They didn't know the publishing industry at all, but no worries, marketing is marketing. Delighted, Rosalie bundled up all the pages to date, stacked them in a shoebox and passed them to Dragonfly.

"Cool," they said.

THIRTY

IF IT HADN'T BEEN FOR SPIRITED JOSIE AND SOLEMN LITTLE HOLLIS I don't know what would have become of us that fall. Those two kids were like tiny seedlings of hope sprouting in a fissured parking lot. If we'd lost Luis alone, things might not have seemed so gloomy, but after having first Angus and then Elizabeth depart, Luis's removal struck a chord more sombre than it might have otherwise. The dogs continued to mope, as they had since Elizabeth left. Lovely Gracie the goat succumbed to old age, leaving her daughter Sara distressed and lonely. Our vaunted commune was listing like a torpedoed frigate. As more than one islander drolly observed, that November's edition of the *Tatler* read like a misanthrope's version of *The Tibetan Book of the Dead*.

Then another low blow. The provincial NDP government—despite its shortcomings, nevertheless light years ahead of its predecessors—rashly called a snap election for early December and was soundly trounced. The province's not-quite-bold experiment with democratic socialism, running on a parallel timeline with our attempt at communal living, was suddenly over, usurped by the revitalized gang of profiteers.

But we didn't give up, not just yet, on the dream of Figurative Farm. "Not to worry," Jess encouraged us. "Remember we started together with a half-dozen communards and we're still holding strong at six, thanks to Josie and Hollis being added to the head count." Yes, there may have been a few particularly dark days when we sank to questioning whether the whole thing hadn't been more farce than social transformation, but mostly we clung like soil to our radical roots.

Then, out of nowhere, Angus appeared at the door one rainy afternoon. We hadn't seen or heard from him for months, but suddenly here he was. Josie was thrilled to see him again and right away wanted to feel his bushy beard as she always had when she was tiny and Angus would cradle her in his arms. "Well, here's how it is," he told us, as earnest as ever. "Jones has decided to sell the farm and move to New Zealand. I could go along, I suppose, but I'm really not inclined to. I think maybe I've already drifted westwards as far as I should." He paused for a moment and looked at each one of us solemnly. "So I was wondering how it would be if I were to rejoin you here. I know I'm a bit of a prodigal son, but...Anyway, think it over, if you will, and let me know. And," he paused for a moment, looking as close to emotional as I'd ever seen him, "I've missed you all a lot this past while."

We talked it over that evening, Jess, Lena, Enzo and I, with random contributions from Josie. Pigs seemed the only sticking point, just as they'd been with Angus leaving the farm in the first place. Persephone was still with us, though we no longer bred her, and she now reigned as a solitary but still grand dowager of the piggery. All four of us were firm that we could not accommodate a return to pig farming, but would happily welcome Angus back otherwise.

The next day I called him at Jones's farm to give him the verdict. "No problem with that," he replied straight away. "I think I've had more than enough of pigs in the last little while." He later told me their pigs had experienced a horrific outbreak of what they thought was coccidiosis, a parasitic disease causing severe diarrhea. The stinking ordeal had dragged on for so long it had been more than enough to permanently sour both himself and Jones on the whole pig-raising business.

Personally I was delighted to have Angus back with us—we all were. I felt again that peculiar male sense of unspoken but rock-solid companionship with him, something I'd never really experienced with either Luis or Enzo. Angus played no games, blew no smoke. What you got with him was him. He remained solitary in a way that might be sad for someone else, but with him just seemed

328

the way it was. I'd never tell Angus I loved him, but in an Angus kind of way I truly did.

Plus, with his return we all realized how much we'd particularly missed having him play his pipes. Jess brought out her banjo again, which she hadn't touched for months, and as we sat of an evening listening to the haunting tunes the two of them would play together, melodies of love and loss and longing, I felt again much the same as on our earliest sweet evenings at the farm.

A growing influx of back-to-the-landers continued to bolster our skinny countercultural ranks. Musicians, theatre people and freelance artistes deepened the roots of community culture. Expanding numbers of tree huggers and general shit disturbers muscled up our small-pond power base. Running for a second term as local trustees, Waldo Gilport and John Thomas were roundly defeated by two of our progressives. All across the region activist networks were springing up to do battle with logging outfits, mining companies, land speculators and shameless polluters. Together we developed a highly refined fetish for marching in protest at the legislature in Victoria. Peace work, the War in the Woods, Native Land Claims, Saving the Salmon—yes! We Shall Overcome after all.

During this time Jess, Lena and Tonya emerged as unabashed champions of a feminist insurgence on the island. Among other initiatives, they helped organize a regional women's festival right here on Conception. What a scene: scores of women from all over the region congregated in strategizing and celebration. Not exactly embraced in every quarter, feminism began exerting an oversized influence on island life. Enthusiasts saw a welcome matriarchy in the making. Tonya, for one, decided she'd finally had enough of hapless Brady watching his oversized TV and suddenly moved out, kids in tow, to join a wimmin's house founded on adherence to the Wicca movement.

The following years were as joyful as any we'd experienced. The kids grew by creative leaps and bounds. Hollis had a dinosaur phase followed by an intergalactic space travel phase; Josie danced like an angel and painted beautiful landscapes. Jess's writing career continued to bloom to the point she was at long last being paid respectable money for her pieces by top-of-the-line progressive publications. With Angus back in harness, the workings of the farm ran more smoothly than ever, and we were producing substantial crops of fruits and vegetables for sale locally. Enzo's crops thrived too. So did the chickens, although the dogs, one by one, eventually died of old age, little Bandy the last of them to go.

By strange coincidence, not long after Bandy died, a card arrived in the mail. From Elizabeth, of all people, whom we'd heard nothing from since her departure. "Amrapali and I have just bought a sweet little house in Carmel. We're both actively involved in the Esalen Institute. Couldn't be happier!!! Hope all's well on the farm."

I eventually earned a teaching certificate and for years served as the local elementary school's substitute teacher, which I truly loved doing.

Once Josie reached high school age—and she was absolutely the smartest, sweetest, cheekiest young woman you could dream of—Lena and Enzo made the impossible decision to move the family all the way back to Enzo's birthplace in Andorra. Family money was available for them to live there and give the kids a quality of education they couldn't possibly access riding ferries and school buses to a high school in Spangler. As much as it hurt them to say so, Enzo and Lena wanted the kids to see more of the world, to expand their horizons of possibility.

We'd never known a sadder day than the morning on which they were all packed and ready to leave. Gathered in the farmyard we hugged and kissed and clung to each of them, professed our love, cried shamelessly, not wanting to let them go. Ever. But off they went, taking a roughly torn-out piece of our hearts along with them.

Soon after, Persephone died one evening. I walked down to the piggery just before dark, as I usually did, to give her an apple for a snack. But there she lay, lifeless yet still magnificent, in her glorious mud. Foolish as it might seem to some, I cried to see her lying there alone. The following morning, Angus, Jess and I dug a deep pit, right there in the piggery, and rolled her into it with great solemnity. We threw a bowl of Jerusalem artichoke tubers in with her for munching in the afterworld.

No sense denying it, our great radical commune was being slowly worn down to a fading memory. With both our impeccable typist and our volatile master printer now departed, the *Island Tatler* soon dwindled and eventually, mercifully, expired. Beyond our farm gate, community life carried on, as it does, with all the kindness and conflict and craziness we'd come to appreciate, but our engagement with it gradually lessened to a much toned-down version of those fiery early years.

Jess's dad, Richard, died at a fine old age, the grief he left his daughter being as sweet as it was sad. As an only child, Jess inherited a considerable sum from his estate. "At least we won't have to ever think again about raising pigs to keep the taxman happy," she joked. But the bulk of what we called "oily money" she put into a charitable trust dedicated to help secure conservation lands and affordable housing on the island. The Richard Trimble Foundation, she called it. "Brilliant, isn't it, Shorter?" she said to me with a wry smile. "After all that scrimmaging with the Waddington gang, we've now got a foundation of our very own!" Sweet indeed.

Angus remained with Jess and me for a good many more years, working steadily and contentedly, the ideal countryman. But with advancing age, his behaviour began altering noticeably. He no longer got up at the crack of dawn and seemed to tire easily through the day. Uncharacteristically, he'd take a long nap in the afternoon but then toss and turn through most of the night. He'd have frequent memory lapses and at times seemed unable to concentrate on anything for more than a few minutes. "Just getting old, I guess," he'd try to laugh it off. But soon he was suffering from severe headaches and seemed increasingly anxious and, at times, despondent. This was a guy who for as long as we'd known him had hardly ever gotten sick. Who never complained. The rest of us might have all been coughing and sneezing from colds or flu or the virus of the day, but Angus invariably carried on without so much as a sniffle. So he had little experience of the medical establishment and little use for it either. But as his symptoms worsened and our concern mounted, it became increasingly obvious that something really serious was besetting him.

The island was blessed with a pair of marvellous doctors in those days and I eventually dragooned Angus into making an appointment. He returned from the clinic looking more morose than when he'd left. We asked him how it had gone. "Bloody hell," he said, "I need to do some tests up at the hospital, but the tentative diagnosis is severe fibromyalgia."

"What the hell's that?" I asked. I'd heard the term but had little idea what it referred to.

"Something to do with the nervous system not processing pain signals properly. A chronic condition. I think I'm bloody done for."

"Surely not," Jess said, putting an arm across his slumping shoulders. It was like seeing Atlas collapse.

Angus tried to work as hard at beating this dismal condition as he had done at everything else. Against his better instincts, he sampled cocktails of antiseizure and antidepressant drugs; he tried to throw himself into aerobic exercises, then tai chi, then yoga. Everything worked a bit, for a while, but nothing worked enough. The incessant pain just kept relentlessly grinding down his spirit. For a long time playing his pipes was his only real solace, but eventually he stopped even that. Jess and I stood powerless against the defeatism that gripped him. Finally, reluctantly, he decided to leave the farm and move into a care facility in Victoria. The day I drove him down to the city he said almost nothing, staring out the window and every so often snuffling quietly. It was as close to crying as I'd ever seen him come. Driving home alone after dropping him off at a facility I knew he'd despise, I felt a great aching melancholy. Dreams evaporating like morning mist.

We were down to Jess and me. The same way we'd first started out half a century earlier.

Still, we were blessed with some fortunate last years together, Jess and I, occasionally looking back, sometimes fondly, other times howlingly, over all that had gone on. What a crazy, wild, beautiful ride it had been. We spent contented hours together puttering in the gardens, still growing far more fruit and vegetables than we could possibly eat, still tending roses, lilies and all the assembled beauties that had graced our days.

I wish more than anything that we might have faded away painlessly together, sharing a couple of final decades in golden dotage. But that was not to be. Nearing her seventieth birthday, Jess was diagnosed with a malignant cancer. We consulted a number of specialists, all of whom advised that chances of successful treatment were extremely low. After an agonizing time of discussing and deciding, then reconsidering, then agonizing some more, she finally decided against the brutal, and likely ineffectual, assaults of chemo and radiation therapy. We'd both repeatedly told each other on the downward slope that neither of us wanted any extraordinary interventions to prolong life, and now that we were up against it Jess wasn't about to abandon that conviction. She would face death with the same fierce strength of purpose she'd shown with most everything else since the day I met her in Grant Park. She wanted to die here at home and in my care.

"I hate to ask it of you, Shorter," she said, feebly taking my hand in hers.

"Anything," I said, choking back tears, wishing that this scene was still years in the future and we could someday, not now, lie dying peacefully together in one another's arms. Wishing that we could have at least a few more seasons of roaming the land we loved so well. To be able to stroll again through the woodlot together, admiring the ancient conifers that had helped draw us here in the first place, and remembering how we'd find sanctuary among them during hard times. To wander along the shores of Ponder and imagine spirits dancing nearby. Or to lie together again among the grasses and wildflowers in the sun-washed meadows of our crazy haying days.

I could scarcely bear to witness her agonizing decline. The viciousness of the pain that beset her. I did my best not to weep when I was at her bedside, or to plead with her to seek firmer medical intervention, but whenever she drifted off to sleep I'd fall apart, crumpled in far deeper grief and sorrow than I'd ever known.

Then came yet another of the miracles that had marked our long journey together. Josie—dear, sweet, magical Josie—appeared out of nowhere. We hadn't seen her for quite a few years; the last we'd heard she was working in a refugee camp somewhere in Africa—Somalia, I think. But suddenly, inexplicably, here she was, a middle-aged woman, but unmistakably our lovely offbeat Josie still. Without a word she and I embraced in a rapturous, sad, sweet, loving hug. As we clung to one another I was thinking there wasn't a person in the world I'd rather have with us at this moment. She made her way to where Jess was snoozing on the couch, bent and softly kissed her cheek.

Jess's eyes slowly fluttered open. "Oh, I thought I was dreaming," she whispered. "Yes. Yes. I was dreaming of you, darling," and Josie whispered back, "I'm glad. You know, I often still dream of you too. I believe we have lovely times together in the dreamworld."

After we'd gotten over the initial excitement of her arrival, Josie filled us in on the latest news about her parents and brother. Despite a lifetime of medical afflictions, real or imagined, Enzo was still very much alive but now institutionalized with extreme dementia. "Mum spends tons of time visiting with him," Josie said, "like almost every day. We all know she's a saint, but it isn't a chore to her, it really isn't. She actually enjoys being with him, even though he's way out there in a very peculiar universe. It's so sweet seeing them together, like you want to cry and laugh at the same time."

"And what about Hollis?" Jess asked in her whispery voice. That firm, assertive voice now diminished to a whisper.

"Oh, he's brilliant," Josie said, sparkling. "I think we all knew that he'd be exceptional right from the start, didn't we?"

"Yes," Jess said with a smile, "he was something special straight away. Were you old enough that you can remember the midwife, Abigail—what was her name, Shorter?"

"Abigail Smythe, astride her black bicycle."

"Yes, Abigail Smythe. She brought both you and Hollis into the world."

"I don't really remember her," Josie said, "but I can remember being beside Mum when she was giving birth to Hollis. How frightening it was, and strange."

"Oh, that was a beautiful birth," Jess said, "just as yours was. Two beautiful birthings. So where is Hollis now and what is he doing?"

"You'll never guess," Josie said with a grin. "He's become a monk."

"A monk?"

"Well, sort of. He lives in a remote monastery in the Carpathian Mountains in Romania."

"Good grief."

"It's centuries old. I think it was originally a Benedictine monastery, but now it's some kind of mixture of Christian and Taoist monasticism. But it involves complete removal from the world. Totally austere. The monks don't venture out, nor do they invite visitors in."

"When was the last time you saw Hollis?" I asked her.

"Oh, it would be seven or eight years ago now," Josie said, "when he decided to join that community. He'd had a flourishing career before that, some kind of systems analyst working in Geneva, but he was never entirely satisfied. Now he doesn't have a computer or cellphone or anything."

"Do you imagine he's happy?" Jess asked.

"Oh, I think so, yes. You know, he never did really seem to fit in the world, the way most of us more or less do."

"Yes," Jess said, smiling faintly, "he was like that from the very start, wasn't he? Abstracted in some indefinable way. Removed."

"An indigo baby after all," I said.

"I believe he's found the perfect place for himself," Josie said smiling. "He writes me once a year at Christmas, the longest letters you've ever seen, and sounds as though he's doing exactly what he wants to be doing. I'm really happy for him. I only wish that we could see him a bit. Visit sometimes."

"Yes, it must be hard for you," I said, "and for your mom."

"It is."

"And what about you?" Jess asked. "Are you settled somewhere or not? Married? Kids? Oh, God, I sound awful! Like some prying auntie or something."

"Not at all," Josie laughed. "I was with a man, a lovely young man, early on, but it only lasted a couple of years. Deep down, neither of us was really the marrying type."

"So you're on your own?" Jess said.

"Not exactly. I have a dear woman friend who I don't see all the time, or even as much as I'd like to, but we're bonded in a very special way."

"Oh, I'm so glad," Jess said. "You know how much joy you and Hollis brought into our lives here. Just by being the dear souls you are. We're delighted to know that you're both living happily. Truly delighted."

Through the early days of Josie's visit, Jess seemed to rally and gain strength. On a couple of occasions she felt strong enough to venture outside and sit for a short while in her beloved flower garden. Perfectly on cue, the herbaceous peonies were in full bloom and the garden glowed in golden sunshine. We set a chair for Jess right beside one of her favourites, the extravagant Japanese peony "Sword Dance" whose big magenta-red petals formed a chalice surrounding a cluster of upright, golden-yellow staminodes. Gently she reached out to touch the silken petals closest to her. "Oh my darlings," she whispered, softly caressing the petals, "my beautiful, beautiful darlings!"

"One thing I should tell you," Josie said at another time, "about my mom."

"What about her, sweetie?" Jess asked. She was lying in the bed we'd set up in the living room for her. From it she had a clear view of the gardens and the orchard beyond and spent stretches of time just gazing out there.

"Well, you know, she never really wanted to leave here in the first place," Josie said, sitting down on a corner of the bed.

"Oh!" Jess and I said at the same time.

"Not at all," Josie continued. "She went along with it, for Dad's sake, and for us kids, and it was probably the best thing to do for us: we did get terrific schooling over there and all that cultural exposure. I mean, on one level it was absolutely right. But really not for Mom. She missed you all dreadfully. And the farm. I'd see a faraway look on her face sometimes and I knew she was remembering this place and you, her dearest friends. She told me once this was the only place she'd ever felt really at home, really part of a family."

I pictured lovely Lena at that point, returning from the hen house with her basket of eggs and little Josie tagging along behind.

"Oh, my dear," Jess said in a whisper, "how dreadfully sad."

"Totally. It's why she didn't write to you more often, or call or visit. She felt guilty that she'd abandoned you, that she'd perhaps helped sabotage the commune."

"Oh, no," Jess said. "I can't stand that she'd worry herself over that. She was nothing but exquisite the whole time she was here."

"I know," Josie said smiling. "But you know how hard she is on herself. Now she's really got Dad on her hands and I suspect she's determined not to make the same mistake again, not to abandon him, no matter how impossible he becomes."

"Much like myself," Jess said with a faint smile. "You wouldn't abandon me either, would you, Shorter?"

"No way," I said jauntily, to stop myself from bursting into tears.

Josie stayed with Jess throughout the remaining painful days, bringing a measure of comfort and, yes, laughter, something I'd been

337

unable to conjure in the growing gloom. We went over the old tales together, the three of us, chuckling away about visiting Willie with Bandy hidden in the satchel, the muddy majesty of Purse-a-pee, the friskiness of baby gloats. A thousand silly stories through which the years melted away and blended into something quite sublime.

And more than that. Josie told us how much she appreciated her childhood on the farm. The beauty of the place itself and of all the people. How much she loved being raised by the whole group of us, watching us trying our clumsy best to create a different way of doing things. "Looking back," she said, "I see how totally right you were in so much of what you were trying to do, like in standing against the desecration of forests. Turning your backs on consumerism. Valuing true community. How you continued trying to maintain your generation's high principles long after so many others forgot them. I'm so proud of you all. Really."

ROSALIE DEEPLY APPRECIATES THESE RECENT PAGES. "OH, YES," SHE SAYS to Shorter, "they ring with the true depth and resonance I'd dare hope for when we began our collaboration. It already seems like a very long time ago, doesn't it? You know," she says, "not long after we began the project, the light bulb went on for me: I realized that what we were doing had less to do with the back-to-the-land movement than with exploring your inner self."

"I know what you're getting at," he says. "It's been totally mind-bending in that way."

"Yes, but how wonderful is that: coming to terms with yourself, putting the pieces of your life into a pattern that gave them meaning and purpose. The living of it and the writing about it somehow conjoined. Even though I had no idea at the outset, it was obviously critical that you didn't just fade away into thankless despondency near life's end."

"Yes, you're right," Shorter tells her. "Muddling around in these memories—besides being fun, it has triggered some sort of rebirth.

And," he adds with a smile, "I freely admit it: before your arrival, that's something I'd come to imagine no longer possible."

Nevertheless, complications have arisen. "More sex and drugs and rock 'n' roll, that's what they're talking about," Rosalie tells him one morning with a splendid rolling of eyes. "They" being the several New York publishing houses that cousin Hattie's been diligently wooing. "Everyone likes the War in the Woods material," Rosalie goes on, "but the whole thing about opposing a little health and beauty spa strikes them as a bit fey. The drug bust is good, they say, but what about adding a few more scenes at the community hall dances where everyone gets stoned and the women peel their blouses off? There's complete agreement that we need more sexy scenes in general," Rosalie adds with mock flirtatiousness. "Can we work up the gay and lesbian component some more? You know, heavier referencing of LGBTQ+ issues."

Shorter starts to say nobody had the mental framework for that back then, but Rosalie is on a roll. "All the Islands Trust blather could be trimmed substantially without any great loss, they say. Instead, why not bring on a heavier dose of the monkeywrenching action—the bit about making propane bottle bombs could have possibilities..."

On and on the proposed revisions go. Rosalie doesn't agree with any of these damn fool suggestions, any more than Shorter does. "But," she points out, "we have to appreciate that Hattie's in a tight spot trying to make the manuscript more marketable. And let's look on the bright side," she adds unconvincingly, "because notwithstanding the setbacks, Hattie's worked her magic to convince several prominent authors she represents to attach their names to blurbs for the jacket, even though they haven't yet read the story."

"That doesn't sound particularly honest," Shorter says.

"Oh, we're far beyond honesty at this juncture," Rosalie laughs. "Just listen to this; it's an advance blurb they've gotten from the novelist Lucinda Weston: 'Bold and beautiful, this is easily the Book of the Year. I can't remember the last time I read anything quite so exquisite.'"

"There!" Rosalie hoots, irony now unmistakably tilting toward mockery. "Our fortune's made!"

"Pretty impressive," Shorter agrees, just to keep the game going. He's come to love Rosalie's zany side, even though it took him ages to actually perceive it.

Fulsome blurbs notwithstanding, Hattie's struggling in her negotiations with various publishers, a major sticking point being what genre the story would fall into. Shorter favours calling it "a reimagined memoir," which Rosalie can live with, but Hattie is insistent that it must be either fiction or a non-fictionalized memoir. It can't be a bit of this and a bit of that, with autobiographical and fictive components jostling for position. Where would you find it in a bookstore or library? Where in the catalogues? No, it's an impossible hybrid. This in turn drags all concerned parties into a squishy quagmire involving the autofictional novel, the semi-autobiographical novel, the self-begetting novel and other subgenres of modern metafiction. No decisions are made.

But shortly after, some truly dreadful news: Rosalie urgently calls Shorter and Dragonfly together one bright summer morning.

"A sad day," she tells them with a mournful look on her face. "Cousin Hattie has been stricken with severe heart failure. She's in hospital just now, in intensive care. Apparently the doctors are optimistic she'll make a full recovery but, to be honest, we really don't know. A frighteningly large percentage of sufferers don't survive more than five years after onset." Rosalie seems closer to tears than Shorter has ever seen her. "One thing is certain: her distinguished career in the high-wire world of New York publishing has come to an abrupt end."

"Sadness," Dragonfly says.

"I'm so sorry," Shorter adds, reaching out to gently touch Rosalie on her shoulder. He doesn't want to admit it, even to himself, but already he's feeling a furtive sense of relief that he's being released from the suffocating pressures of striving for big league success.

JESS DIED AT HOME WITH JOSIE AND SHORTER BY HER SIDE. THEY'D BEEN chatting away about Enzo's illustrious career as a skinny dipper, Jess curled up in her bed and the two of them perched on either side of her. Heavily medicated, she drifted off to sleep with a gentle smile on her face and simply never woke up again. A perfect passing, sad and peaceful both.

Although he'd had a long period of preparation for this moment, once it arrived, Shorter was bereft. Completely hollowed out. Cast adrift in darkness. Notwithstanding their chaotic first time coming together, Jess was absolutely the love of Shorter's life, and he of hers, each the other's rock, their firmament for half a century. He had no idea what he would do without her, no desire to do anything other than to be with her wherever she now was. He surely would have foundered in loss completely if Josie hadn't remained at the farm until the worst of his grief subsided. When Josie finally, reluctantly, left for Europe, for the first time in his life Shorter was entirely alone.

In her will, Jess bequeathed Figurative Farm to him. But what would become of the farm once he'd followed after her? And he surely wanted to follow her, the sooner the better, to be with her in spirit and soul. He had talked his dilemma over with Josie before she left. She definitely had no interest in the farm for herself, nor did Hollis, but she came up with a sensible proposal.

The two of them had already discussed how the Icarus lands, over which the community had battled for so long, had eventually reverted to the Crown after the financial meltdown of 2008 triggered a spectacular bankruptcy of the overextended Zlotnik logging empire. All the equipment was auctioned off and the company holdings dispersed to cover debts. The Icarus lands were now held by the province's Ministry of Environment, Lands and Parks. They were rumoured to come into play as part of the ongoing treaty negotiation process with local First Nations, an impossibly convoluted matter that might require a few more decades of well-remunerated lawyerly discussion before anything substantive was achieved.

Josie's perfectly apt suggestion was that the farm be returned to its original occupants. Of course. "Remember Pauline?" she asked him, "Mom's friend from the band in town?" Yes he remembered her, particularly that remarkable first visit when she and baby Hollis had communed so beautifully. Pauline had visited again a number times over the years, even after Lena was no longer there, invariably spending time among the ancient trees as well as along the shore of Ponder. During her visits it was obvious to anyone with the wit to see that she, and various relatives who sometimes came with her, belonged to this place in a far more lasting fashion than any of the Figuratives ever did. None of us really own any land, they had realized, but the blessed among us truly belong to it.

By this time there was a nascent "give it back" movement aimed at returning certain private properties to the First Nations communities from which they'd been taken illegally in the first place. Easier said than done, of course, as various legalities constrained ownership of land by First Nations. Far easier to seize land in the first place than to try to return it.

After protracted negotiations with officialdom, and in consultation with the band council and with Pauline, who was by then a respected elder of the community, Shorter had his lawyer draw up a will that bequeathed the farm to a trust controlled by the band. He felt good about this decision, and still does, as it offers a sense of completion and rightness. Willie, he's sure, would support it and he knows that Jess would have been all for it too.

Things have shifted a bit over the years since his will was drawn up. Unaccounted for at the time, Rosalie and Dragonfly are now happily ensconced at the farm, the three of them forming a peculiar retro commune of sorts. At a certain point Shorter felt a need to inform them about the provisions of his will.

"Oh, yes, I wholeheartedly endorse the bequest," Rosalie said.

"Even though it leaves the two of you facing the prospect of an uncertain future?" Shorter asked.

"We're cool," Dragonfly said most cooly.

Though neither suggested it, and again in consultation with Pauline, provision was made that the two of them be given lifetime tenancy on the place, should they wish it.

"Oh, but I couldn't imagine living here without you, Shorter!" Rosalie exclaimed when he told her. "That would be the end of the story!"

He loves her for saying so, this peculiar woman who wandered into his life uninvited and proceeded to inveigle him into telling his tale. He remains enormously grateful for her noisy arrival at his door and, despite some rocky patches, for shepherding him through the writing. Teaching him the art of employing the past to redeem the present. The manuscript still hasn't found a publisher, but the point of the exercise has been more than achieved.

"Yes, I'd say that's a wrap," Rosalie announces one morning, as they're standing together, arm-in-arm, by the front door, watching the rising sun splash light across the farm. "Wouldn't you, Shorter?"

"Yes," he agrees, "the tale's been told, for good or ill."

"You ready to start the second half then?" she asks, looking him directly in the eye with that disconcerting way she has.

"Second half?" He's bewildered.

"Of course," she says, "my story. I'm sure you want to hear all the juicy details of my adventures as much as I did yours."

Shorter laughs wholeheartedly and plants a chaste kiss on her head. "Yes," he tells her. "Yes, I most certainly do."

Every so often, in quiet moments, Shorter muses about old Willie's vivid description of Native spirits still lingering around the place. Just as Willie's own spirit surely lingers here too. Shorter likes to imagine that some small remnant of their crazy commune's essence might do the same.

Acknowledgements

I'M GRATEFUL TO MY LONG-TIME FRIEND, PHILOSOPHER JIM CONLON for providing his characteristically insightful commentary on early drafts of this story.

Thanks as well to Jennifer Lee for her encouragement.

I appreciate how the good folks at Harbour Publishing were consistently congenial to work with throughout the publication process.

Luke Inglis in Marketing and Publicity championed *Commune* from the outset.

Publisher Howard White rather dramatically sailed across the Salish Sea to sit with me in our garden and disclose his intention to proceed with publication.

Editor Pam Robertson was a complete pleasure to work with, providing invaluable insights into how the story might benefit from specific deletions as well as advisable additions.

Copy editor Emma Biron was gently but startlingly meticulous in rooting out every inappropriate expression, clumsy construction and muddled word order.

My sincere thanks to them all, as well as to their colleagues at Harbour, for making the entire process so pleasurable.

Lastly, I feel unbounded appreciation and affection for my companion Sandy who restrained her outsized curiosity, allowing me space for solitary scribbling while providing a loving and supportive home environment.

About the Author

DES KENNEDY is an award-winning journalist, environmental activist and seasoned back-to-the-lander. A celebrated speaker, Des has written feature pieces for numerous publications, and has had long stints as a *Globe and Mail* columnist and national CBC Television contributor. He is the author of six books of essays and four previous novels, three of which were nominated for the Stephen Leacock Memorial Medal for Humour. His most recent book is a novel titled *Beautiful Communions* (Ronsdale Press).